UNDER
the STONE PAW

POWER PLACES SERIES

THERESA CRATER

Crystal Star Publishing
BOULDER, COLORADO

Crystal Star
PUBLISHING

Copyright: © First edition, Hampton Roads Publishing, 2006

Second edition, Double Dragon Press, 2011
Third Edition, Crystal Star Publishing, 2016

ISBN-10: 0-9971413-1-X
ISBN-13: 978-0-9971413-1-3

Under the Stone Paw
by Theresa Crater

The Power Places Series

Cover art by: Earthly Charms Designs
Formatting by: Maggie MacLachlan

To Stephen

Part One

The Light Surrounds Me

1

*A*nne signed her maiden name for what seemed like the hundredth time and added the document to the pile in front of her. "And just one more," the legal assistant said as she slid another across the well-polished table. Anne pressed the gilded tip of the fountain pen down again, blotting to avoid ink stains, and signed what she hoped was the last document transferring her aunt's estate to her. Again she wondered why her Aunt Cynthia had chosen her. She barely remembered her.

"Thank you, Ms. Le Clair," the attorney said. "There is one last thing." His somber tones matched the rich wood-paneled walls.

Anne reached for the pen.

"Not another document." Mr. Jefferson pushed a tattered manila envelope across his desk. "Your aunt wanted this given to you in person. She was adamant no one open it but you."

Anne weighed the envelope in her hand. It was surprisingly light. Across the top was scrawled in a shaky hand "For Anne Morgan Le Clair Only." She dropped the envelope into her briefcase. "Thank you for all your help, Mr. Jefferson. My family is indebted to you for your service." She stood up to go.

"Thank you, Ms. Le Clair. It is always an honor working with your family."

Anne smiled faintly. Always the family. She made her good-byes and escaped into the crisp New York winter afternoon.

The Christmas crowd jostling for sidewalk space immediately swallowed her. Anne decided to go home instead of finishing her own shopping. Snow clouds darkened the sky, and all that signing had exhausted her. Besides, she had her own Christmas present to open. Maybe this gift from the past would shed some light on this mystery. She stepped to the edge of the street and raised her arm for a cab.

The snow had begun falling by the time she reached her apartment half an hour later. She ran up the stairs rather than taking the elevator. As soon as she put her key in the door, Anne heard Merlin and Vivienne's welcoming meows. She stepped inside, and the two Egyptian Maus rubbed against her legs, then ran into the kitchen, jumped onto the counter, and waited next to the electric can opener. They'd been a gift from her brother, Thomas, after the divorce; small bundles of fur complete with names and definite opinions. "You'll need company," he'd said.

Anne shrugged out of her coat and dumped her briefcase on the couch, then obeyed their summonses. She opened a can of food and mixed in a spoonful of raw turkey and vitamins.

"You two eat better than I do."

Contented chewing answered her.

She put on the kettle and returned to the living room to check her mail. Nothing interesting. On her answering machine was one message from her secretary reminding her of an early appointment and another from her brother confirming dinner tomorrow.

Anne switched on the small Christmas tree she'd decorated a few days ago, then lit the fire already laid on the hearth. She stretched out on the couch, watching the flames reach eagerly for the long pieces of kindling. She added two small logs when the fire was burning well.

The whistle of the teakettle called her back into the kitchen. She rustled around in the cabinet, but decided against tea. It was a night for hot chocolate. Mug in hand, she went back to the couch and fished the package from the bottom of her briefcase. She turned it over in her hand. Merlin arrived at that moment and sniffed it. "Should we wait for Christmas Day?"

Merlin pawed at the package.

"I agree." She tore open the manila envelope and turned it upside down. A small box wrapped in brown paper landed in her palm. She reached out and tucked the envelope under a log in the fireplace. The brown paper she balled up and threw on the ground for the cats to swat. They began a fast game of soccer.

In her hand, Anne held a small velvet case. She turned it over, but found no imprint from any store. She lifted the top. Nestled against smooth crimson silk lay a crystal pendant on a silver chain. Anne leaned back against the pillows. She'd expected some gem or a ring— but a simple crystal pendant?

She took the necklace out. The three-inch clear quartz point was beautifully fixed in an old-fashioned filigree setting topped with a fleur-de-lis. The hook was old as well. She returned it to the case, trying to slide the chain under the small flaps, but the back of the box shifted. Behind the backing, Anne found a piece of stationery folded over several times. She smoothed out the letter topped with her mother's family crest. There was no date.

Dear Anne—

You probably won't remember me, dear. I stopped seeing you when you were about four. But I knew even then you would be the one to carry on the family tradition. I'm sorry I couldn't train you, but if you delve deeply you may recover some memories of me from when you were quite young. I feel certain, dear, that teachers will be coming to you, and even though I have passed on, call for me in your dreams, and I will come.

Blessings to You,

Cynthia Le Clair

Anne stared at the letter, then reread it, trying to make some sense of the words. Cynthia Le Clair was the aunt who had left her the money, but when Anne had been informed of her passing, she'd had to ask Thomas who this woman was. Anne had gone through some family pictures and found Cynthia in the early ones; a tall, willowy woman riding at her grandmother's, wavy reddish blond hair escaping from her hat.

But Anne had only vague memories of her. In fact, she wasn't certain how she'd died.

Anne put down the note and turned to the crystal. She switched on the lamp next to the sofa, then picked up the necklace and examined it closely. It looked ordinary enough. The stone was clear and cleanly formed, coming to a perfect point, but was almost too large for a necklace. She held it close to the light. As she turned it back and forth, Anne saw small cracks inside the stone. The light played softly inside, changing the hues. She yawned. At that moment, Vivienne returned from destroying the wrapping paper and settled quietly in her lap. Anne stroked her soft fur, and Vivienne closed her eyes and began to purr. The steady hum and the crackle of the fire deepened Anne's relaxation.

The snow fell in earnest now, muffling the apartment like a precious ornament carefully wrapped in layer after layer of tissue paper. Anne felt as if the set of rooms had detached themselves from the outside world.

She was inside a snow globe, some idyllic Christmas scene, her head swirling along with the snow. She settled more deeply into her cushions and dangled the crystal in front of the fire. Anne watched the light dance inside the stone, the purples, crimsons, and golds of rainbows coming and going as the pendant twirled. It slowed as the chain unraveled, then hung still.

Deep inside the crystal, a point of light brightened into a yellow glow, then expanded. The yellow cleared to reveal a scene. A woman appeared. She was young, with long reddish hair, wrapped in a cloak, a crystal in her hand. This scene was replaced by another, a tall woman wearing an elaborate Egyptian scarab necklace and headdress with a solar disk set between two horns, staring intently into a fire, a crystal in her hand. She faded and another woman took her place, her face wrinkled beneath gray hair, staring into a pool in the midst of standing stones. Faint chanting drifted across the open air. Suddenly, the woman looked up and focused her sharp and steady eyes directly into Anne's. She stretched out a withered hand, her gaze holding Anne's firmly. Light flickered in her palm as the twisted fingers opened. Anne reached out for the light without a thought, as if it were the most natural thing in the world. The thud of her own crystal hitting the floor brought her back to the present.

Anne gasped and sat back heavily. Vivienne grunted in protest, extending her claws slightly. The apartment was quiet. Nothing moved. Merlin slept next to her on the couch. The snow fell silently outside. A log sizzled on the fire. Anne shook her head, then leaned over to pick up the pendant. Vivienne squeaked a mild protest and Anne ruffled her ears. She turned the crystal over in her palm once more. It lay there, just a stone. She laughed unsteadily. The sound was loud and hollow.

"Time for bed. I'm falling asleep on the couch." Anne gave Vivienne a gentle push.

The cats ran in front of her down the hallway to the bedroom, jumping up, each claiming a pillow.

"Can I have some room, please?"

* * *

ANNE WOKE before the alarm and lay listening to the faint sounds of traffic from the street below. She swore she'd made no noise, but the cats came running. "Good morning, my magicians."

Merlin found a perch on her stomach, and Vivienne settled on the pillow beside her. She stroked Merlin's long body, enjoying the leisure. Most mornings, she hit the snooze button a few times, then tore around the apartment getting ready. She hadn't gone to sleep as early as she had the night before since she was a child. She looked at the crystal on top of her dresser and frowned. It looked perfectly ordinary in the morning light. She felt like she'd dreamed all night, but she could only remember fragments. They'd been vivid dreams, the kind that seem important, but try as she might, she only remembered one image—an old woman stretching her hand out, a light sparkling when she opened her fingers.

I'm getting as crazy as my grandmother, she thought. She nudged Merlin. "Time to get up, lazy boy."

Anne dressed quickly and left for work. In the office, the meeting with her client went well, even though she'd had to review the files in the taxi on the way in. She had no more appointments for the day, so Anne got her messages, read her mail, and started working on cases. She found herself rereading paragraphs. Once, she went into the firm's library in search of a book, but when she got there, she couldn't remember the title. The mystery of her aunt's crystal and the odd note continued to haunt her.

Why had Cynthia chosen her? Anne had been clear with all her relatives that she would not be drawn into the family drama, yet here she was working for the family firm and getting secret bequests with mysterious notes from long-lost relatives. She slammed the brief she was reading down on her desk and walked to the window. New York had whisked away most traces of Mother Nature's latest appearance. The snow now lay in small brown piles on the edge of the sidewalks that would evaporate by afternoon.

By eleven o'clock, Anne had accomplished next to nothing. At the weekly staff meeting, she schooled her face to show polite interest as she listened to Charles Smyth, one of the partners, hold forth on the progress of his case, his long, thin nose accentuated by reading glasses perched on the end. He wanted three legal assistants from the next crop of students instead of his usual two. The office manager pursed her lips, but held her peace. Her word carried weight, but only if spoken in private.

What about the note? Her family did have a history of peculiar notions. Thomas had explained a little of the esoteric meanings behind the family crest and what he'd called the sacred geometry of the labyrinth on their grandmother's estate. Surely, he was a better candidate for this inheritance than she was. When he was younger, he'd bragged he had inherited the family gift—the Sight, as he called it—but his results had been less than impressive. Anne had never taken any of it seriously. Just romantic stories. All aristocratic families had ghosts in the attic. Her mother had instilled in her a strong respect for the rational, the logical. Anne needed concrete evidence. Proof.

Dr. Abernathy was talking. He didn't fit the attorney image with his ever-present ascot and pipe. Roger Abernathy had been recruited to teach at Tulane early in his career, was christened "doctor" by his students, and the title had stuck with him ever since. Although he was not a blood relative, their two families had very old ties. She smiled at him now, remembering him running into her office to read one of his favorite passages from Dickens on the perfidy of lawyers. He caught her smile and nodded, taking her attention for agreement. Anne nodded back.

Edmund Spear, the firm president, cleared his throat. "Thank you, Dr. Abernathy." Mr. Spear made a show of looking at his watch. "We'll see about your request, Charles. This will be our last meeting of the year." A cheerful rustle greeted this statement. "I expect people to be working, of course." A few laughs came from the back of the room. "We still have business to conduct. Enjoy your holidays."

Anne ducked her eyes at these last remarks. Her work with the firm was more politics than the daily grind of casework, so she didn't work the eighty-hour weeks the other attorneys pulled. Everyone knew this included attending her grandparents' annual Christmas party to hobnob with the rich and powerful. When she'd gone on the job market, Edmund Spear had convinced her it wasn't rational to expect her family connections to be ignored. "Power is more difficult to wash off than grease from fried chicken," he had said, using an uncharacteristically earthy metaphor. "Why work for some poor but noble firm?"

She'd sat on his leather chair, eyeing the Egyptian artifacts peppering his office.

"It would be romantic, yes. But effective? With the Hudson Group, you can pursue your liberal causes. It's what everyone expects of a Le Clair."

Mr. Spear had been as good as his word. Over the past two years, Anne had helped prosecute a large corporation for selling unsafe contraceptives in poor countries, had represented an executive vice president in a race discrimination case, and had helped rewrite legislation for women's health care. Yet her mother still called her a sellout.

Anne exchanged a little congenial chitchat on her way out of the meeting, then slipped into her office. She asked her secretary to order takeout, intending to spend the afternoon catching up on her caseload. Around two o'clock, she pushed away the file she'd reread twenty times and buzzed her secretary.

Susan quickly appeared and sat in front of her desk, notepad in hand.

"I have one small piece of business that needs immediate attention. I have some questions about a case, but I'd prefer not to hire our usual investigators."

"We have several companies on the list. I can call someone we don't use very often."

"Excellent. The questions are about an unusual inheritance from my aunt, and I'd like to keep this discreet."

"Of course."

"I need to know more about her death and activities for, say, six months prior." Anne wrote down her aunt's name and last place of residence. "You can get details from the firm's files, but please don't let anyone know you're looking—even Spear or Abernathy. It's really a personal matter."

"I'll let you know how long they expect the investigation to take." "Thank you."

When Susan left, Anne looked at her calendar. She was meeting her brother at their favorite restaurant for dinner at seven. Maybe she should do a little shopping beforehand. She certainly wasn't accomplishing anything here.

* * *

AT SEVEN, Anne walked into the St. Anthony's Club with her arms full of packages.

The maitre d' sprang into action. "Ms. Le Clair, your party is waiting." Anne checked her bags and coat, then followed the host to a secluded table. Thomas jumped up to hug her, jostling the vase on the table. "Anne, hello. Good to see you."

"You, too." She looked up at Thomas, again wondering where this elegant man had come from. Only the lock of light red hair that kept escaping onto his high forehead held any echo of the gangly older brother she'd grown up with. His well-chiseled chin and nose, his clear amber eyes graced the cover of gossip rags every few months.

A waiter hovered like a hummingbird, so they ordered.

As innocently as possible, Anne said, "Last time I heard you had fathered a set of twins with that actress and were living incognito in a trailer park just outside of L.A. with an ex-prostitute."

Thomas looked like he'd taken a bite of something sour.

"No?" Anne widened her eyes in mock surprise.

"Whatever are you doing with yourself then?"

"If you really must know, skiing with some of the guys in St. Moritz, trying to forget my troubles."

"So, you call the Prince of Wales one of the guys?" "I suppose. Why don't you come along next time? One of those guys asked about you."

"I have a job. Have you heard anything from Janet?"

"Not since her engagement was announced."

"It's a political marriage, Tommy. She still loves you."

"Call me old-fashioned. I want it all. So, how's my baby sis?"

"Pushed around by two cats, that's how I am." Anne could not keep a small smile from her lips.

"Just as I'd hoped."

The waiter arrived with drinks.

"Ready for the grand production at Grandmother's on Saturday?"

"As ever." Thomas raised his scotch. "To the circus."

"To the circus." Anne took a sip of her Merlot. "I signed the last papers from Aunt Cynthia's estate yesterday."

"Oh?"

"I guess it's all finished. I still don't know why she chose me." Anne decided to come to the point. Thomas was her safe harbor in the wild sea of the Le Clair family. "What do you remember about her?"

Thomas hesitated, "Well, what would you like to know? I've known her all my life."

"Really?" Anne set her glass down sharply. Her brother nodded.

"But, I thought—" she stopped. "You thought?"

"I thought she had disappeared from our lives." "From your life, maybe."

"What do you mean?"

The waiter chose this moment to arrive. Thomas dug into his soup.

"How could you have known her? She was never around."

He put down his spoon. "She was never around when Mother was, because Mother demanded she stop telling you 'fables.' She was adamant that you be left out of the family legacy."

"Legacy," Anne scoffed. "In this day and age, how can you take any of those old stories seriously?"

"Then why did Mother insist no one tell them to you?"

"Because she wanted me to be able to function in the modern world, that's why." Anne stabbed an artichoke heart.

Thomas shrugged and continued eating.

Anne looked around the restaurant at the large potted palms, the paneled walls, the watchful staff waiting demurely along the sides, then back to her brother. He'd tilted his bowl and was about to slurp the last of the soup. "Tommy!" Their table was somewhat secluded, so only the waiters were watching.

"I love this stuff." His smile reminded her of when he was ten.

She relented. "So you knew her." "Who?"

"Cynthia, turkey."

"Oh. Mother took *you* away from her when we moved back into the city, but I was old enough to be rebellious. Cynthia was my favorite aunt, so I kept up my relationship with her."

"Why didn't you ever tell me about this? I thought you told me everything."

"Not quite everything."

"So you have this whole secret life I know nothing about?" Anne quipped. Thomas was quiet.

"Oh, my God." Anne put down her drink and stared at him. "You do, don't you?"

"Let's just say I know more about the family than you do. But you knew that already, dearest."

The main course arrived, and Anne began methodically cutting up her steak, wondering how to bridge this gap between them.

"Why do you persist in eating that stuff?" he asked. "You know how much heart disease there is in our family."

"It's from Argentina. No chemicals. Besides, we die from assassinations, don't we?"

Thomas frowned. "Cynic."

"So if you knew Cynthia so well, why didn't she leave you her whole estate?"

"She left me her library, all her papers and research."

"Everybody knows you love the family archives." "Besides, some things have to go through the female line."

Anne sat forward. "What does that mean?"

Thomas considered her. "Do you really want to know?"

"Of course. Oh, you are so exasperating. Why do you all have to be so mysterious?"

"Who else is being mysterious?"

The waiter came to ask if everything was acceptable, and Anne was saved from further comment.

After a moment, Thomas asked, "What is it you're not telling me?"

"You're the one hiding things."

"Annie." Thomas took her hand. "This is your big brother talking to you.

What's the matter?"

Anne looked up at the amber eyes fixed on her. "What's wrong?" he asked.

"Why have you never told me about your relationship with Cynthia before now?"

"Because Mother insisted I leave you out of it, and when you got older, you made it clear you weren't interested in learning more of the family, uh . . ." he hesitated, ". . . legacy. I respected your wishes."

Anne considered this. It was true that when Thomas tried to talk about his ideas or tell her a family story, she resisted him, even ridiculed him. He often flew off to explore the musty libraries of some minor branch of a noble family or an obscure metaphysical organization, but she never listened when he told her about an enticing find. It never excited her. It only served to annoy her that this brilliant man wasted his talents on such pursuits. She'd accepted her mother's view of things as a child and never really questioned her rational worldview. "I guess there's a lot I don't know about you."

Thomas set his glass down and looked across the table at Anne. "I've often wished that was different."

Now the words tumbled out. "I had these weird dreams last night, and Aunt Cynthia left me this odd necklace as a gift, with a very peculiar note."

Thomas glanced around. The tables nearest them were empty. "Tell me what happened. I want to hear about the note and the crystal. Please. This is very important."

"How did you know it was a crystal?" "Tell me what happened."

Anne relayed the story of the crystal necklace, the note from Cynthia, and the faces she'd seen when she was sitting by the fire. When she finished, Thomas studied her for a long time.

"Say something. You're making me nervous." "Actually, that might be an appropriate response." "What do you mean?"

Thomas squared his shoulders. "You need to make a decision and you need to make it quickly. You've always told the family you wanted nothing to do with our legacy." Anne started to speak, but he interrupted her. "Hear me out. If you keep this crystal, then you'll have to learn what it's for and how to use it."

"Use it? It's just a necklace."

"It is far more than a necklace, my dear sister.

You've already had a vision using it." "Vision? I fell asleep on the couch."

"Oh, right." He looked around again, then lowered his voice. "If you don't want to take on the responsibility of being the Keeper of this crystal, then you must give it to Grandmother Elizabeth immediately.

If you keep it like some bauble in your jewelry case, your life may be in danger."

"My life?"

"Quiet." Thomas looked around again.

Anne lowered her voice. "Make sense. How can a necklace threaten me?"

"I'm sorry, Anne. I want to tell you, but we can't talk about this here."

Anne sat back in her chair. "What's the big deal?"

"Are you staying at the estate after the party?"

"I always do."

"Good. We can talk Sunday. I think Grandmother will want to join us. Is that okay with you?"

"What is the big deal?" Anne repeated more emphatically.

"I'll tell you then. Meanwhile, just leave the necklace in its case."

Anne sighed.

"And don't tell Mother." "For God's sake—"

"Please." Thomas watched her earnestly.

"Oh, all right. But I think Mother is right. The family has damaged your common sense."

"Good. Now I've got to scoot." "Big date at the trailer park?"

He smiled. "I'll see you Saturday."

Anne stood and hugged him good-bye, then watched the ripple he left as he moved through the restaurant.

2

───────────

The next morning, Anne woke late and instead of running around getting ready for work, she stayed in bed, absently petting Vivienne. How could a simple necklace be a threat to her? What did her brother have to say that was so important it required a summit with the grand matriarch herself?

She glanced at the crystal necklace on the dresser. Last night had brought more vivid dreams, but she only remembered one. She'd been standing in a room on top of a large castle looking out to sea. She could still smell the salt air, feel the chill of the long, wet winter.

Scarlet and indigo tapestries with intricate Celtic knot borders hung from cold, stone walls. A fire burned behind her. She was waiting for someone. But this was a scene she dreamed often. She certainly hadn't had any more visions, if that was what they'd been.

She glanced at the clock. She should be walking into the office right about now, but she could not bring herself to get up. She called her secretary, who reported there were no messages or appointments and that her speech for the women's health conference was on her desk awaiting her approval. Anne suggested that Susan take the day off.

Munching a bowl of granola and fruit, Anne amused herself watching Merlin and Vivienne knock ornaments off the Christmas tree. Merlin sniffed carefully at the cat reflected in the glass surface, then reached out a paw to touch it. When the ball moved, he couldn't resist swatting it. Vivienne was right behind him. The Christmas fir looked more like an apple tree in autumn, red balls scattered around the bottom.

Around ten, she gathered her shopping list and purse and headed out the door. A stop at Bloomingdale's took care of the nieces and nephews, who had been specific in their Christmas wishes. The toys would be delivered to her grandmother's estate next week just in time for the family gathering. She pushed the large glass door open and hit the sidewalk, going from feeling like a sardine in the packed store to merely a lemming on the sidewalk.

She hailed a taxi and gave the driver directions to a small shop on the edge of the Diamond District. Her grandmother's seventy-fifth year deserved a special gift, and she loved antique jewelry. Anne knew nothing about old jewelry, but a colleague had assured her this shop carried the most unusual pieces in the city and the owner could be trusted to give honest advice. The store was in a narrow street. A bell tinkled when she pushed the door open, and she was greeted by a rush of warm air smelling faintly of dust and cinnamon. Like most antique stores, this one was crowded with merchandise, creating a muffled, intimate environment. The glass cases bulged with rings, pins, cuff links, and tie tacks. A row of black felt mannequin busts wearing necklaces and matching earrings with an occasional tiara lined the counter. More cases lined the far wall. In the corner stood a small bookcase stuffed with catalogs and books. Anne bent to study the brooches in the first case.

A man peeked around the corner from the back room.

About Thomas's age but not quite as tall, he had the same commanding presence. Warm, dark eyes looked out from an open face. His nose curved down to a full mouth and square jaw. He moved like a buck in his prime, precise, with contained strength. He put down the cinnamon roll he was eating and dabbed his mouth with a paper napkin. "Can I help you?" He smiled and pushed a dark lock of hair out of his eyes.

Anne stared for a second too long. She'd expected someone as old as the jewelry. "Oh, yes," she said. "I want to buy a gift for my grandmother."

"What period did you have in mind?"

"Well, I don't really know anything about antique jewelry." Anne felt a blush spreading across her face.

"Don't worry, I can help you pick out just the right gift."

Anne was relieved he had mistaken the cause of her discomfort. "Thank you."

"Did you have a price range in mind?" He cocked his head at a slight angle.

"Not really. She's seventy-five. I want something special."

"Fine . . ."

"My name is Anne."

"I'm Michael." He extended his hand. His grip was warm and firm. "It would help if you could tell me what your grandmother likes. Her collection, what does she have?"

Anne described a bit of her grandmother's jewelry, starting with the pieces Elizabeth wore most frequently. Michael asked about the gems and their arrangements. "Sounds like your grandmother likes copies of medieval pieces and royal heirlooms. We don't really carry anything that valuable."

Anne was not sure they were copies. She asked, "Royal heirlooms?"

"What you've been describing seems like French heraldic jewelry."

"That's true. Our family was from France originally. Before they moved to Scotland."

"Oh?" Michael leaned forward. "How interesting."

"Not particularly." Anne looked into the case, hoping to deflect the conversation away from her background. She hated the moment when people realized they were talking to someone from a well-known family.

"Tell me more about her collection."

This man was comfortable to be with, even familiar in an odd way, and Anne found herself talking to him easily. She described how as a child she had watched her grandmother dress for her parties and had helped pick out the jewelry. "My favorite was a necklace of rubies and diamonds. The rubies were a deep red, but clear. I used to stare into them like I was looking into a lake."

"What did you see?" Michael watched her intently from the other side of the case.

"See? Nothing." Their eyes caught for a minute, then Anne turned abruptly to the case behind her, breaking contact. She studied what was in front of her to regain her composure.

Pictures of pieces from royal collections were laid out like a museum display with a few imitations. Beside several necklaces and two crowns lay scepters and knives with engraved handles. Anne picked up a scepter encrusted with colored glass gems mimicking the rainbow up the wand. It was crowned with a large amethyst. "A little gaudy for Grandmother's taste." She set it down next to a cup engraved with a unicorn and dotted with what looked like rubies. "My grandmother has one of these," Anne said, "except hers is engraved with bees and set with moonstones."

"Bees?"

"Yes. And I just got an odd necklace from an inheritance, a crystal topped with the fleur-de-lis. More French symbols, I suppose."

"Crystal?"

Something in Michael's voice made Anne look up. "A clear quartz. Really the point is too large for a necklace."

"How big is it?"

"About three inches."

"And it's topped with a fleur-de-lis?"

Anne nodded. "It doesn't look very fancy though."

Michael stared off into space for a few seconds.

"I guess it's French, too," Anne said.

"Uh, yes, French." He focused back on her with an odd little shake of his head. "She has quite a collection, your grandmother. I'm afraid we don't have any French pieces. Do you see anything here that might interest her?"

Anne scanned the case. "Not really."

"Might I suggest an Art Deco piece? Medievalists often like those designs as well, and we do have an excellent selection."

"Art Deco," Anne repeated, "that sounds good."

They walked over to another case, and Michael bent to open the lock. He spread several necklaces and brooches on the counter top, turned on a small halogen lamp and began describing each piece. Anne watched him handle the jewelry. His hair kept falling into his eyes and he pushed it back with the same grace she'd noticed before. He had long, well-shaped fingers. His right forefinger and thumb were stained with ink.

"Which one do you think she'd like?"

"Huh? Oh, they're all lovely. What's your advice?"

"It seems your grandmother has quite a few necklaces. How about this brooch?" He pointed to a black rectangle with a star burst in diamonds. "This one is quintessential Art Deco, although it is a bit expensive."

"It's lovely." Anne examined the brooch. "I'll take it." She handed him a credit card.

Michael looked at her name on the card and smiled. After a moment's hesitation, he said, "The clasp is broken, but we can repair that and have it to you by early next week. My uncle will call you. Just write your phone number on the bottom of the receipt."

"Your uncle?"

"Yes, he owns the shop. I'm just helping out today."

"That's too—I mean, you certainly know a lot about jewelry. I thought this was your shop."

"I was lucky. We have similar interests, your grandmother and I."

Anne decided to give her home number instead of the office one. She handed him the receipt.

He took it and they stood looking at each other for a moment. Abruptly, he turned and escorted her to the door. "It's been a pleasure meeting you, Anne Le Clair."

Anne blushed. "And you, Michael—"

"Levy," he answered, extending his hand again.

Anne took it, enjoying the warmth of his grasp. Unable to think what else to say, she murmured, "Well, your uncle has my phone number. Happy holidays."

"Happy holidays."

* * *

ON SATURDAY AFTERNOON, Anne emerged from Elizabeth Arden's with her wheat-blond hair swept up in back and a cascade of elaborate curls falling to one side. Her nails were the color of the balls on her Christmas tree, and her legs had been smoothed into velvet. Her eye shadow deepened her eyes to the color of sapphires. Once a year, she indulged in such frivolity. She was ready for the ball.

As a child, she and Thomas had watched from the third-floor bedroom window as elegant guests stepped from their limousines wearing too little for the weather. The women's gowns glittered in the moonlight, rivaling the lights outlining the doors and windows. The men fit the season in their penguin black and white. Anne had yearned for the day she could join them. In her young imagination, Grandmother Elizabeth's Christmas ball had always been Halloween for grown-ups, who dressed up like movie stars. But as an adult, this yearly transformation startled her. It turned out not to be a game after all. People took it all quite seriously.

At her apartment, she sipped a bowl of soup, not wanting to disturb the artistry that had been lavished upon her. At last, a knock at the door announced the arrival of the limousine her grandmother had sent.

"Miss Anne," the driver greeted her with a short bow.

"Lawrence, how are you doing?"

"Excellent. And may I say you look lovely."

"Thank you, Lawrence, but it's all in the paint."

"Now, Miss Anne."

Lawrence took her overnight bag and gown down the hall and into the garage, then deposited it in the back of the limousine. Anne sank into the leather seat of the car. Lawrence discreetly raised the glass shield. She watched the city disappear and the countryside take its place. Snow on bare branches under a clear sky, the swish of the car through the turns stilled her thoughts and the trip passed swiftly.

The car slowed at a familiar wrought-iron gate, an elaborate fleur de lis in the middle. The gatekeeper pushed a button to open it and waved as they drove through. A cloud of vapor enveloped his hello. Anne waved, but didn't recognize the round face beneath the wool cap. Probably a new hire. National security for all the bigwigs coming tonight wouldn't be so friendly.

The car made its way past fenced pastures. Winter grass peeked through patches of snow. A few horses muffled in blankets grazed in the distance. Venerable old oaks closed over the road as the car climbed, but they fell away at the top of the hill to reveal an old Tudor mansion facing east and commanding a sweeping view over rolling hills. On a clear day, the ocean was visible as a thin strip of blue in the distance.

The main section of the house had been built more than two hundred years ago, but remodeled several times since. The original home had been expanded at least twice, then two more wings added, so the house was now shaped like a crescent. The driveway in front encircled a star-shaped reflecting pool. Anne walked into the grand entry hall, her shoes squeaking on the Italian tiled floor. A large chandelier hung from the cathedral ceiling. The banister of the sweeping stair joining this section to the wings was wrapped with evergreen branches and tiny white lights. The doors to the living and dining rooms had been removed and the furniture rearranged to accommodate the crowd. The house bustled with florists, caterers, and cleaning staff adding their last touches. Anne made it up to her old room without seeing any family.

She unpacked her weekend clothes, then laid her gown out on the bed. Looking out over the hills of her childhood summers, she yawned, suddenly tired, and decided to take a nap. How to lie down without ruining her hair presented a problem. Rummaging in the closet, she found a neck pillow meant for sleeping on airplanes, then stretched out and fell asleep. The dream came immediately, as if it had been waiting for her to close her eyes.

From the top of a stone building, she looked out at an expanse of blue water. The sound of footsteps came from the stone steps below. Another woman emerged from the building and walked over to stand by her side. "Has he come yet?"

"There's been no sign."

The other woman sighed. "Can I bring you something to eat?"

She shook her head.

Silently, the other woman sat beside her. They waited together.

A noise woke her. Now, it was late. She listened into the darkness and heard water dripping from oars, then a boat slide up on the shore. She ran quietly down a flight of stone steps, beneath the sacred wheel of stars, past teaching rooms, their carvings mute in the night, down more steps, then along a long corridor to the west end of the temple. She opened a small door and walked down to the river.

He waited by the boat, wrapped in a dark cloak. She ran into his arms. After a minute, the man pulled back and looked into her face. "It's done."

She shivered against him.

"It was necessary." He stroked her hair. "Meanwhile, you must guard these." He placed something in her hand.

"The night is always so long."

"I will come again with the flood." He bent his head toward her and she kissed him good-bye. He returned to the boat.

She reentered the temple, but this time turned left and walked down the west end. At the end of the hall, she climbed down a small set of stairs to a narrow passageway. She crawled through, then emerged into a passage barely wide enough for one person. Scenes and text covered the walls. She came to a goddess with a lioness head and pressed a stone next to the floor. The stone shifted, revealing a small chamber. She laid the objects inside, then resealed the chamber.

"You must guard the key."

Anne woke with a start and sat up in bed. "What?" She glanced around to see who had spoken to her. "Who's there?" Anne switched on the light and looked around the room again. She was alone. She must have heard someone outside. What had that dream meant? She still felt the arms of the man she loved encircling her. But why had she felt so sad? She glanced at the bedside clock. Half past seven.

"Oh, my God!" Anne jumped up and pulled off her sweats, dressed as quickly as she could, then checked herself in the mirror. The gown had spaghetti straps and hugged her bosom, then fell in luxurious drapes of Maxfield Parrish blue with tiny swirls of gold. After she'd repaired her hair, she picked up the simple string of sapphires she'd chosen to accent her dress and bent her head to fasten them. She looked back into the mirror and saw the crystal necklace hanging there instead.

"For heaven's sake." She unfastened the necklace, tucked it back into its little case, and reached for the sapphires. The crystal pulled her hand like a magnet.

"No," she said and reached for the sapphires. She fastened the necklace and looked at herself again.

The crystal necklace hung around her neck.

"How in the world?" The necklace was no match for the dress or the hair. "If you insist," she said to the stone. Besides, she was tired of all the secrecy. She walked downstairs.

Violins and the hum of human voices filled the air. A variety of expensive perfumes vied for dominance, suggesting the Spice Islands. The party was already in full swing. Anne stopped at the top of the last flight and looked around for a familiar face. The first person she recognized was her mother, who was busy chatting with Senator Rodman. Dr. Abernathy held court in the conservatory surrounded by several important business leaders. Gerald, her grandfather, elegant in a black velvet suit, greeted someone at the front door. The grand dame herself was not in sight.

Someone else claimed the senator's attention, and her mother looked around the room for the next deal to be made. Her eyes met Anne's.

Anne stepped off the stairs and took a glass of champagne from an offered tray. "Mother." She kissed the cheek presented to her.

"And how is my favorite daughter tonight?" Katherine's face was flushed and her voice a bit loud.

"Your only daughter is fine, Mother. I took the day off yesterday. Got some shopping done. You look beautiful."

Katherine's silver gown accented her silver-blond hair, making her blue eyes float in her face like irises in water. She had rounded over the years and now resembled an elder goddess.

Katherine waved her hand dismissively. "Now, I was just talking with the senator, and we both agree you should speak at the next convention."

"What convention?"

"The Democratic Convention. What other convention could I possibly be speaking of?"

"Well, there are thousands of conventions—"

"She wants to introduce some new legislation to improve child care."

"Of course, I have no children. Perhaps—" Anne scanned the crowd for an escape.

"You're perfect. The granddaughter of an old political family, an attorney with a record in . . ."

Anne looked up to see what had silenced her mother.

Katherine had turned pale and was staring at Anne's chest.

"What?" Anne looked down at her dress.

"I see you've decided to embrace your grandmother's occult nonsense."

She pointed to the crystal.

"This is from Aunt Cynthia, for your information. It was part of the inheritance. It has nothing to do with any of that 'occult nonsense.'"

"Don't patronize me, young lady. I know exactly what that is."

"What is it?" Maybe she could get a straight answer from her mother.

But Katherine marched on. "And I know what it means that you're wearing it."

Suddenly, Thomas was at Katherine's side. "Now ladies, people are listening." He smiled amicably.

Katherine visibly drew herself together. "Darling." She kissed Thomas's cheek ostentatiously.

Thomas had somehow positioned himself between Anne and the crowd. "Anne, I'm pleased that you have decided to take on your family responsibilities—"

"Superstitions. You're ruining her chances, Thomas." Katherine's whisper had the force of a shout.

Thomas ignored his mother and continued, ". . . but wearing that to a public event might not be the wisest course of action."

He took her elbow, turned her around, and started walking her up the stairs.

Anne tried to pull her arm away, but Thomas had a firm grip. She could hardly make a scene. Several people had already noticed the loud voices, but her mother was busy smoothing over impressions. Anne had to submit.

Thomas led her into the library on the second floor. Anne jerked her arm away. "Who the hell do you think you are treating me like that? What's wrong with you?" She turned and saw her grandmother sitting in a large leather armchair, as regal and used to command as any queen on a golden throne.

Elizabeth gestured for Anne and Thomas to sit. Anne perched on the edge of a low couch facing the windows, ready to jump back up. Thomas sat on the one opposite.

"I'm delighted to see that you have decided to embrace your legacy at last, Anne Morgan." Her grandmother's voice was unruffled, quiet, and certain of obedience.

"But I'm afraid I must agree with your elder brother." There was a slight emphasis on the word "elder." "Wearing the crystal in public is unwise. In fact, it's dangerous."

Anne wondered how she could have heard what Thomas had said to her downstairs. "I fail to see how—"

Elizabeth turned to Thomas, cutting off Anne's retort. "Did anyone notice?"

"I don't know. How long did you stand on the stairs in full view of everyone?"

"Just a few minutes maybe . . . This was a gift! I can wear it wherever I want."

Elizabeth leaned toward Anne and caught her eye. "I'm afraid not, dear."

Anne met her stare and tried to object, but the calm certainty of those gray eyes won out.

"Thomas tells me you have already been responding to the crystal."

"Responding?"

"That you've had dreams, visions?"

"Well, I wouldn't go that far. I have had a few unusual dreams, but that could be caused by anything."

"Tell me everything."

Beneath her grandmother's gaze, Anne found herself relaying her experiences, just as a child she'd always confessed her darkest deeds despite her determination to stay quiet. Elizabeth stopped her for clarification a few times.

When finished, Anne said, "But those were just dreams. I've been stressed at work, and I always dream when I'm overworking." Anne knew this was not quite true. Work had tapered off.

Elizabeth turned to Thomas. "What do you make of these images?"

"It sounds like she's retracing the crystal's history already. I don't think Cynthia had such vivid dreams so quickly."

"This could mean the time is close at hand."

"What time?" Anne asked.

"Perhaps. Or that Anne is opening up much more quickly than we suspected," said Thomas.

They both looked at her.

Anne was so bewildered she couldn't formulate a question.

Elizabeth put a comforting hand on her arm. "All of this will be cleared up soon."

"What is going on?"

"We can't discuss this now. I have a house full of people. If you wish to accept this legacy, you must be trained. If not, you must hand over the crystal to me immediately."

Anne blinked. "Trained? What are you talking about?"

Elizabeth ignored her question. "I hope you keep it. You've shown an affinity with it already." She watched Anne for a minute. "What will it be, dear?" she asked in a quiet voice.

"If you're not going to explain yourself . . ." Anne reached up and unhooked the necklace. "It's not even that pretty. How much is it worth?"

"This is an important family heirloom, a powerful talisman. It can't be sold or worn casually. I don't have time for twenty questions, Anne. Do as I say."

Anne reached to give the necklace to her grandmother, but something stopped her. Her rational mind told her to give it to Grandmother Elizabeth and get out of the room as quickly as possible. She was furious with all of them: her mother for assuming she'd sold out, her brother for manhandling her up the stairs, her grandmother for demanding the return of a gift unless she undergo some unnamed instruction. She wanted to throw the necklace at them and stomp out of the room. But the crystal felt warm in her palm, and she had to admit she was curious about her dreams, about how it had drawn her hand tonight as she dressed for the party. "What kind of training are we talking about? I already have a doctorate."

Elizabeth and Thomas both laughed. Anne took a breath, but her grandmother forestalled her. "Pardon our manners, dear. You'll be trained how to consciously control the visions and dreams the crystal has been sending you. And more, much more." Her dove-gray eyes shone.

"Sending me?" she repeated. "How can a rock send me dreams?"

"Do you really want to know?" Elizabeth asked.

Anne looked from her grandmother to her brother, who was sitting on the edge of the couch watching her intently.

"Who is this teacher?"

"Someone you know already. I'll leave it to him to introduce himself." Anne looked at Thomas, but he shook his head no. She sat back on the couch, the crystal warm in her hand. She couldn't let go of it, not yet. She decided she would wait to see who this teacher was.

When her grandmother saw she would keep it, she said, "Now put that away in the safe just in case it has been seen. We won't need to chat again in the morning. Both of you go enjoy the party."

3

---

*W*hile Anne danced under New England stars and made polite
small talk with the country's illustrious and powerful, Michael
Levy met with a group wielding a very different kind of power. Tapered
white candles burned in niches on each wall of the room. Two rows of
pews lined the north and south walls and in the east stood a simple but
elegant altar with more candles and a vase filled with red roses.

Michael sat in meditation, waiting for the last of the group to arrive.
After a short wait, one straggler entered and quietly made his salutation
to the east, then, squaring each corner of the room, walked to his seat.
Silence descended for some time. Then, stirring from this silence, like a
lotus gently nudging its head above water, a clear, round vowel sound rose
and deepened as each member added voice to the chant. The group sang
a series of tones together, the women adding the sweetness of chimes to
the resonant bell tones of the men.

Michael felt his body relax and his spine straighten. The silence had
now grown into a deep pool of awareness. Fifteen minutes passed. After
a silent prayer, Michael opened his eyes and waited for the meeting to
proceed. His initial excitement about his news had now quieted to a
confident glow. Perhaps all was not lost, as they had feared.

Guy, the group astrologer, began the meeting. "Pluto and Chiron are
finishing the work they began in their conjunction at the beginning of

the millennium. Their current configuration, along with Uranus and Neptune finishing their journey through Aquarius, suggests that collective consciousness should have shifted dramatically. Yet secular events contradict this. If we are now fighting the Last Battle, as was predicted, we must control the energy to prevent wholesale destruction. Other traditions concur with our calculations, but the shift still hangs in the balance. We must do something to help this transformation occur, but, given recent events, I am at a loss as to how to proceed."

"I have news that may help." Michael addressed himself to the group.

All faces turned to him.

"I had an interesting visitor at my uncle's store recently. A young woman came in shopping for a gift for her grandmother. When she described her grandmother's collection, it became clear she was talking about the crest symbols of one of the Families. When I took her payment, my suspicions were confirmed. She is a Le Clair."

An older man opened his mouth to speak, but Michael held up a finger. "She told me she had just inherited an antique crystal necklace topped with a fleur-de-lis."

The room stirred to life.

"Finally."

"Excellent."

"The crystal has been passed."

Guy's voice rose above the din. "Surely this is a sign for us. The forces brought her to you. Perhaps we will be able to gain access to this crystal after all. Which Le Clair has it now?"

"The niece, Anne."

"Anne. What do we know about her?" asked Robert, the Grand Master. "Our last informant never mentioned her."

"We should investigate her." Guy looked at Michael.

"It would be my pleasure." A light kindled in his eyes.

"Perhaps it should be someone else," Robert said. "We must retrace the footsteps of our last contact to find out what she discovered, and Michael is the best candidate for that job. He could travel under cover on business. He may have to leave the country soon."

"Yes, but he has the most plausible reason to contact Le Clair," Guy pointed out.

Robert looked around at the group. Several people nodded in agreement.

"Then proceed with the niece," Robert said to Michael, "but move quickly. The time may almost be upon us."

* * *

PAUL MARCHANT PUSHED a button on the remote and the next slide filled the screen. "Here you see the Fibonacci spiral on the nautilus." He aimed his laser pointer at the swirl of chambers, his thin arms too long even for his tall form. He pushed the button again. "A pine cone." In a black suit, backlit from the screen, Marchant resembled the thin, attenuated creature from the mother ship who had greeted the scientists in *Close Encounters of the Third Kind*.

He pushed the button again. "Even the arms of our own galaxy spiral in such a way. The Fibonacci series is a basic building block in nature, the number sequence that defines the Golden Mean." He hurried through these basics. "Mathematics describes the basic relationships that form the universe we live in."

Surely everyone knows this by now, he thought.

The next slide showed the Egyptian pyramids at Giza from the air. "How many of you know that the pyramids are laid out on the same scale as Orion's belt?" He squinted his eyes against the lights. Many hands were up. "Good. We don't have to go into that too much. The pyramids serve as a grounding spot on Earth for Orion's energy, a sort of sympathetic echo of the larger system. The pyramids return that energy, setting up a resonant field between the two places. When the pharaoh was laid in the sarcophagus, his spirit was able to return to the galactic civilization that founded ancient Egypt.

"Now let's return to the dodecahedron shape." He pushed the remote several times, clicking back through slides. Finally, the Earth appeared, and superimposed over it was the image of a many-sided sphere made of triangles. "It is no accident that one of the points of the dodecahedron lands at Giza. These points form the Earth grid, the energy matrix making up our planet."

A few murmurs came from the audience.

"If you follow the points, you will see that one rests on Stonehenge." He pointed his red laser at the south of England. "Another at Chichén Itzá." He illuminated eastern Mexico. "Another on Kilauea, the volcano in Hawaii. And so on.

"Ladies and gentlemen, each area is connected to a different star system, and these energy flows are what literally hold the planet together at the quantum energy level, in harmony with the rest of our galaxy. This is galactic gravity, so to speak. Now, when our harmonic resonance drops to zero point, we know what is going to happen."

"Pole shift," said one eager audience member perched on the edge of his seat.

"Exactly," Marchant said. "A pole shift. And most researchers are predicting a disaster of gigantic proportions on that day. Earthquakes off the scale, huge tsunamis that will swamp the land, devastating winds. But this can all be avoided if we reactivate this grid system." He jabbed a bony finger at the audience. "If these stone monuments, the physical markers for these points, can be reactivated, the earth will remain stable through this shift. This is why it is vital my work continue. Are there any questions?"

Marchant took a drink of water as the houselights came up and the floor microphones were adjusted.

A young man spoke from the first mike. "Mr. Marchant, I've always admired your work, but these predictions of doom are reminiscent of the 1990s. Everyone predicted devastating floods, earthquakes, but the world did not end when the new millennium began. As we all recall, nothing of any significance happened. How can you expect us to take your work seriously when you couple it with these doom and gloom prophecies?"

"I disagree that none of these predictions came true." A vein stood out in Marchant's temple. "If you remember, sir, there were floods in the mid-western and southern United States, weather patterns changed dramatically, and there continue to be earthquakes around the Pacific

Rim, in the Mediterranean, Mexico, and California. This pole shift will happen, and it will be devastating if we do not prepare for it."

A woman wanted to know about Edgar Cayce's prediction that a chamber under the Sphinx's paw would be opened soon. An ardent twenty-year-old interrupted her and made a speech accusing the shadow government of stealing Atlantean technology from this chamber when it had been opened in 1999. Marchant was saved from comment. An older man wanted the Platonic forms explained again. Marchant answered this question so quickly that the man mumbled his thanks into the microphone and returned to his seat scratching his head.

And so it went until the emcee walked on stage and took the mike. "Much to our regret, the time is up, but Mr. Marchant will be autographing books in the lobby."

Marchant signed copies and answered questions. He disliked this part of conferences the most, rubbing elbows with every armchair scholar who had never traveled to any of the sites but thought they knew as much as he did because they'd read a few books. At least they were buying his book. That might fund his research for a few more months. As the crowd thinned, a robust man with dark, close-cropped hair and a black leather jacket stepped up to the desk.

"Who would you like me to sign it to?"

"Turnkey." The man's voice was pitched only for Marchant's ears.

Startled, Marchant looked up. Here was a man standing over him, practically announcing his affiliation with the group that was more than likely recovering the Hall of Records. Marchant could not speak.

The man smiled and said, "If you'd like to talk, I'll be in the bar at five."

Marchant returned the book, forgetting to sign it. "I'll be there."

* * *

THE BARROOM WAS full of smoke. The television blared a football game, and several men sat at the bar cheering. Some conference participants at a table nodded in Marchant's direction. He nodded back and walked quickly past them to the man sitting in the back corner.

The man rose and extended his hand. "I'm glad you came, Mr. Marchant. I'm Karl Mueller."

Marchant shook his hand.

"Please have a seat."

Marchant slid into the seat opposite him. A waiter arrived and took his order for a Heineken.

"Your knowledge of ancient geography is impressive, Mr. Marchant—"

"Paul."

"Paul," Mueller nodded. "But there are many who know this information."

The waiter came with the drink and started to pour the beer into a glass. Marchant waved him away.

Mueller took out a black electronic device the size of his palm, pushed a button, and set it on the table. "Now we can speak freely."

Marchant glanced at the machine, then back to Mueller's face.

"You are also schooled in the physics of sound and have some knowledge of primordial languages."

Marchant had never revealed his study of ancient sacred languages outside a very select group. "How did you—"

Mueller raised his hand. "We know a great deal about you. And I'd say you know more about us than we'd like."

"I don't know exactly who 'we' is."

"And you never will," Mueller said flatly.

Marchant blinked, uncertain. Mechanically, he picked up his drink.

"I'm prepared to offer you the opportunity of . . ." Mueller sat back and smiled. "I was going to say a lifetime, but this kind of situation only comes around every fifty-two thousand years or so."

Marchant choked on his beer.

"May I tell my colleagues you are interested?"

Coughing, he answered, "Absolutely."

"We'll be in touch." Mueller picked up his device, threw a few bills on the table, and stood up.

"But . . ." Marchant half stood. "When do we start? I have to reschedule—"

"We'll be in touch."

4

On Monday morning, after stewing for a day, Anne decided to disregard all the conjectures and demands of her family. The Le Clairs resembled not so much a minefield as quicksand. She had repeatedly asserted her independence from them, but the more she struggled, the more she was pulled in. This time she was not going to play. She would ignore them. And she would keep the crystal. She frowned at the thought.

She had left her grandmother's estate early Sunday morning in a cold fury. Her mother's assumption that she had sold out, then a summit meeting with Elizabeth that Thomas had literally dragged her to—it had all been too much. Before leaving the estate, she'd roused her grandmother's assistant and demanded she open the safe so Anne could retrieve the necklace. She had taken it home and set it in its usual place on her dresser, but last night had been filled with dreams, this time of Celtic England or perhaps Scotland, dreams full of mist and stones and chanting. What if Thomas was right? What had he said, that the crystal was reviewing its history with her?

That is ridiculous, she told herself. She closed the little jewelry box and shoved it decisively to the back of her sweater drawer.

Merlin wound himself around her legs, begging for breakfast. "Okay," she reached down to scratch his ears, "tuna or salmon?"

Merlin let out a distinct meow.

"Salmon it is."

After replacing the Christmas tree decorations the cats had knocked down during the night, Anne headed to the Diamond District.

The bell announced her with the same jingle. The same dusty smell filled the air, but this time without the hint of cinnamon. After a minute, she heard a door open in the back. An older gentleman, gray and stooped with many years of bending over watches, necklaces, and gem settings, shuffled up to the counter. He wore wire-framed glasses with a jeweler's eyepiece fitted over one lens, but the same warm dark eyes of the younger man looked from behind them. "Good morning. Please feel free to look around. Just let me know if you have any questions." He half turned to walk back to his room.

"Actually, I'm here to pick up a brooch."

He picked up a list and fumbled with his eyepiece. "What is the name?"

"Le Clair. I had the Art Deco brooch."

"Yes, let me see." From under the counter he lifted a box full of jewelry wrapped in separate plastic bags. He rummaged through the box, each movement deliberate, and finally drew out a small bag. Anne wondered if he always moved this slowly. He found a velvet display mat, brushed it off carefully, then laid the piece out for her inspection. She picked up the brooch, opened and closed the clasp, then smiled. "It's fine." Under the light, the diamonds sparkled, giving dimension to the setting. "It really is beautiful."

"We try to buy only the best antiques. Of course, this is not quite one hundred years old; an antique technically it isn't. Would you like this gift-wrapped?"

"No, thank you. Is your nephew here?"

The man looked up at her. Something in his gaze made Anne explain herself. "It's just that he suggested this brooch, and I'd like to thank him."

"My nephew has returned to his job at the museum. He is a good boy, helping out in my small shop when he has important work. He respects family."

"That's nice," she replied, sensing the man's words meant something she was not catching. "He works in a museum. That explains why he knew so much about medieval family crests."

Michael's uncle peered at her, then nodded. "Yes, our Michael is a smart boy."

"Which museum does he work in?"

The uncle frowned.

"If I might ask," Anne added.

After a moment's scrutiny, he answered. "The Metropolitan. He respects family."

Anne smiled and took the package he held out to her. "Thank you again. I know my grandmother will appreciate this," she said, laying a slight emphasis on the word "grandmother."

Now what was that all about? she wondered.

* * *

ANNE'S TUESDAY luncheon speech was to the International Committee on the Quality of Life of Women and Children, which included members from the United Nations, federal, state, and local governments, plus private philanthropists. The forthrightness of the African ambassador seated next to her cheered Anne and she told him that she would be honored to be his guest in his homeland.

She was glad her speech was short and the topic familiar. Her concentration was suffering.

After being awakened at three in the morning by a nightmare of being chased by assassins down the cobblestone streets of an old Bavarian-looking town, she had decided to do her own research into the crystal. So, after the luncheon, she took a cab to a large New Age bookstore she'd discovered in the yellow pages. The store was in a four-story old brick building in lower Manhattan. Crystals and fairies hung in the window, and books covering topics such as the pagan sources of Christmas, spells for the holidays, and astrology crowded display cases. A stone gargoyle stood by the door. Anne braced herself and entered.

The store was comfortable. Floor-to-ceiling bookcases were crammed with new and used books. Old sofas, overstuffed chairs, and floor lamps turned nooks into comfortable reading areas. A notice announced that tarot, astrological, and psychic readings were available by appointment on the third floor. Anne found the section on crystals, chose several books, and settled into a well-hidden corner.

As she opened a book on minerals, an orange tabby jumped on top of it and circled, trying to find a comfortable place to settle. Anne picked the cat up and put him on the armrest. "How about here?" He stretched out, kneading the already worn fabric, purring softly. Anne turned the pages. The book was largely an encyclopedia of rocks, with a color photograph of each mineral on one page and a summary of its source along with its common and esoteric uses on the facing page. The book stated that quartz crystal conducts energy well and is used in computers, watches, and many modern devices. Under the eso-teric section was a claim that crystal could be programmed to hold information and download it to the person whose energy matched the trigger.

Anne was startled. Could this be what was happening to her? The cat nudged her and she absently stroked his back. He closed his eyes and purred louder.

The next book explained different types of crystals—record keepers, double terminated, self-healed. Apparently, these rocks were quite com-plicated. An article in the back explained how to use windows in the facets for shamanic journeys. Anne found no description of what this entailed. Next came directions for scrying, a process for seeing the information stored in the crystal.

"How do you shut them up?" Anne mumbled. The cat took this com-ment as an invitation to get down on the book in her lap and turn belly up for some serious attention.

"I can see you're a shy one."

"Is he bothering you?"

Anne looked up to find a young woman wearing a store apron and carrying a basket of books standing in front of her.

"Oh, no, I like cats."

"He must like you. He doesn't usually adopt people."

"Then I'm flattered."

The woman turned to shelve books.

"Excuse me, do you have books that explain symbols?"

"Yes, they're on the second floor on the back wall."

Anne stirred and the tabby jumped down with a protest. A book fell to the floor.

"Let me help." The young woman picked up the fallen book and started to reshelve it.

"Actually, I'm buying that one."

"Oh, here," the clerk walked to the back of an aisle and returned with an empty basket. She put the crystal book in it and handed it to Anne. "This should help."

"Thank you." Anne turned and headed up the stairs.

She found the art books first. A book on mystical painters and their work was facing out. Perfect for Thomas. On the next wall was a smaller section on symbols. Dictionaries of angels, fairies, and Hindu gods competed for space. A book purporting to reveal symbols from secret European mystery schools caught her eye. She opened it at random to a picture of a family crest with bees engraved on it, almost a duplicate of her grandmother's cup.

"Oh, my God," Anne whispered.

The caption beneath the picture read, "Bees, like the unicorn and fleur-de-lis, symbolized those families protecting the sacred knowledge."

She thumbed through the book. It had a chapter on labyrinths, another on cathedrals. She decided to buy it. She'd surprise Thomas with it and see what he said.

After completing her purchases, on her way out, she ran headfirst into another customer coming into the store and dropped her bag. "Oh, I'm sorry. I hope I didn't—" Anne looked up into the eyes of Michael Levy. "Hello."

Michael picked up the bag. "What a pleasant surprise. Are you hurt? I'm afraid I was in a hurry."

"No, I'm fine. And you?"

"No damage done, Ms. Le Clair."

"Please call me Anne," she said.

"Shopping, I see." He handed her the bag of books.

"'Tis the season."

There was an awkward silence.

"Well, it was nice to see you," Anne said.

Michael took a quick breath. "Would you like to have something to drink? There's a coffeehouse right next door."

Anne made a pretense of checking her watch. "I think I have time for a cup, thank you."

They walked through the door separating the bookstore from the café and chose a quiet table. Michael went to the front to order. Anne watched him move away from the table, his blue overcoat sweeping behind him like a cape. He was taller than she remembered and moved like a deer skimming over the ground.

Michael returned carrying two large cappuccino mugs. "It's excellent, the coffee." He smiled and set one in front of her.

Anne was dismayed by how much that smile affected her. It had been a year since the divorce was final, two since she'd split with John, and her friends were urging her to start dating. But she didn't miss all the bickering and fighting. She was still enjoying the peace of living alone. But this man, there was something about him.

She took a sip. The coffee was mellow with a good head of foam. "Yum, you're right." Anne licked the foam off her top lip. "I met your uncle, by the way."

"You picked up the brooch. Are you happy with it?"

"It's lovely. I'm sure my grandmother will be pleased."

"Do you have a large family Christmas?"

"We all gather at my grandmother's estate, open presents, eat too much, ride in the afternoon. But this year, I'm not sure I'll go."

"Oh?"

"My family can be a bit demanding."

"I can imagine it's a lot of pressure being a Le Clair."

"Pressure, yes. But all families have their expectations. If I may say so, your uncle seems to be a bit overprotective of you."

Michael's eyes widened. "How do you mean?"

"When I asked about you—" Anne stopped in mid-sentence. "I wanted to thank you for the suggestion."

Michael nodded.

"He kept saying 'Our Michael respects family.' Now, what was that all about?"

A look of chagrin came over Michael's face. "Well, you aren't a nice Jewish girl."

Anne mouthed an "Oh" over her coffee mug.

"Nice, yes. Jewish, no."

Anne nodded to acknowledge the compliment and decided it was best to change the subject. "Your uncle told me you work at the Metropolitan Museum?"

"Yes, I specialize in Egyptian and Middle Eastern antiquities."

"Really? What led you into that?"

"Personal interest. Family history."

"Family?" Anne shrugged off her coat.

"You know all about that, I'm sure."

Anne sighed, "I've had enough family for a while. But Egypt?"

"Some aspects of Judaism are intertwined with ancient Egyptian beliefs."

"Really?"

Michael just nodded.

Anne leaned back, cradling the warm mug in her hands. "So tell me about yourself. You're an Egyptologist? How did you end up selling me an Art Deco brooch?"

"I have a Ph.D. in Egyptology from the Oriental Institute in Chicago. I did fieldwork in Luxor for two years and was offered a job at the museum in New York. I've stayed here ever since. I teach a few classes at Columbia and City College, and help my uncle out from time to time. His son is away at school in Israel." He shrugged, a bit embarrassed.

His shyness touched her. "Where did you grow up?"

"The Bronx."

"So you're a native."

Michael picked up his coffee mug and settled back in his seat. "Yes, but enough about me. How about you? Where did you grow up?"

"Manhattan and New England. My brother and I spent summers on the estate, the school year here."

"And college?" Michael prompted. "After all, I ran down my resume."

Anne grimaced. "Le Clairs are required by law to attend Harvard."

"I hadn't realized there was actual legislation."

"Oh, indeed."

"And is a major specified?"

"Law, of course."

Michael laughed. "Silly question. When do you run for office?"

Anne thumped her cup down on the table. "Never. I draw the line at that. But somehow they managed to get me to work for the family law firm."

Michael studied her face. "Looks like you're not too happy with that."

"I used to be. I felt like I'd reached a compromise I could live with, but ever since this inheritance, the family is at me again."

"Inheritance?" Michael asked.

"My aunt recently passed away and left me some property and heirlooms. I think I mentioned it."

"Anything like your grandmother's collection?"

Anne folded her arms. "Nothing so elaborate. Just a simple necklace. Nothing your uncle would be much interested in."

"Then why the family fuss?"

"You tell me," Anne answered. "Actually, this crystal is a bit puzzling. But you're an Egyptologist, and the fleur-de-lis is French."

"Well, I do know quite a bit about symbol systems, if I may be permitted to say so. And some aspects of European history and Egyptology are intertwined."

"Is everything intertwined with Egyptology?" Anne asked wryly.

Michael laughed. "I suppose I'm a bit prejudiced. If you have questions about your necklace, I'd be happy to look at it."

Anne considered him. Just as she was about to answer, a young man with dreadlocks and several hemp bracelets approached the table and addressed Michael. "I was hoping to ask you a question before class started tonight, if I'm not interrupting."

Michael looked at his watch. "Oh, I hadn't realized how late it was. I'll be up in a couple of minutes. Then we can talk."

The man nodded and walked back into the bookstore.

"Before class?" Anne asked.

"I teach here also."

"You teach here?" Anne could not keep the dismay from her voice.

"A class on Egypt."

"Of course, but why here, when you work at such a prestigious museum and teach at Columbia?"

Michael studied her a long moment. "Because some things cannot be said in such places."

"Now you sound like Thomas."

"Thomas?"

"My brother."

Michael smiled mysteriously. "What?"

"Nothing. I hope this discovery does not discredit me in your eyes."

Anne just looked at him.

"Because I would like to see you again. May I call you?"

Anne hesitated. "I'm all out of business cards at the moment. Do you have one? Then I can call you."

A sad smile lifted the corners of his mouth. He reached into his pocket and wrote his home phone number on the back of his card. "I hope you do call, Anne." He looked as if he wanted to say more, but only wished her good evening.

She watched him leave. *Such a knowing smile,* she thought. But she was disappointed. How could he bring himself to teach alongside fortune-tellers?

Anne bundled up in her coat and walked down the block looking for a cab. She did not notice the man in the sports car parked across the street.

* * *

MUELLER PICKED UP a cell phone, activated a small scrambler, then dialed.

"Barbarosa Travel, may I help you?"

"This is Turnkey 592."

"Hello, Mr. Mueller."

"Put me through to Mr. Spender."

After a moment, a gruff voice answered. "Karl, what is your report?"

"Our first subject is maintaining his normal schedule. Perhaps our intelligence that he is leaving the country was incorrect."

"Do you think he is one of the six?"

"We have not been able to ascertain that as yet."

"Time is short, Karl. Perhaps you should be more aggressive in your methods."

"I understand. There is a new development with this subject. A woman met with him at the old Jew's shop. She returned a few days later."

"Did she leave with a package?"

"Yes."

"Perhaps she was Christmas shopping." Mr. Spender's sarcasm was cold enough to freeze the line.

"I thought so at first, but tonight she met the subject at a local café."

"Find out who she is and what she knows. Use whoever you need."

"Yes, sir."

"Is that all?"

"One more thing. Our contact is considering our proposal."

"Considering?"

"He will comply. The psychological profile suggested he needs the illusion of control."

"We must find it. Do not disappoint us." Spender hung up.

Karl Mueller checked his rearview mirror in time to see the blond woman getting into a cab. He turned the sports car and followed at a discreet distance.

5

On Friday evening, Anne arrived at Dr. Abernathy's estate around six o'clock. "To the house, not the office," his voice on the answering machine had said.

She glanced over her shoulder. The black Ferrari she'd been noticing off and on all week was nowhere to be seen. She lifted her hand to ring the bell when Abernathy's wife and their two daughters swept out the front door.

"We're going to the city," one daughter called over her shoulder.

"To go shopping," the younger finished, with a conspiratorial smile.

"I'm sorry to rush off, darling," Grace Abernathy pecked Anne on both checks European style, "but you two are likely to talk business, and you know how the girls squirm. He's in the dining room waiting for you," she added over her shoulder. "Ta, ta."

Anne waved good-bye. She had grown used to Grace's flamboyant ways and, more important, had lost her discomfort with the vast differences between Dr. Abernathy's aristocratic reserve and his wife's excesses. Beneath her veneer, Grace Abernathy was a solid support for her family, with brains to match her husband's.

Anne paused in the entryway to gaze at her favorite stained-glass window, which dominated the landing of the stairs—a knight dressed in white kneeling before a brilliant golden star. The banisters were a dark oak, the carpet a burgundy that matched tones in the knight's tunic and the red roses in the border of the window. She glanced through the French doors to her right, where palms and sofas filled the back wall of the large living room. Every time she came to Dr. Abernathy's house, she felt as if she'd entered a chapel. She stood for a moment in the silence.

Carrying this calm with her, she walked down the hallway to the left and into the dining room. Dressed in a shirt, khaki pants, and his habitual ascot, Dr. Abernathy was as relaxed as he ever allowed himself to be. He offered her a glass of wine. "I hope you don't mind that we are dining alone tonight. We do have business, and Grace and the girls need to spend some of my money." He rolled his eyes.

"Thank you." Anne accepted the glass and took her seat at the long table next to Dr. Abernathy, who sat at the head. They started with a pumpkin soup with some complex spicing that Anne tried to decipher with each bite. "This is delicious."

"I'll tell the cook."

"How was your trip to Washington?"

"Very busy. I think I'm getting too old for politics."

Anne laughed. "That'll be the day."

Dr. Abernathy paused to consider her, wineglass in hand. "It's true, you know. This public life is not my true vocation."

Anne looked up, surprised. "So are you going to retire and become a gardener? Sail off to the islands?"

"No, my place is here with your family."

"But you are family." Anne was touched by his wistful tone. "Now tell me about this mysterious case of yours. I'm eager to put my teeth into something."

Rather than answering, Dr. Abernathy rang a small bell beside his plate and the cook carried in the next course. "Our compliments on the soup, Lois."

"Thank you, sir."

Anne surveyed her plate, a small portion of bean loaf served with wild rice and haricots verts. "Has Thomas talked you into becoming a vegetarian?"

Dr. Abernathy laughed and patted his stomach. "Just want to eat light when I have the chance." He looked at her, a serious expression on his face. "Before we talk business, tell me what's bothering you."

Anne set down her fork. "Bothering me? Why do you think something is bothering me?"

"Well, let's see; you disappear from your grandmother's without a word, you've been distracted at the office, you come here asking about business so quickly. Shall I go on?"

"There's more?" Anne looked a bit chagrined.

"You've been looking tired lately. And preoccupied. Is it anything I can help you with?" Dr. Abernathy softened his tone.

"It's just the family trying to take over my life again."

"More than usual?"

She sighed. "Thomas and Elizabeth seem to think that accepting an inheritance means accepting their demands about how to handle it. And my mother . . ." Anne picked up her fork again. ". . . thinks I've completely gone over to the other side."

"You know, it's too bad Katherine has divided the family when we're really all on the same side."

"Well, you can hardly blame her." Anne turned and looked at Dr. Abernathy as his comment registered. "What side would that be?"

"That is one of the things I was hoping to talk to you about tonight."

"What are you talking about? I thought we had a case to discuss."

Dr. Abernathy chuckled. "In a manner of speaking, we do. If you're finished, let's adjourn to the library for sherry."

The library held a large collection Anne had never fully explored. As a child, she'd loved to climb the spiral staircase to the second floor of books surrounded by a small walkway protected by banisters. She and Thomas had often played pirates here, making each other walk the plank or pretending they were at the top of a mast searching the ocean with their scopes. Now a fire burned brightly in the stone fireplace framed by two comfortable sofas, an overstuffed chair, and several reading lamps. A decanter of sherry, a pitcher of water, and glasses waited on an end table. Anne curled up on the sofa and wrapped herself in a chenille comforter. Dr. Abernathy handed her a glass of sherry.

"You know, I've never really liked this stuff," she confessed. "It's too sweet."

"Would you like something else?"

"No, thank you." Anne put the glass down on the coffee table. "Now tell me what this is all about. I confess, you have me puzzled."

Dr. Abernathy paused over a sip of sherry, then studied her.

"What? This is Anne, remember? Your honorary niece?"

Dr. Abernathy settled back on the sofa and reached for his pipe. "I've been trying to figure out how to tell you this ever since it became apparent that you were the heir to . . ." He hesitated, and Anne's heart thumped. ". . . to the crystal."

"The crystal." Anne sat forward. "What do you know about the crystal?"

"Quite a bit, my dear." He looked into her eyes for a long moment. "I am the teacher your grandmother said would be contacting you."

Anne stared in disbelief. "You?"

"Yes, your old uncle is also a mystic."

"How can that be? You've always been so . . ." she reached for a word, "rational."

Dr. Abernathy smiled at this. "I'll show you how mysticism is also rational and follows natural laws."

Anne stood up suddenly, "Oh, so now you are going to start telling me how to run my life? Well, I don't think so. Not you, too."

Dr. Abernathy made no move to stop her. "I can understand you feel betrayed."

"You're damn right I do, and I'm leaving."

"If you want to leave, please do."

"I will leave, and I don't need your permission." Anne's face was flushed.

"I'll never force you to do anything against your will. The job you have before you is too dangerous, the training too rigorous, the attunement too refined to be forced. You must be one hundred percent committed to succeed."

By the time Dr. Abernathy finished this speech, Anne was halfway across the room. She stopped and turned on him. "What job? What is this legacy you all keep talking about? Why did Aunt Cynthia give this to me when I hardly knew her?"

"That might be a good place for us to start tonight," Dr. Abernathy said quietly.

"Are you going to conjure up her spirit and ask her?"

He ignored the sarcasm. "I don't think we'll have to go that far."

Anne stared at him, at a complete loss.

"I only know part of the story. As children, your mother and Cynthia were unusually competitive. Katherine was the older, but by only eighteen months. By tradition, the eldest daughter is usually the heir."

"Everyone inherits from Grandmother. She's been clear about that always." Anne was still standing halfway across the room.

"I'm not talking about money or property."

"Then what are you talking about? Why does everyone keep secrets from me?" Tears welled up in her eyes and she shook her head against them, annoyed with herself.

"Because your mother insisted, darling. But now it is time to tell you the truth."

Anne walked back over to the sofa and sat on the edge. "I would like to know the truth."

Dr. Abernathy took a sip of sherry and sat back, his attention turned inward for a moment.

Anne picked up her drink and finished it off in one gulp. Dr. Abernathy raised an eyebrow and Anne shrugged. "I think I need it."

He chuckled. "It's not all that bad, you know. Your family holds a particular responsibility with historical roots that go back—well, quite far. I'm going to leave it to Thomas to tell you the intricacies of the family history. Most people think aristocratic standing can be traced back to ancient landowners. But it's not that simple. Some families get their standing because special abilities are passed through their line. Your family has a long history of metaphysical talent."

Anne snorted.

"The family's public obligation stems from this talent."

Anne started to interrupt, but Dr. Abernathy forestalled her. "At least hear me out."

She held her hands up in a gesture of surrender.

"Each generation is trained to use their psychic senses. The men, as you know, are trained to rule. And now perhaps the women," he conceded when he saw her arched eyebrows. "We've been living through a dark night. When I say 'we,' I mean humanity in general. Enlightened leadership can lessen suffering during the dark times. That's been half your family's job.

He paused to light his pipe. "But this night will end and when it does, it's important that the Le Clairs and others like them be in positions of power to bring certain knowledge to light. This is the second half of the family responsibility." Dr. Abernathy's eyes glowed with a depth of feeling she'd never witnessed in him before.

"You really believe this stuff, don't you?"

"I have reason to, Anne. I've seen many things."

"Those are lovely sentiments. Reactionary, but sweet. What does this crystal have to do with it?"

"There's so much to tell you." Dr. Abernathy closed his eyes for a moment.

"Then tell me what happened between Katherine and Cynthia."

"As I've said, they were competitive as children. As the elder, Katherine was in line to be the Keeper, but her sister was much more talented. Katherine didn't have the patience for the training. She was undisciplined and headstrong. Eventually, Cynthia was chosen instead of her. I don't think Katherine ever forgave her."

Anne nodded. "Well, that fits my mother. She thinks she should be ruling the world."

"We're not sure what brought about the complete break. It happened after Katherine had married and moved to the city."

"But you promised me the truth. What was it she was supposed to be the keeper of?"

"The crystal."

Anne shook her head. "Always the crystal."

"This crystal is so ancient that we've lost part of the knowledge of its use and origin. We can trace it back two thousand years. As I said, Thomas will explain the details to you. The legend is that one will be born to the Le Clairs who will know how to unlock the secrets of this stone and use it to bring in the light."

Anne could contain herself no longer. "Well, that lets me out, since I know nothing about it. This crystal is just a necklace, for God's sake. You're spouting medieval superstitions. How can a rock do anything like that? How can you take any of this seriously?"

"How has it been affecting you since you've had it?"

Anne drew herself up. "It hasn't affected me at all."

Dr. Abernathy studied her for a long moment. "If you want me to tell the truth, I would appreciate the same from you."

"Oh, all right, I'm having a lot of dreams. That's it."

"Tell me about them." His tone was clinical and detached.

Anne began to recount the dreams she'd had since receiving the crystal. As she continued, even she was impressed by their number and intensity. When she'd finished, Dr. Abernathy nodded. "Any more?"

"I think that's it."

"How long have you had the crystal?"

Anne counted. "Ten days."

"Have you ever had dreams like this before?"

Dr. Abernathy's calm step-by-step questioning reminded her of how a case was built in a court of law, and she started to relax.

"No, not that I can recall. I used to have intense dreams as a child, but they faded."

He picked up his glass and said casually, "Thomas thinks they're more than dreams."

"He said something about the crystal downloading its history to me, but how can a rock talk?"

Dr. Abernathy poured Anne another glass of sherry. "Actually, crystal transmits energy quite well. It is used in computers, watches—"

Anne interrupted, "Yes, I've read about it."

"You have?" She had surprised him.

"I've done a little research on my own."

"That's my Annie." He tipped his glass to hers. "Interrupt me if I repeat what you already know. Crystal can be programmed with information, like a file in a computer. This information can be placed or retrieved psychically. It's really not such a strange notion when you understand the crystalline structure."

Dr. Abernathy looked around for a piece of paper. "This idea has been called the lattice defect theory. The structure of quartz crystal is silicon dioxide, one silicon atom bonded to two oxygen atoms forming a hexagon. That's why crystals have six points." He drew a small crystal.

"Okay, that makes sense."

"In the latticework of a crystal, the silicon atom is sometimes missing, leaving an empty energy space." He drew a representation of this. "There can be millions of such spaces in even a small crystal. It is believed that this space can be occupied by pulsed energy, or human thought."

"What?" Anne shook her head. "How can that be? Human thought isn't energy."

"It isn't? So what are they measuring when they take an EEG?"

"Electrical energy."

"And how is this different from thought?"

She sat back. "Well, I guess you have a point, but it still sounds like science fiction."

"This crystal could have been programmed thousands of years ago with information to be passed down and retrieved much later, when humanity wakes from its long sleep."

"A letter from the past. But how do we read it? We don't even speak the same language now. Besides, they were cave men, weren't they?"

Dr. Abernathy rubbed his temples. "We have a lot of information to go over in a short time. And I want to leave the history for Thomas. The thought impulse is not necessarily encoded in language, actual words, but in intention. The current mind will translate the impulse into images, perhaps words, that make sense given its context. For now, let's see if we can find out anything about why Cynthia gave this crystal to you."

Anne's forehead wrinkled. "Okay, how do we do that?"

"I'd like to use hypnosis to access any early childhood memories you might have of your aunt."

She frowned. "But hasn't hypnosis been proven unreliable? Aren't people arguing that therapists can plant false memories?"

"Possibly, if used incorrectly, but I know what I'm doing. Do you want to proceed?"

"What do I do?"

"Lie down and get completely comfortable."

Anne lay back on the couch.

Dr. Abernathy covered her with a blanket.

She smiled. "Just like when I stayed overnight as a kid and you tucked me in."

"Your metabolism will drop when you go into an altered state," he explained. "Now close your eyes and just listen to my voice." Dr. Abernathy began a standard hypnotic induction, beginning with her breathing, then asking her to relax each part of her body in turn, starting from her feet and working his way up. He took a long time and soon Anne was floating in a quiet, peaceful state.

"Now I want you to go in your mind to the place you feel safe. Lift your finger when you're there."

Anne immediately lifted her right forefinger.

"Tell me where you are."

"In Granny's rose garden," said Anne in a childlike voice.

"Describe it for me," Dr. Abernathy said.

"It's so beautiful, with a birdbath in the center and all colors of roses planted around. In the back is a trellis with red ones growing all over it. In the summer, I can hide on the bench behind it and no one can see me. The air is full of the roses' smell."

Dr. Abernathy went on. "Now, Anne, I want you to go to a time when you were with your Aunt Cynthia."

Anne's first memory was of riding her pony with Cynthia over the estate. The pony ride melted into Christmas morning, which gave way to a pillow fight with Thomas that Aunt Cynthia stopped. Dr. Abernathy's voice whispered above her somewhere as memory after memory played out before her eyes. Then Anne was alone with Cynthia, before a burning candle.

"Tell me what is happening," Dr. Abernathy said.

"Aunt Cynthia is drawing in the air with a knife and we're holding hands. Now she's sprinkling me with water." Anne's nose wrinkled. "It tickles."

"How old are you?"

"Four."

Incense burned on the altar beside the candle. A bowl of water and a bowl of salt stood on the other side. The crystal necklace lay in the middle surrounded by rose petals. Cynthia turned to Anne and asked, "Do you remember why you were born?"

"Yes, Auntie, we all came to change the world."

"We?"

"Many of us. We're here to make things good again." "You remember this?"

Anne nodded solemnly.

Cynthia kissed her forehead. "I'm going to tell you a secret, darling, and let's keep it between us. Is that okay?"

Again, Anne nodded.

"This crystal is going to be yours one day, and you're going to use it to make things good again for all the people on Earth. Do you want to do that?"

"Yes, ma'am."

Cynthia smiled. "Now I'm going to chant. It's like singing. Then we'll both hold the crystal together, and this will bind you to it."

"But I already belong to it, Auntie."

Cynthia's eyes widened.

"When I was in the castle and even before."

"You remember?"

Anne nodded.

"Good, this will make your memories stronger." She began to chant again and the atmosphere deepened. After a few minutes, Cynthia picked up the crystal and placed it in both their hands. She called on the highest ones. "Bless this child and strengthen her abilities. Return her memories and her knowledge from past initiations. Protect her and lead her. Lend her your grace, for it is clear she is the one. This one will turn the key."

As Anne recounted the prayer, tears seeped from the corners of her eyes.

When Anne stopped talking, Dr. Abernathy counted her back to the present moment.

Anne opened her eyes and smiled up at him. "Imagine that," she said. "I remembered past lives as a child. I knew the purpose of my life then. If only I'd kept that knowledge."

"Excellent. I wondered if you would retain full memory." Dr. Abernathy handed her a glass of water.

"Thank you." She sat up and drank it down.

"Tell me what else you remember."

"After the ritual, Mother found out we'd been together and insisted I tell her what had happened. Then she called Cynthia on the phone and I remember a screaming fight. She kept saying, 'You'll never see my daughter again.' And I never did. I cried and cried. I really missed her, even though I dreamed about her often."

"So now we know why Katherine broke so completely with Cynthia. She couldn't stand for Cynthia to teach you." He looked at her for a moment, his eyes shining. "Now it's certain. You are the one. We feared you would never accept this."

Anne sighed. "But can it be true? I've spent so many years not believing in any of this. I've pushed down any psychic abilities I may have had. Maybe it's too late."

Dr. Abernathy sat back on his sofa. "This session is a good sign. You went into trance very rapidly. And—"

Anne interrupted him, "Yes, as you were getting me to relax, I remembered that Aunt Cynthia had done this with me many times. She also taught me a special sound used to meditate. I did it every day as a child, and I still do when I'm tired or worried. I'd forgotten where I learned it, I've been doing it so long."

"That is another excellent sign. You've meditated most of your life, so you'll be able to learn how to open to your dreams and visions easily."

"I don't know. It all seems so unreal."

He smiled at her. "Do you want to continue?"

Tears filled Anne's eyes. "Very much. I feel as if I've uncovered some hidden treasure I never imagined I had."

"Excellent. I think we've done enough tonight. You'll sleep well. I'll be in touch with you soon." Anne nodded.

"I'll call for a taxi. I don't want you driving after this session."

Anne smiled. "Ever the protector."

"That's my job, my dear. You can't imagine how accurate you are."

6

$\mathcal{M}$ichael usually found comfort in the group's Friday night ritual, and he hoped tonight would quiet his thoughts. He lit a candle, breathed a prayer, and walked the corners to his seat. He closed his eyes to meditate, but his mind still toyed with his predicament. How could he win Anne's trust? Since their chance encounter on Monday, he'd heard nothing from her. The look on her face when she'd discovered he taught at the bookstore made him fear that he would never hear from her again. Yet he knew their destinies were linked. During the week, he'd sought guidance during meditation (and from those very methods that had alienated Anne). He'd seen a flurry of images when he'd asked about past lives. He was *certain* they'd known each other in the past, worked together, in fact.

He'd also searched for information along more conventional lines. In news archives, he discovered many photos of her. As he scrolled through the pictures, he watched her grow from a bundle in her mother's arms at her uncle's state funeral to a golden-haired child atop her first pony to a graduate of Harvard. Along the way, those blue eyes had lost some of their initial sparkle. When he came to the announcements of her marriage, Michael felt a twinge of disappointment, but five years later, he discovered a rude article speculating on the reason for her divorce.

But these public documents did not contain the kind of information he needed.

Michael chided himself for his impatience and doubt. Doubt was the worse, because it could influence the outcome. This quiet feeling would be broadcast to the subtle energies almost as a set of instructions: "Give me what I fear the most." Michael had done spiritual work long enough to know he must return to a quiet trust in the universe to bring them together at the right time. With this thought, he focused again on his meditation and felt some measure of peace enter his heart.

After the silence came the chanting. Michael felt the power in the sound around him. He was grateful for the quiet strength of his companions who had honed their minds and hearts with years of discipline. He would not fall when he was held in this net of safety.

After the chanting ended and the group grounded themselves in the present, Guy asked for the floor. He looked at each member to gather their attention. "We have discovered the time."

A current of excitement ran through the room, but no one spoke. Twelve sets of eyes were on him.

"On Imbolc, an alignment takes place more powerful than the configuration in May at the turn of the millennium. It has escaped the attention of uninitiated astrologers because it is less obvious." Guy looked around at the curious expressions on the faces of his friends, savoring this moment. "It is the Star set in the thirteenth degree."

Shocked silence greeted this statement, and then the silence burst. Robert raised his hands for order. Gradually, the room returned to silence. He addressed himself to Guy. "The Star, on February first? How could we have missed this most important sign until it's almost upon us?"

"Recently, a member in Germany circulated an article discussing reconciling certain changes in the calendars, especially the ones made by Pope Gregory." He looked around. "Everyone will recall he added ten days to correct the Julian calendar, which was off already. This article points out the necessity of including certain star configurations and other celestial phenomena such as black holes—"

Robert raised his eyebrows and Guy cut himself off midstream. A pained expression crossed Guy's face and he refocused his comments. "At any rate, some of these phenomena have only been recently charted, but our colleague recognized their description in some ancient texts. To sum up, the information has just now become available."

Robert covered his smile by scratching his beard. "Thank you, Guy." He glanced around the circle. "This is certainly momentous news. I can hardly believe I've lived to see this day so close upon us."

A chill ran through Michael. Two chance meetings with Anne in a week. Discovering the new Keeper only four weeks after the death of the old one. It made sense now.

Robert took a breath to continue, but it caught in his throat and his eyes teared up. He closed them and whispered, "God give us strength to complete our task."

From around the room others joined his prayer. "God grant us wisdom."

"And guidance."

"May we be found worthy."

After a moment, the group members opened their eyes and Robert, master of himself again, continued. "Michael, my son, are you prepared?"

Michael smiled at the man who'd taught him so much, who was indeed his spiritual father. "I can only do my appointed duty. The miracle will come from above."

"Well spoken. And the girl?"

A shadow darkened Michael's eyes. "I've had a setback with that contact." He recounted his meeting with Anne at the bookstore.

"How can a holder of the crystal disrespect the mystical?" Miriam asked.

"I gathered from our talk that her training has been incomplete. Some resistance from her mother."

Various members frowned or shook their heads. Miriam continued. "The crystal rite cannot be done by the uninitiated. The result could be disastrous."

Robert agreed. "This doesn't bode well for the project. Even a well-trained practitioner would have difficulty completing this job."

"She has training from many lives. And she is gifted," Michael said.

Robert shook his head. "That's no substitute for work in this life. How could the Le Clairs have allowed this to happen?"

"Perhaps we should try to take the crystal. At least we know how to use it," another member suggested.

Everyone was silent for a minute.

Michael broke the silence. "We certainly know how to use the crystal, but I'm not sure we have all the information we need."

Robert said, "That is an extreme solution. The Le Clairs are a respected family. We should try speaking with them before carrying out so drastic a plan."

"If we speak with them, they'll be alerted we know of their crystal and who holds it," Michael pointed out.

"Yes," Robert conceded.

"These are drastic times," the other member pushed his point. "Many groups holding the sacred trust have been infiltrated or become corrupt."

Others nodded.

"Still, breaking spiritual law will weaken us," Robert pointed out. "Let Michael try again in the time he has left." He turned to Michael. "You must leave the country very soon. Can you make arrangements at work?"

"As a matter of fact, I've been invited to speak in Egypt at an international conference shortly before this date."

"A synchronicity. Excellent sign," Robert said. "Have you booked your flight?"

"Not yet."

"Good. You'll have to leave a few days earlier. I'll explain what you must do." Robert looked around at the group. "Everyone has a part in this. Each of you knows your duty. We've trained for many years for this day. Don't neglect your meditation and prayer in this crucial time."

The group spontaneously stood and joined hands. Robert spoke a long benediction to end the meeting. Michael made an appointment with Robert and left for his apartment, even more concerned about Anne.

* * *

PAUL MARCHANT CHOSE a table in the hotel bar toward the back and ordered bottled mineral water. It was essential he remain sharp during this meeting. He surveyed the room and was satisfied to see the place was almost empty. He preferred having no witnesses, but had hesitated to let the man come to his apartment. He might see something Marchant hadn't meant to reveal.

His contact entered the front of the bar and Marchant raised his hand to catch his attention. The man bought a draft from the bar, then walked to the table. "Good to see you. It's been a while since you were in D.C."

Marchant returned the handshake. "Good to see you, too, Donald."

Donald looked around. "I don't like meeting in public. If someone saw me, that would be my clearance."

Marchant attempted a smile. "Then let's come to the point. Were you able to decode those files I sent you?"

Donald spoke with contained excitement. "I was. We knew they were tunneling in Egypt, but now we have proof."

Marchant sat forward, his eyes fixed brightly on Donald. "Do you have the pictures?"

He slid a manila envelope across the table. Marchant put it in his briefcase immediately. "And the contact?"

"This one must be deep cover because official military files list him as dead."

"Dead?"

Donald nodded, satisfied to have surprised Marchant. "Karl Mueller was born Adam Ardsen in Detroit. His father was a Vietnam veteran who never recovered from combat. He started to drink heavily and do crack and heroin. The father was killed by a gang in the inner city, and the mother moved the family to an uncle's ranch in Montana.

"As a teenager, Adam got involved with a fringe group up there with a vague neo-Nazi agenda. Joined the marines on his eighteenth birthday and was promoted quickly. He was involved in several insertion operations in the Middle East, Eastern Europe, and Central America.

Then official reports say he was killed in a training op." Donald smiled dryly. "That's what they say when one of their boys bites it on a cover mission."

Marchant listened, swiveling his head from side to side.

"His file indicates he spent a good bit of time at secret Nazi settlements in the Andes. Hell, some say Hitler is still alive there."

"I've heard stories," Marchant commented.

"I'd say our boy just got a promotion."

"To?"

"That's where the trail ends." Donald sat back in his chair and took a long sip of his beer. "This guy is involved in some deep-cover black ops, for sure. He works for the real government now, the multinationals."

"So he's legitimate?"

"Legitimate?" Donald leaned forward. "His information is good, but he'll show you only what he wants you to know. These guys are danger- ous, Paul, and they're powerful. They answer to no one. They operate outside the law."

"They're uncovering the Hall of Records."

"Paul, are you listening to me?"

Marchant waved a hand dismissively. "But who else would open it? Who else has the money, the technology, the access?"

"After they're done with you, they'll leave you in the garbage dump just on the other side of the Giza Plateau." Donald thumped the table with his forefinger.

Marchant looked through Donald at some shining future. "They need me."

"Look, man, if you go in, just leave some insurance with me. A taped conversation, photos, something. That way, you might have a chance of making it out."

The smile did not fade from Marchant's face. "They don't understand what they're uncovering. Once I get in, they won't be able to touch me."

Donald frowned. "What does that mean?"

Marchant only smiled in answer.

"Just leave something with me."

Marchant glanced at Donald, but his eyes strayed back to his brief-case. "Whatever you say." He pushed a smaller envelope across the table. "Thank you."

Donald put the envelope in his inner jacket pocket and stood up. "Okay, man. Knock yourself out with those pictures."

Marchant waited ten minutes before leaving, and then made sure he wasn't followed.

7

Anne awoke at twelve on Saturday to the concerned meows of her two cats. She fed them and straightened up the Christmas tree again. The phone rang.

It was Dr. Abernathy. "How are you this morning?"

"I feel wonderful. I haven't felt this peaceful in years," she said.

"Excellent. You don't have cold feet?"

"I have to admit I'm intrigued. I certainly didn't expect to remember anything about Cynthia."

"Good. Dreams?"

"Not last night."

"That makes sense. You needed time to incorporate the work we did. Now, if you're game, I want you to start on a new regimen. We need to get you up to speed as quickly as possible."

"Okay, coach."

Dr. Abernathy laughed. "I've sent a courier over with some suggestions. Let me know if you have any objections or need clarification. If they meet with your approval, then get started as soon as you can."

They hung up. Elizabeth had chosen the perfect teacher for her, Anne thought. With the door open to leave, Anne felt free to stay.

She sat with her teacup in front of the fire, remembering the single flame of her faith as a child. Wordsworth had been right about young children trailing clouds of glory. It had all been simple then. The memories they'd uncovered last night surprised her, as did her easy acceptance of them. She felt whole somehow, like she'd found a long-forgotten box in the attic. Dr. Abernathy's explanations seemed rational. It felt right to continue.

* * *

HIS PROPOSED REGIMEN, however, would seriously cut into her time. It included two one-hour meditations a day and a session with the crystal each night. Plus she was to keep a journal of her experiences during those sessions and record her dreams.

By Monday, she was enjoying meditating and reading so much she decided to take yet another day off. Her dreams, now that she was waiting with pen in hand, seemed to have disappeared. No images formed in the depths of the crystal, but her inner silence was deepening. When she asked why everything had gone dark when she was finally paying attention, Dr. Abernathy told her to be patient, that these things had their own timing.

On Tuesday, Anne went into the office to finish off loose ends before the holiday break. Sorting through the papers on her desk, she found a note from Susan telling her the private investigators had finished their report and that she had an appointment at their office this afternoon. It took Anne a minute to remember that she'd asked them to investigate Cynthia's death.

Anne made her way to the Madison Avenue offices of Lynx and Associates, and was ushered into the main investigator's office immediately. Sitting behind a massive desk topped with a green banker's lamp was John Lynx. Overweight with a round face and bald head, he looked every inch the CPA, not a private eye.

He rose and shook her hand. "Please sit down. Can we get you anything?"

"I'm fine, thank you."

At a nod from Mr. Lynx, the secretary closed the door. He assumed a look of commercial sympathy, which transformed him into the perfect undertaker. "We're sorry for your recent loss, Ms. Le Clair. I know it's difficult to talk about the recently departed, and it can be even more upsetting to discover anything . . ." He waved a hand and looked up into the air, searching for the most delicate word.

"Untoward?" Anne suggested.

Mr. Lynx nodded gravely.

"Let me set your mind at rest, Mr. Lynx. I didn't know my aunt well and, as an attorney, I've had some experience with criminal cases. Please be perfectly frank with me."

Mr. Lynx underwent another transformation into a straightforward businessman. He opened the file in front of him and cleared his throat. "Your aunt had some unusual contacts for someone of your family's standing—a Rosicrucian group with connections to a Jewish mystical sect in the city."

Anne suppressed a smile.

"About six months before her death, she had several meetings with this group, followed by travel to Israel and then Egypt. Did your aunt have business in the Middle East?"

"Not to my knowledge."

He nodded. "It seems she met with a historian in Jerusalem, a man connected to the group here in New York. They caused a bit of a stir when they were found trying to enter a restricted area near the Wailing Wall late at night."

"Excuse me?" Anne said. "I wonder why my aunt would want to go to the Wailing Wall."

Mr. Lynx ran a well-manicured nail across the page in front of him. "It is puzzling. Her activities in Egypt seemed normal for a tourist, except she hired a guide who specializes in leading New Age groups." Mr. Lynx sniffed. "They traveled to most of the major sites it would seem. Your aunt did rent the Great Pyramid for one evening."

"Rent the pyramid? For what?"

"Apparently, people like to meditate in it." Mr. Lynx shrugged, obviously at a loss.

"Now here is the unfortunate part. A few days after her return, your aunt's apartment was broken into. Nothing was reported stolen, which is unusual since she had some rare artifacts—silver, jewelry, and the like—in the residence. Three days later, your aunt had a heart attack and died the next day. However, before her trip she'd had a medical checkup and was reported in perfect health. Her physician and her personal trainer were both surprised by her death." He paused. "Ms. Le Clair, I believe your aunt was murdered."

Anne's stomach twisted. "Murdered? But why?"

"That is always the question. I'm afraid we have no suspect."

Anne grabbed for her briefcase. She needed to get out. There had been another assassination in the family. She thanked the private detective and gathered the report he'd prepared for her.

He walked her out. "If we can be of any assistance . . ."

She thanked him and hurried home. Dr. Abernathy was not in his office, Thomas did not pick up his phone, and the butler informed Anne that her grandmother was out. She left messages with all of them. Then she noticed that the light on her answering machine was flashing. She heard Dr. Abernathy's voice and felt a rush of relief.

"Sorry I missed you at the office. I wanted to let you know there's an extremely important session tomorrow night at your grandmother's estate. You'll need to fast all day if you plan to participate. Hope to see you there."

Anne sat down. She read through the report, which simply added details to what she'd already been told. All she could do was wait. Who had killed her aunt and, more importantly, why? She leaned back on the couch and thought about meditating, but she could not imagine any success in her current state. Merlin butted her arm with his head, a concerned look on his face. Vivienne turned circles on the couch. Anne hugged Merlin to her, and the unshed tears finally fell onto his sleek coat.

* * *

ON WEDNESDAY NIGHT, Anne arrived at her grandmother's estate just as the sun set. She ran up the curving staircase and deposited her overnight bag in her bedroom, then found Dr. Abernathy waiting for her in the library.

"Anne, I'm pleased you're joining us," he said. Then he saw the look on her face. "What's the matter?"

"Didn't you get my message?"

"Yes, but I didn't have time to call. We've been preparing for this ceremony all day."

"I have some disturbing news. Before we talked, I decided to do some investigating into Aunt Cynthia's life."

Dr. Abernathy sat forward, a look of alarm on his face.

"A reputable firm," she reassured him. "Someone the office uses from time to time."

"And?" Dr. Abernathy pushed back into the sofa and crossed his arms.

"She may have been murdered, that's what."

Dr. Abernathy nodded his head.

"Murdered. Assassinated," Anne repeated more loudly.

"Yes, we know."

"You know?" she shouted. "So why didn't you tell me? Why is there no investigation? Why hasn't the family been notified?"

"Those who have chosen to take on their responsibilities as Le Clairs know about it," Dr. Abernathy said forcefully.

"But Mother doesn't know about it," she protested.

"Just as I said. We have kept a lot from your mother since she has shirked her responsibility to the family. And it is being investigated. It has just been kept from the press."

Anne sank down onto a nearby chair. "Why would someone kill Aunt Cynthia? Uncle James, yes, but why her?"

"We aren't sure. The FBI is investigating a Jewish mystical group with links to extremists in Jerusalem." He shrugged. "It could have been some other group or a person acting alone. This is a powerful family."

"Could it have anything to do with the crystal?" Anne's voice was almost a whisper.

Dr. Abernathy considered her for a minute. "We don't know. I'll let you know what we discover. Rest assured the situation is being handled."

Anne was somewhat relieved. "Why didn't you call me back? I was very worried."

"As I said, we had to prepare for tonight. What we're about to do is vital to the success of your mission."

"If it's vital, why did you tell me it was optional for me to come?"

He sat forward. "Everything you do must be from your own free will. Now, are you ready to focus on tonight's business?"

"I suppose so. I did as you asked, fasted all day and meditated with the crystal."

"Excellent. Now tell me, why might we have an important ritual tonight?"

Anne looked at him blankly.

"Do you know what tonight is?"

"Wednesday," she answered quickly.

A short laugh escaped Dr. Abernathy. "Yes, and it is also the winter solstice. According to the old ways, it is midwinter. The Druids started the seasons on the days that mark the halfway points between the equinoxes and solstices. The winter began on Samhain—Halloween. That's the beginning of winter, according to the old ways. The solstice marks midwinter. Tonight is the longest night of the year, the deepest point of winter. Tonight the darkness triumphs, and in that triumph lies its defeat. In the old religion, on the solstice we celebrate the rebirth of the sun."

"Okay, but what does all that have to do with us?" Anne asked.

"Even in the city we're affected by nature, by the seasons, by the length and intensity of the light." Dr. Abernathy reached for his pipe, but changed his mind. "Do you feel the same in the spring as you do now? In the heat of summer?"

"Well, of course there are emotional differences," Anne conceded.

Dr. Abernathy's eyes kindled. "The differences are much more profound than even modern science understands. Even city cats don't go into heat until the days have reached a certain length. Why? The pineal gland, the master gland in the center of the brain that helps produce altered states of consciousness, reacts to the sun's light, which turns on the reproductive cycles of cats. The pineal interacts with the pituitary and hypothalamus."

Anne frowned, little lines appearing at the corners of her blue eyes. "You're suggesting the sun affects consciousness?"

"Yes. Certain texts discuss the interaction of the pituitary and pineal glands in the production of soma, which is a chemical made by the body under certain circumstances that allows for the expansion of consciousness. The old rituals aren't just ceremonies to mark the agricultural and herding cycles. They take advantage of the effects different times of the year have on human consciousness. When the light is at its lowest, we turn inward. We honor the womb that gives birth to the light. We face the darkness, and in so doing, the light returns."

Anne tucked her feet under her. "As if Aunt Cynthia's murder wasn't enough."

"That is upsetting, but we must focus." Dr. Abernathy's eyes lit with sympathy. "Winter solstice is a good night to see what's hidden from view. We will do some scrying with your grandmother's large crystal. Did you bring your own?"

Anne pulled the small stone out from beneath her sweater. "It looks harmless, doesn't it?"

"Wear it and the robe I'll have delivered to your room. And nothing else." To Anne's raised her eyebrows, he replied, "And I mean nothing. Synthetic fibers interfere with the energy."

"Isn't that a bit excessive?" Then seeing his frown, she said, "Okay, okay. No more questions."

"I'll come get you in a few hours. You can nap, have tea, meditate, whatever you want. Just don't eat anything."

* * *

SHORTLY BEFORE ELEVEN O'CLOCK, Anne was reading in her bedroom, dressed only in the black robe she'd found draped over her bed and the crystal necklace. She'd tucked a comforter around her bare feet. There was a knock on her bedroom door. She put her book down, smoothed her robe, and opened the door.

Dr. Abernathy stood outside, also barefoot and garbed in a black robe marked with an equal-armed red cross.

"Black?" Anne pointed to her robe, then his

"Black absorbs energy. We'll be casting a circle, creating an energetically pure environment. Black helps us use the energy we generate more efficiently. And we're honoring the darkness. Follow me."

Anne followed him down the staircase and into the foyer. "Where are we going?"

He held his finger up to his lips and refused to answer.

Anne followed him to the back of the house into the ballroom that had been one of the later additions. He walked to the left wall.

"But—"

Dr. Abernathy shushed her forcefully, then turned and pushed something in the wall. A panel swung open, revealing a small entry.

Anne caught her breath. She'd never realized that the ballroom didn't run the entire length of the back of the house, that there was a secret room at the end.

Thomas stood just inside, also in a black robe. "Who desires entry?" he asked in a formal tone.

"The Protector," Dr. Abernathy replied.

Thomas shifted his gaze to Anne and asked again, "Who desires entry?"

Anne looked from her brother to her uncle, amazed by this archaic exchange.

"The Keeper," Dr. Abernathy replied for her.

Thomas stepped aside for them to enter.

Candles glowed from each corner of the room. In the center stood a low altar dominated by a large crystal ball illuminated by white candles and other accoutrements. Against one wall was a table with a decanter of wine and a loaf of bread, also surrounded by white candles, sprigs of holly, and Christmas flowers. She took a step forward and felt carpet beneath her feet. Looking down, she saw woven into the rug a large pentagram that took up a full third of the room.

Her grandfather Gerald, her cousin Rebecca, Winston and Cordelia Stuart, Mary Shak, and Julia and Bill Hardy, all family friends, stood in a circle along with a few people whose names she didn't recall. Everyone smiled or nodded, but no one spoke.

Elizabeth stood in the middle of the room, regal in her black robe, her hair loose and flowing down her back in a river of silver. She held out her hands for Anne. "I can't tell you how many times I have prayed for this. Stand here, dear, and don't say anything until I tell you." Elizabeth kissed her cheek, then turned to the north and raised her hands. She held a long knife, its blade elaborately carved, which she pointed across the room.

"I call upon the powers of the North, powers of earth and winter," she intoned. "We ask your guidance and protection in our circle as we honor the rebirth of the sun."

Anne noticed everyone had turned to face north and was holding up similar knives or just bare hands. When Elizabeth finished, she drew in the air with a flourish, which the group mimicked. Then everyone turned to face east. Elizabeth recited another invocation. By the time she turned to the south, Anne felt a shift in the room around her, a buzz, even a slight tingling on her skin, as if the air were charged with electricity. After invoking the four directions, Elizabeth lifted her hands and looked up, inviting the Solar Lord into their midst. Then she knelt and spoke to the Earth Mother.

Anne would have dismissed this as superstitious nonsense if she hadn't felt the atmosphere growing more vibrant as each direction was added to the circle. She vaguely remembered Cynthia doing something similar during the ceremony with the crystal when she was four.

Elizabeth stood and nodded. Rebecca picked up a silver bowl engraved with a simple star and an evergreen sprig from the center altar and walked the circle her grandmother had just created, sprinkling water and chanting softly. Anne couldn't make out her words. Once she had walked the circle, she went to each person and sprinkled each in turn. When she came to Anne, a warm smile lit her face. "May you be purified," she whispered. Drops of water fell on Anne's face and mouth. She tasted salt.

When her cousin finished her rounds, Thomas took up a stick of incense, lit it from the candle, and walked the perimeter, waving smoke in the air as he went. Following Rebecca's path, he waved incense around each person, intoning the same phrase, "May you be purified."

He looks exactly like a priest, Anne thought, amazed by how comfortable he seemed in the role.

She was beginning to feel light-headed, although she wasn't dizzy. Looking around the circle, she noticed the light had intensified, but she hadn't seen anyone add candles or a lamp. She wondered what had happened. Beneath her uncertainty was a growing lake of calm. She felt a stir in the air, a fresh breeze, but knew no one had opened a window.

Her grandmother looked at Anne and smiled. "The circle is complete," she said simply.

As if this were a cue, Gerald stepped forward and began to speak:
"We meet again on the longest night.
When dark has triumphed over light.
On this night we find it right
To seek within our inner light."

They all closed their eyes, so Anne followed suit. A soft wordless chant began. Anne floated on the sound, feeling her breath quiet, her body grow lighter. The crystal resting on her chest stirred to life. She lifted it out from beneath her robes.

Behind her came the voice of Elizabeth:
"Deep in the darkest night,
We feel a stir of light.
The Goddess groans and into the world
Is born the infant light."

Anne felt a hand on her shoulder. Mary handed her a few candles. She took one and passed the rest. Her cousin Rebecca moved behind her grandmother, lighting each candle in turn. The group chanted, "Hail the return of light." Once the candles were lit, everyone moved into a circle around the main altar. To her great surprise, they sang a Christmas hymn, "O Holy Night."

When the song finished, people found places for their candles around the room. Now Anne could see altars on each of the four walls. She placed her candle on the closest, the east, then joined the circle forming in the middle around the crystal ball. Her grandparents had cushions. Others sat cross-legged, their hands resting loosely on their knees.

Elizabeth spoke, "Tonight it is my great joy to welcome my granddaughter Anne into our circle. She is appointed Keeper. We bless the spirit of the past Keeper and pray for her enlightenment. May she guide this new one."

The group murmured welcomes to her.

Elizabeth continued, "Now we will search for guidance from the wise ones. We face a difficult challenge. This one is new to her responsibilities, yet the time presses in upon us. How shall we uphold our duty and fulfill our sworn oaths?" Elizabeth looked around the circle at the shining eyes of thirteen men and women. "Let us begin."

The group turned their attention to the crystal. A few began a low wordless chant. Anne followed the directions on scrying that she'd found in one of the books she'd bought. She looked at the crystal ball, focusing just inside the surface of the sphere. As the group's trance deepened, the chant gradually fell away.

Anne floated in the vibrant silence as if on a stream. Gradually, images formed inside the crystal. She saw a bonfire, heard other voices chanting. A pool of clear water appeared and a voice said, "Gaze into the water, but don't focus too closely. Allow yourself to drift." In the water, she saw reflected the face of the old woman she'd seen on her first night with her own crystal.

A glow started in the depths. It spread and encompassed her entire vision. Images formed. A long line of people walked through hot sand, some riding donkeys. Her throat burned with thirst for a few seconds. Then came the sound of splashing water. Women soaked in a Roman-style bath. Then a man sat in a study, hunched over amidst books and odd instruments, reading by candlelight. Next she was on a ship, desperate to escape, huddled with two small children. Again came the sounds of chanting from a circle of large standing stones. Then a man on a horse charged toward a group of men in white with swords, a large stone fortress behind them.

The images flowed so quickly she had trouble registering them. She grasped her own crystal to steady herself, but the contact only quickened the pace. More images exploded in her mind. She stood in the midst of a group, each holding a crystal, each chanting very particular sounds, each focusing as if the fate of worlds rested on their shoulders. The chanting grew more insistent, the weave of harmony more complex. Anne saw a large crystal in front of this group, the largest she'd ever seen. It soared over her head, taking up her entire field of vision. As the chanting grew to a pitch, the room began to hum, the floor to vibrate, the walls to quiver.

Suddenly, the space around and within her imploded, as if the world had sucked itself up into one tiny point, and then the enormous crystal before her exploded with light. A beam of purest white shot from the crystal and irradiated the room, the air, the walls. The light expanded into an enormous column, rising out of the room and flowing out through the domed ceiling into the night sky. If Anne's ears could have heard the sound, it would have burst her eardrums. Every cell in her body reverberated with this note that was also light. She felt as if she were etched into eternity. She gasped for release, for vision, for breath, but none came. She was burning in the fire of that radiance. She could stand it no longer. She lost consciousness and slumped to the floor.

* * *

"SHE'S COMING TO," Elizabeth said.

Anne glanced around at her childhood bedroom in her grandmother's estate. "What happened?"

"We were hoping you could tell us that," Thomas said, trying to keep the concern out of his voice. "You've been out for almost half an hour."

"How did I get here?" She started to sit up, but fell back on the pillow.

"I carried you," Thomas said. "Tell us what you saw."

Anne tried to recall her experiences. "I saw images, a lot of them. There were people in the desert, then in a community bath. I was in a library, on a boat." She closed her eyes wearily. "There were so many."

"Take your time," Elizabeth said. "There's no rush." This wasn't quite true, Thomas thought, but it wouldn't help her to know that now.

After Anne recited the visions she could remember, Grandmother Elizabeth asked, "What happened right before you passed out?"

"I was in some sort of room chanting with a group of people. It was a special chant, and we all had crystals." Her eyes widened as she remembered the enormous crystal in the middle. She tried to describe it. "It was as tall as a two-story building. And it exploded, only not really. It just suddenly . . ." Anne grasped for words. "There was a huge light, but it was also sound. I felt like I was on fire, only the pain was exquisite somehow. And then I guess I passed out."

There was a long silence in the room. Then Elizabeth said, "This is very promising."

"Promising? I fainted," Anne said.

"Yes, dear, but next time you won't."

"Next time?" Anne's eyes widened.

"Now I want you to go to sleep. I'm having some warm milk with sedative herbs sent up. Drink it all. You need to rest now. Tomorrow, we'll answer all your questions."

Anne tried to object, but Thomas could see she was still pale.

"Yes, Granny." Anne winked.

＊ ＊ ＊

DR. ABERNATHY, Elizabeth, and Thomas returned to the group to enjoy the traditional wine and bread after the ritual.

"How is she?" Julia asked as soon as they appeared.

"She's resting now," Dr. Abernathy said. "She went too deep, too fast. She's still a beginner, after all."

"Except for what she saw," Thomas amended.

Elizabeth handed each of them a plate of gingerbread with lemon sauce. "You both need to ground yourselves. She wasn't the only one who went deep. We have important news to digest. Members of our association in France report that their astrologers say we have an important opening coming up. This is an ancient configuration, the Star Alignment—one that has only recently been reinterpreted. It may be the sign of the rebirth. And there have been signs in nature and in dreams."

"Excellent," Rebecca said.

"This configuration will take place on the first of February."

There was a moment of stunned silence.

"Of this coming year?" Dr. Abernathy asked.

Elizabeth nodded, looking at each member in turn. "This makes our task all the more difficult, and our success all the more essential. If only Cynthia had told us what she discovered in Egypt before she died." Her knuckles were white on the arm of her chair.

"We should retrace her steps ourselves," Thomas said. "I could travel to Egypt and speak with her contact."

"Do we know his name?" asked Rebecca.

"No, but I know where to get it."

"If the time is so close, perhaps Anne should go with you," Gerald suggested.

Elizabeth shook her head, "She's not ready. We have so much to teach her. Damn it, Katherine!" She muttered this last softly, then drew herself up to her full height. "Anne must be prepared. We cannot carry this knowledge for so long only to fail at the last moment."

Dr. Abernathy placed a hand on her shoulder. "Perhaps this explains the intensity of her vision."

Elizabeth struggled with herself for a moment, then turned her eyes to him and nodded. He proceeded to tell the group what Anne had told them.

"But this is promising," Rebecca said. "She's accessing deeper information. Perhaps this is a clue to the use of the crystal."

"May I suggest a plan?" Thomas asked.

Elizabeth nodded.

"I'll try to find out what Cynthia discovered and return as quickly as possible."

"This seems unavoidable." Dr. Abernathy looked at Elizabeth. "We must put Anne on the fast track, focus night and day on her instruction."

"And we must have faith," Rebecca added softly, "that her spiritual training from past lives will come through for her."

Elizabeth studied the faces of the people she had worked with all her life, then nodded.

Dr. Abernathy spoke up. "There is one more piece of business. Our investigation of Cynthia's death turned up some disturbing possibilities. The cause of death is still a mystery."

"I thought she had a heart attack," Gerald said.

"She did, but why? We looked for designer drugs, the kind the CIA uses to induce heart attacks, but found nothing we could identify—no puncture marks, no trace drugs in her system. It could be a brand-new substance. We also discovered unusually high activity in Egypt by the Illuminati. We must consider the possibility that Cynthia was killed by magic." Dr. Abernathy looked around the circle.

"Magic?" Elizabeth said. "Cynthia could protect herself. Surely one of us would have picked up residual impressions. Who could do such a thing?"

"I can think of only one person," Dr. Abernathy said. "Alexander Cagliostro."

Rebecca inhaled sharply. "You mean he's still alive?"

"I thought he was only a myth," Bill Hardy said.

"No, he exists all right," responded Dr. Abernathy.

"Anne is definitely not ready to meet Alexander Cagliostro," Elizabeth said.

* * *

ANNE WOKE LATE on Thursday morning and sat up in bed, looking around to orient herself. The crystal rested next to her on the nightstand. Her memories of last night's ritual were vivid. She felt an unaccustomed happiness, like champagne just uncorked. Her stomach growled and she realized she was ravenous. She finished her morning ablutions quickly, pulled on jeans and a turtleneck, and hurried to the dining room.

Thomas sat at the table, dressed in riding clothes, drinking tea and looking out the expanse of windows. She joined him.

"How are you this morning?" he asked.

"Famished."

"I'm not surprised," he laughed and rang the small silver bell on the table.

The maid arrived shortly from the kitchen, and Anne asked for an omelet, hash browns, and juice. Meanwhile, she poured a cup of tea and took a scone from the basket on the table.

"Why are you not surprised?"

"About?"

"That I'm famished," she spoke carefully around a bite of scone and jam. "Where's the clotted cream?"

"Double cream, you know." Thomas pushed the bowl toward her.

"It's the holidays. I can eat over the holidays." Anne lavished her half-eaten scone with a spoonful of cream.

"Aren't you hungry?" she asked.

"I ate a snack last night after the ritual. Psychic work tends to make people hungry, but I'm used to it."

"How long have you been doing these rituals?"

"Ever since I left mother's house and started living on my own."

"But you spent holidays and summers with Grandmother while you were in boarding school."

Thomas looked thoughtful. "You're right. I guess since I was thirteen."

"I didn't know anything about it. I never realized that room was even there." Anne took another bite.

"You seem to have had a change of heart. How was your sudden conversion accomplished?"

"Dr. Abernathy helped me remember Cynthia. I remembered when she bonded me to the crystal. I think I was four or so."

"Where is your famous skepticism?"

Anne shrugged. "I'm willing to consider the evidence, and so far he's been able to provide perfectly rational explanations for my experiences."

"I'm glad to hear that," came a voice from the doorway.

Turning, Anne saw Dr. Abernathy, dressed in corduroy pants, a sweater, and ascot. He took a seat at the head of the table. "How is the star performer this morning?"

"Star? I don't think so," Anne said. "I feel wonderful."

"Dreams?"

"Can't recall any."

"You're consistent. That's good."

Estelle arrived with Anne's food and she plunged in. After a few more bites, Anne asked, "Were you able to make any sense of what I saw last night?"

Thomas and Dr. Abernathy looked at each other.

"What?" Anne demanded.

Dr. Abernathy nodded for Thomas to speak. "It's like I said before. The crystal is downloading its history to you. It's just that you've gone much deeper than Cynthia ever did in her lifetime."

Anne put down her fork. "How can that be? I'm a beginner."

"Not exactly. Remember, you've been meditating all your life," Dr. Abernathy corrected her. "Plus you've probably had spiritual training in past lives."

"Let's hope I can remember it," Anne said.

"I want to catch you up on the meeting last night." Dr. Abernathy gave her a brief version of the astrological information they had been given, then continued, "So you can see that we might be on a rather tight schedule. I'd like you to consider reassigning all your cases to another attorney and working full-time here to finish your training."

"Finish? I've just started."

"Which is exactly the problem."

"But I have a speech at the end of the month."

"You can deliver that. I'm just asking you to dedicate the next six weeks to your training."

Anne pushed her now empty plate away and took a sip of tea. "I suppose I could do that," she said at last. "Whatever happened last night was very intriguing, and I'd like to know more." She put her cup down and gazed out the window for a long moment, then murmured, "Mother is going to have a fit."

Thomas snorted. "If it weren't for Mother, we wouldn't be in this predicament."

Anne opened her mouth to defend Katherine out of habit, then stopped. "You're probably right."

Dr. Abernathy stood. "Excellent. I'll see to the office. I'll give you the day off, except for meditating. Shall we start tomorrow?"

"Deal." Anne shook his hand in mock seriousness. She looked up to see Thomas beaming at her.

"It's great to be working with you, Annie. When you feel up to it, we've got a lot of history to cover."

"Let's go for a ride," she said.

Thomas grabbed his riding gloves. "Sounds perfect. I was planning just that."

They spent the morning riding over the estate and the adjoining bridle paths. Anne felt the joy and vigor of their old childhood days. In the afternoon, she went home to the city since she'd only left the cats enough food for a day. They greeted her with demanding yowls. "Oh, you're such abused kitties." They purred and rubbed her legs as she prepared a dinner for them.

She had two phone messages. The first was from Susan telling her she understood Anne was taking some time off from the office and that she'd e-mail the speech. Anne made a note to mail Susan's Christmas packages to her home.

Next was a male voice Anne didn't recognize at first. "Anne, this is Michael Levy. I sold you the Art Deco brooch and had coffee with you at the metaphysical bookstore. I hope it's okay that I'm calling. I was wondering if you'd like to have dinner." He gave his phone number.

Anne sat looking at the machine for a moment. After all she'd done in the last few days, she certainly couldn't hold a class at a New Age bookstore against him. She decided to call him—if, she thought ruefully, her new schedule would permit a date.

8

$\mathcal{P}$aul Marchant paced around his hotel room, wondering how best to spend a Thursday evening in New York City. The Solstice Seminars conference would end tomorrow, and he was one of two keynote speakers. But his slides were ready, his talk almost routine. He wasn't interested in Broadway shows or films, or any of the Big Apple's cultural events. There were several rare books on his list, but he didn't feel like making the trip to used bookstores.

The conference organizers had invited him to the speaker's dinner, but he couldn't bear listening to self-important, part-time theorists. He'd read their books, and if he talked too much, his ideas would end up in the next article one of them wrote, with no credit given to him. He took out the worn envelope holding the satellite pictures and Donald's report. He'd pored over the photos and run calculations of the tunnel angles revealed in the shots, but there were so many channels. If these pictures were any indication, there could be several Halls of Records. In fact, he wouldn't be surprised if a whole city was hidden beneath the sand.

What had him puzzled was the math. He knew there had to be a pattern. He was looking for the place that matched the location of the Orion Stargate, but he hadn't been able to piece the photos together to reveal the whole Giza complex. Some pictures overlapped and some didn't connect at all. Plus he wasn't used to looking at these types of pictures. Ground-penetrating radar created an unusual image. And they were labeled poorly. Pure laziness on the part of some government flunky. He controlled his frustration and laid them out on the kingsize bed, trying to create a picture of the plateau.

After a few minutes, there was a knock on the door. Muttering under his breath, he walked over and looked through the peephole. Standing outside was Karl Mueller.

A tension, of which he hadn't been fully aware, left his body. He'd imagined Mueller changing his mind, going to someone else, but had reassured himself that these people didn't let you know of their existence casually. If he weren't going to be included in the project, they would never have contacted him in the first place.

"Just a minute," he called. Rushing over to the bed, he picked up all the pictures and stuffed them into their envelope. He tried to push the envelope back into his briefcase, but now it didn't fit. Several pictures were folded over and some stuck out of the top. Exasperated, he pushed the envelope under the bed, then partially unbuttoned his shirt. Marchant walked to the door and opened it. "Please come in." He started to button his shirt again.

Mueller walked cautiously into the room and looked around at every corner.

"I'm alone. I was just getting dressed." Marchant tucked his shirt in and gestured toward two chairs next to the window. "Please sit down." He glanced again at the table. His briefcase was open, but no papers were visible. He closed the case and placed it beside the table. "I was reviewing my talk for tomorrow."

Mueller took out his small black electronic device, pushed a button, and placed it on the table. Only then did he speak. "Have you had time to consider our offer?"

"Yes, I want to be a part of the team." Marchant sat down in the chair next to Mueller.

"I thought you would." Mueller's smile resembled a black panther bearing its fangs. "Let's get down to business."

He opened a case and took out a laptop with a few add-ons Marchant had never seen before. Mueller turned the screen away from Marchant, dialed a number, then waited. Marchant could hear the machine connect as it began some internal rumblings. Then Mueller typed. In a moment, he turned the computer back to face Marchant. On the screen appeared the same pictures he had just hidden under the bed, only these were clearer, with coordinates and location.

A rush of triumph filled Marchant's chest, but he schooled his face to show nothing. His hacker had found the real deal. He reached for the machine, but Mueller pushed him back. "I'll show you the series, then the overview."

One enticing image after another filled the screen and Marchant was soon lost in the pictures. He saw pieces, but was still frustrated. These muscle types didn't understand the basics of math. He needed to see the overview first, but the images themselves were tantalizing. The plateau was filled with tunnels—tunnels over tunnels. Cayce had been right, but no one had imagined how many chambers were beneath the sand. He sat forward, barely able to contain himself. Finally, the image he'd been waiting for came on the screen. The whole Giza complex—three large pyramids, six smaller ones, and the Sphinx—stood as ghosts on the surface of interwoven passageways. The tunnels seemed to be at different levels, many stretching far into the west, which surprised him. Some branched to the north, others to the south. Most of them headed for the pyramids. He reached for his calculator. There were several things going on here.

Mueller exited the program and then turned off the computer.

Marchant let out a grunt of protest.

"Based on what I have shown you, do you think you could figure out the harmonics of the plateau?"

Marchant sat back in his chair, alarmed at the sophistication of Mueller's question. "Yes, but you must give me time. There are many more tunnels than I anticipated. I must sort through the levels, find the correspondences. If you leave the pictures with me—"

Mueller's bark of laughter cut him off. "These are highly classified. You may study them only under controlled conditions."

Marchant nodded, trying not to let satisfaction show on his face. He'd seen enough to rearrange his own hard copies. He didn't have the overview, but he felt certain he could find the order now.

"There is one more thing," Mueller said. "A chamber has been found—a large room. We have not been able to access it."

Marchant's entire being focused on Mueller's words. *This is* it, he thought, *this is it.*

"We have not been able to ascertain the exact nature of the . . ." Mueller studied Marchant's face for a moment. ". . . energy field that is blocking it. We think it may be sound-coded."

An almost uncontrollable shiver ran the entire length of Marchant's spine. His flesh pebbled. *This is it,* he thought. *This is what I was born to do.* "Go on," he said aloud.

"Do you think your knowledge of the arcane languages will be sufficient to penetrate this block?"

"I'm absolutely certain," Marchant said. He was certain he could gain access to that room, the room that had haunted his dreams as a child, the room he'd searched for his entire life, through all his studies, his painful, self-enforced isolation, the hours and hours of rigorous work on subjects so arcane most people did not know they existed. "Just take me there."

Mueller nodded. "Clear your schedule for January and February. We're going to Egypt."

* * *

ON FRIDAY EVENING, Michael Levy waited patiently as Paul Marchant continued his presentation, apparently unaware that he'd significantly run into Michael's time. The conference organizers had flashed Marchant several signals, which he'd missed. Finally, the emcee walked on stage and caught his attention.

"Oh, am I out of time?" Marchant stopped in midstream.

"I'm terribly sorry, but we still have another speaker. Can you wrap it up in a couple of minutes?"

Marchant nodded and turned to the crowd. He summarized the sacred geometry of the Earth grid, then added his plea. "So you can see why my work is vital to our future. We hope, with proper funding, to find the means to stabilize the grid and prevent any disasters in the years to come."

As Marchant finished up, Michael walked through the rear door of the auditorium and headed backstage. He'd have to shorten his talk, but most of the information was available now that his book had been published. People could read the details. Walking up the stairs to the stage, he heard applause, then the voice of the emcee.

"Remember, Mr. Marchant will be signing books in the lobby at the end of the evening. Now it is my great pleasure to introduce to you tonight a man who has uncovered the heritage of ancient Egypt for us. Michael Levy's work in ancient history reveals a hidden continuity in the past, from predynastic Egypt through European metaphysical secret societies that are now opening their knowledge to the modern world."

Michael walked to the podium, squinting against the light. "Good evening," he said. "It's an honor to be living at a time when knowledge that has been held in trust over the centuries is now being revealed to us." He glanced at the audience again, but could see no one. He looked to the side of the stage. "Could we bring up the houselights just a bit? Can we still see the slides if we do that?"

The emcee nodded from backstage. Michael turned back to the micro-phone. "What I want to talk to you about tonight is how the European metaphysical traditions have their origins in Egypt. Understanding Egypt is the key to unlocking our own past. But let me begin at home to show how this is true."

Just at that moment, the houselights brightened and, as his eyes adjusted, the audience became visible. "Ah, there are people out there," he said. "Excellent." Then he saw her. Anne Le Clair was sitting a few rows back, her blond hair gleaming under the lights. She stood out in the crowd, a tall, elegant lily in a garden of smaller flowers. "It's good to see you," he said, hoping she would understand he was not addressing the whole audience.

Light laughter rippled through the auditorium.

"Now for our founding fathers, the Masons." Michael pushed a button and a slide appeared showing an aerial view of the White House and Capitol building. "Most people don't realize that in 1793, when George Washington laid the cornerstone of the Capitol building, he was wearing full Masonic regalia. Why? Because our capital city is laid out using sacred geometry. These buildings are in a proportional relationship to each other so that the president's office in the White House receives maximum energy for clarity and communication. In fact, if the holder of the office is in a high state of consciousness, it can be used as a stargate."

A murmur followed these words.

Michael showed a slide of the dollar bill with its many Egyptian symbols. "The Eye of Horus, the pyramid, these are Masonic symbols coming straight from Egypt, which I'm certain you are familiar with already. The number thirteen was used repeatedly. Thirteen colonies, thirteen arrows in the eagle's claws, to name only two. Twelve disciples and one master teacher. Twelve signs of the zodiac and one hidden sign, Ophiucus, between Scorpio and Sagittarius. Thirteen months in a lunar year. This number has great metaphysical significance."

Then Michael began a quick explanation of how the Knights Templar came to America to escape the churches of Rome and England, which had tried to suppress the spiritual teachings the group was sworn to protect. "This group is a primary keeper of an ancient spiritual tradition. The kings from this tradition, the Merovingians, rule in true service to the people, so it was thought best not to replicate the monarchies of Europe, which had become corrupt, but to begin a true democracy."

Michael began his series of slides on Scotland. "Those who speak of a shadow government taking over today don't realize that ever since the Templars came to America—earlier than Columbus, by the way, because Henry Sinclair from Scotland mounted an expedition as early as 1398— there has always been a secret government in the U.S. But this secret government was to rule spiritually, if not politically. It was not always corrupt and, to this day, elements of it are still pure."

Michael could not stop himself from looking at Anne. He heard mumbling in the audience, but couldn't make out the specifics. He knew this would be a point of contention.

"Now, William Sinclair was a descendant of the Templars, the head of the order once it relocated to Scotland, and he lived in the township of Roslin, just outside Edinburgh. His family built the famous Rosslyn Chapel. This chapel has many Druid, Gnostic, and Celtic Christian secrets built into the architecture; has the most Green Men in one place in all of Europe; and was also built using sacred geometry. In fact, Rosslyn Chapel is also a stargate on two levels. It receives energy from a large Earth grid beginning in Spain and running through the heart of England, and is also built to mimic that same Earth grid. All cathedrals are built as stargates. 'As above, so below' works not just in a dualistic mode, but also as a series of Chinese boxes. The same design used to build the capitol of our country can be found in this chapel.

"These stargates create a vortex of energy that amplifies human consciousness. This allows the people using them to access their psychic abilities much easier, to do conscious astral travel, even bi-locate if the person is an advanced mystic."

This caused a stir in the audience.

"To shift gears a bit since time is short, let's talk about another spiritual group. Many people associate the Rosicrucians with Germany, thinking them separate from the Masons, but actually this designation comes from the eighteenth degree in the Masonic order, called the Rose-Croix degree. Due to various political pressures, the groups have been separated at times during their history, underground at others.

"Many argue these groups sprang from two earlier organizations whose job was to protect the knowledge of a lineage that can be traced back through the Merovingians to Jesus, the Christ. He inherited an ancient spiritual knowledge from the Essenes, a group that can trace its lineage all the way back to Egypt. In fact, the Merovingians didn't just pass on his knowledge; they are the direct descendants of Yeshua, or Jesus, and Mary Magdalene."

Michael heard laughter in the audience. As long as this information has been out, it still comes as a surprise to some, he thought.

"The knowledge of this lineage has been so thoroughly suppressed by the church that it seems like the wildest science fiction to us now." Next he showed a slide of Notre Dame. "The Priory of Sion is a group that has always protected this lineage and passed on their teachings. This cathedral is, of course, dedicated not to Mother Mary, but to the divine priestess Mary Magdalene. This priestess role is another aspect of the tradition thoroughly suppressed by the Church of Rome. This cathedral contains the same sacred geometry that all cathedrals do. The details are fairly well known and are also in my book.

"The military wing of the Priory of Sion was the Knights Templar." Here Michael showed a picture of a knight in white with a red cross on his chest. "In school, we were taught about the struggles of these groups, but they were not given their proper names. Many of these wars were political struggles for power, but they were spiritual conflicts as well. The Crusades, the War of the Roses in England, the Hundred Years War in Germany, even the two world wars of the twentieth century—all these conflicts and more have hidden within them elements of this struggle between two forces, one that wanted to hide certain information and one that wished to preserve it.

"In the early part of the last millennium, the Inquisition attacked all forms of spirituality in Europe, whether indigenous, the Jews, Muslims, or other types of Christianity. The Cathars were destroyed, and the Knights Templar were attacked on Black Friday, October 13, 1307, perhaps the origin of the superstition that Friday the thirteenth will bring bad luck. They'd been forewarned, and many had already moved from France to Scotland. What's important to realize is these groups kept alive the teachings of the Essenes, the Jewish mystics whose own knowledge came from the temples of Egypt."

Michael touched on the Arthurian legends and their role, and talked about the temple teachings in Egypt, then looked at his watch. "I don't have time to go much further. Let me tell you where my research is going now. All the groups I've talked about tonight can be traced back to Egypt. Recently, I've discovered that this ancient spiritual system may still be alive in that country. To find this tradition and learn from them is my hope. In Europe, it's fortunate that all this knowledge wasn't lost completely, even though much effort was spent to extinguish the light. Those groups holding pieces of the truth are coming together . . ." He glanced at Anne. ". . . restoring the teachings and revealing them to the world."

There was a spontaneous burst of applause.

He smiled at the crowd. "Yes, it is an exciting time we live in. More details can be found in my book and in the works of many excellent researchers. Thank you for your attention."

Michael acknowledged the enthusiastic applause that followed his talk, then quickly made his way back to the table in the lobby to sign books. He hoped to catch Anne, but the crowd was thick. A group of people gathered, some to ask him to sign his book, others to ask if he knew this or that piece of miscellany. Usually, he enjoyed talking with people, listening to their ideas, picking up tidbits to track down later, but tonight he kept glancing around for Anne. Then he spotted her. She was leaning back against a wall, watching him with a bemused smile. Apparently, she was waiting. He relaxed and turned his attention to the crowd.

When the knot of people surrounding him had finally dissipated, she walked up to the table. "Well, I hadn't realized what a celebrity you are." Her blue eyes twinkled mischievously.

"Only in a very small community. But I'm surprised to see you here. After our last encounter, I got the impression you didn't have a high opinion of metaphysics."

"Well," Anne turned her palms up, "a lot has changed since then."

"Really? That was only, what, a week and a half ago?"

Anne counted back. "Yes, but it seems like months."

"That long?" The corners of Michael's mouth turned up.

Anne suppressed a laugh. "Let's just say it's been packed with surprises, this being one of them." She picked up his book and turned it over.

"My gift," he said spontaneously.

She looked up, surprised. "Why, thank you, sir."

"I would love to hear about all these changes. May I sign your book over a drink?"

She hesitated.

"If you're too busy, I understand."

"No, it's not that. It's just that I'm not drinking alcohol or caffeine these days. No meat. I guess you could say I'm in training."

She's finally waking up, he thought, containing a rush of excitement. *The family's decided to assume their responsibility.*

"Excellent," Michael said. "Perhaps sushi or a bowl of miso soup?"

"That would be lovely."

After thanking the conference directors, Michael joined Anne, who was waiting by the door. "Shall we walk?" he asked. "I know a place a few blocks away."

"Certainly."

He offered his arm and, to his great delight, she took it. They strolled along quietly for the first block, enjoying the crisp air after the press of the auditorium.

"So what brought you to my talk tonight, or did you come to hear the esteemed Mr. Marchant?"

"Actually, it was my brother's idea. He thinks highly of your work." Anne seemed to be measuring her words.

"I'm flattered. Does your brother teach or write?" Michael winced at his continued deception, but how could he tell her how much he knew? If she revealed a bit more, he could do the same.

She glanced at him sideways. "He's the family historian."

"Oh?"

"Surely you know something about my family, given the talk you just gave."

Michael laughed, relieved. "I confess I do. But you seemed not to know when I first met you and so I didn't know how much I could say."

"I can't say I agree with all your conclusions," Anne said. "After all, the Stuart family tree that traces its lineage all the way back to Adam and Eve can hardly be taken as more than propaganda."

Michael didn't respond, as they had arrived at the restaurant. He held the door for her and was pleased to see that the place was only half full. Anne ordered a bowl of miso soup and Michael decided on California rolls. "They have a brown rice and green tea that is excellent. Shall we try it?"

Anne nodded, then fixed him with her azure eyes. "How much do you know?"

"Excuse me?"

"About my family history?"

"Well, not the details of course. Surely your brother is the one to ask."

Anne put her spoon down. "He told me it would save him time if I read some books. Yours was on the list, so I came to hear you instead."

"I know your family has a spiritual legacy that is the true reason for its political prominence. Your ancestors came from France to Scotland along with the Knights Templar, carrying certain artifacts to escape the Catholics who were trying to eliminate all other spiritual traditions in Europe."

"And these Templars, they dressed in white with an equal-armed red cross?"

"Yes."

Anne's eyes took on a faraway look. She picked up her bowl and sipped the remaining liquid, then dabbed her mouth with her napkin.

Michael watched her, thinking she made this breach of etiquette look like grace itself.

She looked up and caught him watching. "I guess I was hungry."

"The chef is excellent."

"I don't understand what importance all of this information could possibly have in the modern world. Let's face it, most people are secularists—agnostics or atheists even. Royal families are no longer relevant."

Michael filled her teacup. "I suppose that explains the public's indifference to the marriage and death of Princess Diana. Or how your uncle was able to electrify the country during his administration."

Anne shrugged to admit his point. "But surely our job is to move forward, not backward. These Masons established a democracy when they came to the New World, not a monarchy. If their true secret purpose was to reestablish this ousted lineage, then why not do just that?"

Their purpose was much deeper," Michael answered. "The Masons escaped the political rule of European monarchs and the Church in order to keep specific knowledge safe, to establish a power base from which to reveal that knowledge when the time came. And to keep certain artifacts secure."

"Ah, certain artifacts." She smiled sphinx-like over her teacup. "Such as?"

Michael decided to keep it academic for the moment. "Many historians speculate that during the Crusades, the Knights took sacred artifacts from beneath the Temple Mount in Jerusalem and transported them to Europe. To keep them safe from the Muslims, of course, although the roots of Islam are the same as Judaism and Christianity. One of those artifacts could be the Ark of the Covenant."

Anne set her cup down abruptly.

"Yes, the famous Ark. Some think it's buried beneath Rosslyn Chapel, along with other, less powerful objects, and a few were taken when a branch of the Sinclairs moved to the States."

"Not the Le Clairs?"

Michael only smiled. The teapot was empty and the waiter had taken their plates long ago. He asked, "May I escort you home?"

This time she didn't hesitate. "Yes, let's take a taxi."

Michael and Anne settled into the back of a yellow cab and the conversation lulled as they rode across town. Michael enjoyed her presence, the soft weight beside him, the play of the city lights on her face as they drove. He breathed in her scent, then put his arm on the seat behind her. She settled under his arm, a perfect fit. He pulled himself back from turning her face to his, letting himself be content with her closeness. They arrived too quickly. Michael paid the cabbie.

Anne walked to the door. "I wonder where the doorman is." She searched her purse for the key. She slid a plastic card into the slot and the door opened with a buzz. "This is odd," Anne said. "There's always someone here. Do you mind coming up?" She blushed. "It's just that this is so unusual."

"At your service." Michael squeezed her hand to reassure her.

They took the elevator to the top floor and Anne pointed the way to her apartment. She drew close to him as they walked down the dark corridor. She stopped outside a door and started to put her key in the lock, but the door swung open at her touch. She stopped dead in her tracks.

Michael pushed her behind him and eased himself into the apartment, all his senses alert. He listened, but heard no sound. Walking a few steps inside, he searched the darkness as his eyes adjusted. He saw the huddled shapes of furniture, things scattered on the floor. Stretching his senses across the apartment, he searched psychically for another person, but found no one. He returned to the front door and said, "There's nobody here."

Anne stepped inside and switched on the lights. A jumble of overturned furniture, emptied drawers, and torn cushions met their eyes. "Oh, my God," she said. She walked into the living room, looking around. "The cats," Anne cried. "Merlin, Vivienne, kitties?" There were no answering meows. Anne walked through the apartment calling them, but there was only silence. She began looking underneath the purple cushions strewn over the floor, behind the armoire close to the wall, anywhere there was a small hiding place, but they were nowhere to be found.

"Cats?" Michael asked. "They're probably hiding. They'll come out when they feel safe. Shouldn't you call the police?"

"I suppose you're right, but first I have to call the family." At his surprised look, she added, "The police means the press when your name is Le Clair."

"Ah," Michael murmured. "Do you want me to wait?"

"Please."

Michael perched on a chair and watched as Anne dialed the phone. "Dr. Abernathy, someone's broken into my apartment." She walked away from Michael as she continued the conversation, so he heard only murmurs.

In a couple of minutes, Anne walked back into the room. "Dr. Abernathy's calling the police. He'll be here soon." She began milling around, picking up things at random.

"You should probably leave things as they are."

"I guess you're right." She walked into her bedroom. Michael followed and stood in the doorway. Anne opened drawer after drawer of a tall jewelry case.

"Everything's still here."

Michael bit back the question.

Anne smiled at him and lifted the crystal from beneath her blouse.

"Thank God," he said before he could stop himself.

"It's safe." Anne tucked the necklace back under her clothes. She looked around the floor at her sweaters and started searching. After a few minutes, she stood. "But the box it came in is gone."

"Was there anything in it?"

"A note from my aunt I would have liked to have kept."

At that moment, there was a knock on the door. Two police officers showed their badges to Anne and then walked into the apartment. Immediately, one of them took Michael aside and began asking him questions. The man in charge questioned Anne. More police arrived and they carefully sorted through the apartment.

By the time the officer finished with Michael, the apartment was full of various officials checking out the crime scene. He looked around for Anne and saw her in the living room, surrounded by police, with an older man wearing an old-fashioned ascot. Standing just beside the door was another man dressed in a chauffeur's uniform.

"Pack a bag. You can't stay here," Michael heard the older man say.

"I would recommend you stay somewhere else, Ms. Le Clair," said the officer in charge. "We want you to be safe, and the detectives need to go over the apartment with a fine-tooth comb."

Anne looked from one to the other. "Oh, all right. But please find my cats." She walked into her bedroom.

Michael decided it was best to leave. Anne had enough to deal with and it seemed she'd forgotten him in the crisis. He walked to the front door of the apartment, then glanced back into the room. The man in the ascot was watching him carefully. He turned to the chauffeur. "Please tell the lady I will call tomorrow."

"Yes, sir," the man said neutrally.

Michael suppressed a sigh of frustration and walked down the hall to the elevator. At least Anne and the crystal were safe for now.

* * *

KARL MUELLER STOOD in the back of a richly appointed conference room, wishing he were anywhere else.

"It is evident the Le Clairs are planning to make their move in February, during the alignment." A tall man dressed all in black sat in front of a gold statue of Isis alleged to be from the tomb of King Tutankhamen. "We must stop their bid for power. Spender, what do you have?"

"Our attempts to gain control of the Le Clair crystal are ongoing."

"In other words, you don't have it."

"Not at this time."

"When may we expect it?" The man in black looked past Spender to Mueller.

Mueller shifted his weight to both feet and stood at attention. "The niece has moved into the family compound. It would be best to wait until she goes to Egypt, if that meets with your approval."

"At least we took care of the previous Keeper. This new one is untrained. She'll never be able to do the job." The man turned and addressed a woman seated at the table. "Miriam, your report?"

"Our crystal bearer travels to Israel, then Egypt, the second week in January."

"How much does the group know about the mission?"

"They believe they'll be restoring the world to light, bringing in a new age of enlightenment through a ritual with the keys. Michael hopes to find remnants of the wisdom tradition in Egypt. He thinks they will know the details."

The man in black sat silent, but Mueller knew from experience that he could be speaking mind to mind with the other adepts in the room. The man nodded his head, as if agreeing with someone, then looked up. "Spender and Mueller, gain control of the keys before the alignment. You'll be looking for six in all. The crystals will draw the Keepers together." He looked around at everyone sitting at the table. "We've put all the pieces in place. We must squash this final attempt to wrest control from our alliance. Don't be misled by our enemies' apparent weaknesses. They are quite resourceful."

9

Anne woke with a start. Something was wrong. She sat up in bed and looked around. Sun streamed through the window, lighting the chaise lounge and marble-topped mahogany dresser of her childhood bedroom at her grandmother's house. Then she remembered the robbery. The pillow beside her was empty. The cats were missing. She swung her legs over the side of the bed and held her head in her hands. Her eyes felt heavy and her head ached. What herbs had her grandmother given her to make her sleep? She glanced at the clock and saw a note on the bedside table:

Meet us in the library at 11:30. We have much to discuss.
Grandmother

The clock read quarter after ten. She would have time for breakfast. What else could her grandmother possibly have to tell her after everything she'd heard from Michael?

Anne pushed herself into the shower and stood beneath the hot stream until her head cleared. She quickly dried her hair, dressed in jeans and a turtleneck, then made her way to the breakfast room. No one was around. She pushed open the door to the kitchen and was greeted by the smell of pumpkin pies. Several faces looked up from their various labors.

"Miss Anne, you finally woke up." Estelle was rolling pie-crusts, her apron and face dusted in white. "I saved some breakfast for you." Estelle nodded to a slight woman who pulled a plate out of the refrigerator and stuck it in the microwave.

"Thank you, but I don't want to be any trouble," Anne protested.

Estelle just shook her head. "You need your breakfast," came the familiar answer. "The city is not safe, Miss Anne, if you'll pardon me saying so." Estelle's face was the picture of worry.

"Well, I really can't argue with you today, can I?"

Estelle just shook her head and went back to her dough.

Anne was amazed at the flurry in the kitchen. In one corner, loaves of bread were being crumbled and mixed with herbs smelling strongly of sage. Another helper chopped up onions, her eyes streaming. A young man stood at the stove stirring something that smelled intoxicating.

"What's the occasion?" Anne asked.

Everyone turned to stare at her.

"It's Christmas Eve, my dear," Estelle answered.

Anne blushed. "I forgot."

Estelle smiled indulgently. "That's understandable. Now, tea or coffee?"

"Tea, please. But I can get it."

Estelle shook her head. "We're too busy to have an extra body in here. Go have a seat and we'll bring you your breakfast."

Anne walked into the breakfast nook and sat at the long table. She still hadn't seen any of the family. All the extended relations would begin arriving in a few hours. Not to mention her mother. Anne dreaded another confrontation.

After breakfast, Anne went in search of someone to ask about her cats. The house was as busy as the kitchen, full of people polishing, vacuuming, and putting the final touches on decorations. But no one had seen Dr. Abernathy, Thomas, or her grandmother. She made her way to the library early.

When she opened the door, Thomas raised his head and gestured for her to join them. "Did you sleep well?"

"Like a Yule log," she said, frowning slightly at her grandmother.

"It was necessary, my dear." Elizabeth dismissed the unvoiced objection. "Have my cats been found?"

"There's no word yet, but I sent Lawrence to gather your things. He'll check," Dr. Abernathy said briskly. "Now, we have business."

Anne sat on the couch, looking from face to face. "Why so grim? It was a robbery."

"We're not so sure of that, Annie," Thomas said.

"What do you mean?"

"No jewelry was taken, no silverware, no artwork. Only the case the crystal came in, along with Cynthia's note," Dr. Abernathy said. "And, as you discovered already, your Aunt Cynthia was murdered. We can't take any more chances."

Elizabeth leaned forward slightly. "We've decided the time has come for full disclosure. You deserve to know the risks of what you're involved with."

"And the importance," Thomas added.

"Full disclosure?" Anne said faintly. "You sound like the CIA."

Grandmother Elizabeth didn't smile. Nor did Thomas or Dr. Abernathy. Anne looked from one serious face to another.

"Thomas, you begin," Elizabeth ordered.

Thomas glanced at Anne, a worried look in his amber eyes. "I've asked you to do some reading. How much have you been able to ascertain?"

Ascertain?" Anne repeated, marveling at the official tone of the language everyone was using. "Last night I attended the Solstice Seminar lectures. I got a crash course in sacred geometry, half of which was over my head. And I heard Michael Levy speak. He claims many of the royal families of Europe were engaged in a secret spiritual war, that they were involved in passing on some metaphysical tradition forbidden by the Church. He said this knowledge they so jealously guarded can be traced all the way back to Egypt." Anne watched the faces around her as she spoke. She couldn't bear the heaviness any longer. She turned to Thomas. "That must explain why you worship cats."

To her relief, he laughed. "Well, that's a good start. Let me add some finishing touches to that basic outline and you'll have some perspective on what we're doing."

Anne nodded.

"All ancient traditions—by ancient, I mean teachings from the Vedas, from the Maya, from Egypt, that sort of thing. Anyway, they all explain that the Earth goes through a long cycle in which humanity changes from being fully enlightened and in harmony with all natural rhythms to living in base ignorance and violence, a state in which humans have lost all connection to the principal intelligence of the universe. Then we go back again. We rise into enlightenment. Human consciousness rises and falls like the ocean tides, but the cycle is thousands of years long. The Vedas teach that these cycles are not equal in length, that the time of enlightenment is much longer than the darkness."

At a slight rustling from Elizabeth, Thomas interrupted himself. "Well, I guess the details aren't important right now. Simply put, now is the time of reawakening. While these cycles occur over thousands of years, the transitions are sudden and dramatic, just like the sunrise. You can see the sky lightening for a long while, but when the sun lifts over the horizon, the effect is transforming."

"We have reason to believe that sunrise will occur very soon," Elizabeth said.

Anne looked from her to Thomas. "Dr. Abernathy told me about this already, but I wonder if we aren't deluding ourselves. The world has always been a mess. Now it's getting even worse." She sat forward. "We're threatening our own existence. We're destroying the ecosystem. War has reached into almost every continent. A few people enjoy luxury while many starve. How can you say we are entering some sort of age of enlightenment?"

Dr. Abernathy spoke up, "The times of transition are always the most difficult. Darkness has ruled for a very long time, and it has fully flowered by the end of its reign. The old saying is true, 'The darkest hour is—'"

"'. . . just before dawn,'" Thomas finished for him.

"Great. Now you're quoting song lyrics," Anne said.

"Just as the full flowering of enlightened civilization happens right at the setting of the sun," Dr. Abernathy persisted.

"But where's the evidence of this enlightened civilization?" Anne asked.

"Right in front of our eyes in the ancient monuments of Egypt, the pyramids in many places around the globe, Stonehenge, the Bimini road," Dr. Abernathy answered immediately.

"In hidden documents," Thomas said.

"Suppressed by the authorities," Elizabeth said.

Anne stared at them all.

"You've had such a conventional education, my dear," Elizabeth said in an attempt at a soothing voice. "That education shapes you to accept certain ways of looking at the world and automatically to ridicule other ideas without giving them serious consideration. All this is understandable given the intense effort that went into suppressing the truth, but when the yoke of the Church was finally loosened, scientists threw out the baby with the bath water. Instead of examining the traditions the Church tried to eliminate, educated men rejected all spiritual traditions and tried to start from scratch. Science has been helpful in many ways, but its underlying assumptions are flawed."

Dr. Abernathy cleared his throat.

Elizabeth looked at him and raised her hands in a helpless gesture. "There is so much to teach her and so little time."

Dr. Abernathy smiled sympathetically, then turned to address Anne. "Has nothing you've experienced in the last couple of weeks made you question your rational world view?"

"Science can't fully explain my affinity with the crystal, the dreams, the experience I had on solstice night." Anne had to concede this point. "Even though some of it could be explained as posthypnotic suggestion, that doesn't account for my sense that I must pursue this, that there's something important in it for me. That feels genuine enough."

"You've already experienced that human consciousness is more than science has so far understood. The universe is not the result of some accidental crapshoot. Matter is not inert, as science says. Quantum physics is now beginning to guess what metaphysics has understood all along. That everything has consciousness, everything is interactive. The universe is alive, guiding us forward on our best path."

"It's a comforting thought," Anne said.

Thomas said, "When consciousness begins to wane, those who are most conscious try to save the knowledge. They formulate teachings that are passed from generation to generation, often within certain families or groups, hoping that some light will still exist, some small candle will still be burning at the end of the long night."

"And we're such a family." Anne shifted impatiently. "I sort of gathered that already."

"When the dawn begins, certain souls are born to shepherd humanity through these transitions. Our family is a conduit for these souls because of our DNA. We do teach basic metaphysical truths. We try to offer enlightened leadership. That's been one of our primary functions through the ages. But we also have a very particular task. Our family is a Keeper of one of the six keys."

"Six keys?" Anne asked.

Thomas nodded.

Anne slowly lifted the crystal from beneath her shirt. "Is this it?"

Thomas nodded again.

"So what is it a key to?"

Dr. Abernathy spoke. "We aren't entirely sure. As I've already told you, the tradition states one will be born who will remember how to use the key. The exact wording is that this stone will be used to 'restore the flow.' We think the crystal is a key to something in Egypt, since that is where it came from originally."

Suddenly, Anne remembered a dream, walking through a narrow hall with a low ceiling, looking for a place to hide something precious she'd just been given.

"We are certain of one thing, Anne." Dr. Abernathy waited for her full attention. "You're the one we have been waiting for all these years. You'll unlock the stone's secrets and use it to shift the balance of power on Earth. You are a vital part of ushering in the next age of enlightenment."

Anne stared at Dr. Abernathy as if he had taken leave of his senses. "What the hell—me? Bring in the age of enlightenment? Are you crazy? I can't even enlighten myself."

Dr. Abernathy just watched her.

Anne looked desperately around at her grandmother and brother. They both studied her earnestly, obviously in full agreement with Dr. Abernathy.

"You're all mad." Anne stood up and started to walk out of the room. Then she whirled around. "If it's so important . . ." She held the crystal aloft. ". . . what the hell am I doing with it? I haven't been trained for any of this. I'm just an ordinary person."

"No, you haven't. Katherine tried to turn you from your destiny, but now you are training," Elizabeth said quietly.

"You're a Le Clair," Dr. Abernathy said.

"So what?" Anne spit out. Then she remembered something Thomas had just said, and something Michael had mentioned about the Knights Templar. She remembered the stained glass window in Dr. Abernathy's house and the red cross on his robe the night of the ritual. She looked at Thomas. "What do you mean, 'because of our DNA'?"

Thomas smiled. "The Le Clairs are descended from another person whose job it was to bring in the age of enlightenment, to save the world from darkness, a man himself descended from a long line of teachers."

Anne had a sinking feeling she didn't want to hear this.

"Our ancestors can be traced back to the Merovingian dynasty who ruled in southern France prior to the rise of Charlemagne. They were descended from a man who restored the ancient Jewish line of divine kings."

Anne remembered Michael's words from last night just as Thomas said, "They were the direct descendants of Mary Magdalene and Jesus, the Christ."

Anne felt as if she had been hit in the stomach. "No." She sat down heavily on a chair near the door and stared at the floor. After a long moment, she looked up. "You're trying to convince me that our family is related to Christ? What kind of fanatics are you?"

"Surely, Michael Levy spoke about this in his lecture last night," Thomas said.

Anne nodded. "Yes, but it sounded just like the kind of myth that springs up about royalty. The Stuarts went to a lot of trouble to construct a bloodline all the way back to Adam. But it's nothing to be taken literally."

"It's true, Annie." Thomas's eyes begged her to believe him. "Not the Adam and Eve bit, but Mary Magdalene escaped from Israel with her children and settled in the south of France. Her descendants and their followers formed a country, Septimania, which was later conquered by the Catholic Church."

Anne shook her head. "But he was celibate. He never married."

"Is it so crazy to believe a rabbi was married? Or would you prefer the perfectly rational belief that a virgin gave birth?" Elizabeth asked. "They've even tried to erase Jesus' siblings."

"But there's no evidence," Anne shouted.

"So says the Church, the same group of men who declared that women don't have souls, who tortured and burned alive any who disagreed with them, who taught primitive people that their gods were devils. It was this group of men who decided which books would go into the Bible and which would be destroyed. But they didn't get everything." Elizabeth's eyes burned through her. "Our family and others have preserved the true teachings of Christ, teachings older than two thousand years, teachings that can be traced back to the end of the last age of enlightenment. And we have preserved certain archives that prove what we are saying is true."

Anne sat stunned. Several times she opened her mouth to speak, but couldn't voice the shock she felt. What her family was suggesting was unthinkable, beyond any fantasy she could have imagined, yet clearly they believed every word of it. Finally, she gathered her wits and said, "I want to see the archives."

Elizabeth nodded. "So you shall."

Anne turned and ran out of the library, heading for the back door. She grabbed an old overcoat hanging in the mudroom and walked quickly across the lawn. When she reached the end of the grass, she broke into a run, not really seeing where she was going. All she knew was that she had to get away—away from these crazy ideas, away from the eyes watching her every reaction, away from the dreams and visions, away from the expectations.

Out of breath, she stopped and looked around. She was standing in the rose garden she'd so meticulously described to Dr. Abernathy during her hypnosis. She sank onto the seat under the trellis.

What have I gotten myself into? she wondered.

She stared at the bare garden surrounding her, the trimmed brown bushes, the mulched leaves piled on the beds. The bare branches of the climbing rose laced the trellis. The bower gave little shelter in midwinter.

Anne tried to piece together everything that had happened to her since she had inherited the crystal. She thought if she could just lay it all out, somehow it would make sense. Dr. Abernathy's guidance had been a light touch. He'd always given logical answers to her questions. Her decision to follow this path had seemed reasonable. The dreams, the visions, the experience in the solstice ritual had all been real, undeniable in their power. So how had it all ended in the ludicrous assertion that she was going to bring on an age of enlightenment by using a crystal necklace in a yet undiscovered way? She was a lawyer, not a mystic, and certainly no savior.

The rest of it was simply beyond belief. Her mind kept circling back to her brother's claim that they were descended from Mary Magdalene and Jesus, the Christ. If that weren't outrageous enough, Elizabeth had topped it off with the wild claim that the family knew the true teachings of Christ and the rest of the world had it all wrong. This sounded like the ravings of a street prophet, not the words of the matriarch of one of the country's most powerful political families. How could she make any sense of this mess? Who could she talk to?

Michael's face appeared in her mind's eye, but she rejected this idea immediately. She doubted that he'd be objective. Clearly, he believed she was descended from the son of God as well. He had said as much in his lecture, although she hadn't grasped the full implications of his words until her brother's announcement. But Michael was Jewish. Why would he care about her alleged family line? And he had a doctorate from a prestigious university. How could he believe such nonsense?

Anne picked up a stick from the ground and prodded the brown grass. She sat lost in thought for a long time.

* * *

A VIOLENT SHIVER shook her from her reverie. Her breath was visible, a cloud of vapor in front of her face. The temperature had dropped significantly. Looking up, she saw the shadows had crept out from the grove of cherry trees to the west of the rose garden and were stretching across the lawn.

She wanted to call a cab and go home to her apartment, get away from her family, but she knew she wasn't safe there. Even if she returned the crystal to her grandmother, as she'd half decided to do, whoever was searching for it would think it was still in her possession. Her aunt had been murdered over it. She couldn't take the risk of going back to her apartment now. She'd have to stay here, at least until after Christmas. Then she could find a place to go for a while. She needed to get away to think, to reconsider her life. Perhaps she'd move, take a job with a firm that had no family ties. But one thing was certain. She would not continue the training. She would not allow herself to be drawn into the family delusion. Anne knew the moment had come to stand up to her family once and for all.

Feeling like a recalcitrant member of some lunatic cult, Anne made her way back to the big house and snuck up the stairs to her bedroom. She didn't see anyone. Once safe in her room, she locked the door and took a long, hot shower. On Christmas Eve, the family usually attended the celebration at King's Episcopal, then came home for a gathering. No one was likely to corner her in the middle of services. Deciding this would be the best course of action, she dressed for church. The family gathering afterward would be the challenge. She braced herself and walked downstairs.

Luckily, her distant cousin Christine from California was just loading up a station wagon with her brood. Anne took the diaper bag from her, kissed her cheek, and said, "You could use some help. Shall I come along with you?" Without waiting for an answer, Anne climbed into the back next to the car seat. On the way, she listened to Christine's family news and entertained the youngest by making faces. The baby strained in her car seat, trying to reach Anne's dangling earrings.

But when they arrived and settled in the family pew, there was one thing she hadn't thought of. It was Christmas Eve and she was going to hear about her alleged ancestor all night. Evergreen boughs tied with red velvet ribbons hung from the ceiling of the familiar old church and tall red candles surrounded with holly burned on the altar. The beautifully painted nativity scene to the side of the pulpit had intrigued her as a child. Anne had loved Christmas then. In this church, she'd lost her sense of the modern world and floated away on the sounds of hymns. She'd always waited impatiently for the candle lighting at the end of the service, when golden beeswax candles draped in red crepe paper were passed down the aisles by women dressed in red and green. When the minister had described the significance of lighting a candle of faith and holding it aloft to the world, Anne had stretched her small arm as high as she could reach.

Now she wished for the simple faith of that little girl. She listened with an acute sense of loss to the familiar Christmas story and softly sang the hymns that had fueled her childhood devotion. She tried to reason with herself that it was a faith she'd lost long ago, that she hadn't thought seriously of this story in years, yet the ache in her throat turned into a burn and her head began to throb with the strain of not crying. She lowered her eyes to gain control of herself and saw the eyes of her cousin's children large with wonder. Then the tears fell. Anne bent down, pretending to pick something off the floor to hide her face.

The congregation sat and, under the cover of the noise, Anne blew her nose. The choir stood and a lone soprano voice sang out the first line of the next hymn, "O Holy Night." Anne's head came up abruptly. The solstice ritual with her family flooded her memory. That night, Anne had marveled at the beauty of how the two beliefs intertwined like the Celtic knots of old. She'd enjoyed the depth of the atmosphere created by that ritual, much as she'd reveled in the Christmas Eve service as a child, and had felt a surprised joy that she'd recovered a lost part of that childhood on a different path. Now she felt flat.

Anne was relieved when the service ended. She rode back with Christine and helped her herd the children into the large living room. When Christine asked if she was all right, Anne said she thought maybe she missed John, her ex-husband. Christine accepted this at face value. Elizabeth, Thomas, and Dr. Abernathy seemed to sense her need for silence. None of them spoke to her. In fact, they avoided her, and she relaxed. The hustle and bustle of the family's Christmas Eve was a welcomed relief. She sat in the background and enjoyed her nieces, nephews, and younger cousins, all dressed in crushed velvet dresses or suits with bow ties, as they stared at the enormous tree and speculated about their presents, so colorfully wrapped and piled high under the tree. Estelle brought in spiced cider and paper-thin ginger cookies, a specialty from her German family.

When the children were finally being put to bed, Anne walked into the now-empty ballroom. She gazed out the wall of windows onto a quarter moon shining its waning light on the rolling hills. The noise of a door opening behind her drove her into the shadows. A wave of familiar perfume told her who had followed. She heard footsteps cross the room, then stop.

"Mother, now is not a good time." Anne turned to fend off the argument she expected.

Her mother, however, didn't speak immediately. She stood studying her. Anne dropped her eyes under the close scrutiny. Katherine set her eggnog down on the window ledge and took Anne's face in her hand. She turned it up to the light. After a moment, she said, "They told you, didn't they?"

Anne jerked away. "Told me what?"

Katherine didn't answer her directly. She pulled a chair out and sat down heavily. Shaking her head, she said almost to herself, "Oh, Mother, why? Why did you do this to my baby?" She looked up at Anne. "I tried to keep it from you."

"What?" Anne's voice was urgent.

"The family albatross, our two-thousand-year-old ancestry, the loneliness of knowing what no one else knows, what other people would never believe." Katherine's shoulders sagged. "I'm so sorry, darling." Tears glistened in her eyes.

Anne reached out for something steady, but found only the glass behind her. She sank to the floor next to her mother's chair and sat staring up at her. Her mother's confirmation had driven all doubt from her mind and left an empty spot where all her old certainties had stood. This woman would not believe in nonsense. Abruptly, she leaned her head on her mother's knee and sobbed.

Katherine stroked Anne's hair until the tears were spent. Minutes later, Anne sat back and looked for a tissue. Katherine handed her a cocktail napkin, and Anne blew her nose loudly. She took another napkin and wiped her eyes, then picked up her mother's eggnog and took a drink. Finally, she spoke, "How can this be?"

Katherine shrugged. "It is. I've seen the documents. And that woman . . ." She pointed her finger at the door behind her. "She never let me forget it. The stories she told us. And the secrecy. 'If you ever tell anyone, Katherine, you will be endangering the safety of all your family. You cannot jeopardize the sacred mission.' Always the sacred mission. And who could have told anyone such a thing?" Katherine looked out the window, but saw only the past. "Imagine trying to date, trying to have ordinary friends. I constantly had to be careful not to say something about the family rituals." She looked at Anne now. "People would have thought I was a freak."

"When did she tell you?"

"When I 'became a woman,' as she put it. After the first menses, the girls are told the full story. The boys at thirteen. But we're prepared before that with family stories. Just listen to the little Christmas story she tells the children tomorrow morning. For immediate family, there's more. I was told I had to marry only from a select group so as not to weaken the bloodline or risk an outsider revealing the secret."

Anne shivered.

"I swore I would protect you from all that lunacy. And I did. You were a happy teenager, weren't you, darling?" Katherine's eyes begged her.

"Yes, Mother," Anne answered gently. "Except for the divorce, I was happy."

"But that is something many children bear. It's not some dark secret lurking in the shadows." Katherine waved her hand in dismissal.

"I suppose not." Anne felt as if the stone to her mother's heart had been rolled away and she'd found standing there, not a dragon, but a frightened child trailing her teddy bear, needing to be picked up and comforted.

Katherine visibly gathered herself. "So what is it they want you to do?"

Anne was momentarily startled by the sudden businesslike tone. "Learn to use the key."

Katherine sniffed. "Nobody knows how to use that damned thing, nobody. I lost my sister to it. I will not lose my daughter."

"But," Anne put a hand on her mother's knee to stop her from rising, "I've had visions."

Again, Katherine waved her hands as if clearing clutter off a table. "Of course you've had visions. All Le Clairs have visions. So what? They don't have to run your life." She smoothed out her skirt.

"I didn't have visions before I got this crystal."

"Of course you did. I just—" Katherine realized what she'd said and looked down, unable to meet Anne's eyes. "I just told you they were bad dreams. After a while, you stopped paying attention and they subsided."

Anne stared at her. "You mean to tell me—"

"I did it for you, don't you see? I was trying to free you, to let you live in the modern world, not be shackled to some medieval oath to save the world. For God's sake, Annie."

Anne stood up suddenly. "I have to be alone." She walked toward the door and, for once, her mother did as she asked. She did not follow.

Anne walked toward her room without seeing. Her mind was dark and silent, bruised by too many revelations. She opened her door and sat on the edge of the bed. A tray stood on the bedside table. A mug of warm milk still steamed, and beside it were three gelatin capsules filled with her grandmother's sleeping potion. She immediately swallowed the capsules with a glass of water and then drank the milk. She set down the empty mug, then stood and stripped off her clothes. Without washing her face or brushing her teeth, she climbed into the bed where she had lain as a child so many Christmas Eves, waiting for Santa to bring her presents. Tonight she waited for the gift of understanding. And forgiveness.

After a minute, out of the dark came the sound of familiar meows and the pad of soft feet. Two cats jumped on the bed and snuggled down on the pillow beside her.

"My darlings." Anne gathered the two sleek bodies in her arms. "I thought I'd lost you." Two sandpaper tongues licked the tears from her face and then settled down next to her. They fell asleep together.

* * *

WITH CHRISTMAS DAY came the chaos of opening presents and the fanfare of the family feast. Elizabeth thanked Anne for her new brooch, and it sparkled from the head of the table where she sat. Anne went through the motions of the day without any real enjoyment. Thomas and Elizabeth still left her alone, but Katherine was chummy in the way of those who share some kind of suffering. Anne found it comforting and annoying at the same time. She finally escaped in the afternoon for a long horseback ride alone, skipping her grandmother's special Christmas story for the children. She'd heard it a dozen times. Now that she knew, it was obvious. The private story of Christ coming to England with a special secret with a group of children who would carry on his teachings.

When Anne returned from her ride, she found a stack of documents in her bedroom. On top was a note: *If you're interested.* Thomas. An old manuscript lay on the table in a plastic envelope to protect it from the elements. The front was illustrated with an old Celtic capital letter, intricate with intertwined birds. The colors were still brilliant. A copy of another old manuscript and a collection of gospels and history books were stacked beside it. Some she had heard of: The Gnostic Gospels, The Gospel of Thomas, and The Dead Sea Scrolls. Others were unfamiliar: The Talmud of Immanuel, The Gospel of Mary, and another attributed to Mary Magdalene. She saw Michael's new book along with others she wasn't familiar with. All the books bristled with her brother's yellow sticky-notes. It was a good thing she was a lawyer and used to reading stacks of material at one sitting.

She took the manuscript from its plastic envelope and spread it in her lap, hoping the cats would take a long time with the turkey she'd brought them from the kitchen. It was written in Middle English, but Anne was able to pick out the main story. It was an early Arthurian manuscript, and told the story of how Morgan le Fey, the Queen of Avalon, was descended from Elaine Du Lac, the French matriarch. These women were called priestesses in the story and referred to as the Keepers of the Grail, the vines of Christ. It appeared they were connected by blood to the Magdalene and were carrying on part of her priestess duties. Anne had thought Morgan was from the Druid tradition, a pagan tradition of the Celts that the Christians had opposed.

The cats, full from their meal, curled up next to the hearth and fell asleep, so Anne felt safe leaving the antique manuscript out while she read through the photocopied one. It was a family history, penned in different hands, beginning with Mary Magdalene and going through the now familiar progression. Much of it was unreadable because of the variations in old French and then English. She turned to the pile of books. One by one she opened them to read the marked passages. Gradually, the whole tale unfolded. Some details were disputed, like whether Joseph of Arimethea was Jesus' uncle or a wealthy merchant, or if it was Jesus himself or his son, Jesus the Younger, or even Joseph who had come to England and founded the Celtic Christian Church, but all the books told basically the same story.

Jesus was a rabbi from the Nazarene sect, which was a group working to overthrow Roman rule. The city Nazareth hadn't even existed during his lifetime. He was connected to the Essene mystics, whose teachings formed the basis of his message. He'd most probably been born in March, perhaps 7 A.D. Centuries later, when the Roman Empire converted to Christianity, December 25 was chosen to coincide with the Roman holiday of Saturnalia. Also, the whole manger scene had been a fabrication.

The books revealed that the Church of Rome developed its own version of Christianity, and from the fourth to fifth centuries, the gospels and documents disputing the new dogma were ruthlessly suppressed, almost entirely destroyed. Various mistranslations of the scriptures, coupled with the political domination of the Roman church, all led to the story of Jesus told today. The Celtic Church and the Cathars, among others, held to different versions of Christianity, but these groups had almost been eliminated. Many alternative gospels had been hidden, and several had been uncovered in the twentieth century, such as the Nag Hammadi Gnostic Gospels.

According to this alternative history, Jesus was of the royal house of David, son of Jesse, a descendant of Judah, the rightful king of the Jews. His ministry was political as well as spiritual, an attempt to overthrow Roman domination and to make Judaism less legalistic and more experiential. All the books agreed that Jesus was married and left descendants, and the new Roman church went to great pains to hide this lineage. The evidence of his marriage, once Anne overcame her automatic rejection of such an unfamiliar idea, turned out to be convincing. Jesus married Mary Magdalene. The famous story of her washing and anointing his feet, then drying them with her hair, was a description of a well-known royal betrothal ritual. In this way she proclaimed him publicly as the Messianic heir. Mary had used a particular oil, spikenard, reserved for royalty. She was supposed to carry this oil with her until he died, at which point she would use it to anoint his body. That was why she was called to his tomb. Authors argued that the wedding feast at Cana, when he made wine out of water, was likely his own. It was the responsibility of the bride's father to offer such a feast. One book claimed that the facts about this marriage and subsequent lineage had been well known into the Middle Ages and had once been part of Catholic liturgy.

Most of the books agreed that Jesus continued to walk the Earth for years after the crucifixion. Some said the crucifixion had lasted only three hours and Jesus had then been put into a tomb that symbolized a spiritual death or excommunication. His "resurrection" was simply the spiritual leader forgiving him for his offenses and allowing him back into the community. Others argued that the drink given him on the cross contained a powerful potion that produced a state simulating death. Once he was in the tomb, the Essene healers administered the antidote and mended his wounds. One writer stated that Jesus *had* died, but then achieved what the Tibetans called the Light Body Enlightenment, a state in which the consciousness of the individual, joined with the Universal Mind, transmuted the body into pure energy. Thus he could manifest his physical body any time he wished to do so.

These alternative histories traced the movement of Jesus, the Magdalene, and their children. Most agreed that they'd separated, Jesus going to India, she to Gaul, to avoid being hunted down. The books verified that several great cathedrals in France—Notre Dame, Rheims, Chartres— had indeed been dedicated to Mary of Magdala. One claimed that the red mantle she was often depicted wearing showed she was a bishop, a fully functioning priestess, able to preach and administer rites—an equal in all respects to the other disciples. One writer provided a long list of the female disciples who were priestesses in this same way.

Apparently, the plan had been to hide Jesus' bloodline. To do so, the roles of women in his ministry and life had been hidden or the women themselves discredited. In fact, the evolving church decided to silence women altogether, denying their power and role in spiritual life. Over and over Anne read that when the role of female power was denied, the resulting spiritual teaching would inevitably be severely imbalanced. Finally, Mary Magdalene had been turned from a royal wife, a queen, and a priestess into a common whore. Jesus' mother, Mary, was changed from a spiritually advanced woman with a normal family life into a literal virgin, and the role of any other women involved with Jesus' teaching distorted or completely obliterated.

Anne piled the books on the table beside her chair and replaced the antique manuscript in its plastic cover. She stretched out on the chaise lounge and stared into the fire. What she had read was logical and well documented. After she'd overcome her initial resistance, Anne found herself more and more persuaded. This version of Christ's life made more sense than what she'd been taught in church, and this vision of women's roles fit her own convictions. Her ancestors were priestesses and leaders. She could see how the Le Clairs were upholding this practice, even in a small way today. She would take her place in that tradition.

10

---

*M*ichael paced back and forth in his office, avoiding the large crate of Egyptian artifacts he'd been examining. He hadn't heard from Anne since the night they'd discovered the break-in at her apartment, and now it was Monday, the day after Christmas. He'd forced himself to wait through the Christmas holiday, but his patience was completely worn out. He had to know how she was and what had been discovered about the break-in, but most of all he needed to find a way to tell her he would be leaving the country soon. How could he ever explain to her that she needed to come, too? He hadn't yet revealed to her the depth of his own involvement in the task ahead. Maybe he could start with the astrological configuration in February. But how could he impress on her that the crystal holders had to be in Egypt on that day?

Shortly after nine, he took out the card she'd given him and dialed her home number. He thought she might be there since many people took off the whole week between Christmas and New Year. The phone rang twice, then switched to a series of familiar beeps and a recorded message, "We're sorry, but the number you have reached has been disconnected. Please check the number—" Michael hung up and redialed, carefully watching his fingers as he punched the buttons. He looked at the phone display and saw Anne's number lit up in green. This time he knew he'd dialed correctly, but the same thing happened. The number had been disconnected. Frustrated, he turned her business card over and called her office.

A brisk voice answered, "Ms. Le Clair's office."

"Yes, can I speak with Anne, please?"

"May I ask who is calling?"

"Michael Levy."

There was a short silence. "I'm sorry, Mr. Levy, which case are you calling about?"

"I'm not a client. This is a personal call."

"I see. Hold, please."

Michael expected to hear Anne's voice next, but instead he found himself listening to recorded music. He swung around in his chair and looked out the windows of his office. Sparrows and pigeons often visited the ledge, but today it was empty. He was on hold for a full five minutes. He was about to hang up and redial when a male voice suddenly addressed him. "May I help you?"

Stifling his frustration, Michael smoothed his voice. "Yes, Anne Le Clair, please."

"And who is calling?"

Michael repeated his name in measured tones.

"I see. I hope you'll pardon the question, Mr. Levy. Do I know you?"

A sigh of frustration escaped Michael. "I'm not really in a position to answer that question, sir, since I don't know who I am speaking with."

The man gave a short bark of a laugh. "This is Roger Abernathy. I'm a senior partner in this firm."

I see." Michael did not see, but he introduced himself anyway. "I was accompanying Anne the night she discovered the break-in. She attended my lecture that night. I didn't have the opportunity to introduce myself then. You were busy with the police and Anne. I was concerned about her."

"Anne is fine. She is taking a leave of absence to attend to other matters."

"I see. But . . ." Michael hesitated. ". . . her phone has been disconnected. Is there a way I can reach her?"

"Mr. Levy, I hope you'll pardon the inquiry, but in light of recent events, I'm sure you will understand. Are you associated with the Zohar Group?"

Michael was stunned. This was not a group many people knew existed, and he'd only discussed his consultation with them inside his own spiritual association. They would never have divulged this information. "Excuse me?"

"Cynthia Le Clair Middleton visited with the Zohar Group shortly before her death. And I find you with Anne Le Clair the night her apartment is broken into." Dr. Abernathy paused for effect. "You can see my problem."

Michael burst out with a retort before he could gather himself. "If I was with her, how could I have broken into her apartment?"

"I assume you didn't work alone."

"What are you—I never—how can you even suggest such a thing?"

"We will be investigating you, Mr. Levy, rest assured. In the meantime, I highly recommend you avoid the Le Clair family." The phone clicked as Dr. Abernathy hung up.

Michael was left staring at the receiver. Slowly, he returned it to the cradle, but continued to stare at the telephone for a few minutes. How anyone could have leapt to such a profoundly ludicrous assumption was beyond his imagination. He stood up and started to pace. On the second turn, he ran smack into the crate.

"Damn." Michael grabbed his leg and sat in a side chair, grimacing. He inspected the leg and found a lump forming. The skin wasn't broken.

Sitting back in the chair, he tried to make sense of the situation. Why would he want to break into Anne's apartment? And this Abernathy character had implied there was something suspicious about Cynthia's death. This could mean his own life might be in jeopardy.

He jumped up and began pacing again, this time avoiding the box. What was he going to do? He had to speak with Anne. He needed to tell her what he knew. After this demonstration of ineptitude, he no longer trusted that the Le Clairs had the same information.

A flash of inspiration sent him back to his desk. He dialed the fund-raising office for the museum. He introduced himself to the woman who answered, then said, "I understand the Le Clair family is interested in donating some jewelry from their collection, but I've misplaced the message. Do you have the number for Elizabeth Le Clair?"

"I'll have to check." After a pause, the woman gave it to him, emphasizing it was unlisted.

He thanked her, pressed for a dial tone, then called the number. After two rings, a neutral female voice answered, "Le Clair residence."

"Yes, I'm calling for Anne Le Clair. Her secretary suggested I try her here. It's a matter of some urgency."

"I'll check to see if she is here, sir. Your name, please?"

"Michael Levy."

"Just a minute, please."

Again, Michael was put on hold. He stared at the green display on his phone, wondering what he would say to her. After a minute, the same woman's voice came back on the line, "I'm sorry, sir. I can't locate Miss Anne. May I take a message?"

Michael suppressed a sigh, gave both his office and home number, and asked to have her call as soon as possible. "This matter is urgent."

"I'll relay the message, sir."

Michael hung up the phone. What a pretty mess this was.

* * *

ON WEDNESDAY EVENING, Michael made his way down an alley on the Lower East Side and knocked three times on a door with peeling brown paint. A faded curtain moved slightly behind the grilled window. Then Michael heard the bolts being pulled back. The door opened.

He was greeted formally with, "Shalom aleichem."

"Aleichem shalom, Reb Mordechai," he replied.

"Come in out of the cold, Michael," the man said, pronouncing his name as it would be spoken in Hebrew, with the accent on the last syllable.

At one time, the old rabbi must have been about six feet tall and powerfully built. Now his shoulders were permanently stooped and he walked with a slight limp. His hair and beard, mostly a whitish gray, showed occasional strands of red. A royal blue yarmulke was almost lost in his mass of curls. He gestured at the only couch in the room, surrounded by a diverse assortment of armchairs, all in various states of disrepair.

Michael sat on the vinyl couch, which made a small squeak when he leaned back. An old oak teacher's desk stood in the corner of the room. The walls were filled with an assortment of bookcases, all jam-packed.

"Tea?" The man shuffled toward a side table that held a hot plate, tea kettle, and tin of sugar cookies.

"No thank you, Rebbe. I don't want to put you to any trouble. Are the others coming?"

"No, I wanted to speak with you alone." Rabbi Mordechai walked slowly to the oak desk and rummaged through a pile of papers. "Here we are." He walked back to a chair next to the couch and carefully sank onto it.

Michael moved over quickly. "Please, sit here."

This chair is good for my back." The old rabbi spread an astrological chart on the stained coffee table. "I don't know if your group has noticed, but a Mogen David alignment is forming on February first." He pointed to the chart.

"Guy mentioned this, but he said it's even more elaborate than the Star."

Rabbi Mordechai smiled. "Excellent, yes. Neptune and Pluto are forming strong aspects as well. I think this is the Day of Opening. And you, Michael—your own chart is aspected very auspiciously by these alignments." He pulled a second astrology chart from the tattered folder and spread it next to the first. He pointed a finger, the joints swollen with arthritis, at the top of the page.

Michael leaned forward and put on his reading glasses.

"Already you need these?" Rabbi Mordechai chided.

"I do a lot of close work."

"Uranus will be making its final pass over your tenth house, which rules your career, in late January. On February first, Pluto, Saturn, and Neptune all aspect your Sun, indicating this is an important day for your life's mission. Pluto is directly conjunct your Mercury, allowing you to see into the great mystery. All these planets are either involved in or aspect the Mogen David alignment."

Michael nodded. "There have been many signs."

"Good, then you are aware of what is unfolding."

"Yes, but you've added some new information."

"Excellent. Now, have you been able to discover the identity of Cynthia Le Clair's contact in Egypt?"

"No." Michael sat back on the couch, which let out another squeak. "And I'm not going to make any progress with the Le Clairs." He told Rabbi Mordechai about his last phone conversation with Roger Abernathy. "Who is this man?"

The rabbi smiled. "A man with a sacred trust, one in a long lineage."

"But he isn't a Le Clair."

"No, but one sworn to protect them."

"Oh." Michael's eyes widened as he realized Abernathy's status. "Then I'd better be careful. I was striking up a friendship with the new crystal bearer, Anne, but she hasn't returned my calls since her apartment was broken into, and now I don't believe she will. I'm going to try to make contact with her again."

"You must hurry. Who Cynthia saw in Egypt we do not know, but I gave her the name of the man who does. He's a second cousin, an obscure Kabbalist and historian in old Jerusalem, also a member of the Zohar Group. His name is Moishe ben Zvi. Moishe understands the route the knowledge took, and he knows there are those who still keep the wisdom in Al Khem."

Rabbi Mordechai looked around for a clean piece of paper. Not finding one, he started to stand up, but Michael gestured for him to stay. He walked over to the desk and rummaged around, finally finding a smudged piece that was otherwise blank. Mordechai took it and carefully wrote out an address, then started to draw a map at the bottom of the page. After a minute, he stopped. "There are too many turns and I am old. This is the name and address and general neighborhood. You are a young man. You will find him."

The old rabbi blew on the paper to dry the ink, then carefully folded it and handed it to Michael. Michael took the paper, but Rabbi Mordechai did not release it. He looked deeply into Michael's eyes. "May the Abbisher, Baruch Hashem, guard your steps, my son, for now is the darkest night and the sunrise rests in your hands."

11

$\mathscr{A}$ cold cat nose woke Anne on Thursday morning. She opened her eyes to Vivienne who greeted her with a small peep. "You know you aren't supposed to wake me up, Ms. Viv." She looked at the alarm. The clock read nine-thirty. "Were you wondering if I was going to sleep forever?" She ruffled Vivienne's ears. "Who's hungry?" she called out. Merlin let out a loud meow and jumped on top of Anne, pushing under her hand. "Okay, okay," she said, laughing, "let me up."

After putting down some dry food for the cats' breakfast and finishing her morning ablutions, Anne settled on the couch and began her daily routine. First she spent a few minutes calling on the directions to create a mobile ball of light around herself. Grandmother Elizabeth had taught her what she called psychic self-defense. Anne noticed a stag in the east, a black wolf in the west. Once her visualization of this circle was strong, she asked for protection against any energy not in her highest good and a signal if significant negative energy was directed her way. Then she started to record her dreams from the night before, but they'd fled with the morning light. She closed her eyes and relaxed, allowing images to surface. Nothing came. Dr. Abernathy had told her dream recall could be aided by lying in the same position she'd slept in, so she lay down on the couch and let herself drift. After a minute, a memory surfaced.

Elizabeth had come into her room and asked Anne to follow her. Anne got up and walked down the hallway, but noticed little things had changed about the house. The walls looked lighter than usual, and when they reached the spiral staircase, the old chandelier from Anne's childhood hung from the ceiling.

Elizabeth led Anne into the ritual room where people were gathered over the large crystal. Anne nodded to her cousin Rebecca, Dr. Abernathy, and several other members of her grandmother's group. She looked into the crystal and saw an unlikely scene, the Sphinx with the face of a lioness surrounded by water and green palms.

Surprised, she looked up and saw a tall, willowy woman smiling at her from the other side of the circle. She was vaguely familiar. Anne turned to ask her grandmother who the woman was, but found herself staring into a tall silhouette of light. She looked down at her own arm and saw that it was glowing as well. She wondered what had happened to her body. With that thought, she woke up in her bedroom. Anne had sat up and looked around, then turned over and gone back to sleep.

Now on the couch, Anne sat straight up again, scattering two cats and the journal. "Oh, my God." During her lesson in self-defense, Elizabeth had promised to come wake up her astral body and take her on a journey. This must have been it, although Anne had imagined something more exotic than a trip to the ritual room. Anne threw on a pair of blue jeans and a T-shirt and went running in search of her grandmother. She found Elizabeth in the office dictating to her private secretary and came to an abrupt halt just inside the door.

Elizabeth held up a finger while she finished the letter she was dictating and gave instructions for its distribution. Anne thought she caught a tiny smile behind the serious face. Elizabeth turned to her. "What is it that can't wait until our appointment, my dear?"

After the secretary shut the door behind her, Anne plopped in a chair in front of the expansive desk and explained what she'd just remembered. As she talked, Elizabeth's smile widened. Anne finished with a barrage of questions. "Did it really happen? Do you remember it? Why did the house look different? Who—what was that tall being of light I saw?"

"One at a time, please." Elizabeth counted off each answer on her raised fingers. "Yes, it really happened. I'm pleased you remembered the experience. Two, the house looked different because the astral plane is not an exact duplicate of the physical, as you saw. Physical objects leave a signature that can last for a while, although that chandelier isn't new. You probably saw it because you liked it so much as a child. The mind has a stronger impact on that level of existence. Three, I didn't see any tall light being."

"I still can't believe I did it."

"You did. Congratulations. And the rest of your assignment?"

"The rest?"

"You were supposed to search for your spiritual guides."

"Oh, Thomas took all afternoon and part of the evening telling me family history. I fell asleep meditating when I got back to my room."

Elizabeth chuckled. "He can have that effect at times. He's a walking encyclopedia, although when he speaks to the public, he has some of your Uncle James's charisma. How far back did he get?"

"To the man himself. I'd pretty much figured out the flow of things, but Thomas felt compelled to dot all the i's and cross all the t's. This afternoon, he's promised to explain the current balance of power—as if I don't understand that."

"There are certain things you'll see differently now." Elizabeth sat looking at Anne for a moment, then roused herself from her reverie. "Well, tomorrow Dr. Abernathy will be back and you two can meet for instruction. I'm pleased you remembered our little jaunt. Perhaps we'll do it again."

"Let's go somewhere exotic."

"We go where we need to. Now back to work."

Anne returned to her room to finish her morning routine of meditation and work with the crystal. She closed the blinds and cradled the small crystal in the palm of her hand. Closing her eyes, she allowed her mantra to settle her mind and breath. The silence deepened. After about ten minutes, Anne sent a mental request into this quiet: *I want to meet my spiritual guides.* Then she returned to the silence.

Vivienne rubbed against her, but settled down on her left. Merlin took up a post at her right hand. She returned to her mantra to regain the depth of silence, then sat waiting. After a moment, she saw a glow beginning in her forehead. Trying to follow Dr. Abernathy's instructions, she didn't reach for this glow, but continued to observe it neutrally.

The glow spread and brightened, then began to take a human shape. Again she saw the woman from last night's excursion—tall and willowy with reddish blond hair. The woman moved closer and sent the thought to Anne, "Hello, Anne."

"Hello," Anne sent back. "Do I know you?"

The figure shifted slightly, the face growing more solid and slightly older. Suddenly, she was wearing riding clothes and Anne saw the two of them riding across the estate, Anne on her favorite childhood pony.

"Cynthia?"

"Yes, darling, I am near you always now. You must go to Egypt to finish what I began. You will receive guidance."

A noise from outside distracted Anne momentarily. The figure of her aunt faded and she could not make out all of her last words. Something about trusting someone. Anne tried to return to the silence, but no images formed after repeated requests.

Anne remembered her aunt's words on the letter that had accompanied the crystal: "Call for me in your dreams, and I will come." When she'd read that letter, she'd never imagined that Cynthia literally meant for Anne to call her, that Cynthia would respond—with advice, with emotional support. Anne returned the crystal necklace to its accustomed place around her neck. She'd come a long way in a few short weeks. Maybe she didn't have to do this alone after all.

She glanced at the clock on her bed stand. Eleven already. Time to meet Arnold for another training session. The martial arts he'd taught her in her early teens were returning more easily than she'd imagined. She had to see Thomas at two o'clock. She sincerely hoped he wouldn't drone on as he had yesterday.

After she'd succeeded in throwing Arnold across the gym, Anne's spirits were high. It wasn't every day you put the family's head of security flat on his back. But it was quarter past two and she hadn't eaten. She stopped by the kitchen to request that lunch be sent to the library for her. "And tea for two, if you don't mind."

Estelle nodded. "I'll send someone as soon as I can."

Thomas was ending a phone conversation when she arrived. "Thank you, Ralph. We'll need to leave in a few days." He motioned for Anne to come in. "My secretary will make the hotel arrangements. Let her know when you have a flight plan." He hung up.

Anne raised her eyebrows in a question.

"Just a quick trip to verify some information. I know you'll miss our discussions."

"Your lectures, you mean."

Thomas laughed. "Ready for more?"

"Estelle is sending up lunch."

"Let's sit."

Brother and sister settled down on the two couches in front of the fireplace, facing one another. "First, do you have any questions from yesterday?"

"Just one. How do you remember it all?"

"Actually, we learned this from the branch of our family that descended from the priestesses of Avalon. The Druids, especially the bards, had to memorize long ballads and stories. We've retained certain mnemonic devices from that time. Any other questions?"

"Why do I get the feeling I'm about to be tested?"

"Oh, how perceptive you are. Now tell me the flow of our ancestry."

"Okay, but do I have to remember all the names?"

"No, that's my job." Thomas wove his fingers together and sat back, ready to listen.

Anne closed her eyes and recited the story of their family from Jerusalem to France, then to Scotland and on to America.

"A passing summary." Thomas's eyes twinkled. "I'm glad to see you can learn while you're asleep. That is usually an ability only long-term adepts develop."

Anne opened her eyes and saw Thomas's lips twitching. "Then there's Lila Mae, your current wife, the ex-prostitute," she said.

"The same profession as Mary," Thomas pointed out. They both burst out laughing. Someone knocked on the library door. "Yes," Thomas asked, between guffaws.

"Lunch for Miss Anne."

"Oh, excellent." Thomas jumped up and opened the door. Anne took a bite of her salad. Thomas poured himself a cup of peppermint tea, stretched his legs in front of him, and began to narrate another series of historical events.

"You'll notice the Romans have been responsible several times for hunting down our ancestors and attempting to eliminate them. The Romans in the form of the empire and in the form of the Holy Roman Empire, and then the Roman Catholic Church. These empires had certain characteristics in common. A strong military. A militaristic culture. Oppression of women. A patriarchal family structure." He ticked them off on his fingers. "A belief in the ultimate superiority of their own group of people and enslavement or oppression of others. The broader Christian Church shared some of these as well, plus an enforced allegiance to a set of beliefs that if questioned could result in torture and murder. They added to the mix a conviction that other spiritual beliefs are evil or demonic." Thomas looked pointedly at Anne who paused with her fork midway to her mouth. "In fact, they invented the devil as we know him today. Does all this sound familiar?"

"Invented the devil?" she asked.

"Used the image of the pagan god of fertility. The Horned God—Pan in southern Europe, Cernunnos in the British Isles."

Anne scowled. "Why did they hate sex so much?"

"I think it was part of their attempt to suppress the priestess tradition, but we don't have time to talk about that today. . . . During the eighteenth century, the French and American revolutions loosened the grip of the corrupted aristocracy and church, which spread across Europe in the nineteenth century. In the twentieth century, however, the philosophy of control went through another revival, especially in central Europe."

"Thomas, they do still teach history in some four-year colleges. Even the occasional high school." Anne finished off her salad.

Thomas ignored her. "The roots of this movement we're discussing go all the way back to 1776, when a man who was from a distant branch of our family, Adam Weishaupt, was seduced into the abuse of power. In turn, he accused the British branch of the order of being corrupt. In truth, there was some corruption in both groups. Weishaupt was the head of the Bavarian Illuminati, a group most likely descended from the Teutonic Knights."

"That sounds vaguely familiar."

This was the group Hitler attempted to resurrect in the Third Reich when he tried to create the third Roman Empire."

"Ah." Anne wiped her hands and pushed away her empty tray. "Same philosophy, different century."

"Exactly. Our concern today lies with the Nazis."

"But they were defeated." At Thomas's look, she quickly said, "Okay, some of them may still live in the mountains in South America, but so what? They have no real political power."

Thomas pursed his lips. "So most of the public believes, but the real situation is much more complicated. During the war, certain industrialists and politicians supported the Nazi agenda. Some were just doing business, supplying the gas, the ammunition, building their own financial empires. But some had ties to an old mystical order, the Knights of Malta. This group also fell from the light and still recruits the brilliant and powerful in a certain well-known American university, using an old Templar symbol, the skull and cross bones, but that's an entirely different subject. Anyway, when Berlin fell at the end of World War II, certain elements within the industrial and governmental alliance brought German scientists over to continue the research they'd been pursuing. You may have heard of Project Paperclip? They also protected the Nazi governmental officials they'd made deals with. Thus the Teutonic Knights and the Knights of Malta joined forces."

Anne got up and poked the fire. "Thomas, are you reciting a plot from *The X-Files?*"

"No, my dear sister, they leaked information to the American public."

She turned around to stare at him. "So now everything is a conspiracy."

"You tell me how they killed Uncle James and got away with it, not to mention the Kennedys, Martin Luther King Jr., Malcolm X—" He gave up counting. "All the others."

She was silent for a moment, remembering her shock when she'd realized the official government report about her uncle's assassination was only a cover-up. "I guess you have a point, but wasn't that a simple coup? A combination of forces that refused to allow him to change the course of the government?"

"Yes, a combination of forces. That's exactly what I'm explaining to you."

Anne sighed as she settled back on the couch. "Okay, Thomas. Actually, this kind of conspiracy is much easier to believe than certain other wild notions you've managed to convince me are facts."

Thomas nodded. "This group includes international industrialists, bankers, scientists, politicians, and high-ranking military and intelligence officers. Since the Second World War, this group has conducted advanced scientific study in many areas, including continuing work in physics that was begun by the Manhattan Project and work in genetics that was started in the concentration camps."

Anne shuddered.

"It is grisly. All this clandestine research necessitated recruiting people within legitimate government agencies; thus black ops began with the OSS, which developed into the CIA, and with the FBI, NSA, and branches of the military. These people operate outside the law. Add to this the private armies, if you will, of corporations and the world's wealthiest families . . ."

Thomas sat forward, warming to his subject. "In fact, that is what makes this group so invisible to the average person. They think in terms of nations, of diplomacy, of international law being administered by the United Nations, a group made up of nation states. But the twentieth century was really run by this loose association of people whose agenda was dominated by economics. That's who is really running the world."

He jabbed the air with his index finger. "Politics is a camouflage, a decoy to keep public attention from seeing the real power. Affairs of state are largely controlled by these forces. It's obvious the American presidential election was controlled, but people dropped that fact from consciousness as soon as the war began. If they'd remembered it, perhaps they could have seen the other agendas at work."

"Well, to be absolutely accurate, Thomas, Uncle James didn't exactly win fair and square either."

Thomas closed his eyes for a minute, then looked at her. The depth of sorrow she saw there surprised Anne. "Thomas." She reached to touch his hand, but he waved her away.

"It's okay, Annie. It's just that the amount of corruption on the other side would have swept us away, and we felt we had to do something. And by other side, I don't mean political parties."

"Why maintain the pretense of a democracy then? Why don't the forces just come out of the shadows?"

Thomas gave a cynical laugh. "Because it's easier for them this way. People believe they're living in one world, and the powers that be don't want to jar them from this happy dream. And we want the idea of democracy to still be taught to people, because the Constitution, the Bill of Rights, is the embodiment of the Davidic ideal of government. We can't throw that away just because it's not being followed now. If we play our cards right, we can regain control and make it real again."

Now his eyes shone. "Besides, it's not that simple really. There are positive forces within the shadow government. There are highly developed souls who've incarnated into these families to try to turn the course of history. And the projects some of the groups are doing involve psychic activity, work that necessitates the development of spiritual abilities. This is a dangerous game for the shadow organizations, although I don't believe they realize it, because this type of effort is the way souls evolve. People developing their psychic abilities to spy on other factions sometimes have a spiritual awakening and begin to work for the light."

Anne put her tea, long cold, on the tray. "Why not recruit them?"

"We do. But most often we ask them to stay where they are. Their very presence affects the shadow side. This is a game of consciousness as well as physical actions. Our aim is to raise the consciousness of the world so that there is so much coherence, so much light, that the negative power plays melt away like snow in the sun." He pointed out the window behind him, then frowned when he realized the sun was on its way down.

Anne nodded toward the growing darkness. "That sounds very much like wishful thinking. Believing that some magic wand might return our influence could be just a way to ease your wounds." She softened her voice. "You know you can never run for office. You might as well go stand in front of a target at the shooting range."

Thomas looked up at her with a smile. "Yes, but don't you see? All that does is free me to work behind the scenes where the real action is anyway."

Anne studied her brother for a minute. Tall, handsome, articulate, brilliant—he was made for leadership. "I'm sorry, sweet prince."

Thomas waved her words away. "Thank you, Annie, but I believe this, you see, so I'm not as sad as you imagine."

Anne stirred on the couch. "Where do we stand now?"

With the crystal. As I told you the other night, the prophecy is for this time. Many religious and spiritual groups—the Maya, the Aztec, the Hopi, the Western metaphysical groups, the Vedic masters—point to now as the time for the return of the light. It's the turn of a major cycle in astrology, the beginning of the Age of Aquarius. We must do our part to bring in this age. We must uncover the secret of the crystal and get you ready to use it. And we must find the other five."

"I'm working hard."

Thomas nodded. "Has Grandmother told you about the Star Alignment?"

"No, but Dr. Abernathy did."

"So you know the date when you're supposed to use the crystal?"

Yes, the alignment will take place February first—but that's only a month away. Oh, my God, Thomas, I'll never be ready. There must be a mistake."

Thomas shook his head. "There's no mistake. And you will be ready."

* * *

ON FRIDAY around ten o'clock in the morning, Anne, flanked by two Secret Service men, got into the back of a limousine. Arnold rode up front and a man she was not familiar with had replaced Lawrence, the regular chauffeur. She thought this was overkill. After all, whoever was after the crystal had only broken into her apartment. It was unlikely they'd attack her in public, but her grandmother had insisted.

Anne thought two guards would have done, but the family didn't entirely trust the Secret Service. At least they were trained to be discreet, not just in public, but to allow the privacy of their subject as much as possible. Neither of them met her eyes or addressed her unless she spoke to them. Anne settled back in the leather seat with a sigh and closed her eyes, trying to relax.

She'd spent the week meditating long hours, scrying until her eyes crossed, studying with Dr. Abernathy, and training with Arnold. Now she was able to drop into an altered state almost at will and during scrying had discovered historical information about the crystal that Thomas had verified in large part. Her dreams had returned in force as well, showing her scenes from Celtic Britain, Jerusalem, Tibet, Mexico, and Egypt. These she puzzled over.

Dr. Abernathy was pleased with her progress, but she still felt frightened and woefully ill prepared. Today was the thirtieth of December, almost the end of the year. She had one month to hone her skills, discover the other five crystals, and find out where they should be used and how. It seemed impossible.

Anne looked out the window as the freeway exits zoomed by. This trip was a welcome distraction, a return to familiar territory. The speech, scheduled for months, was a fund-raiser for a United Nations committee on International Women's Rights. The speech was pretty much routine, a plea to improve the harsh conditions many women lived under, to ensure women had the money to raise their children, to encourage the availability of birth control, education, the vote—all the rights Western women had gained less than one hundred years earlier. People forgot that. It always helped to remind them. As she leafed through the eight pages of her speech, she reflected how, when she'd written it, she could never have imagined how her life or beliefs were going to change. She smiled as she imagined adding a paragraph about the erasure of women from the history of Jesus, explained by one of his granddaughters, many centuries removed.

They arrived and Anne began the slow process of taking her seat—greeting people she knew, posing for the press, listening to news from colleagues or pleas for her support, and giving polite, noncommittal responses. Finally, she made it to her place on the podium and the formalities began with a brief welcoming address from the chair of WomenWatch, one of the committees sponsoring the gathering. As she listened, Anne suddenly felt an odd prickling at the small of her back. Surreptitiously, she stretched her shoulders and rubbed the back of her neck, but the sensation only increased. Puzzled, she tried to move to a more comfortable position in her chair, but the sensation didn't change.

After a minute, she realized with a shock that this was the warning she had requested if negative energy was sent to her. The morning protection ritual had become almost a habit, something she gave little thought to. Furtively, she glanced around the room. She didn't notice any unusual behavior, but found her eyes kept returning to one table where a muscular man with dark hair and sharp eyes sat, not noticeably looking at her. But by now, Anne trusted her intuition. Just as she was about to dismiss him as a candidate, he looked directly at her and the prickling at the small of her back intensified. She felt a chill as their eyes met, but she schooled her face not to show any reaction and kept her eyes moving. Instead of feeling afraid, she was pleasantly surprised that her new tools had worked.

Turning her attention back to the front table, Anne noticed lunch was quietly being served as the chairperson finished her introductions. Anne's mouth watered when she saw the plates were piled with mounds of mashed potatoes, gravy, and mixed vegetables surrounding a good cut of steak. She took her fork in hand when her plate arrived, but she found only mixed vegetables, a fruit salad, and a small mound of cottage cheese. Anne tried to smile as she thanked the waiter. Her neighbor to her left pretended not to notice, but she mouthed "Doctor's orders" to him, and he nodded politely, obviously not understanding.

I thought we were trying not to draw attention to our activities, she mentally addressed herself to her grandmother.

She ate quickly, preparing to be called to the podium. After everyone else had been served a tiramisu and coffee, the chair introduced Anne.

Once behind the podium, she warmed to her subject, surprised how much she was enjoying this brief return to what had been her normal life.

"The suffering endured by women under the Taliban rule captured our attention and opened our hearts to the plight of women everywhere, but now that the war against terrorism has become old news, let us not waver in our resolve." She outlined her own plan of action, which just happened to correspond with the committee's own platform, which she as a member had helped to formulate. When she finished her speech, she acknowledged the enthusiastic applause, then took her seat and listened attentively to reports from various countries on their progress. She almost forgot about her new responsibilities.

After another hour of socializing with the committee's financial supporters, Anne worked her way through the crowd, assuring colleagues she would be back, she hoped in the spring, and answering personal questions from the press with the simple phrase, "Family business, I'm afraid."

Once outside the room, Anne told Arnold about the man she'd noticed, including exactly what seat he'd been in, and carefully described him.

Arnold went back inside, leaving her with the Secret Service men for a minute. They ushered her outside. Waiting for her limousine to pull up, flanked by two men in black suits, each with a small earphone and wire stretching under his collar, Anne suddenly noticed a familiar face in the crowd. Michael Levy stood behind the first row of onlookers, a slight frown on his face as he scanned the crowd.

She called out, "Michael."

His head turned around sharply and a smile broke out on his face.

12

*M*ichael stepped toward Anne, relieved by her greeting. He'd been standing outside waiting for quite some time and his feet in the thin-soled shoes were heavy with the cold. He'd telephoned her several more times during the week, but she never returned his calls. He hadn't known what to think, except that her family had convinced her he was somehow involved in Cynthia's death. He'd been afraid she would think he was stalking her or some nonsense like that, but he was determined to see her. Their business was just too important to allow potential embarrassment or even legal trouble to stop him.

Her face had brightened at the sight of him—at least he hoped he was not imagining it—and now she stood in front of him, or at least behind a rather intimidating man in a dark suit who was looking at him with cold, detached eyes.

"It's all right. He's a friend," he heard Anne's voice explaining.

The man turned and whispered in Anne's ear. She nodded and turned back to Michael. "Would you mind terribly going with this gentleman for a moment? He'll escort you to my car."

Michael hesitated, looking from what looked like a Secret Service agent to Anne. He saw a slight movement of her eyes toward the press, who had already snapped a few tentative pictures. "Oh, of course," he said, and followed the agent inside.

The man walked into the manager's office behind the front desk and motioned for Michael to follow. Once they were both inside, the agent shut the door.

"Empty your pockets, please, sir."

Michael, though a bit offended, complied.

The agent sorted through his keys and change, then produced a small metal wand that he passed over Michael's body. He nodded. "You may come with me, sir."

Michael returned the items to his pockets, then followed the man into the garage. Anne's limousine was pulled over to the side, waiting. The man opened the back door for Michael, who got in next to Anne. Then, to his even greater surprise, the agent got in behind him and sat on the opposite seat facing them. All in all, Michael counted four security men in the car.

He turned to Anne, "Did I miss the announcement? Are you running for president?"

"I'm so sorry." Anne looked distinctly uncomfortable. "After the break-in, my family insisted I take every precaution."

At his hesitant nod, she went on, "We've had an assassination in the family, remember, and other attempts in the past that are not generally known about."

Michael looked from Anne to the two Secret Service agents, who now were scanning the streets as the car drove off, studiously ignoring the two.

"Don't worry. They won't disturb us," she said.

Michael gave a short laugh, "Won't disturb us? But they're right here. I was hoping to talk to you."

"Go ahead. They aren't going to leave me alone."

"Okay, then. May I ask why you haven't returned my phone calls?"

"Calls?"

"You haven't gotten any of my messages?"

Anne shook her head, a slight frown wrinkling her forehead.

"I've called you at least six times."

"I can't imagine why no one gave me your messages. That's certainly not like the staff."

Michael sat back against the leather seat. He felt disoriented, rather like a rabbit scooped up by an eagle. "Well, I have an idea." As he said this, he noticed one of the men in the front seat studying him through the mirror on the back of the visor. He turned back to Anne. "Can we go somewhere to talk where we might have a bit more privacy?"

Anne chuckled. "They do take some getting used to." She addressed one of the agents. "Is there some place that's been cleared for us?"

He turned to the driver. "Take us to the St. Anthony's Club."

Michael looked down at his casual shirt and pants with dismay, then up into Anne's blue eyes.

"Don't worry," she said, "we'll go to a private room. I mean, you look fine. It's just that—well, we want some privacy. Then we can talk."

They settled back and Michael tried to enjoy the ride, only now seeing the luxurious appointments of the automobile. It was equipped with a television, phone, computer jack, and bar, and the leather of the seat was smooth to his touch. He glanced at Anne, her oval face soft above her navy-blue business suit. He wanted to talk, but held his peace.

When they arrived at the club, Anne spoke to the maitre d', who quickly ushered them past open rooms with lush carpets, fine furniture, and perfectly polished chandeliers into a private suite furnished with a luxurious sectional couch in front of a gas fireplace. Behind the couch next to windows overlooking Central Park stood a dining table. Off to the left was a rather elaborate bathroom.

"We don't wish to be disturbed," Anne told the man who'd shown them to the room.

"As you wish, madam."

She turned to Michael. "Would you like something?"

"Oh, I'm fine." Michael looked around, a bit lost.

Anne turned to the waiter. "Nothing, then."

"As you wish, madam."

Michael had the fleeting thought that if she ordered an assault rifle, the man would repeat the same phrase with the same neutral look on his face.

The man left and Anne turned to the one remaining security guard. "Can we be alone, please, Arnold?"

Arnold favored Michael with a particularly dark look, then said to Anne, "I'll be right on the other side of that door."

"Thank you, Arnold. He's been frisked."

Still he hesitated.

"I think with our sessions I can handle him," she joked, but Arnold only glared at Michael once more, then left the room.

Once they were alone, Michael found that the words were now stuck in his throat. He sat kitty-cornered to Anne on the sectional, staring at his hands.

In a gentler voice, Anne asked, "So you called me? Was there something particular you wanted to talk about?"

Michael looked up to see Anne's blue eyes lit with amusement.

"Now that we're alone, I'm having trouble thinking where to begin. I've never had an experience quite like this before." He pointed to the closed door.

"I guess it is odd. I've been around the Secret Service all my life." She shrugged. "You said you had an idea why your messages didn't reach me?"

Michael felt his stomach tighten, but he plunged ahead. "Yes, I do. I'm afraid I have a confession to make."

"A confession?"

"Yes." Suddenly, he blushed. "I, uh . . . well, you see . . ." He stumbled to a stop.

Anne blushed, too. "Well, I can't say I hadn't noticed."

"No, it's not that."

Anne flushed and sat back on the sofa, back straight, arms crossed.

He rushed on. "I mean, yes, there is that, but there's more. Much more."

Anne sat watching him, but he couldn't make out what she was feeling. "Go on."

"Well, you see, as it turns out, when you first came to my uncle's shop, I didn't recognize you at first. I mean, I'd never met you, but as you described your grandmother's jewelry collection, I began to suspect you were a member of an important family, spiritually that is. You weren't the first member of that family I'd had dealings with. You see, I knew your Aunt Cynthia."

Anne's face didn't change, but Michael felt as if the room had grown colder. "You knew Aunt Cynthia?"

Yes." Michael studied his hands for a moment, then took a deep breath, feeling like he was about to jump off a high dive. "Cynthia consulted with a spiritual group I work with from time to time. She was searching for a contact, someone who would know the answers to some questions she had."

"Yes." Anne's face was the picture of neutrality.

Damn these politicians, Michael thought, then said aloud, "She was looking for information about the crystal."

"So you knew about the crystal before I even mentioned it."

"Yes, but I had no idea who it had passed to. I was delighted that circumstance had brought you to me, and I wanted to talk to you immediately, but you seemed not to understand its significance." He looked into Anne's eyes. "I'm very sorry I kept things from you, but I felt it was necessary at the time. I didn't understand how you could be in possession of such a powerful artifact and not know anything about it. I had to be cautious."

"So your interest has always been professional." Anne's voice wavered slightly.

"Yes, I mean, no. Oh, damn it!" Michael stood up and started to pace in front of the fireplace. "The last time we talked, you seemed more open. You came to my lecture. You told me your family was training you."

"I never said that to you."

Michael stopped in mid-stride. "You're right. I assumed it. Was I wrong?"

Anne was quiet for a minute, then simply said, "Go on."

"I was worried about you after we discovered the robbery. I called, but your phone had been disconnected. I called your office and was put through to a Mr. Abernathy."

"Dr." Anne corrected him out of habit.

"Yes, Dr. Abernathy. It seems he'd discovered my connection to Cynthia and assumed the worst."

Anne's eyes widened. "The worst?"

"Yes, he warned me not to try contacting you. He said he was going to have me investigated."

"Investigated? For what?"

"I thought Cynthia died from a heart attack, but based on what he said, I think he suspects foul play."

"And he suspects you?"

"Apparently. Anne, I swear to you, I had nothing to do with Cynthia's death. I was trying to help her discover the other keys and the secret of their use."

Anne took in a sharp breath. "You know about the other keys?"

"I know there are six crystals, that they must be used together, and soon."

"February first."

Michael stared at her. "Thank God you know."

"But how did you know?"

Michael shook his head in frustration. "There is so much to tell you." He sat back on the couch and took a deep breath. "I'm also a member of a secret spiritual organization, one that goes back many centuries, one that passes on knowledge much as your family does." He paused; then he closed his eyes and asked, *Is this the time to tell her?* Immediately, he felt a warm glow in his chest, a clear affirmation.

He opened his eyes and looked again at her, this woman he'd worked with centuries in the past, this woman he'd loved before, this woman he knew he loved now. He pulled on a chain hidden by his collar and out came a crystal very similar in size and shape to her own, only topped with a Mogen David.

Anne stared at him, dumbfounded.

"It was no coincidence that you came to my uncle's shop. We were destined to meet. Cynthia knew I held a matching crystal and we tried to find out more information. She sent me a message that she'd discovered something, but I never got the chance to find out what."

Anne stared at him, her eyes filled to the brim with unshed tears.

He pressed on. "Tomorrow, I'm leaving for Israel to consult with the man I sent her to. He'll be able to tell me what he told her. Then we'll know more about how to use the crystals."

"Your group doesn't know?"

"We know some things. Cynthia and I shared some information, but we don't have time for that now. They all work together somehow. Together they will turn the key."

"But to what?" Anne asked.

"We aren't certain of that either, but we think it is February first, like I said."

"That's so soon. How will we ever be able to figure it out?"

Michael looked deep into her eyes. *The walls were limestone, carved with figures and hieroglyphs. They stood on steps just outside a temple. It was near dawn. He felt a heavy sadness.*

He felt Anne remembering the same moment.

"It was you," she said.

"Yes, I came to you," he said.

"What did you give me?"

"It was in Egypt."

"Yes."

They stared at each other.

Michael spoke first. "I knew you were the one."

Anne shook her head. "I wish people would stop saying that. I'm the one playing catch-up. At least you've known this all your life. I'm trying to cram a life's worth of learning into six weeks."

"What happened?"

"It's a long story. My mother forbade the family to tell me anything."

Michael frowned. "How could she do that?"

"She thought she was saving me from feeling like a freak when I was a teenager. And I think she was jealous of her sister's talent."

Michael snorted. "The things we allow to get in our way."

Anne nodded. "Michael, how will we ever do this?"

Michael took her hands in his. "We must trust that everything will come together. Just look at the miracles that have unfolded so far. You found me. Your family has told you the truth about your ancestry and you've started learning." He paused, considering whether he should say more, but now was not the time for secrets between them. "Anne, you aren't learning these things, but remembering them. You've been very powerful in the past. I'm sure of it."

She smiled. "Let's hope that person takes over when the time comes."

He nodded. "We'll pray for divine intervention. You must come to Egypt."

I know. They're making arrangements to send me soon."

"I'll find a way to contact you when I know something."

"Good luck."

"Thanks. Be careful." He opened the door and saw four security men standing there. He wished he could borrow one.

* * *

KARL MUELLER SAT in a well-appointed office across the desk from Spender, whose lean, sharp face was lit by his desk lamp.

I followed enough of Paul Marchant's calculations to be sure he can do the job," Mueller reported.

"Why didn't you get them?" Spender took out an expensive cigar and clipped the end.

"We still need the sound codes."

Spender favored him with a glance, then lit his cigar and took a long draw. "Always get as much as you can, Mr. Mueller, even if we already have it."

Mueller nodded, showing no reaction to this criticism. He accepted the chain of command.

"And the girl?"

"Anne is holed up in the family compound. We were able to place a few cameras and confirm she has the crystal before our monitors were discovered. She did make a public appearance, but was surrounded by Secret Service and family security." Mueller kept his gaze as neutral as his voice. When there was no comment, he continued. "On her way out, she met with Michael Levy. We've been observing him closely. He plans to leave the country tomorrow."

"Yes." Spender turned to one of the computers behind him and touched a button. The screen lit up, revealing a travel itinerary. "January first he flies to Jerusalem on El Al, leaving at 2:22 P.M. from La Guardia, arriving the next morning. The following week, he'll continue to Egypt. His return ticket is booked for February third. Now what do you suppose is so important to our Mr. Levy that he would risk a trip to Israel in the midst of these violent and uncertain times?"

"He's retracing Cynthia Le Clair's footsteps. One of our best men is trailing him. We must discover what the Egyptian contact knows. Then we can get the crystals."

"Why not bring in the contact?"

Mueller looked at Spender for a moment, then replied in the same flat voice. "I prefer to leave no trace, sir. To abduct a well-known Egyptian citizen could bring attention." He shifted his feet. "But if those are your orders . . ." He ended this thought with a sweep of his hand.

Spender laughed and put down his cigar. "I agree. What about the other crystals?"

"We are aware of the location of three. We have a reasonable scenario that places a fourth somewhere in the Middle East, but not with the old Kabbalist. Two seem 'lost in the mists of time' is the phrase our researchers used, I believe."

Spender's eyes narrowed. "As they may be if they don't find the keys." He fixed his gaze on Mueller. "You must bring the crystals together on the first of February. Otherwise we may lose control of the situation." He paused, then punctuated his next words with stabs of his forefinger. "If you do not succeed, the result will be worse than death."

"Yes, sir." Mueller knew this was no idle threat. He'd seen Alexander Cagliostro at work.

"We killed this Jew before, you and I. Do you remember?"

Mueller shook his head. He avoided the mystical side of things, preferring to work with what could be seen.

Mr. Spender leaned forward and spoke with emphasis. "This time we must destroy his soul."

Pure hate flashed through Mueller, which he quickly subdued.

"We've set up this conference as a cover. Even the people producing it don't realize where their money is coming from. Both of them will speak. Perhaps this will lure the others out."

"Yes, sir."

"Be there."

Mueller left the meeting and went straight to Michael Levy's apartment building. He thought of calling for backup, but decided he'd rather handle this alone. After half an hour of surveillance, Michael walked out the front door of the building and headed for the subway. Mueller waited five minutes before he got out of his car and strolled across the street. He passed the front door, continued around the corner of the building, and then, checking to be certain he was unobserved, entered the alley.

He wrapped his hand in a piece of cloth and broke a basement window. He slid through, careful of the glass. Using the back stairs, he ran up seven flights. Michael's apartment door, secured with five locks, presented no challenge. Once inside, he put on latex gloves and began to search methodically, carefully noting the exact position of each item before he touched it. Everything had to be returned to its precise position. If he was lucky, Michael had headed to Times Square for New Year's Eve, but he doubted it. Michael wasn't the type.

It was a two-bedroom apartment with a large living room, no view to speak of, and a narrow kitchen. One bedroom was sparsely furnished—a bed, dresser, nightstand, and lamp—but the walls were lined with bookcases. A half-packed suitcase lay in the middle of the bed. The other bedroom served as an office. Overstuffed bookcases covered two of the walls, and under the window stood a desk crowded with papers, a wild assortment of news articles copied off the Net, New Age magazines, a few astrological charts, and letters. Not bothering to read anything, Mueller took out a small camera and snapped pictures of the charts and letters. Thinking of his recent dressing-down, he also took pictures of the articles.

He turned to the file cabinets in the corner. In the third drawer, he found a whole section on crystals. Knowing he didn't have time to record everything, he began to scan, looking for references to Egypt and Orion, as he'd been instructed. He snapped pictures of all the information he found. He also took pictures of the bookcases, so the eggheads could retrace Michael's knowledge base.

Mueller checked his watch. He'd been in the apartment just under an hour. He had no idea if he had the rest of the night or one more minute. Next he systematically checked for safes by running a scanner over all the walls and insides of the closets. No hidden compartments. He examined the suitcase, looked for a false bottom, and carefully unpacked the clothes. Finding nothing, he replaced them just as they'd been before he'd touched them. He looked through the dresser and nightstand, and scanned the mattress. He examined the lamp to see if it contained a secret section. Nothing.

He moved his search to the kitchen, going through all Michael's food in the cabinets, refrigerator, and freezer. He searched under drawers, inside pots, in the garbage, even the garbage disposal. Just as he'd started searching the bathroom, he heard footsteps and a key inserted into the lock. He stepped into the bathtub and pulled the shower curtain closed.

The door creaked a little as it was pushed open, and Mueller heard footsteps heading into the living room. After a minute, classical music played softly. Next, footsteps sounded in the kitchen. The refrigerator door opened and liquid was poured. With the utmost care, Mueller finished his sweep of the bathroom, waiting for an opportunity to leave. He hadn't found the crystal or a potential hiding place for it. A toiletry bag sat next to the sink. Mueller searched it, listening carefully, but heard nothing.

Suddenly, the phone rang. Mueller stood perfectly still, a bottle of shaving gel in his hand. He heard Michael walk toward the office.

"Hello." Michael's voice was muffled.

Mueller breathed a sigh of relief. His escape would be simple. He pushed open the bathroom door and looked around.

Michael's voice carried from the other room. "Guy, thank you for calling."

Michael's coat was thrown over the back of the sofa. A glass of orange juice sat on the coffee table.

"Yes, I'll be sure to ask about that when I see him."

Mueller checked Michael's coat for the crystal, then slipped out the door of the apartment. He must be carrying the stone, and it was too early in their plans to take it from him by force. Mueller looked around, but no one was in the hallway. He took the back stairs to the alley and returned to his car by a different route.

* * *

ON NEW YEAR'S DAY, just three days before he was scheduled to leave for Egypt, Paul Marchant fulfilled an obligation he didn't look forward to. He visited his mother. Not that she would know it; she had advanced Alzheimer's. When he was in town, Marchant visited her every week, watching her lose her memory, her ability to care for herself, her sense of self. If anyone had asked why he saw her so regularly, he'd be at a loss to answer, but there was no one to ask such a question. Perhaps he went because he wondered if he would suffer the same fate and thought that watching the progression of the illness would somehow provide a talisman against it. He noticed that if he didn't visit when he could, his concentration suffered, and this he could not tolerate, particularly now.

Mrs. Marchant was seated in her favorite chair in front of a south-facing window that looked out onto a small park. An old spreading oak stood next to the building, its bare branches making a latticework for the sky. Wrapped in a blue robe with matching blue slippers, Mrs. Marchant was quietly talking to herself. "Now, Jacob, you know how much I liked that drive we took the other day. Can't we go again? I get tired of being cooped up in this house all day long." She paused and looked vaguely through watery blue eyes at her son.

"Hello," he said. He'd stopped calling her mother. It only confused her.

"Hello, young man." She turned back to her conversation with her long-dead husband. "Jacob, do you know where I left my knitting?" She looked down at her hands. "I just had it, but I seem to have misplaced it."

"How are you today?" Marchant asked.

Mrs. Marchant looked back at the son she didn't recognize and asked, "Have you seen my knitting? I seem to have misplaced it."

"I'm sorry, no." Marchant pulled up a chair beside his mother, took her hand, and sat looking out the window. His mother resumed her private conversation, but he took no notice. He felt oddly content sitting with her, watching the winter sparrows outside jump from branch to branch, fluffed up against the cold.

A nurse came by and greeted Marchant. "She's still doing well physically. Her mind is about the same, but she hasn't had any more episodes for a few weeks."

He thanked the nurse. It amused him that they called the fits of rage or uncontrollable weeping his mother was subject to "episodes." After a time, Marchant began to talk. He believed that although his mother's mind was badly impaired, her spirit was still present, so some part of her would understand him. "I'm going to be leaving the country in a couple of days. I wanted you to know I won't be visiting for a while. I'm not sure when I'll be back."

She looked at him and smiled. "Hello," she said. Then she turned back to gaze out the window.

"I'm going to do what I came to this Earth to do," he said, thinking it ironic that now he could tell his mother the truth about his life. "I'm going to recover the knowledge of ancient Atlantis."

Mrs. Marchant turned her head and looked at her son for a long moment. Something seemed to flicker at the bottom of her eyes.

"If I can find a way to heal you, I will." Marchant's throat felt constricted. I better not be catching a cold, he thought. He stood to go. "Good-bye," he said and kissed her on the forehead. As he began to walk away, he heard his mother's voice.

"Be careful of these men, Paul. They don't mean you any good."

Stunned, he turned on his heel to stare at his mother, but the clarity left as quickly as it had come. Her gaze became confused. "Have you seen my knitting?" she asked.

"I'll have someone bring it to you."

"You're a good boy."

Marchant's eyes filled unexpectedly with tears. He pulled himself straighter, blinking them away. "Thank you," he said and turned to leave.

13

On Monday, the second day of the New Year, Anne sat on a cushion in the ritual room looking out at the garden, waiting for Dr. Abernathy. Every day, she meditated, recorded her dreams, scryed with the crystal, and tried to contact her guides. She ate like a Zen monk and trained like a Shaolin priest. She was beginning to notice some results. Her meditations were clearer and her visions more detailed, but she was bored. The sessions with Thomas had helped, but he'd left on a research mission the day before New Year's and would not be back until tomorrow evening.

Anne looked outside at the gray winter sky, studying the labyrinth in the west garden.

The door opened. "Happy New Year, my dear." Dr Abernathy walked over and kissed her briskly on the cheek.

"Happy New Year."

"How's the star pupil doing?"

"Hardly a star."

Dr. Abernathy dragged two large pillows into the center of the room and settled onto them. "Actually, you're doing remarkably well. I've had your grandmother's reports. Increased dream activity, beginning contact with guides, improved scrying, past-life memories, conscious astral travel."

Anne was taken aback. Dr. Abernathy had a way of restating things to make them sound better than she'd thought they were. She grunted. "But I'm not ready to do whatever it is I'm supposed to do."

He laughed, "How can you be certain, since we don't know exactly what that is?"

"Exactly my point," Anne returned.

"Perhaps today we'll discover more. Let's see what we can find out about this mysterious mission."

Anne lay back on the cushions she'd already arranged and placed her left hand over the crystal, ready to begin.

Dr. Abernathy laughed. "A few weeks ago I would've had to tell you how to start."

"Okay, so I'm making progress, but I'm not ready to save the world."

Dr. Abernathy didn't answer. He stood and made a quick sweep around the room, reinforcing the circle of protection that always existed here, then returned to his seat. "Now close your eyes and just float. Allow yourself to relax." He continued his hypnotic induction, his voice even and slow. After a few minutes, he said, "It's time to ask for guidance about using the crystal. Ask exactly what it is you're supposed to do to return the flow."

Anne heard Dr. Abernathy's voice as if from a distance. She floated in a warm sea of light, content. She allowed the phrase he suggested to pass through her mind, and waited. After some time had passed, she asked a second time, this time fueling the thought with the deep need she felt to know more. She continued to wait. Feeling she was losing some of the silence, she picked up her mantra, sinking deep again. She repeated the question a third time and waited.

After what seemed like a long time, Anne detected a small glow in front of her. She continued to watch as it brightened and took on the shape of an exceptionally tall human. The glow grew brighter and Anne realized the figure had wings, or was it a large aura of light? The face had just the suggestion of features. A wave of deep love flowed from the presence, love like she'd never experienced before, completely accepting and uplifting. Anne was overwhelmed with the surge of light that came with that love and basked in it. Here there was no hurry, no time. She wondered if this was the being she'd seen on her first astral trip with her grandmother. Affirmation radiated from the spirit.

She started to repeat the question in her mind, but before she could form words, the figure turned slightly and stretched out its hand. Anne looked and saw a gigantic lioness lying before her in the classic feline pose, paws stretched out in front, back legs tucked beneath her. Suspended above the head of this noble cat was a great solar disk. The enormous cat looked not at her, but into her. She realized she was looking at the true form of the Sphinx. She'd thought the Sphinx was male. A slight wave of amusement rose from the great cat in response to this thought.

Can you tell me—

Before she could finish her thought, Anne's consciousness stretched into the surrounding desert and the huge stone pyramids rising into the sky. She heard a deep hum, like a large engine running deep in the ground. The cat stretched Anne's awareness down now, into the sand, where she felt lines of energy running, converging on one spot, located somewhere behind her, since she had now merged with the Sphinx. Their awareness became the whole Giza complex, the flow and interweaving of many energies. Their third eye opened and tidal waves of energy flowed in, galactic energy, energy from the stars, not just one, but many, so many she was losing track of them all.

Then Anne stood in a room with limestone walls and an alabaster floor, holding the crystal before her. The crystal was white with light and there were others, each with a crystal held before them, each pulsing with a light too bright to be contained, each person chanting. Then the room began vibrating more deeply—the floor, the walls, Anne herself. The vibration spread through the sand, into the pyramids, which in turn lit up with white light. Anne noticed there were more than three pyramids now. The vibration increased in pitch until Anne lost track of where her body ended and another started, where her own mind ended and another began.

Anne opened her eyes and sat up with a gasp, but the ritual room wavered. She lay back down until the dizziness passed, then sat up straight, planting her feet on the ground, and scanned her body for imbalances. She felt as if she were suspended about three feet above the top of her head. Slowly, allowing her breath to steady her, Anne returned to the here and now. She reached for water. After gulping down half a glass, she massaged her temples until she started to feel better. She looked up into Dr. Abernathy's concerned eyes.

"Take your time," he said.

"I'm all right."

"Are you sure?"

"Yes, it just happened so fast I was startled."

"What happened exactly?"

She told Dr. Abernathy what she'd experienced.

"Interesting."

"Interesting? Is that all you can say?"

Dr. Abernathy shrugged. "What do you think it means?"

"Clearly, the crystal will be used in Egypt. Under the sand." Anne took another sip of water. "Which is, of course, impossible."

"Not necessarily."

"Excuse me?"

"There are tunnels under the Giza Plateau."

"Tunnels? I've never heard that. Where do they lead?"

"Who knows? To my knowledge, no permits have been granted to explore them since the early twentieth century when George Reisner's son drowned in one."

"Drowned?"

"Yes, many of them are full of water."

"Water?"

"Yes, do you need some help collecting yourself?"

"Why do you say that?"

"Because you keep repeating everything I say."

Anne laughed. "That's because you're saying very unexpected things."

Dr. Abernathy steepled his fingers and studied her. "This was a very productive session."

"Productive?"

He smiled at the repetition. "We now know where the crystal is to be used: Egypt. We know when: February first. We know the crystals will be activated by sound vibration, most probably chanting. In your vision, the other crystals were present. This suggests the hidden powers will guide the other Keepers of the Keys to the site."

"Ah." Anne was silent for a minute, trying to think how to bring up her next topic. "Speaking of the other crystals."

"Yes?" Dr. Abernathy turned his penetrating gaze on her.

Anne had the fleeting thought that she'd had just about enough of people seeing into her. "I've discovered who is keeping another crystal."

Dr. Abernathy stared at her, completely still. It was the stillness of a leopard ready to pounce.

"Say something."

"Who?" he asked, never taking his eyes off her.

"Michael Levy."

Dr. Abernathy's eyes became hooded, but he continued to watch her.

Flustered, Anne tried to explain. "I saw him after my talk last week. He was just standing there," she said, sounding like a teenager squirming out of an incriminating situation. "He wanted to know how I was. He had some things to tell me, so we went to the St. Anthony's Club." She waited for Dr. Abernathy to respond. When he didn't, she burst out with, "They frisked him."

"So I heard."

Anne suppressed her annoyance. "Michael has another crystal. He showed it to me." She forgot his disapproval. "It looked a lot like mine, only the setting was different. He said he worked with Cynthia, that she knew he had a crystal. Anyway, he's left the country, gone to see the man Cynthia saw in Israel, to find out what he told her." She stopped short, aware of Dr. Abernathy's growing censure. "You still think he was involved in Cynthia's death, but I'm certain he's innocent."

Still Dr. Abernathy was silent.

"He's on our side, for Christ's sake."

"How are you so certain of this?"

"I just know."

Dr. Abernathy favored her with a look.

"Okay, consider the evidence." Anne's attorney self surged to the surface. "He's had a few opportunities to steal the crystal already. At first when I didn't know what I had, he could easily have talked me into loaning it to him for study. He could have taken it after his talk. Besides, have you read his book? Have you heard him speak? He's the most unassuming scholar I've ever met. He is kind, considerate."

"Handsome?" Dr. Abernathy asked.

Anne blushed a dusky rose. "What exactly are you implying?"

Dr. Abernathy put a hand on hers. "Annie, I'm just suggesting you might not be entirely objective in this matter."

She hesitated, then took a deep breath. "There's another thing. I've known Michael in a past life. I think this had something to do with the crystals."

Dr. Abernathy raised a bushy eyebrow. "Indeed? Tell me."

Anne relayed the story of the dream she'd had the night of her grandmother's gala, the memory that had flashed between her and Michael that afternoon in the club. "We were in Egypt. He gave me something to hide. It felt vitally important, sacred. He said something about the flow being stopped."

Dr. Abernathy sat lost in thought for some time. Then he said, "This is suggestive, but I have two problems. The first is the same as I've said before. Apparently, in the life you have recalled, you two were lovers. Thus I have to repeat that you are not objective. Second, people, especially adepts, can change. The more advanced one becomes, the more one is subjected to tests." He paused, searching for the right word. "Temptations shall we say. Michael may have become corrupt."

"But he is a crystal holder," Anne repeated with force.

"Yes, but that doesn't guarantee he has remained pure of heart. I still want to know beyond a shadow of a doubt that he was not involved in Cynthia's death, that he's not working for the other side."

Anne sat back. "Okay, investigate him, but hurry up. We haven't got much time." Anne's eyes lit. "It was such an amazing experience. We were sitting there talking and suddenly we both remembered at the same moment. It was like we were both watching the same movie. We both knew the other saw the same thing."

Dr. Abernathy watched her. "One more thing. You are not to see him again until I give you my permission."

Anne didn't answer immediately.

"You risked your own life and put Arnold's job on the line. Do you hear me?"

"I wish I could say what I would have said two months ago."

"And what is that?"

"I would have asked what gave you the right to tell me what to do."

* * *

ON TUESDAY MORNING, Michael leaned against a wall in the old city of Jerusalem, trying to find room to consult his map out of the way of the pressing crowd. The trip had been long, but he was a seasoned traveler. After settling into his hotel room, he'd walked to the Wailing Wall to pray as the white stones of Jerusalem turned to gold in the setting sun. There, among the quiet murmurs of men from many different lands touching the ancient stones, he'd found his center again. He'd returned to his hotel room with a sense of quiet confidence. But now the twisting alleys of the old city had gotten the best of him.

"Can I be of some assistance?"

Michael looked up to find an older man in a black suit and white shirt standing in front of him. The tassels from his tallis hung below his jacket.

"Thank you, sir. I'm looking for Ha'Omer Street."

His gaze went to Michael's bare head, then to his face. "A map is not so good in the old city. Too many turns." He gestured for Michael to turn around. "Go back two blocks, turn left. Go another block, then right, then the next left, and the street is the third right."

Michael repeated the directions, then thanked the man, who nodded and hurried on. Michael set off, making his way through the narrow streets. He finally found the address Mordechai had given him.

The house was tall, narrow, and crowded into a row of many similar ones. He leaned back against the railing of the porch and looked up at the four-story building. On top, a small round TV dish jutted from a tangle of foliage like an overgrown morning glory. He rang the bell and waited. The sound of footsteps came from behind the door, and then a grate being slid back. A woman's voice asked, "May I help you?"

Michael tried to look through the grate, but the light was dim. "I'm Michael Levy. I believe you're expecting me."

"Just a minute." The grate slid shut and Michael heard the sound of several locks being opened.

Just like New York.

The woman opened the door. "Please come in. He's waiting for you."

Michael followed the older woman in a dark dress up two flights of stairs.

He stood in the doorway and saw that the room was small, but every nook was filled. Across from him was a wall filled floor to ceiling by a built-in bookshelf, stuffed to capacity, with more books stacked on the floor. An old desk stood against the right wall, overflowing with scrolls and papers. A modern laptop running a fractal screensaver stood in the middle of this profusion of paper, completely out of place. Two faded green armchairs sat side by side on the left wall, each with a reading lamp. A knitting basket sat next to one chair. The other held a stooped, grayed man who gripped the arm of the chair and struggled to stand.

Michael hurried to the old man's side and leaned down to offer his hand. "Sir, my name is Michael Levy. Your cousin Mordechai in New York sent me to speak with you."

The old man shook Michael's hand and settled back into his chair, wrapping a shawl around his shoulders. "Moishe, please call me Moishe. Mordechai sent me an e-mail telling me about you. Sit, sit. Just put those papers on the floor." Moishe watched with the bright eyes of an eager bird as Michael cleared off the faded green armchair. "That I should live to see this day I am very grateful."

"I take it you know a great deal about my task."

"Yes. To meet you at last is an honor."

Michael waved this comment away. "I have yet to earn any honors, sir. In fact, I have many questions, and the success of our mission is far from assured." He took some time explaining where the situation stood at present. "I believe you met Cynthia Le Clair, the holder of a key, and that you sent her to a man in Egypt who has knowledge about the crystals."

"Yes, did you speak with her?"

"Briefly, but before we could have an extended meeting, she died."

The old man sighed. "I heard about her death. Most unfortunate."

"How did you know, if I might ask?"

"Her nephew just visited me."

"I see. So the family has been in touch with you?"

"Yes. And now you."

"I thought she died from a heart attack, but the family suspects foul play." Michael paused, "In fact, they suspect me."

Moishe shook his head. "This is not good. The Keepers must work together. The family is trying to piece together in a month what Cynthia spent a lifetime learning."

"Then I assume that you know the crystal has been passed to the niece, Anne, and that she is not properly trained." Michael explained what he knew about Anne's relationship to her family.

Moishe frowned, the wrinkles on his brow and around his eyes deep with age. "This is bad news, and yet you must walk the path that the Abisher has laid before you." The old man leaned forward. "I may be able to help in some small way. I know some details about the history of the stone you carry that may have been lost."

"I would be greatly indebted to you. Information has been scarce."

"It is my service." Moishe's eyes strayed to the gold chain showing beneath Michael's shirt.

Without hesitation, Michael pulled the crystal over his head and handed it to the other man, who carefully took it and held it to the light of his reading lamp.

So small," he mused, "and so powerful. This stone, Michael"—he said the name with its Hebrew pronunciation just as his cousin had—"has traveled a long road. Your family must have told you that the crystal went to Germany to escape the Roman invasion and was held by them and various members of the Rosicrucian Order for many centuries. Certain members of the Levite priesthood who kept to the old knowledge have always been interconnected with the Rosicrucians, since their teachings share the same roots. Your grandfather watched the rise of the Nazis and, knowing they would seek possession of all the ancient mystical talismans, fled to America to keep it from them."

Michael nodded.

What you do not know is that the crystal came to Israel with the Exodus. And the story you have been told about that is wrong."

Michael leaned back in his chair, preparing for a long tale.

"First of all, you must have realized by now that the pyramids and monuments of Egypt were not built by slaves. The Torah teaches that the Hebrews were put at hard labor and treated harshly by their Egyptian task- masters. But the real Exodus took place much earlier than what is now believed. Freud, the old goat, hit closest to the mark when he declared that Moses had been a priest under the Pharaoh Akhenaten."

"I've read his essays on the subject."

Moishe nodded. "It fell to Akhenaten to revive the truth in a time of great darkness. The priests of Amun had become corrupt, as is inevitable in a time of ignorance. Akhenaten's mission was to restore the understanding that one consciousness lived behind the different gods, but the priests resisted his teachings. They were so corrupt he decided to build an entirely new city."

Moishe leaned forward, his eyes bright. "The entire city of Amarna was built using sacred geometry, a series of interlocking golden mean rectangles, moving down from the city's relationship to the hills in the east, to the buildings and rooms." Moishe gestured vaguely toward his computer, where the screensaver was happily spinning out fractal pattern after fractal pattern. "In this energetically charged city, Akhenaten established the worship of the highest reality, but the people needed some representation, something concrete after so many centuries of worshiping images. So he used the solar disk of Aten and the images of himself and

Nefertiti to illustrate that each person could attain the consciousness of this highest plane.

"Of course, this teaching has been lost and Egyptologists assume Akhenaten was an egomaniacal king bent on forcing the people to worship himself and his queen." Moishe shook his head. "So many of the great teachers are misunderstood. The Amun priesthood did not just stand by and give up their power either. They opposed him openly at first, but because he was pharaoh and the religion they had created deified the king, they were in a bind. They acted against him in secret. Eventually, they murdered him and attempted to assassinate the entire royal family to wipe out his line. They had to kill Tutankhamen as well, because he followed in Akhenaten's footsteps, but once this boy king was dispensed with, the old priesthood returned to power and reestablished their religion. During this turmoil, many of Akhenaten's followers escaped."

Michael sat forward, but Moishe anticipated his comment. "Yes, this was the Exodus we know of today. The followers of Akhenaten fleeing Egypt. And they took these teachings with them, which became the basis for Mosaic Judaism. But like all things in the age of darkness, this light became distorted when it mixed with the teachings of the Amun priests."

"And the crystal?"

"Two crystals made the trek across the desert with Akhenaten's followers. One you hold. The Le Clairs have the other. But the origins of the stones were much earlier. They were formed during the previous age of enlightenment, during the height of the predynastic civilization." The old man sat back. "Who knows? Perhaps they are even older and span the cycles of time themselves, appearing when the light returns, and kept in trust during the dark of night. Their ultimate origin is unknown, at least to me and the historians of the order."

Moishe studied the stone for a moment. "This is why you must go to Egypt, back to the land that birthed the stones, to learn the use of this crystal." He handed the necklace back to Michael. "The man you must seek out is well known in Egypt, but his true identity is unknown to most. He is a keeper of the indigenous wisdom of the ancient civilization."

Michael felt a shiver as Moishe spoke these last words. "You're certain the tradition is still alive in Egypt?"

"It is, and you must go to study with him."

"I've been invited to speak at a conference there at the end of January."

"Excellent, but be careful. There are those who wish to control the crystals, to use the energy for their own purposes. There will be agents in Egypt bent on stopping you," he paused to catch Michael's eye. "By any means."

"I'll be careful."

"The man's name is Tahir Nur Ahram. He lives in the village of Nazlet el Samman, two blocks east of the Sphinx, next to the perfume shop called Secrets of the Nile."

* * *

ANNE DIDN'T FEEL ready to leave for Egypt next week, but Grandmother Elizabeth and Dr. Abernathy had years of experience in metaphysical practices. They'd insisted the final stage of her training must take place in the hands of what they called an indigenous elder, the man Cynthia had consulted and Thomas had found, a man who knew more about ancient Egypt than anyone else. He would be able to tell her more about the crystal. She'd finally agreed. She wondered if there would be initiation rites, going without food, taking hallucinogens. The last few days of her monkish routine hadn't brought any great revelations, just a growing confidence in scrying with crystals and a sense of contact with Cynthia.

Today she had to meet with her colleagues who'd be taking over her cases to explain details and give hints about how to deal with some of her more ticklish clients. This took the whole morning. Over lunch from her favorite Chinese take-out—if she was leaving the nest, she was going to eat what she pleased—she and Susan sat in a conference room going over her schedule of public appearances, picking replacements when possible, or simply canceling if there was enough time to give proper notice. The cover story was simply that she was taking a break to attend to family business at the request of her grandmother. Attending to family was always good publicity in this political climate, especially for a woman. And it was the truth.

Just as they finished clearing her schedule, one of the receptionists appeared at the door, slightly breathless. "I'm sorry, Ms. Le Clair, but she insisted—"

"Since when am I not welcome here?" Katherine sailed by the receptionist into the conference room.

"Mother," Anne said simply, as if that one word summed it all up.

Katherine fixed an eye on Susan, who quickly gathered the calendar and paperwork off the table and excused herself.

"I'll speak to you before I leave," Anne said as Susan walked out the door.

"Which is apparently more than you were going to do for me," Katherine spit out.

Anne took a deep breath. "Shall we take this into my office, or would you like the entire firm to be in on it?" Without waiting for an answer, she straightened her shoulders and marched down the hall. Once there, she instinctively put her desk between them, settling into the large executive chair and pointing to a side chair for her mother. Susan quietly closed the door after them.

Katherine did not sit, but leaned over the desk as if she owned it. "I thought I raised you to have better sense. What in the world has gotten into you, spending your valuable time locked away like some nun, meditating, staring into crystal balls? And now, you plan to traipse all over Egypt trying to find the answer to some medieval riddle."

"The mystery is older than the Middle Ages."

"And how do you know that? Been listening to family fables again?"

This was too much for Anne. "Family fables? You're the one who convinced me they were true."

Katherine's mouth worked. She sat down abruptly, took a deep breath, and began again, a few decibels lower. "Just because one small part of the story is true doesn't mean you have to buy it all. Yes, we seem to be descended from Yeshua ben Yusef, or Jesus, if you prefer. But that doesn't mean the story about the crystal is accurate. I've never found any evidence to support it. And as for all that psychic mumbo jumbo—"

"You said I had visions as a child." Anne's voice was creeping up again. "You said they were real, that it was inherited."

"So we're intuitive. So I sometimes know things before they happen. It's just something scientists haven't explained yet. Give them enough time and they will. But crystal balls? Ancient legends? You're an attorney, for God's sake."

Anne pushed back in her chair. "Dr. Abernathy's explanations make sense."

"Dr. Abernathy—" Katherine forced herself to take another deep breath. "All right, if you want to spend your time chanting in black robes with your ridiculous relatives, that's your business. I hoped to spare you all that foolishness. But I will not allow you to risk your life on this trip. It's simply too dangerous. A war might break out at any minute."

"A war has been breaking out in the Middle East since the fifties. Besides, Egypt is in Africa, not the Middle East."

"Don't split hairs with me."

Anne took a quick breath to respond, but then noticed her mother's eyes were filled with unshed tears. "Mother."

Katherine squeezed her eyes shut. "Damn it."

"It's okay. In fact, it's much more persuasive than yelling."

"Anne, I'm so frightened for you." Katherine's voice sounded small. "I've lost both my brother and sister. At least Cynthia's death was from natural causes."

Anne tried hard not to react.

"I don't want to lose you."

"Arnold will be going with me, along with another bodyguard. I'll be perfectly safe." Anne sounded as if she were quieting a child.

"That's what James told me a month before he was assassinated."

"But why should I be in danger?"

"Haven't they told you? For God's sake, Annie, don't be so naive. The Illuminati are behind the current administration. They believe in magic as much as your grandmother does. They'll kill for something they consider to be a powerful talisman."

Anne frowned. "First you tell me it's all just silly legends. Now you tell me you believe in the Illuminati, that they're secretly in charge."

Katherine shook her head. "People only think we've escaped feudalism. If they only knew."

"What do you believe, anyway?" Anne was thoroughly exasperated. "Why did you never tell me any of this? You knew I'd end up in public life somehow, that the media would never just leave me alone. How was I supposed to conduct myself without knowing the truth?"

Katherine's smile held the satisfaction of a raccoon who has successfully broken into the kitchen cabinet. "You were doing just fine, my dear. You were my proof that we could escape the past, that we could live in the twenty- first century, not the . . ." She waved her hand, searching for a date. "Sixth," she said at random. "You were my trump card."

"I am not a card in a game, Mother." Anne spoke each word with emphasis. "I will not be played."

"Oh, you won't, will you? Did you ever before in your life want to go to Egypt? Did you believe in crystal balls last year? Would you have put your entire life on hold to research some superstition?"

Anne was silent.

"I thought not."

They looked at each other for a long moment.

"All I'm asking," Katherine said, "is for you to reconsider. Get away from your grandmother for a few days. Away from Thomas and Dr. Abernathy. You can stay at my place in Malibu. They won't follow you out there. I'll leave you alone."

"But I—"

"For God's sake, Annie, please. Don't throw your whole life away over some new whim. Think about what you're doing." Katherine gathered her purse and coat and stood up. "Let me know if you want the keys."

Anne nodded, trying hard not to show any reaction.

"Don't I get a hug?"

Anne stood and embraced her mother woodenly.

"Just think, my darling." Katherine kissed Anne's cheek, then turned and left.

After the door closed behind her, Anne sat for a long time. Her mother was right. Three weeks was a very short time for such a dramatic change. But her mother had lied to her all her life. If she hadn't, perhaps she'd be prepared now. She wadded up a piece of paper and threw it into the recycling bin.

In actual fact, they'd all lied to her, every single one of them. A chill crept over her. She found herself wishing she could talk to Michael. But hadn't he lied as well?

In the end, she had to decide for herself. She couldn't deny the power of her experiences. Regardless of how much she thought about what had happened, tried to puzzle out all the angles, she knew one thing. The crystal called to her. When she held it in her hand, she felt as if something she'd been searching for, even without knowing that she searched, had been restored at last. She felt complete. She had to follow where it led. It was well past dark before Anne called for the driver to take her back to the family estate.

Part Two

The Light Comes Through Me

14

$\mathcal{P}$aul Marchant walked along the street of the village bordering the Giza Plateau, dodging local villagers, tourists, hawkers, small cars, and piles of camel dung, oblivious to the sales pitches of the vendors. He turned toward the ticket booth in front of the Sphinx, bought a pass, and made his way over the wooden pathway leading to the opening to the monument's enclosure. But he didn't go in.

He'd have access to the real secrets of the Sphinx. This thought spurred him past the enclosure and up the hill toward the pyramids. He wondered if Michael was already here. Marchant had followed him to La Guardia Airport on New Year's Day, keeping his distance. Michael Levy hadn't seen him, at least he didn't think so. Michael had gotten on a plane to Israel. Why Israel? Maybe it was some family visit. Anyway, Michael would be in Egypt for the conference. His name was on the program.

After Marchant had watched Michael board his plane, Marchant tried to break into his apartment. Getting inside the building had been simple, but he had no skill in picking locks and didn't want to share his business with anyone who did. But Michael had probably taken anything of importance with him, and it was easier to get into hotel rooms. He'd give Michael's room a good search once he arrived.

About halfway up the hill, Marchant sat down on the stone wall surrounding one of the tunnels. Closed off by a grate, the tunnel dropped straight down into the sand beneath. Pretending to fish a stone out of his shoe, he peeked over the edge down into the dark pit scattered with litter. He pictured the ground-penetrating radar map in his mind and tried to superimpose it over the land surrounding him. Where did this shaft lead and where exactly was the chamber? He was finding it difficult to pinpoint, but he knew it was close, somewhere beneath him, within a few hundred meters.

Tonight he'd meet Mueller somewhere in the middle of Cairo. Marchant wondered if he'd meet the big cheeses immediately or if Mueller was going to play cat and mouse with him a little more, just to make himself feel more important. Whatever Marchant had to put up with was well worth the reward. He was the only man who really understood the math and language codes. Otherwise they wouldn't have come to him.

* * *

THAT SAME AFTERNOON, Michael Levy made his way through Egyptian customs. The conference was still a couple of weeks away, so he'd been prepared to take a cab from the airport. He had been surprised, therefore, to find a driver waiting for him. The drive was slow, but he enjoyed the hustle and bustle of Cairo. When he arrived at the Mena House, he asked to see the manager first. Michael had shipped a box with museum labels to the hotel, hoping the reputation of the institution in Egypt would ensure its safe arrival. International cargo was never completely safe. He'd taken the risk, not wanting to schlep his books and slide show all over Israel. He was relieved to find them waiting for him.

After handing a hefty tip to the manager, he carried the box back to the lobby where his luggage sat. Two bellhops took his burdens from him, ignoring his protests that he could manage alone, and led him to his room in the annex, a room with his favorite pyramid view. After the bellhops lined up his luggage beside the closet, and after another hefty tip, Michael was alone.

He felt a bit disoriented. On all his previous trips to Egypt, he'd arrived after at least a ten-hour plane ride from an entirely different time zone. Since he'd just come from Israel, he was fresh and full of energy. He wanted to punctuate the moment somehow, to set the stage for this final phase of his journey. He settled into the armchair and crossed his legs under him, preparing to meditate. But a better idea occurred to him. He should go visit the Sphinx. What better place to declare his spiritual intent? He grabbed his hat and headed out. In the hotel lobby, he caught a glimpse of Paul Marchant. Michael raised his hand in greeting.

Marchant's face clouded for an instant, then he nodded back at Michael and smiled.

What an odd duck, Michael thought. He wondered for the hundredth time if Marchant held a key. He hoped not. He would be tricky to work with.

Michael decided to walk across the plateau to prepare himself for his visit to the grand matriarch of Egypt. He always thought of the Sphinx as female. He walked quickly up the hill and purchased a ticket at the nearby gate. The familiar exhilaration overtook him as he strolled toward the massive stone pyramids rising in front of him. Careful not to smile at the many hawkers offering camel rides, turquoise-colored scarabs, calendars, postcards, and bottled water, he made his way around the pyramids and toward the causeway. The sun was halfway down the western sky and the temperature had dropped a little. Michael took a deep breath, enjoying the smell of dust and stone, even the camel dung. He was home. He was in Egypt.

He slowed as he walked down the hill toward the small conical head of the Sphinx that stuck out from her enclosure. Rounding the Sphinx enclosure, he stopped to run his hand over a large piece of granite lying discarded close by. It was carved with multiple contoured angles, smooth as glass. Copper chisels couldn't have done that. Not much on this plateau could have been carved with crude Stone Age tools, but this didn't stop his colleagues at the museum from believing that was how they'd all been made.

Michael walked over to the gate and took his place in line. Already he felt the statue alive before him. A deep purr radiated from her, filling his chest, the sound of an enormous lioness. His heart swelled. He reached into his pocket and wrapped his hand around a small lump of lapis lazuli.

Welcome, my son.

The words sounded deep in his mind and his eyes teared involuntarily. Michael looked down to blink them away.

The time is near. I have much to tell you.

A woman in a long dress and headscarf stood by the opening. She nodded to him and pointed out the already familiar entryway. Michael wanted to find a corner in the granite antechamber and sink down on the alabaster floor, allowing it to support him as he gave himself over to the great mother lioness speaking to him even now, but he knew this would only attract attention, so he followed the small crowd up onto the viewing platform. He rounded the corner and there she stood, majestic, magnetic, vibrating with a deep resonant power.

Mother. The word came unbidden to his mind. He saw her turn and look at him and the impact of that gaze knocked him into a seat against the wall. Luckily, no one was close by. It was late and the monument would be closing soon. With a small part of his mind, he noticed that the crystal key hanging around his neck, concealed beneath his shirt, had started to tingle, vibrating in harmony with the Sphinx.

Mother, I need your help. I can't do this without you.

My vigil is almost finished. The six are gathering.

Please, show me the way.

Go to him now.

Michael rose without hesitation and started to walk away. But then he remembered his manners. He glanced around. No one was watching. He took a step forward and gently dropped his piece of lapis over the edge of the platform. Then he walked down the steps and out of the Sphinx enclosure toward the village.

Michael fished the small piece of paper with directions to Tahir's house out of his pocket. He walked to the first block and looked at the street corner. The street wasn't named. He searched the front of the first building. There were no numbers either. Funny he hadn't noticed this before. He crossed the street, narrowly avoiding a cart packed with open boxes of spices, and walked past the stores, their windows crammed with replicas of antiques, Egyptian scarves, jewelry, and postcards. Down the next street, he spotted the shop next to a vacant lot that seemed to be the home of two white donkeys. Michael walked past them and took the two front steps of the shop in one bound.

Three men looked up sharply from their customers. Michael stepped back, chagrined that his excitement had got the better of him, and took in his surroundings. The walls were mirrored and filled with shelves of colorful perfume bottles, gold, blue, red, and green. He caught the gleam of gold from farther in the room. The floors were tile, covered with intricate but faded rugs. Customers sat on dark wooden benches.

"May I bring you something to drink?" One of the men had finished with his sale and approached him.

"No, thank you. I'm looking for Tahir Nur Ahram."

"Tahir. He is my uncle. A great man. His home is next door." The man gestured to the west wall of the store.

"Thank you." This time Michael took the steps one at a time and walked to the house next to the shop. It was multi-tiered with balconies on every floor, similar to the one he'd just left in Israel. He knocked on a heavy wooden door.

After a minute, the door opened. A boy, somewhere in his midteens, dressed in blue jeans, T-shirt, and sandals, looked Michael up and down, then spoke in English, "May I help you?"

"My name is Michael Levy. I'm looking for Tahir Nur Ahram."

"My father is away in the south on a tour."

"I see." Michael's chest fell.

"But he'll be home late Thursday."

"May I come to visit him?"

"Friday in the evening is the best time."

Michael thanked the boy and turned to make his way back to the hotel.

He wanted to go back through the plateau, but the guards were just closing the gate, so he flagged down a taxi. The Sphinx was silent, dozing in the gathering twilight. A cab finally arrived and after a brief haggle over price, Michael got in. As the taxi turned around on the busy street, he noticed a man lounging next to the ticket booth. He wore a Fedora over a hooked nose. Something about him seemed familiar. Had he seen him at the airport? Was he just an innocent tourist out for his first experience of Giza or was he a tail? Michael would have to keep an eye out for this guy.

* * *

LATE THE NEXT NIGHT, Paul Marchant crouched near the low buildings next to the Sphinx ticket booth waiting for Mueller. About twenty scrawny cats picked through the Dumpsters across the street from him. He turned his eyes away from their meager meal and scanned the street. Just a few locals walking home. The shops were closed for the most part. During their meeting the previous evening, Mueller hadn't revealed anything new. They'd reviewed the maps, discussed the math, although Marchant was certain it had all gone over Mueller's head. Marchant wondered if he were being watched or videotaped. After they talked, they were served hot hibiscus tea and stuffed grape leaves. Mueller seemed anxious for Marchant to partake. Assuming he would not be poisoned, he'd grudgingly eaten a few bites. Then Mueller told him to be waiting near the Sphinx the next night, sometime around midnight.

Marchant had been here since eleven. He shifted his weight to ease the dull ache in his knees, then heard the crunch of tires turning off the street toward the building and moved back to avoid the headlights. He followed a jeep down the road behind the wall. The vehicle was obviously new, green with black roll bars instead of a roof. It looked like army issue, an impression reinforced by the glint of a machine gun held by a chiseled man dressed in khaki pants and shirt.

Mueller swung out of the backseat and walked toward him. "Ready?"

"Yes." Marchant was equally abrupt.

Mueller pulled a sash out of his back pocket. "Just a precaution," he said, as he fit the blindfold around Marchant's head and tied it snugly over his eyes. Marchant allowed himself to be led to the jeep and guided into the backseat. Mueller got in beside him.

The jeep backed up and drove down a smooth road for about one hundred yards, then turned to the right. Marchant knew they'd driven around the sound and light show area and were headed out of the bus parking lot toward the plateau. The jeep lurched to the side and Marchant grabbed the bar next to him just in time, stifling a protest. He heard the grinding of gears and the roar of the engine, then he was thrust back in his seat as they climbed a hill.

After two similar turns and a trip up and down another hill, he lost any sense of direction. He wondered if they were going out into the desert to a secret entrance or if Mueller had directed his men to drive in circles just beside the plateau to confuse him. After a few more twists and turns, the jeep came to a halt and the engine cut off.

"You can get out now," Mueller's voice was close in his ear. Once Marchant was standing, someone took his arm. "Wait here." It was Mueller's voice, apparently directed at the jeep driver. Then he felt pressure on his arm and they walked a few steps. More pressure pulled him to a stop. Suddenly, a hand pushed his head down. "The ceiling is low. We're going down some steps."

Marchant steadied himself on the wall to his left, crouched down, and slowly began descending, counting as he went. Thirteen steps went straight down, then there was a turn to the right, and they climbed down again. He counted three such turns, and then a rush of air hit him, smelling of dust and, oddly enough, moisture. He sensed space around him. Mueller took a firm hold on his arm and they started to walk forward. Marchant listened intently to the sounds. Their footsteps echoed from a distant wall and he thought he heard the sound of flowing water. They were in a large underground cavern or room.

After about two hundred feet, Mueller told him to duck again. "Just like going into the pyramid."

Marchant assumed the familiar duck-walk posture and went through what felt like a tunnel. He fought the sudden claustrophobic fear of being crushed below tons of earth, forcing himself to keep going. Soon he emerged into a second chamber. The floor was smooth beneath his feet, maybe stone. He heard Mueller scramble out behind him. Then the blindfold was pulled from his eyes.

Marchant blinked in the glare of the electric lights mounted around the room, willing his eyes to adjust rapidly. The walls on each side were lined with pillars, and in front of each pillar were large statues of Neters. First, the tall muscular Anubis stood with his black dog's head looking avidly toward the entrance they had just emerged from. He saw Osiris, Horus, and Ptah. On the opposite side were their counterparts, Isis, Hathor, and Sekhmet. The floor was alabaster with an intricate inlaid blue and gold tile forming a six-pointed star within another six-pointed star with six circles at each point contained within a square.

"Of course," Marchant muttered. He stepped forward. At the end of this underground temple, two massive white alabaster pillars marked where the entrance to the Holy of Holies should be. But instead of an open door, a shimmering blue sheet of some kind, like a fog full of fireflies, blocked the entrance.

Marchant silently asked for permission to enter the temple and paused for an answer. He thought he saw Anubis's huge head nod once and felt an inner affirmation. Reverently, his head slightly bowed, he made his way past the long line of watching Neters and stopped a few feet in front of the six steps that led up to the inner sanctum of the temple. Here he could see the blue sheet was not cloth, but an energy field of some type, just as he'd been told. The field pulsated gently, giving off tiny golden star bursts. He had expected to feel prickling on his skin, irritating like static electricity, but standing before this magnificent curtain of energy was soothing, like being in front of a waterfall.

Marchant turned to the walls on either side, searching for clues. A scene depicted Thoth with an ibis head holding out an ankh to Seshat, whose head was decorated with a seven-petaled flower. She stood with her arms extended in front of her, palms down. Next to them was Ma'at, whose head was topped with a feather. There were no hieroglyphs of any kind.

Moving from the walls, he returned to his position in front of the curtain. He closed his eyes and listened deeply for a sound, a frequency, any hint of the resonance of this guardian energy. After a minute, a sound began in his mind, faint at first, then growing in volume. He matched the sound with his own voice and began to hum softly. He opened his eyes and watched the energy. Slowly, he increased his volume, but nothing happened.

Marchant closed his eyes and listened again. He had the right tone. Then he felt a warm glow in his right pocket. The key. He reached into his pocket and took the stone in his hand, placing the root of the crystal against the energy center in his palm and the point aligning with his index and middle finger. Again, he hummed the tone, steadily increasing the volume. A small spark of light appeared in the center of the energy field and spiraled out to the edges. He heard a gasp from behind him. He'd completely forgotten anyone else was in the room. Again he hummed the tone, louder this time. Another burst of energy spiraled through the field and the color began to shift from a deep royal blue to robin's egg. He could see the room behind the curtain emerging.

"All right," Mueller's voice grated on his finely tuned nerves. "That's enough for now." The energy field snapped back to its deep blue color, completely obscuring the room behind it.

Marchant reached out to it, then turned on Mueller, infuriated. "This is delicate work. You must not interrupt me like that again."

Mueller looked amused for a second, then his face assumed the familiar mask. "I have my orders, Mr. Marchant."

Marchant struggled visibly to master himself, then nodded. "As you say. Besides, it is not the time."

"What do you need to further your work?" Mueller asked.

"Photographs of these walls." Marchant pointed to the identical panels on each side of the energy shield.

"This can be arranged. Anything else?"

"And the floor."

"We can give you computer access to these files, read only."

"That will do."

Mueller held up the blindfold. "Ready when you are, Mr. Marchant."

Marchant took a deep breath, swallowing his fury. Why was Mueller so mockingly calling him by his last name now? Because he'd seen Marchant knew what he was doing? He swore a silent oath he would come back. Somehow he would find the entrance and come to this temple alone.

Anything was possible in Egypt with the right amount of baksheesh. He needed to work away from this barbarian. He bowed his head, submitting to the blindfold for the moment.

✷ ✷ ✷

MUELLER WOKE EARLY the next morning after only a couple hours of sleep. He shook the grogginess off in the shower and went to his favorite restaurant for a cup of Turkish coffee. He thought about the night's events as he sipped the murky liquid, wondering if they would gain access today. Perhaps this was the endgame. The organization would have access to the technology it needed. If what the eggheads said was down there really worked, he'd get a huge promotion. Hell, he could even retire. Maybe he'd buy some island near Micronesia. Their victory would end all the pockets of resistance in the Third World. Order would finally prevail and he could relax on his own estate. He'd travel, maybe pay back some old scores.

Now fully awake, he headed back to the compound to make his report. Mr. Spender was waiting along with two Egyptians. The first man was dressed in an Egyptian military uniform and sat drinking a cup of chai. The other was familiar, the real, not the nominal, head of the antiquities police. Mr. Spender pointed to a fourth chair around the table and Mueller sat down.

"Was our mission a success?"

"Yes, sir." Mueller slid a large manila envelope across the table to Spender. "Here is the recording and the crystal. I switched it during the ride home with the duplicate we made. I'm certain he didn't notice. He was too wrapped up in his own schemes."

"Tell us what happened."

Mueller told how Marchant had examined the raised reliefs on either side of the curtain, how he'd chanted, but had needed the crystal to make the energy field begin to shift. "I stopped him before the field completely disappeared. He asked for access to pictures of the panels and the design on the floor. I told him he could see the files, read only."

"And how did he use the crystal?"

"He held it in his right hand, point out, like this." Mueller demonstrated with a pen that was lying on the table. He knew better than to touch the crystal around Spender.

Spender rubbed his hands together. "Perhaps we are done with Paul Marchant. Gentlemen?"

The other men nodded and Spender picked up the phone next to him. "Bring a car around front." They walked down the hall, a procession of power. Spender almost had a spring in his step.

A BMW with darkened windows was waiting for them outside. They got in and headed for the Giza plateau. The roads were crowded, as usual, but they arrived at the antiquities police office in just under half an hour and made their way by jeep to the entrance to the site. Inside the chamber, Mueller took his position next to the door, melting discreetly into the background. The three men walked past the watching Neters without a glance.

"Shall I do the honors, General Ahmed?" Spender asked the military officer in a quiet voice.

Mueller could hear every word. The acoustics of the chamber were perfect.

Spender took the tape recorder out of the envelope and rewound the tape. He positioned the crystal in his right hand and hit the play button. Marchant's voice filled the chamber and Spender pointed the crystal at the royal blue energy field. Nothing happened.

Spender rewound the tape and turned up the volume. Again the energy curtain did not respond. Cursing under his breath, Spender tried a third time, stepping closer, almost touching the field with the crystal. Again, nothing.

"Perhaps we should chant. Maybe the live voice is required."

The three men stood in a line before the blocked entrance. Spender replayed the tape and after a minute, the three joined in. The energy field remained an opaque navy blue. Even the gold energy bursts stopped.

"God damn it," Spender said. "Karl." He wheeled around.

"Yes, sir." Mueller took a few steps toward the group, suddenly acutely aware of the statue of Anubis.

"What did you leave out? Think, man."

"Nothing, sir. He stood in the exact same spot you're in and held the crystal exactly as you are. I was very careful in my observations."

Muttering, Spender turned toward the energy curtain again and repeated the procedure several more times with no results. "God damn the man. I'll strangle him with my own hands." He kicked at the wall next to him.

Mueller studied the floor.

Squaring his shoulders and taking a deep breath, Spender turned to the other two men. "Any theories?"

"Time," General Ahmed said. "Perhaps the field must be opened at a certain time. Let's come back in the early morning and try again."

"It's worth a try. Other ideas?"

"Is the recording distorted in some way? Can we clean it up, get a perfect duplicate of the voice?" the head of the antiquities police asked.

"Karl?"

"I'll get right on it."

"Tonight then, gentlemen."

* * *

ON THURSDAY EVENING, Michael was walking toward the Mena House. Since he had to wait for his meeting with Tahir, he'd decided to fulfill some business obligations and had spent the evening with a family who was well connected to the Cairo Museum. Dinner in a wealthy neighborhood near the Nile had been pleasant, if conventional both in manners and Egyptian theory. He had asked his cabdriver to drop him off a good ten blocks from the hotel so he could walk off the heavy meal. The shops were still open even close to eleven o'clock, hoping to bring in the tourists who were returning to their rooms. He walked past a teahouse, where men sat outside playing backgammon, hookah pipes next to them. An argument had broken out at one of the tables and the men were shouting at each other, faces red, but Michael knew from experience that it was all just for show. As soon as someone won the game, all the players would break into song and hug each other in celebration. Then the whole drama would be repeated, an argument over some play, almost coming to blows, then another celebration.

Ahead he saw a merchant pacing the sidewalk in front of his shop with a sharp eye out for customers. Rather than be dragged into his shop, Michael took the next alleyway and found himself walking past houses, most closed up tight. As he rounded the next corner to walk back up to the street, a car came screeching to a halt in front of him, cutting him off. Before he could turn around, someone grabbed him from behind, pinning his arms. A blindfold was forced over his head, then he was shoved into the car. Another squeal of tires threw him against the seat.

"Who are you? What do you want?" The men were European or American. He'd seen that much before they'd blindfolded him. He thought the car was a steel-blue Mercedes. "I'm well known in Egypt. You'll—"

"Shut up, Mr. Levy. We know exactly who you are and that you checked into the Mena House alone."

The accent was American.

"What do you want with me?"

A hand grabbed Michael's throat.

"We'll do the talking."

The fingers tightened and Michael nodded. The man released his throat, and Michael tried not to cough.

"We know why you're here, Mr. Levy. And we know what you carry."

Michael stilled, praying the fingers would not start searching his pockets. He desperately wished he'd followed his instincts and left the crystal in the hotel safe, but he wasn't by any means certain it would be safe there.

There was a short, bitter laugh. "Don't worry. I'm not after that. We wouldn't stoop to murder to take the artifact, like you."

Michael blinked beneath his blindfold, confused.

"Go near her, and I will kill you."

"Who?"

"I think you know, Mr. Levy. You tried to contact her before you left New York."

Anne. They had to mean Anne. They still think I was involved in Cynthia's murder, he thought.

"But we have to work together—" Michael heard the car door open. The tires hummed louder over the dirt road. Suddenly, he was shoved and this time he couldn't stop the scream as he fell from the car.

Braced for a hard landing, he was surprised to feel something soft beneath him. Then the reek hit him. He tore off his blindfold and looked around wildly. All he saw were lights through a cloud of dust. He looked down. He was sitting in a large pile of dung. Next to it was a stable bursting with horses and camels. One gray stallion stretched his nose through the gate of the stall and blew air noisily through his nostrils. Two camels lay against a far wall, mildly gazing at him as they methodically chewed mouthfuls of hay.

"Shit." Michael stood and started picking bits of straw from his suit. Beneath the straw was dung, now smeared all over the buttocks and down the leg of his best suit. "Shit!" Michael took a few tentative steps. At least the pile had broken his fall. He was unhurt. He walked off toward his hotel, planning to avoid the lobby.

15

Something woke Anne. She sat up and found herself in the small pull-out bed on board the family jet.

Egypt, she thought. *We must be there.*

She threw back the covers and went to the window. Lights dotted a black velvet ground. She glanced at her watch, but that didn't help at all. It was still on New York time. Grabbing a light blanket to wrap around herself, she walked into the main cabin.

Bob, the new security man, looked up. "Couldn't sleep?"

Anne slid into the seat opposite him and pressed her face to the window. "Something woke me. Like electricity. Some kind of buzz."

Bob just nodded. He seemed to have adjusted to the peculiarities of the Le Clairs.

"What time is it?" she asked.

"Almost eleven at night, Egypt time."

The cockpit door opened. "Time to wake up her—oh, you're up."

"Her highness is awake," Anne said.

"Excuse me, ma'am."

"No problem."

"Time to buckle up. We're cleared for landing."

Touchdown was smooth. The plane taxied a short distance and stopped.

Anne went to the back room that converted between a bedroom and conference room and quickly changed clothes. After repacking her toothbrush and nightgown, she pulled the suitcase off the bed and walked back into the main cabin. The door was already open and the stairs pushed up to the plane. Bob took the suitcase from her, peeked out the door for a moment, then proceeded down.

The air was cooler than she'd expected and smelled of dust, flowers, and jet exhaust. They walked quickly into the terminal and down a long, featureless hallway to customs. She squinted against the harsh fluorescent lights. The line at customs was short, but Bob walked behind the waiting people and into a windowed office.

The man behind the desk stood and extended his hand. He was short with dark hair and dressed in a khaki uniform. "Miss Le Clair."

Anne shook his hand, suddenly self-conscious of her blue jeans and T- shirt. Where was her family training? She'd expected an anonymous arrival, but you could never count on that if you were a Le Clair. She sat down quickly.

"May I see your papers, please? A formality, I assure you. We are honored by your visit."

Anne handed over her passport and the money for two visas. "You're very kind. The honor is all mine, I assure you." She slipped easily back into her public self.

I've been cooped up in Grandmother's house too long, she thought.

"And yours, sir?"

Bob slid his papers across the desk.

"You will be staying where?"

"The Mena House," Bob answered.

"How long?"

"I think we'll be in Egypt for at least a month. There is so much to see, so many national treasures," Anne said.

The man smiled and stamped both passports quickly. "Enjoy your visit."

"I'm certain I'll enjoy your beautiful country."

The official stood when she did. Anne and Bob made their way into the main terminal. It was late at night and she hoped there would be no more special attention. Maybe she could sneak into her room without fanfare when they arrived at the hotel, but already a woman was approaching them with a formal smile. She breathed a sigh of relief when she caught sight of Arnold right behind her.

"All clear?" he asked Bob.

"Yes."

"Excellent." He turned to Anne. "Did you have a good trip?"

Anne nodded.

"This is Shani, our guide's daughter."

Anne extended her hand. "I'm pleased to meet you. The family is grateful for your assistance."

"Welcome home to Egypt." Shani's round face lit in a smile.

"Uh, thank you." Anne's eyes darted to Arnold, who shrugged.

"My father sends his apologies for not greeting you himself, but he asked me to be sure you got settled."

"I appreciate your help," Anne said.

Arnold grabbed the large suitcase. "The car is this way."

Anne followed him out the sliding glass doors with Bob behind her carrying a smaller case and Shani on her left. Anne slid into the backseat of the waiting limousine while Arnold loaded the luggage. When everyone had taken a seat, the car pulled away and Anne watched the outskirts of Cairo pass by her window.

After about ten minutes, Shani said, "On the right you'll see the Citadel. It was built by Saladin before the crusades, around the twelfth century."

The fortress was a large stone structure on the side of the road. The walls were golden under the lights still illuminating it even at this hour.

"The stones were quarried from pyramids at Giza," Shani said.

The car took a few curves, and then headed for the ring road. People, mostly men, still walked the streets. Some sat together in front of street-side cafés, smoking hookah pipes, drinking tea, or playing board games. A few women looked out of second-story windows, white scarves covering their hair above black robes. Some were bareheaded. More people were sitting outside grocery shops. Tubs full of mangoes, bananas, potatoes, broccoli, and some kind of nut lined the front of the shops. Next came a store with racks filled with shoes up to the ceiling. Anne had never seen so many shoes in one place before.

"The population of Cairo is eighteen million. It's the most populated city in Egypt." Shani's voice narrated the scene as it unfolded through the window.

They drove up a ramp and across a long bridge. The water, dotted with large boats, flowed dark beneath. Behind her on the right, Anne saw a tall, brilliantly lit hotel. On the other side of the river, tall apartment complexes lined one street. Each apartment had a small balcony; clothes dried on a few, others sported plants.

"Was that the Nile?" Anne asked as the car slid away from the river.

"Yes. It's the longest river in the world, starting in Ethiopia and ending in Alexandria. It flows south to north."

Anne nodded.

"Hapi is the Neter of the Nile, a hermaphroditic god because the river contains both female and male elements. The Nile was the lifeblood of Egypt before the dam was built. The yearly flood of the river began in late July, shortly after Sirius began to be seen on the morning horizon."

Anne looked up, surprised.

Arnold chuckled. "We thought you'd need a special kind of guide."

"Tomorrow I'll take you to meet my father."

"Mr. Ahram?" Anne asked.

"Yes, but everyone calls him Tahir."

They rode in silence for a while. Anne marveled at how crowded the streets were even at this hour. She sat back, trying to relax, but a subtle energy worked its way through her body, like celestial espresso. It was pleasant and annoying at the same time.

The car traveled along a canal, sporadically littered with garbage. Hotels, shops, and restaurants lined the street. Then the car turned and drove slowly along a smaller street, again lined with shops and a few restaurants. Anne snorted with disgust when she saw a Pizza Hut on her left. Would American fast food become dominant just as American corporations had? The car pulled over and stopped. Anne looked up in surprise. "This is the hotel?"

"Not yet," Shani said. "Since you are a special visitor, I thought we should come here first."

Anne wondered just how much this guide knew about her mission.

She opened the door and gestured for Anne to follow. Arnold got out first and looked around, then extended his hand. She took it just to keep him happy. They stood in front of a low fence with a grocery store on the right and on the left a Dumpster, which was being picked over by a group of cats. A few looked up suspiciously. Anne stooped down and called to them. A mostly orange calico came running and rubbed herself against Anne's legs.

Shani chuckled. "Now that is a sign."

"I love cats."

"I can see that, but these cats are wild. They don't trust most people."

"Then I'm doubly honored," Anne said, scratching the cat behind her ears.

"Now may I introduce you to the supreme cat of all Egypt?"

"Excuse me?" Anne stood up, brushing hair from her hands. Shani was pointing into the darkness in front of her. Anne walked up to the fence and peered into the mist. After a moment's search, she saw a form, a conical shape. Suddenly, she realized she was staring at the Sphinx. "Oh, my God! It's so much smaller than I expected.

You just wait until I get hold of you. The words traveled across the span of sand between the statue and her. Shani went on with her explanations, but Anne did not hear. She'd found the source of the energy she'd been feeling since she woke on the plane. She stared into the darkness, almost making out the Sphinx's features, her mouth slightly open, caught up in the currents of energy flowing around and through the site.

After a minute, Arnold cleared his throat.

"We're coming back tomorrow?" Anne asked.

"Yes, everyone should see the Sphinx first," Shani answered.

Anne shot a glance at Arnold, who was frowning. "Okay, let's go."

The party got back into the limousine. The driver turned the car around and they drove around the Giza complex. Anne strained to catch a glimpse of the pyramids, but it was too dark, the mist too thick. She hadn't expected mist in a desert. She sat back, wondering about those words she'd heard.

Thankfully, the hotel lobby wasn't crowded and Anne checked in quickly. In her suite she found the fridge stuffed with bottles of water, fruit juices, pop, plus some chocolate wafers. A vase of red roses from the hotel manager sat on the small desk.

Arnold dropped her suitcases near the luggage rack, then turned to leave. He turned back. "Only drink bottled water."

"I know," Anne laughed.

"I'd recommend it even for brushing your teeth."

"Thank you, Arnold," Anne said in a slightly formal voice.

"Good night, then. I'm just next door."

"Would you relax?"

Arnold shot her a look, then left, shutting the door behind him.

Anne was exhausted, yet still swimming with the electric energy. She took a warm shower, hoping this would take the edge off, and then stretched out in bed, preparing to sleep. But sleep refused to come. Instead, the weird energy intensified. She fished out two melatonin tablets from her toiletries bag and swallowed them with the bottled water. Then she tried to meditate lying in bed. That usually put her to sleep, but instead the energy increased until Anne's limbs felt like they were vibrating.

Relax, she told herself. *It's just jet lag. It will pass.*

But when she relaxed into the sensation, the energy amplified again. She felt as if her whole body was being shaken, only there was no movement. There had to be some explanation. Sometimes Anne had this feeling when she'd done too much psychic work. It felt like an overload, but this energy was much more intense than any she'd encountered before.

Just let it happen. It was the same voice she'd heard at the Sphinx enclosure.

She resigned herself. It seemed she'd signed up for a roller coaster ride without knowing it. Suddenly, Anne felt herself surrounded by an enormous lioness. Now the energy sounded like a purr, but that was an innocuous word for such a tremendous force. Anne opened to the vibration more and it spread quickly through her whole being. She felt like she was being shaken apart. Finally, she stopped fighting. The energy grew to a fever pitch and Anne lost awareness.

Minutes or hours later, Anne felt a quickening in the silence that had become her consciousness, like a light breeze blowing over a still pond. She lay still, feeling the Earth tilt toward morning. A bird lifted its voice, declaring the coming end of darkness. Next the voice of a *mu'adhdhin* lifted to God, summoning the people to prayer. Anne rose and dressed quickly. She walked down a carpeted hallway of arabesque arches and dark wooden panels, past the empty bar with its amber chandelier, down the steps, and across the lobby. The sky was just beginning to lighten in the east. She headed toward the pool and surrounding garden, then looked to her right. And there they stood. The pyramids, massive solid stone anchors in the earth.

Anne found a quiet corner beneath a palm tree to watch the sun rise. The birds had now begun a full song, flitting from bush to bush, but the *mu'adhdhin* had stopped. The sun finally lifted his head above the horizon and the scent of jasmine filled the air. Gradually, the sounds from Alexandria Street made their way across the garden to Anne's corner—truck horns, the rush of cars. She heard people talking, the bray of a donkey. A man arrived with a large net on a long pole and started skimming leaves and flower petals from the pool. He nodded at Anne. Time for breakfast, she decided.

She walked across the lawn to the Greenery, the toes of her shoes damp from the morning dew. After getting a table, she went over to the sumptuous buffet. She piled her plate high with fresh strawberries and melons, a croissant, scrambled eggs, and a few black olives. When she returned to her table, she found hot tea. Anne settled down to eat, completely content, the difficult night forgotten.

"Excuse me, are you here for the conference?"

Anne looked up to see a tall spindly man peering at her. She recognized him, but the name did not come. "Oh, yes, Mr.—" She paused, but he didn't supply his name. "I heard you speak in New York, at the Solstice conference."

"Paul Marchant."

"Yes, of course. Please forgive my memory. I'm Anne." She offered her hand, but his were full of a breakfast plate and newspaper. He stood there a moment longer.

"Would you care to join me?" she finally asked.

"May I?" Marchant put his plate down. "Coffee," he called out to a waiter passing by.

"Are you here for the conference?" he asked again.

"Yes, I'm certainly looking forward to your presentation. I have to admit the math is a bit steep even for me, but your ideas are fascinating." Anne wondered if she was overdoing the dingbat routine. Thomas had told her Marchant was someone to watch out for.

"I'm hoping to go into much more detail while I'm here." Marchant looked at Anne, cocking his head at a peculiar angle that made Anne think of a praying mantis. "But you're early. What are you planning to do before the conference begins?"

"Sightseeing, shopping, all the usual things." She hesitated. "I don't suppose . . . no, I'm sure all your time is spoken for."

Marchant took a breath as if to speak, then hesitated. "I am quite busy, but I'd certainly be happy to suggest an itinerary. Of course, we'll be visiting all the usual places during the conference, but perhaps I can clear a morning or two to show you a few of my favorite sites."

"Could you? I would be most grateful." Anne gave him a dazzling, well-practiced smile.

Marchant pulled a pen out of his shirt pocket. "I'll make a list of must-sees." He looked around for a piece of paper and found a large paper napkin.

Anne spent the rest of breakfast listening to Marchant discuss the sites he'd listed. She didn't like deception and was not a particularly good spy. She'd have to find something she liked about him if she was going to win his confidence. Before she left the Greenery, she secured a promise that he would visit at least a few of the sites with her.

* * *

EARLY FRIDAY EVENING, Michael caught a cab to the other side of the Giza Plateau to the village of Nazlet el Samman. Finally, he was going to meet Tahir. He'd spent the day reviewing his notes so he'd be prepared.

The cab pulled up in front of the Sphinx enclosure and Michael got out. She was awake but said nothing as he paid his respects from the street, then found his way to Tahir's door. This time a young woman with short coiffed hair opened the door.

He introduced himself. "I was told this would be a good time to see Tahir Nur Ahram."

"Oh yes, we heard someone had come by. Please come in."

The woman led Michael into a central room where a man in his sixties had just risen from a cushion on the floor. He was lean and unusually tall for an Egyptian. The white turban around his head contrasted with his brown face, and he wore a flowing brown *gallabiya*. Warm green eyes looked out of a slightly wrinkled face, eyes that seemed used to squinting against the sun and blinking against the dust. Before Michael could introduce himself, Tahir smiled and offered his hand. "*Ahlan wa sahlam.* Welcome home to Egypt. I've been expecting you, Michael."

In his surprise, Michael forgot to shake the offered hand. "Expecting me? Did Moishe call you?"

"I didn't need a telephone to feel you coming. Please, sit."

Michael took a seat on the adjacent couch and Tahir walked to the open-air porch and shouted across the street, "*Azzizi, etneen chai.*" He took his seat on the floor again and Michael slid off the wooden couch and onto the floor across from him. Two children chased each other into the front room, then back again, the little girl screeching in delight.

A man rushed in carrying a silver tray with tea, two cups, and a sugar bowl, took off his shoes and set the tray on the rug in the middle of the room. Michael looked at Tahir again, who picked up his tea. He gestured for Michael to pick his up. "*Bilhana Woshefer,*" he said, "to the success of our mission."

Michael stared at Tahir, then quickly raised his cup to his lips as Tahir took a sip. Michael swallowed the hot tea, then repeated, "To the success of our mission. But, please, how did you know?"

"I have been waiting for this time all my life." The children reappeared, this time running around the tray. Tahir spoke sharply to them in Arabic and they ran from the room, laughing.

"So you know."

Tahir chuckled. "You sound surprised."

"Please forgive me. It's just that I grew up with this carefully guarded secret passed on in strict ritual. I'm not used to—"

Tahir laughed again. "How can we be used to this time that comes only every fifty-two thousand years?"

"Indeed. Moishe ben Zvi told me how to find you. I must say I'm relieved you know the purpose of my visit."

"And how is Moishe? I haven't seen him in several years."

"His health seems good. He sends his regards."

"He told you I would be able to explain the story of the stones, how they left Egypt, and why they are now returning."

A rush of gratitude filled Michael, followed by a shiver of fear. "Are they returning?"

"Yes, the time has come. Surely you have questions?"

"A couple hundred."

But before Michael could begin, there was a knock on the door. Tahir looked up expectantly, his eyes shining.

The same woman opened the door and they heard muffled conversation, then footsteps. Michael leapt to his feet when the visitors walked into the room. "Anne."

* * *

"MICHAEL!" Anne was so relieved to see him she had to stop herself from stepping into his arms. "But how did you find your way here?"

"My group gave Cynthia her contact in Israel." He shrugged almost apologetically.

Tahir stepped forward, his arms open. "Anne Le Clair, welcome home to Egypt."

"I am honored to meet you, sir." She returned the hug, a bit uncomfortable, then stepped back. At that moment, Arnold stepped in front of Anne and glared at Michael, who blanched and took a step back.

"Arnold, stop it. I've told you Michael is innocent. You just heard what he said. We must work together and how can we if you're always threatening him?"

The bodyguard looked from Michael to Anne, then grudgingly moved to the corner and took up his post.

Tahir walked to the porch again and shouted for more chai. Anne settled next to Tahir, Michael in his old place. More cups of tea appeared from across the street.

Tahir raised his cup again. "To the Keepers of the Keys. May our mission be successful."

Anne stared at Tahir, forgetting to take a sip.

"He knows everything." Michael's quiet voice reached across the room to her.

She looked at Michael, then suddenly started to laugh. "Of course he does. That's why we're here." She raised her cup. "To the success of our mission. And what exactly is our mission?"

Tahir looked around from face to face. Anne felt a spark of recognition as those twinkling green eyes looked deep into hers. An expectant quiet spread through the room. "Before we discuss what we're going to do, I think I should fill in some gaps concerning your crystals." He looked at Anne. "I'm sorry, but your man may not hear this."

"Arnold."

"My orders forbid me to leave you alone with him." He looked hard at Michael.

She stood up and faced him. "We need privacy. You and I need to come to a compromise."

Arnold looked around the room and the adjoining porch. Anne followed him. The back wall was open at shoulder level, giving a good view of the Sphinx. "I'll sit here." He pointed to a bench pushed against the outside wall. "I can be in here in a few seconds if you need me." He walked up to Michael. "I'm sorry sir, but I'll have to frisk you."

Michael looked at Anne. "Is this really necessary?"

She took in Arnold's set shoulders and glowering eyes. "I apologize, Michael, I really do, but this is the only way he'll leave the room."

"Just don't ruin *these* clothes, please."

Anne looked from Michael to Arnold, her forehead wrinkled.

Arnold patted Michael down, then left the room. The door clicked shut behind him and Anne took her seat again. She addressed herself to Tahir. "I'm sorry. My aunt was murdered, as I think Thomas told you, and my apartment broken into. We found cameras in my grandmother's house. My uncle was also assassinated some time ago. It tends to make my family overly cautious."

Tahir dismissed this apology with a wave of his hand. "We will welcome the protection on our trip."

"Trip?" Anne asked.

But Tahir ignored the question. Instead he gestured for them to join hands. He closed his eyes for a moment, then began to chant in a language Anne had never heard before. When he was quiet again, she felt a tingle in the air, like she'd felt during the solstice ritual at her grandmother's estate. She looked up. Tahir was watching her intently. He nodded his approval, then said, "I believe you know these crystals came from Egypt."

Anne and Michael looked at each other and then nodded.

"What you don't know is how long ago. Michael has heard the story of how they left Egypt." He nodded at Michael, inviting him to retell the story.

Michael hesitated, then relayed the tale Moishe had told him about the Exodus and the Jewish connection with Akhenaten. "So my crystal traveled across the desert to Israel almost three thousand three hundred years ago."

"Both your crystals made this journey," Tahir corrected. "Anne, your crystal was given to the Davidic line and thus inherited by your ancestor, the great teacher Yeshua."

"So I've been told, although I still can't get used to it."

Tahir smiled. "You carry his DNA, and hers, the Magdalene, who brought the line of Benjamin into the union. This is one reason the crystal responds to you and not just any random person. As you have no doubt been told, the crucifixion was staged as a way for the family to escape the Romans, but some of the plans leaked out, forcing Yeshua to part from his beloved. He left the crystal with the Magdalene because these things pass through the female side. What you do not know is this crystal was once in the hands of the Queen of Sheba."

"The Queen of Sheba?"

"Yes. Ethiopian tradition holds that Menelik, the son of King Solomon and the Queen of Sheba, stole the famous Ark of the Covenant from the temple, and this relic may now reside in Axum. It may be true, it may be false, but this does not concern us now. He did take another artifact more powerful in some ways than the Ark, although much less impressive to look at. He took your crystal. His mother felt that these power objects belonged to her since she had become the head of the family through their marriage, but my order disagreed. It was not appropriate for one person to hold so much power during the time of darkness, so after her death we took the crystal back and returned it to the Davidic line. I'm sure you know the history of your stone in Europe."

"Thomas gave me a test on it, in fact, before he would let me get on the plane."

Tahir smiled. "Your brother is a most excellent man. Now for yours, Michael. You have been told the crystal was held by the Levite priesthood, then by the Rosicrucians, our order in Europe, that it was taken to Germany to escape the Romans."

Michael nodded his agreement, too absorbed to speak.

Tahir continued. "Our family's crystal"—Anne sat bolt upright—"has never left the motherland." He reached into the capacious pocket of his *gal-labiya* and brought out a necklace. He laid the crystal, similar in size and shape to their own, on the table before them. "The first triad is reunited," he announced, with all the solemnity of a priest speaking the crowning words of a ritual.

"Oh, my God!" Anne whispered. She and Michael both leaned over the crystal to get a closer look. Anne's crystal began to tingle.

"Yes," Tahir agreed. "We will need the help of all the Neters to complete our mission successfully."

Anne and Michael waited in silence.

Tahir studied each of them for a moment, then resumed his narrative. "Before the Greeks came to Egypt, even before the land was called by that name, before the kings reigned and claimed their power as the embodiment of Horus, an ancient civilization existed in this land. It was called Khemit, the Black Land, after the rich, dark soil deposited by the yearly floods of the Nile. These people carved the Sphinx and raised the great pyramids you see outside. And they did all this thousands and thousands of years before 2500 B.C., as my colleagues now say. The crystals come from this civilization."

Tahir looked at Anne. "You ask what our mission is? Our mission is to use these keys to restore the flow."

Anne felt goose bumps as she heard the exact words from her family's story repeated by Tahir.

"Our mission is to ensure the coming of the Awakening. Together we will open the Hall of Records. But first you both must be initiated. Tomorrow we travel to the south of Egypt."

16

*O*nce it was clear she and Michael would be traveling together, Anne had to deal with Arnold. He whisked her away in the limousine, which turned out to be very impractical on these narrow streets. She much preferred taxis, but Arnold didn't like the security risks. Once they got back to the hotel, Arnold adamantly refused even to consider the trip. He would not back down from his orders to minimize all contact with Michael Levy until he was cleared of any involvement in Cynthia's death.

"This is ridiculous, Arnold. The whole purpose of this trip was to meet with Tahir and learn how to use this crystal. Now we know what it's for, at least, and he says we must all work together—the first triad, he called it. You don't realize what is at stake."

"I don't know anything about your mystical goings-on, Anne. All I know is I'm supposed to keep you alive and Michael may have killed your aunt."

"Oh, right. He's a big scary secret agent. *You* intimidate *him*. By the way, exactly what did you do to him? What did he mean about ruining his clothes?"

Arnold merely smiled.

They finally contacted Dr. Abernathy. Anne couldn't risk using her cellular, but it was difficult to find a secure line in Egypt, so Arnold pulled out some fancy scrambler and hooked it up to the hotel phone.

Dr. Abernathy was delighted with Anne's progress, praising her a bit too much, she thought. A positive attitude did much to influence the outcome of events, but she detected a strain in Dr. Abernathy's voice. He was definitely worried.

Then she was summarily dismissed and Arnold talked with him at length, about security plans for the trip, she guessed. She wasn't able to get any details from Arnold about the conversation for the rest of the evening and he frowned at her suggestion to meet Michael in the hotel bar.

"Three-thirty wake-up call," he said, looking at his watch. "You'll get five hours' sleep if you hit the rack right now."

"Hit the rack? I'm not one of your little soldiers, you know."

"And tomorrow we need to do some sparring."

"For Christ's sake."

After repacking for the trip south, Anne went to bed and slept soundly, much to her surprise. Arnold woke her in the middle of the night. They met Michael in the hotel lobby. Arnold marched him through the metal detector, then frisked him and rifled through his luggage before piling it all in the trunk of the limousine along with hers. They stopped in the village for Tahir, whose small overnight case sat by his sandaled feet on the ride to the airport through the dark of night.

They were flying Egypt Air to Aswan and, as it turned out, Tahir, who was now functioning as their guide, had booked economy. Anne had forgotten how small the seats really were, but she dismissed any such concerns when Michael sat next to her, after Arnold had frisked him a second time. Tahir sat across the aisle, but the setting was too public for any serious talk. Anne buckled her seat belt just as the pilot announced the fog was too heavy for takeoff.

Anne turned to Michael, glad of a chance for an intimate chat, but he was snoring softly, his head against the seat, mouth slightly open.

"I'm glad my company is so scintillating," she whispered. She studied him as he slept, the halo of soft brown curls, the strong nose and jaw, the powerful shoulders and arms ending in long, graceful fingers. He was a delicious combination of opposites. After a few minutes, Anne closed her eyes and fell asleep listening to Michael's breathing.

The plane taxiing down the runway woke them two hours later. By late morning, they'd checked into the New Cataract Hotel in Aswan and gone to lunch together. Anne left Michael and Tahir tucked away at a table in the restaurant, talking endlessly about obscure points of Egyptology that were over her head.

She sat by the pool in the early afternoon sun, a glass of cold hibiscus tea called Karkaday in her hand, looking out at the rocks of Elephantine, watching the feluccas come and go on the Nile. Bob, Arnold's backup, sat at the bar behind her, chatting with the waiter. The warm sun relaxed her.

What did it really mean to open the Hall of Records? Edgar Cayce had made the whole idea famous with his trance channeling in the thirties. He claimed there was a chamber beneath the right paw of the Sphinx containing records from Atlantis. Cayce, along with many New Age teachers, believed Atlanteans founded Egypt, bringing their advanced knowledge and technology with them. They had taught the native people and built the civilization that now lay in ruins around her. According to Thomas, the Western metaphysical tradition claimed some connection to the ill-fated isle.

Supposedly, crystals had powered Atlantis. Legends told of a crystal matrix chamber with an enormous clear quartz point that stood more than two stories high. Perhaps the keys would fit into some sort of device, turning on an ancient machine that would hum to life again after thousands of years. But that didn't sit quite right with her. Too mechanical. She wondered what Tahir would say about the whole idea.

Tahir had said that her DNA carried a particular vibration, making her able to attune to her crystal. But how did that work? Surely after two thousand years, many people carried strands of the same DNA she did. She'd seen enough genealogical charts in her family to know that once you got going, it seemed everyone on the planet was related. Her theory was that the DNA wasn't so important as the story that was passed down. The best way to keep knowledge alive was to pass it through a family line or religious order using strict ritual and precise language rigorously memorized. Even with this, her family had lost most of the knowledge.

All but that one phrase Tahir had repeated, "to restore the flow." She wondered if he'd known that or if Thomas had told him.

Michael and Tahir finally arrived at Anne's spot in the sun. "Ready?" Michael asked.

Bob was magically at her side.

"Just five minutes," she said. Anne went back to her room and quickly changed into jeans and a light shirt. She grabbed a water bottle and hat, then joined the men at the pool. "Now I'm ready."

Michael looked up surprised, then turned to Tahir. "She really meant five minutes. I thought she'd take twenty."

"Oh, please," Anne said. "I've been waiting for you since lunch."

"*Ya la.* Let's go," Tahir repeated in English. "Khnum awaits."

They scrambled down to the dock. Tahir had arranged a felucca to take them to the island. As soon as they had set out in the smallish craft, a Nubian boy about the age of ten paddled up to them in a little boat that looked like a canoe, but was one-third the size and open at the bottom, like an inner tube. "Where you from?" he asked, his dark face broken by a huge smile and brilliant white teeth. He was dressed in a white undershirt and shorts, and was underwater from the waist down.

"America," Michael said.

"Row, row, row your boat," the boy promptly sang.

They burst out laughing. The boy gestured for them to join in, so they sailed slowly along singing with the young Nubian boy, who had latched onto the side of their sailboat with one hand. After this song, he began a Nubian chant. He sang a phrase, then waited for them to repeat it. Once they'd learned the basic phrase, he began the song, nodding to them when it came time to repeat the chorus.

Anne noticed another boy in a similar vessel paddle up to another felucca and ask the same question, "Where you from?" She did not hear their reply, but this boy launched into a rendition of "Frére Jacques" and his stunt produced the same roll of laughter.

"The Nubians are famous for their music," Tahir said, handing the boy a few Egyptian pounds after the songs were finished.

Anne reached for her wallet, but Tahir shook his head. "I take care of the baksheesh."

"But—" she began to protest.

Their boat hit shore and Tahir jumped out, ignoring her attempt to hand him money.

Michael got out next, then turned and offered Anne a hand. "Later," he whispered in her ear. "It's customary to tip the guide at the end of the trip."

They climbed the hill and Tahir started to talk. "At the top is a museum. You can look around and then we will visit the temple. Khnum is the divine potter, the Neter of form and the source of our physical bodies. He is a ram-headed Neter. After the museum, we will walk in silence from the door of the temple to the *mamisi*."

Anne listened intently, trying to remember all the new words she was hearing.

"There we will do our ceremony. The Holy of Holies in this temple is now too difficult to reach." Tahir looked at Anne. "The *mamisi* is the birth spot in the temple, where women would come to give birth. But it is also the place to cleanse ourselves before entering the Holy of Holies."

Anne nodded, a puzzled look still on her face.

"Do not worry. We have many temples to visit. You will understand by the time we return to Cairo."

Tahir took a seat outside and talked with the keepers of the site. Anne and Michael walked through the museum, leaning their heads close over old jewelry and talismans, admiring canopic jars. Bob followed at a discreet distance. Anne watched Michael scrunch up his eyes to see the detail on a small statuette of Isis. His hair fell into his face and he brushed it away. She reached out to touch it, but caught herself. She felt at home with him. Perhaps they could find some time to talk about ordinary things, get to know one another.

Michael looked up to find her scrutinizing him. "What?"

"Nothing."

He watched her for another minute, then saw Tahir stand up and look inside for them. "I guess it's time to go," he said, inclining his head toward the door.

"Lead on."

Once outside, they climbed the terraced steps and walked around to the front of a stretch of ruins. On the other side of the museum stood three houses, each with a small garden. Goats grazed on the far hillside. They made their way down a long line of granite that had once been a wall. Halfway down, Tahir pointed. "Here are the remains of a Jewish temple built by Menelik, the son of Solomon and the Queen of Sheba. He stopped here for a few years on his way back to Ethiopia with what he claimed was the Ark of the Covenant and your crystal, Anne."

She looked around, but had a hard time imagining what the temple must have looked like all those years ago. All that was left now were huge limestone rectangles lying on the ground. Michael had a faraway look in his eyes. Perhaps he could see the past. He was trained for it. Then, Tahir put his finger to his lips and without a word started walking across the ruins toward a small building still standing on the left curve of the hill. Anne followed behind Michael in silence, her senses alert. Her ever-present bodyguard trailed behind. The crystal hung quiet between her breasts, perhaps not remembering its residence on this island or, at least, having no comment.

Once inside the small structure, Tahir gestured for them to stand in a circle holding hands. Then he started to chant in the ancient language. Anne felt a small point behind her on the top of the hill stir to life and spiral outward. Her body swayed to the unfolding energy. A strong sense of vitality and joy filled her and she laughed out loud. She felt pressure on her hand and opened her eyes to see the two of them smiling at her.

Tahir inclined his head toward the entrance to the room. They walked outside to a stone statue of a ram with wavy horns. "Now we'll pray to Khnum for health and strength." He put his hands on the ram and closed his eyes. Michael and Anne followed suit, and this time Bob decided to join them.

Suddenly, Michael let out a yell. Bob pushed himself in front of Anne. She looked around him to see Michael holding his rear with one hand and waving his other at a large gray goat who had a patch of cloth hanging from his mouth. "He bit me."

"Are you hurt?" she asked.

"Just my pants."

Tahir started to laugh, then Anne. Even Bob chuckled.

"Thank you very much." Michael's face broke into a large grin. "This trip is turning out to be inordinately hard on my clothes." He took a jacket out of his pack and tied it around his waist.

"Problem solved," Anne said. "Perhaps we can go shopping. Do they sell pants in Aswan?" She looked at Tahir.

Tahir nodded, then pressed his lips together, trying to stop laughing, but it only made things worse. Soon the whole group was roaring. They walked down the hill and back around the shoreline to the waiting boat, joking with Michael that his prayers had been answered and he should be glad his sacrifice was accepted by a goat and not a ram.

Once on the boat, Tahir directed the captain to take them around the island. On a high hill, he pointed out the tomb of Aga Khan, the father of Aly Khan, the famous playboy who had married Rita Hayworth. Aga Khan, according to Tahir, had been married to a former Miss France.

"Aswan is good for love," Tahir said to the air. "Tomorrow even more."

Anne studiously avoided looking at Michael. The felucca rounded the northeast shore of the island and they admired the long line of tour boats piled six and seven deep at the piers across the river. It was near four by now, and the river had filled with feluccas. The white, orange, and blue sails were like colorful streamers against the dark blue Nile. Soon another young boy paddled up and asked the inevitable question, "Where you from?" and they all sang, even Bob, full of vitality and joy, as the boat tacked back and forth, circumnavigating the island. No one would have imagined this jubilant group to be in any danger.

* * *

MUELLER PICKED UP the digitally mastered copy of Marchant's chant only an hour before reporting to Spender's office.

Spender looked up when Mueller walked in. "Give it to me."

Mueller handed the CD over. Spender swiveled around in his chair and popped it into the bank of equipment behind his desk. A pure sound filled the room.

"Our Mr. Marchant sounds like a diva." Spender picked up the phone and buzzed his secretary. "Is Ahmed here yet?"

"He just called, sir. He'll be right over."

"Egyptians," Spender addressed himself to Mueller. "Can't ever be on time. What's the surveillance report?"

"Marchant spent the day walking on the Giza Plateau."

"What was he looking at?"

"Snooping out the other tunnel entrances."

"Predictable. And the other two?"

"They left this morning for Aswan."

"Together?"

"Yes, sir."

"Anyone else?"

"They hired an old guide from the village—Tahir Nur Ahram."

"Blabbermouth. Always telling the tourists fanciful tales."

Spender's secretary ushered Ahmed into the office. Spender pushed a button and Marchant's purified voice filled the air. "What do you think?"

Ahmed raised his hand in the air in a dramatic gesture. "You perform magic, again."

"Let's go." Spender grabbed the CD.

The three men got into the BMW, and Mueller battled Cairo traffic. They arrived at Giza just as the sound and light show started. ("Damned nuisance," Spender growled.) A guard recognized them and jumped to open the gate. Mueller pulled through and drove the BMW up the narrow desert road.

"If you get us stuck, you'll be digging all night."

"We'll be fine, sir."

He parked on the road and the three walked to the stairway. They hurried down the stairs and into the second chamber of the temple. The energy field shone, a dark luminescent blue. It looked like cellophane but was as impenetrable as Fort Knox.

Mueller arranged the portable sound system on the top step leading up to the blocked room, and Spender handed him the CD. Spender took Marchant's crystal out of his inside jacket pocket. He positioned the stone in his right hand, point out, and stood close to the blue curtain. "Ahmed, if you will." He gestured for the man to join him. Once the two were in position, Spender nodded and Mueller pushed play.

A beautiful chant filled the chamber, reverberating off the flat limestone walls. Before either man made a move or a sound, gold specks immediately appeared in the energy field and slowly started to circle. Spender pointed the crystal at the curtain and the two joined in the chant. The energy field lightened from midnight to royal blue. The gold specks swirled faster.

Spender moved the crystal closer and the curtain changed from royal blue to robin's egg. He touched the curtain with the crystal and it snapped back to a dull, midnight blue.

He pulled the crystal back and they started again. The same sequence unfolded, first gold specks circling, then the curtain changing from dark to a lighter blue. But they couldn't get it to come down. Even when it was a sky blue and the room behind it almost visible, the curtain kept them out.

Spender signaled to start the chant again. Mueller pushed the button. Spender didn't give up until around three in the morning. He turned on Mueller, but to Mueller's surprise, Spender gave him the crystal key. "Get this back to Marchant before he figures it out. We're going to have to get him down here again. Find me one more crystal. One can't do the trick. When you've got another one, we'll take Marchant's and try again."

* * *

SUNDAY MORNING DAWNED bright and the birds sang the sun up with all the abandon of a kindergarten playground. Anne was beginning to see the wisdom of the schedule Tahir had laid out for them. Up at dawn, out to the sites early to beat the heat and the other tourists, a late lunch, and back to the hotel to nap in the afternoon. Evenings would be spent answering questions or just relaxing. She reached into her drawer to pull out a T-shirt, but found the one she'd wanted to wear at the bottom, slightly wrinkled. It surprised her. She was usually careful to fold her clothes because she hated wrinkles and ironing equally.

She dressed in a khaki skirt, cotton T-shirt, and a broad-brimmed straw hat, then knocked on Arnold's door to receive her escort for the day, this time the man himself. They headed down for the breakfast buffet. As early as she was, Tahir was already sitting before a plate piled high with scrambled eggs, fruit, and bread. Anne filled her own plate and joined him. Arnold sat at an adjoining table.

"You slept well, I trust?" Tahir asked.

"Yes, now that the Sphinx has decided to let me be."

He looked up. "What happened?"

Anne described her experience the first night she'd arrived in Egypt. In the middle of her story, Michael joined them with a plateful of eggs, hummus, olives, and pita bread. Arnold nodded cordially to him. Apparently Dr. Abernathy had put an end to the frisking. Anne filled Michael in on what he'd missed.

"So what was that all about?" she asked Tahir.

"You Michael? Any experiences with the Sphinx?"

"I always feel that I should see her first thing every time I come to Egypt, and she welcomes me," he said. "This time she told me to go see you."

"It is appropriate to begin with the Sphinx," Tahir said. "Why do you say 'she'?"

"The voice has always sounded female to me."

"According to our tradition, the Sphinx's proper name is Tefnut. You know Nut?"

"Yes," Michael said.

Anne shook her head.

"I will show you as we go to the temples. Nut is the great cosmic mother of all. She is the vault of the sky, the darkness behind the stars."

"Like the Black Virgin?" Anne asked. "Thomas told me about her."

Tahir raised his eyebrows.

Michael explained. "The Black Virgin is the Christian version of the primordial dark mother."

"Nut is shown as a woman. Her hands and feet are on the ground, her back is the sky and stars in the background of blue. In the beginning of the current cycle, Nut spit on the Earth. From that came the Sphinx. The name 'Tefnut' means 'spittle of Nut.' Tefnut was the first manifestation on the planet of the ancient civilization. She is an aspect of the Great Mother, which is why you felt overwhelmed by her energy, Anne. When she pounces, the lioness can frighten the cub."

Anne smiled at the idea.

"How old is she then?" Michael asked.

"This particular statue? At first it was an outcropping of limestone where the people used to go to energize themselves. People have been going there for at least fifty-six thousand years."

"But—" Anne began.

"So you're telling us that the civilization of ancient Khemit goes back that far?" Michael asked, nonplused.

Tahir nodded.

"How can that be? Human civilization started in the Sumer around 4000 B.C.," Anne said.

"Khemit is older. The scientists made a mistake. They think writing is a sign of advanced civilization. Actually, it is a sign of the coming darkness. During the time of light, no one needs writing. We speak mind to mind and tradition is passed orally."

"But don't the stories get lost, distorted?"

"Nothing is ever totally lost. Distortion begins only when the sun has set," Tahir said.

They piled into a taxi, Arnold up front, the rest of them squeezed into the back. After half an hour, they arrived at a dock bustling with vendors, hawkers, and boat owners. Tahir arranged for a boat and they all boarded the small craft. When two men selling beaded necklaces tried to board, Tahir turned and had a heated conversation with the Nubian sailors. Eventually, the salesmen got off and they pushed off from the dock.

Tahir sat in the prow of the boat facing them, looking out of place surrounded by water in his turban and *gallabiya*. "Today we are going to visit the temple of Isis at Philae. You know the story of Isis and Osiris?" he looked at Michael.

"Yes, of course, everyone knows that myth."

Tahir nodded, obviously waiting for Michael to recite it.

"Isis and Osiris are the daughter and son of Nut, as are Set and Nephthys, their opposite pair. Osiris was the wise king and Isis his sister and wife—"

"Wife," Tahir interrupted, a touch of scorn in his voice. "Ancient Khemit was a matriarchy, as were all societies during the time of Aten, the time of the light. The women owned the land, the home, and inheritance was from mother to daughter. My own mother, she knows one hundred percent that I am her son. But my father?" He shrugged his shoulders. "Who can say? In ancient Khemit, it was only important who your mother was."

"But if two people are married—" Anne began.

"Marriage did not exist in Khemit. Not in the way we understand it. In all relationships, the woman chooses. The head of the household chooses the one who will rule in her name. The woman's house was called the *Per Aa*." He leaned forward in the boat. "*Per* means 'house' and *Aa* means 'high.' The high house, *Per Aa*. Isis is the one who rules and, by her choice, Osiris becomes king. *Per Aa* is the origin of the Greek word *pharaoh*, by the way."

"You mean the pharaoh was actually the woman?" Michael asked, astounded.

Tahir threw back his head and laughed at Michael's reaction. "Yes, the woman rules."

"Well, my grandmother would agree with that," Anne said.

The boat pulled close to a crowded dock and the men in front grabbed a boat that was docked and started to pull it away. The crew of that boat shouted at them, waving them away. They pulled up to another boat and the same procedure was repeated with the same results. The third time they found a boat that was ready to leave, and Michael, Tahir, and Anne quickly got off before someone could pull their boat out from under them. They walked up a slight hill to a tourist shop and thumbed through postcards while Tahir bought the tickets.

"I wonder if I should send some cards," Anne mused. "I feel exactly like a tourist. I expected much more rigor, like my grandmother imposed on me."

Michael smiled down at her. "It's rather pleasant, isn't it?"

Arnold cleared his throat and Michael took a step away from Anne. She shot Arnold a look.

Tahir arrived with the tickets and continued the story Michael had begun in the boat. "That is why Isis carries the throne on her head. She is the throne, and she is the woman of power, the *hemeti*. She should sit on a chair, her feet on a stool, and be honored."

"I hope you're taking notes." Anne smiled sweetly at Michael.

He rolled his eyes.

"The story goes that Osiris was a good king, but his brother, Set, was jealous. One day Set presented Osiris with a gift, a fine coffin carved from cedar. He encouraged Osiris to try it out and, when he did, Set's people nailed the lid shut and threw the casket in the Nile. Isis searched all over for Osiris and finally found him in Lebanon. The box Osiris' body was in had become part of a tree that had been cut and shaped into a pillar. It stood in the court of a king. Isis became the nursemaid for the young son of the household and every night she would hold the infant in the fire, granting him immortality. One day the mother found her son in the middle of the fire and screamed out."

"Wait," Anne said, "I thought Demeter did that."

"Demeter is Isis under a different name. Once interrupted, Isis had to snatch the boy from the fire. She revealed who she was and the household fell on their knees before her. They offered her a gift to make up for their ignorance, and she asked for the pillar."

Michael and Anne followed Tahir to the *mamisi*, which was full of columns topped with the head of Hathor, the goddess with the cow horns and round face. From here they strolled through the temple, down the hypostyle hall. Tahir continued his story. "She took the body of Osiris out of the box and was preparing to return it to life, but Set knew of her plans. He chopped up the body of Osiris and distributed the pieces all around the country."

By now they were close to the end of the temple and Anne noticed a group of Japanese tourists following them, listening carefully to one of their group translate Tahir's story. Arnold moved closer to her.

"There's always been a debate about how many pieces he was chopped into," Michael said.

Anne made a face. "This is important?"

"Actually, it is." Tahir smiled at Anne's discomfort. "Osiris was chopped into forty-two pieces."

"Forty-two. I've never heard that one," Michael said.

"There were forty-two tribes in ancient Khemit," Tahir explained, "each entrusted with a piece of Osiris."

Michael's eyes took on a hooded look as he tried to work out the implications of this new piece of information.

Tahir pressed on. "Isis went in search of the pieces of Osiris, eventually finding all except his—" here he made a gesture toward his lower hips.

"Phallus," Michael supplied the word for him.

The group had stopped next to a series of raised reliefs toward the end of the temple. The tourists were standing in a tight circle with Anne and Michael, listening avidly. Arnold was right behind Anne.

Tahir continued, "But even this did not stop her. She fashioned what she needed from a piece of acacia wood and, in the form of a swallow, hovered over the body of Osiris and became pregnant. She gave birth to their son, Horus, the falcon-headed god." Here Tahir pointed to the relief of the baby Horus on his mother's lap. "So, Anne, what is Isis the Neter of, then?"

"Huh?" Anne was taken by surprise. Perhaps this was not going to be a vacation, after all.

The Japanese were talking amongst themselves. Then the man who had been translating for them said in a heavy accent. "She Egyptian Quan Yin? She mother?"

Tahir smiled at the man. "Yes, I know the Chinese Quan Yin, the goddess of compassion."

"Yes, yes." The man turned and translated for his group.

"Anything more, Anne?" Tahir looked at her again.

"Resurrection?" she asked. "Transformation?"

"Exactly. She is the vehicle through which man is transformed from the good king into the enlightened one, the resurrected hero. Horus is the Greek form of the Khemitian Heru, and the source of the word "hero." Isis enlightens us. She is the bringer of immortality."

The Japanese group burst into applause.

"*Domo arigato*," Tahir said, bowing his head in acknowledgment, then he walked down a narrow hall and began to point out a series of reliefs. Osiris held an ankh up to the nose of Isis. "The breath of life," he said. In the next, the god held the ankh to her heart and in the third to her crotch. "The water of life," Tahir said. "Isis is also Neter of the sacred procreative alchemy."

They turned from the wall panels and walked into the Holy of Holies, a large stone slab in the center of the room, the walls covered with hiero-glyphs. They went through quickly, then down the other side of the temple.

"Our ceremony?" Anne whispered to Tahir. "Wasn't that the place to do it?"

Before he could answer, two of the temple guardians dressed in flow-ing white *gallabiyas* stood up and shouted, "Tahir Nur," their arms outstretched.

Tahir turned and shouted their names in turn, but Anne couldn't make them out. Tahir embraced the two men, kissing their cheeks ceremoniously. Then he slipped them some baksheesh, which to her great surprise they kissed before putting in their pockets. The three men talked, then the guardians led them to a chain with a wooden sign that read "No entrance." They pulled the chain back and with great ceremony invited the group into the restricted area. It turned out to be a small Hathor temple. They leaned against the wall, studying the tops of the columns, enjoying a bit of shade.

After a few minutes, Tahir turned to them and said in a low voice. "Now we're going to a place not many people visit. Before the dam was built, the temple stood on the original power spot on the island of Biga. This is where we shall do our ceremony." They returned to the boat and reloaded. Tahir said, "Now we will approach the Holy of Holies in silence."

Gradually, they pulled away from the other feluccas and all that could be heard was the boat moving through the water, the wind gently lifting the sails. The water was a deep blue. They sailed across the lake to an island with tall cliffs, the boulders a deep orange in the sun. Birds flew back and forth from nests in the rock hollows. Anne looked over at Michael, who sat across from her, slightly turned, looking out over the water. His hair blew back in the wind. He looked like a buck testing the air, his body relaxed, but always ready to spring into action.

Sensing something, Michael turned and, when he saw her watching him, his brown eyes lit with a warm fire.

The boat slowed at a spit of land with overgrown granite blocks lying just beneath the soil, suggesting a formal landing site some time in the distant past. An arch still stood at the end of the spit, ushering them into a thicket of trees and undergrowth. Tahir picked his way through the trees until he found the spot he was looking for. Much to Anne's surprise, Arnold stayed with the boat, as did the Nubian sailors.

Tahir gestured for Anne and Michael to sit. Anne settled on a fallen log. Michael took off his jacket and sat on it, completing the circle. They joined hands and Tahir began to chant in the language she'd heard him use before. She felt unsteady, like she was still bobbing around in the boat. Anne closed her eyes and the sensation intensified. She slipped onto the ground and leaned back against the log, giving herself over to the sounds and sensations.

Tahir's voice intensified and, after a few minutes, Anne found herself floating up, hovering in the space above their circle. Suddenly, Isis was before her, dressed in flowing blue robes, a golden sash wrapped around her hips. The Neter gestured for Anne to follow her into a golden barge. They floated across the water to a small island that held a temple of golden stones. Anne followed the Neter through the temple into a room with a large, flat altar stone surrounded by priestesses. On their heads sat elaborate headdresses, some with the throne of Isis, others with the softly curving horns of the Neter Hathor.

One of the priestesses took Anne's hand and led her forward. She laid Anne on the stone and moved away. Tahir's chanting was now laced with the voices of women adding an intricate harmony. She looked around and saw an elaborate ceremonial chamber with beautifully painted reliefs, oil lamps burning, priestesses with gold headdresses all chanting. She was naked, lying on cushions covered in red silk. Suddenly, radiance lit the room and a man walked toward her, his skin golden with light, his phallus erect. He joined her on the altar and, as the chanting intensified yet again, gently entered her. The chanting built to a pitch and they rocked to the chant, sensation building on sensation until they ignited like a starburst.

Anne opened her eyes to two concerned faces looking down on her. Embarrassed, she tried to sit up, but dizziness stopped her. She looked from Michael to Tahir, finding him safer. "What happened?"

"You . . ." Tahir searched for an appropriate euphemism.

"Shouted," Michael offered.

"Yes," Tahir nodded, "and fell over."

"Oh." Anne took Tahir's extended hand and sat up. She noticed Arnold had joined the circle.

"What happened?" he asked.

"She fainted," Tahir said. "The energy is very intense today. The island has recently been beneath water."

Arnold frowned at Michael, then asked Anne. "Are you all right?"

"Yes, nobody did anything to me. I'm safe."

Arnold crossed his arms and stood next to Anne.

"Can you tell us what you saw?" Michael asked.

"Uh," Anne hesitated. She looked at Tahir again. "Some kind of ritual."

Tahir's eyes lit. "Excellent." He seemed to know not to ask for details. "And you, Michael?"

"I felt an enormous amount of energy, like I was being shaken, but I didn't see anything. I'm not always visual."

Tahir nodded again, clearly satisfied.

Anne was relieved he hadn't asked her to explain more. She had the odd feeling he knew already. She stood up and brushed herself off, feeling a damp stain on the seat of her skirt from where she'd been sitting on the ground. She took a few wobbly steps. Michael steadied her, then put his arm around her for support. They made their way back to the dock. Without hesitation or permission, Michael lifted her into his arms and carried her into the boat. She sank against him, half from relief, half from desire.

Michael settled her on the narrow seat on the boat, then sat beside her, firmly ignoring Arnold's attempt to intercede. She leaned her head against his shoulder. A hint of musk from his neck mixed with the smell of sweat reached her. She was acutely aware of the warmth and solidity of his body. Anne closed her eyes, trying to get control of herself. The Nubians pushed off and soon they were sailing back. Anne wished she were alone with Michael, but was at the same time grateful she wasn't.

They sailed across the dammed-up river in silence.

17

Anne went straight to her room after they arrived at the hotel, saying she needed to rest. What she really needed was to regain her composure, to separate her feelings for Michael from the experience on Biga. She'd been attracted to him from the beginning when he popped his head out from the back office of his uncle's jewelry store, licking cinnamon off his fingers. Then she had discovered they'd shared a life here in Egypt sometime in the distant past. She had loved him then, but they had never married. Perhaps that was the source of the sadness she'd felt, but Tahir said there were no marriages in the old civilization. Their fates were tied together as Keepers of the crystals, but Tahir also held a key and she didn't remember any lifetimes with him, although there had been a spark of recognition when she first met him.

Michael was handsome, that was certain, but it didn't stop there. He was intelligent and successful in his field. She'd checked him out online and found he'd authored two dozen articles in respected magazines and another dozen in alternative publications. Not to mention his book. Sophisticated, well traveled though he was, he was kind and considerate to everyone—the servants, waiters, cabdrivers.

Was she in love? She had to admit she was teetering on the brink, but today she would have taken him farther into the spindly trees on Biga if they'd been alone. How much of that feeling was residue from the Isis initiation? She marveled even now how quickly the vision had come and how vivid it had been. But what did it mean? Perhaps it had been the sexual alchemy Tahir spoke of. Anne had embodied the essential feminine, the divine lover, all sense of individuality subsumed by that power. She'd become Isis, and the man who'd come to her had embodied the divine masculine, Osiris. This was separate from the individual Michael and Anne.

Or was it?

After a long nap, Anne woke feeling more like herself. It was all right to slow down. The family still hadn't cleared him. She dressed in a floral print dress and walked to the Sultan's Terrace to join Michael and Tahir for tea. As usual, they were deep in conversation. Tahir was smoking a hookah pipe that had been set next to the table, looking like the caterpillar in *Alice in Wonderland*. Both men stood up when she arrived and Michael pulled back a chair for her. "How are you feeling?"

"Better. I needed a good sleep."

And you?" she directed the question at both of them.

"Good, but my knees need a rest," Tahir answered. "You will enjoy the market without me slowing you down."

Anne was taken aback. Here she had decided to go more slowly with Michael, and fate immediately put them alone, *or practically alone,* she thought, glancing over to see who had followed her. Tonight it was Bob.

"Perhaps a shopping excursion then," Michael said. "I need some pants, remember?"

Anne laughed. "Yes." Turning to Tahir, she said, "When we came on this trip, you said we were going to be initiated, but, I hope you'll pardon the question," she added, seeing his lips purse, "I feel just like a tourist. Egypt is beautiful, but—"

Tahir laughed at her diplomatic tone. "So you are wondering what are these initiations? They are not what you expected?"

"Yes." She was relieved he'd come straight to the point. "I thought we'd be learning more about . . ." She glanced around, leaving the rest unsaid.

"We are tracing as near as we can the pattern of initiation students underwent in the past. Of course, then the ceremonies were much more elaborate and people prepared for them longer. But we don't have time for a lifetime of study. Besides, you've both done this in the past."

Anne looked up quickly. "We have?"

"Most certainly. And the temples are no longer in our hands." His eyes looked sad for a moment. "But the energy is still here. The sites themselves are the keys, or perhaps the—how you say?" He made a gesture of turning a dial back and forth.

Michael said, "Combination lock?"

"Exactly." Tahir clasped his hands together. "The combination to open us to the Neters within us."

Anne's forehead wrinkled.

"The Neters, what people call the gods and goddesses of Ancient Egypt, live in us," Tahir said. "The Neters are principles, attributes of the one unified consciousness. By visiting the sites, we turn on that aspect of our own awareness. You've already experienced this." Seeing Anne's face, Tahir changed his example. "Weren't you full of energy after visiting with Khnum?" He looked at them both.

"Now that you mention it, I did feel more energetic than I have in a while," Michael answered. "I just thought it was from finally having some fun." He smiled at Anne. She dropped her eyes and took a quick sip of tea.

"Khnum rules our physical existence, our survival," Tahir explained.

"First chakra," Michael added.

"You could say this, but it is simplistic. Just as it would be too simple to say Isis is the second chakra, even though this is partly true." He glanced furtively at Anne. "Each temple is a vital link in the chain, or a part of the combination that will prepare us for our ultimate goal: restoring the energy flow in the most vital temple on Earth."

"And the Hall of Records? What is it exactly?"

Tahir sat back in his chair. "This is not something that can be explained in words. It is an experience. By the end of our time, the knowing will come to you."

A couple walked up to the point and stood close to their table. "Beautiful, no?" said the man, commenting on the sunset in a Spanish accent. They all looked up to see the sun poised on the western horizon, the sky streaked with orange and purple. The rounded rocks on Elephantine Island took on shape and definition as the sun baked them a warm gold. The Nile turned a deeper shade of blue.

Tahir's tall form drooped a little in his chair. Anne and Michael decided to leave him to watch the sunset rather than drag him off to their rooms for further instruction. They got directions to the open-air market, then stood up from the table.

As they turned to leave, Tahir said, "Remember, tomorrow we sail downriver to meet the great Neter Sobek and face our fears."

The Spanish couple began asking Tahir questions about the temples they'd visited. When she and Michael were out of earshot, Anne said, "He's getting to be just like my grandmother, full of solemn pronouncements."

"He reminds me of Robert, my teacher in New York."

In front of the hotel, Michael raised his hand and a cab pulled up. Bob sat in front, but kept a close eye on Michael. On the way, Michael told Anne a bit about Robert and his group. "He's a learned man. He's dedicated his life to uncovering and preserving metaphysical knowledge. I was truly blessed to work with him."

"I only wish my own training hadn't been interrupted." She told Michael a bit about Cynthia and how her mother had pulled her away after the dedication ceremony. She chose her words carefully, aware the driver might overhear. Soon they arrived at the market.

The market stalls were stuffed with colorful *gallabiyas,* brilliant silk scarves, statues of various pharaohs, queens, and Neters, papyrus paintings, jewelry, and tourists viewing the wares. Between the tourist shops, Anne caught glimpses of spices, vegetables, and huge wedges of meat hung toward the back of shops. As they walked, the sellers in the stalls called out to them about how much money they would save if they shopped with them. She took Michael's arm so as not to lose him in the crowd. She saw a promising shop with beautiful *gallabiyas* hanging from every square inch and steered him in that direction.

"What do you think? Should I go native?"

"Absolutely. You'd look ravishing in these."

"But the women here don't really dress in these. Where do they shop?"

"These are so much more colorful. Support the local economy. Buy something."

"Only if you get one."

"Actually, I own several already, but not quite so bright," Michael said, pulling out a tangerine with gold trim.

Anne made a face. "Why haven't you worn them?"

Michael shrugged. "I usually wait for an occasion. Certainly, at the conference cocktail party." He pulled out a royal blue with gold trim.

"Nice," she said. "We'll wear them to face our fears tomorrow."

"Actually, I'd advise pants. It may involve some crawling through tunnels."

"You know already. Tell me." Anne put down the dresses she had slung over her arm and grabbed Michael's hand. "Tell."

He looked into her eyes and she was suddenly aware of the warmth of his skin. She let go of his hand.

"*I* didn't know the first time. Why should I tell?"

"You've done this before?"

"Not with Tahir, but I think I know what part of the temple we'll be going into."

"No fair." She stuck out her tongue impulsively, exactly like a ten-year-old girl.

The edges of Michael's mouth turned up into a smile and she stood gazing up at him. He leaned a bit closer.

"You like the blue? I have good cotton. I make you best price."

Anne turned to find the anxious shopkeeper holding out the *gallabiyas* she'd just put down. "Yes, and the pink please. Do you have a dressing room?"

The man frowned slightly, not understanding.

"Is there a place I can try them on?"

"This way." The shop owner ushered Anne to the back of his booth where a small area was enclosed on four sides by canvas.

"*Sukran.*" Anne was trying to learn a few words in Arabic and she'd mastered "thank you."

"*Afwan,*" the man said, pulling the curtain aside for her to enter.

The *gallabiyas* were quite voluminous, so Anne decided just to try the garments over her dress. In the middle of pulling the royal blue over her head, Anne heard something rip. "Oh, no," she said, but then realized the tear had been too loud to be cotton.

Someone grabbed her, pulled a piece of torn canvas from the tent over her head and dragged her out the back of the stall. Anne screamed and stomped the instep of her assailant's foot as hard as she could, but her tennis shoes were no match for his boots. The man cursed under his breath and another set of arms fastened around her. She struggled to get free, to breathe.

"Anne!" she heard Michael yelling for her, then sounds of a scuffle. The two men wrapped the canvas around her more tightly and one slung her over his shoulder. As soon as her feet were off the ground, she started kicking, trying to find a vital spot. The other man grabbed her legs, tightening the canvas even more, and they carried her exactly like a rolled carpet. Anne continued to make as much noise as she could. She scrunched herself up, then pushed out, trying to loosen the canvas.

They put her down on the ground and one pinned her while the other started searching her body. They felt all around her waist and her pockets. So this was not attempted rape. They were after the crystal. She had no leverage wrapped in this bulky material, but tried to turn and get an arm or leg under her so she could push off. The hands stopped at a lump in her front pocket.

Oh, no, she thought. *They're going to get it.*

Then she heard the hard crunch of fist on bone. One of the men staggered. She heard the thump of a blow landing hard. The man lost his hold on her and, kicking out at the second man, she rolled free. Anne struggled to escape the suffocating shroud. She heard more blows land, the sound of feet running. Finally, she freed her head and took a big gulp of air. She looked around wildly.

She saw Bob holding a wiry Arab man down, one of his arms expertly twisted into a pretzel. The other man had apparently escaped.

"Are you all right?" he asked.

"Yes, and you?"

He nodded.

"Only two?"

"I saw a van tear off just now. No license plate." He shot her a wicked grin. "I guess they didn't expect you to be able to fight."

"Michael." She looked around the alley the men had carried her down. "Where's Michael?"

"No time," Bob said. "I have to get you out of here."

* * *

THOMAS LE CLAIR sat in his alcove in the family archive room at his grandmother's estate, patiently going through Cynthia's papers for the fifth time. His painstaking search was not very exciting or even dangerous, but the fate of the mission depended as much on his attention to every detail and nuance as it did on Anne's initiations. He hadn't heard from his contact in the Vatican for three days and was beginning to worry. What if they'd caught him breaking into the records of the vaults where the church kept the scrolls, secret books, gospels, and artifacts they'd accumulated over the centuries? What if they'd seen the computer files of the documents he'd scanned? Intercepted the fax? Thomas shook his head and tried to concentrate on the manuscript he was studying. There was no use speculating. If he hadn't heard from Rudolfo by tomorrow, he'd fly to Rome himself.

He put Cynthia's files away and took down another plastic envelope holding an old Templar document that had been partially burned. Vital sections were missing. It detailed, but in code, the disposition of various treasures. Perhaps today he could read between the lines. Thomas leaned closer to the page, but still could not make out some of the words. He took out a magnifying glass and bent closer still. *"Le clef secrete avec Jacques de Molay,"* the phrase read. But Molay had been caught and tortured before he'd been burned at the stake. Under those circumstances, he'd probably told them something.

The Templars had probably left the key in Paris, thinking the church needed to find something of value; otherwise they'd know the main treasure had escaped them. At the time, perhaps the crystal hadn't seemed vital. It was attached to a vague prophecy about an unspecified time in the future. The new head of the order had known the time would be coming at the turn of the millennium, but had he been in Paris when this decision was made? Probably not. They'd most likely resolved to retrieve the key at a later date. This was the task Thomas now faced.

The fax suddenly hummed to life. The documents he'd been expecting. Finally. It was late afternoon in Italy. Rudolfo must have waited until the offices of the Vatican were not so crowded.

Thomas began to read. It was the church report about the Templar massacre, written in code. "Damn it," he muttered. Now he'd have to dig up the code and translate it. He'd hoped Rudolfo would do it for him, but perhaps he'd been watched and hadn't had the time. Thomas turned back to the machine, which was still pushing out pages. He took them and found the rest of the Latin document, then the beginnings of a translation. "Thank you," he whispered.

He took the pages over to a low table and spread them out. After a brief description of the Templar massacre, Thomas found a list of the property the church had confiscated. The list included a document proving the marriage of Yeshua and Mary Magdalene. Birth records of the Merovingians going back to this couple. A case of jewels. The Crown of Three Frogs. The Sword of Clovis II. An amethyst crystal skull. A crystal necklace topped with an Egyptian glyph. Documents transferring ownership of many properties to the church.

Thomas's blood boiled as he read the list of artifacts, some belonging to his own family. Why had the Templars left such important documents in Paris? There was a scribbled note from Rudolfo at the bottom of the last page, stating that, as far as he could tell, the crystal necklace was still in the vaults. Rudolfo was going to try to find it himself. Thomas grabbed these papers, stuffed them into his briefcase, and went to find someone to go with him into the city. Grandmother Elizabeth had put her foot down and forbidden him to travel alone. "You are just as vulnerable as Anne. You must take at least one bodyguard with you wherever you go."

Soon they were speeding toward the city in his silver Jaguar, the new security man trying not to grab the roll bar as the tires screeched around turns. It was imperative they get this crystal out of the vaults and to Egypt. He wished Arnold were here, but he knew Anne needed him more. Arnold was such a good thief; he'd come up with a way to penetrate the Vatican vaults if anyone could. Thomas hoped Dr. Abernathy would know who to call for the job. Maybe he could convince him to recall Arnold for a night. Cairo was closer to Italy than New York was.

They arrived at the law offices and Thomas jumped out of the car, making his bodyguard hustle to keep up with him.

"I'd appreciate it if you'd let me do my job, sir," the man growled as the elevator door closed.

"Oh, sorry," Thomas said, "I'm rather distracted."

"Even more reason."

Thomas hurried down the hall and requested entrance from the secretary by pausing. She waved him in. Dr. Abernathy was sitting at his massive desk reading. He looked up.

"Do you have news?" he asked, seeing Thomas's expression.

"Yes." Thomas took the fax from Rome out of his briefcase and handed it to him. "The last page suggests a fourth crystal is being held by the church."

"Fourth?" he asked.

"Anne has one. Michael has a second, and Tahir assured me he will be able to locate a third in Egypt. This is the fourth."

Dr. Abernathy scanned the pages before him, then got up and walked to the window. He stood lost in thought for a minute. Thomas waited, his foot jiggling. Finally, Dr. Abernathy turned back to him. "I wish we could spare Arnold."

"Why can't we pull him off Egypt for a day or two? Rome is close enough."

Dr. Abernathy shook his head. "I've had some news—"

At that moment, the door to his office opened again and they heard his secretary say, "He's in a meeting, ma'am."

Katherine swept into the office. She took a seat and nodded at Thomas. "I'm glad you're both here."

"Mother." Thomas greeted her with a perfunctory kiss on the cheek.

Dr. Abernathy gestured for his secretary to close the door. "Katherine, to what do we owe—"

"Something's happened," she said. "Is she alive?"

Thomas looked from his mother to Dr. Abernathy, alarmed.

"Of course, she's alive. What are you talking about?"

Katherine's jaw tightened. "Don't lie to me, Roger."

"My dear Katherine . . ."

"This afternoon I was working in my office and suddenly I felt panic, like I was being suffocated. I felt hands searching my body."

Thomas took a sharp breath and looked at Dr. Abernathy, who pushed back in his chair.

"As a matter of fact, I've just had Arnold's daily report. Anne is quite safe. Nothing has happened."

Katherine leaned forward. "I told you not to lie to me."

Dr. Abernathy held Katherine's eye. "I promise you Anne is perfectly safe. We're taking every precaution."

"Then maybe this is a premonition." Katherine didn't look convinced.

Dr. Abernathy shifted in his chair. "Perhaps," he said. "Your sensitivity is significant. I'll convey your experience to Arnold."

Katherine regarded him through narrowed eyes, then her shoulders dropped. "Please do, because if anything happens to my daughter, I'll hold you personally responsible."

"As well you should," he answered. "Now if there isn't anything else, we're in the middle of a very delicate operation."

Katherine snorted, but gathered her purse and stood up. Unconsciously, she smoothed her dress. "Keep her safe, Roger."

Dr. Abernathy got up and escorted Katherine to the door, his arm around her shoulders. "You have my solemn word."

"Good-bye, Thomas," she said.

"I'll call you for lunch soon."

"Good."

Dr. Abernathy closed the door behind her and turned. "It's really too bad she never trained properly."

Thomas frowned.

"As I was just about to tell you, Anne was attacked in the market at Aswan."

"What?" Thomas grabbed the arms of his chair.

"She escaped unharmed. Arnold was pleased with her response. They were clearly after the crystal."

"Was it Michael?"

"Arnold thought so, but no. I just received the final report from our investigators. Cynthia was killed by a toxic agent available only to the top echelons of the intelligence community. Michael and the Zohar group could never have gained access to it. It's looking better for our Mr. Levy, although he's not one hundred percent in the clear as yet."

"I have a feeling he's trustworthy," Thomas said.

"Now, about this fourth crystal . . ."

* * *

PAUL MARCHANT WAITED in the shadows next to the north gate of the Giza Plateau. Two guards had just locked up and were strolling down toward the pyramid ticket booth. In a few minutes, another guard appeared. Marchant handed over a hefty bribe, and the man unlocked the gate.

Marchant passed through, handed him an extra twenty pounds, and said, "I've just always wanted to climb the pyramid. Please don't tell anyone. I don't want to get caught." He hoped he looked sufficiently nervous.

"No problem," the guard said, pocketing the money. "Just be down before dawn."

Once inside, he headed toward the middle pyramid. Usually, nobody went there at night. The moon was waxing toward full, lighting the desert sand before him. Careful to stay in the shadows as much as possible, he made his way across the back end of the plateau.

Mueller hadn't shown up for their scheduled meeting that afternoon. Last night Marchant had dreamed about Mueller sneaking into his room to steal his crystal, but it was there on the nightstand beside him when he woke up.

Yesterday, when Marchant was supposed to show Anne Le Clair around Sakkara, she'd been nowhere to be found. Come to think of it, he hadn't seen Michael Levy for a few days either. He'd been busy investigating various openings on the plateau, searching for the underground room Mueller had taken him to. He'd chosen the most crowded times of day when the pyramids were crawling with tourists, camel jockeys, guides, and local kids selling water or plastic scarabs. Of course, the locals had sharp eyes, not to mention the antiquities police, but Marchant had discovered long ago that he had a knack for being invisible in a crowd. His explorations had given him what he now thought was a complete picture of the tunnel system. Tonight he was going to the blue wall alone.

It took almost half an hour to hike to the south of the site where he thought the entrance was. He slipped around a small hill, but the sand lay unbroken in the moonlight. He walked west until he came to the next hill. He walked around and there it was, a low entrance that looked exactly like the tombs next to the Sphinx enclosure. He saw no guard. Surely they wouldn't just leave the place open. Marchant paused for a long while, listening for sounds. No footsteps, no voices, no jeep engine, nothing. Satisfied no one was around, he put on a pair of goggles Donald had procured for him. They were a bit old, but they'd have to do. He pushed a button on the side and looked again at the site, scanning for infrared signals. He pushed the button a few more times, going through the light spectrum. The place was clear.

Marchant crept to the opening of the stairway and discovered a locked gate two steps down. Before Marchant had left New York, Donald had given him a quick lock-picking lesson. This lock proved to be fairly simple. Probably if they'd put too sophisticated a device on this gate, it might have drawn attention. He went through the entrance, then arranged it to look like it was locked. He turned and took the steps two at a time, his heart throwing itself against his chest.

The stairwell led into a tunnel large enough to stand up in. He followed it for a short distance, and it opened up into a large underground cave. He took out a flashlight. A path of footprints in the dust led the way. About fifty yards in, the cave walls gave way to limestone blocks with incised reliefs. He didn't stop to see what they depicted. Rounding a corner, Marchant stopped dead and gaped. Before him was an enormous underground temple. Two Sphinx statues, much smaller than the original aboveground, sat at the bottom of broad limestone steps that led to an open plaza. A large statue of Osiris lay on its side toward the back of the temple. He hadn't expected to find this particular Neter here. A series of columns stood against the back of the cavern, holding up a roof that was now covered from above by sand.

Marchant walked a few steps into the temple, awed by the majestic architecture. If they'd built this place after the fall of Atlantis. . . . Farther to the left was a lake, full even now. The desert was still alive with ground-water. This explained the moist smell he'd noticed on his first visit. The lake was lined with small blocks of limestone, indicating it was man-made.

The footprints continued along the side of the cavern and around another curve to a wall with a small passageway cut into it. Marchant duck-walked through to the other side and emerged in the inner temple where he'd been taken on his first trip. He flushed in triumph. Finally, he was here without that insufferable musclehead breathing down his neck. He turned to face the statue of Anubis and mentally asked permission to enter. A wave of welcome emanated from the statue. He walked past the other Neters without acknowledging them, thinking that later he would decipher the code they represented, and climbed the six steps to the blue wall.

It was a deep midnight blue, vibrating slowly. Spirals of gold came and went. He closed his eyes and listened. Subliminally, he heard its song. He stood for a moment longer, making sure of the frequency. Taking his crystal in his right hand, allowing his energy to harmonize with the field, he intoned an "ah" at the same pitch. Marchant chanted for a full five minutes, losing himself in the energy and resonance of the chamber. When he finally opened his eyes, the energy curtain was almost transparent, revealing a small chamber behind it.

The room was empty.

Marchant took a sharp breath and the energy field darkened slightly. He hadn't expected this. This had to be the entrance to the Hall of Records.

It matched all the stories that had been passed down, except it was not exactly beneath the paw of the Sphinx. The more agitated he became, the darker the energy field grew. Taking hold of himself, Marchant forced his breath to slow and lengthen. Again he closed his eyes and chanted, asking for support from the Neters. Immediately, he felt a strong flow of encouragement from the statues behind him. When he'd returned to a place of balance and peace, he opened his eyes again. The field was transparent. He reached out and touched it. It felt like a cool gel, completely smooth, but his hand couldn't penetrate it. The Hall was still not ready to yield its secrets.

Marchant studied the room behind the curtain. It looked bluish, but he thought this might be a reflection, not a tint or paint. The walls were rose granite like the sarcophagus in the king's chamber, and blank. No hieroglyphs, no reliefs of any kind. He looked carefully at the crevices between the granite blocks, hoping to find indications of a door or some kind of passageway, but they were smooth and uniform. On the floor lay an intricate inlaid pattern in gold and shades of blue, a smaller star tetrahedron matching the one outside the chamber. This reassured him. He understood the geometry.

Surely this was another antechamber, yet another test to open the real Hall of Records. Perhaps the wall would open onto another hallway that led closer to the Sphinx. Perhaps Cayce had been close. But he was satisfied with his night's work. Now he knew that at least one other crystal was required to access the room and to open the smooth walls that hid the treasure he'd trained for so many lifetimes to uncover. Marchant had no doubt he would lead the team, since he held the Orion crystal. He stood in front of his goal, a hair's breadth away, yet it was still unattainable. Patience, he must have patience. The alignment was just a little more than two weeks away.

18

$\mathcal{M}$ ichael woke with a groan and sat up quickly. His head protested. Gingerly touching his temple, Michael found a large lump and newly dried blood. He must have been out for a while. His hand went to his secret pocket. Empty. They must have gotten the crystal. Then the memory returned, handing Tahir his crystal while they waited for Anne. Something had nagged him. He was relieved he'd acted on his intuition.

He looked around and found he was in a narrow alley probably a few blocks from the bazaar. It was silent and the sky through the buildings was dark. A lone star shone weakly down on him.

Anne, what had happened to Anne? He'd heard her screaming and seen two men wrap her in some heavy material. He'd run after her and grabbed one of the men, whirling him around and landing a satisfying crack on his jaw. The man had fallen, but just as Michael had turned to run after the other, someone had hit him on the side of the head and he'd blacked out.

He had to get back to the hotel. He had to notify her people, perhaps the police. Tahir would know what to do. He stood, took a few wavering steps, then steadied himself against a wall. He made it out to the street, but it was deserted.

You're only alone in Egypt when you're in trouble, he mused.

He made his way up a couple of blocks, stopping occasionally when he got dizzy, and finally found a main street. It too was deserted. It must be very late. Michael looked up at the sky, but saw no signs of dawn. He waited a few minutes and finally a taxi appeared a block up. He threw his hand up, but the driver took one look at him and turned the other way.

Michael looked down at his torn, bloody shirt. The lights of a hotel a block down caught his eye and he walked to it. The man at the front desk frowned at his appearance, but Michael ignored him and found the washroom. He examined the cut on his temple. A small scratch ran up into his hair, but scalp wounds bleed heavily, which explained all the blood. He washed his face, then took off his shirt and washed it. Better wet than bloody. He shivered when he buttoned the cold, wet shirt over his chest.

At the front desk, he asked the man to call him a cab. His request elicited a raised eyebrow, but no comment. "*Sukran,*" he said, reaching into his pocket for a tip. His wallet was missing. "Damn it," he muttered. "Never mind," he said to the man. He'd never convince a taxi to take him to the hotel with no money at this time of night. He started to walk. He reached the river in about half an hour. The water was dark, the air heavy with the smoke of so many boats. His head throbbed and his ribs had begun to ache.

Michael walked down the sidewalk next to the river, passing the Internet café and various stalls and restaurants. He reached the New Cataract just as the rosy fingers of dawn stretched into the eastern sky. A bus full of tourists was loading. He walked into the lobby and immediately spotted Tahir talking to a policeman.

Michael called to him.

A look of relief lit Tahir's face. "I was just giving your description to the police. Are you hurt?"

"I'll be okay. Where's Anne?"

"In her room. She's fine."

Arnold walked across the lobby and joined them. "Where can we talk?"

Tahir's room was closest, so they followed him there. Michael gingerly sat down in one of the armchairs by the window and Tahir perched on the edge of the bed.

Arnold stood with his hands on his hips. "Tell me what happened."

Michael relayed the events. "I tried to follow, but there must have been a third man. He hit me with something and I blacked out."

Arnold looked closely at Michael's temple, then grunted. "You'll have a headache for a few days. Nothing serious." There was a look of deep suspicion in his eyes.

"I had nothing to do with this."

Arnold just stared at him.

"For God's sake—" Michael sat back heavily against the chair. He turned to Tahir. "You're sure Anne didn't get hurt?"

"Yes," Tahir said.

"She knows how to fight. I guess your men didn't count on that," Arnold said.

"Goddamn it, they weren't my men. When are you going to get it through your thick head that I'm one of the good guys?"

Arnold surveyed him calmly. "When I have proof. Meanwhile, we're going to have extra security for the rest of the trip. And a private boat. Don't get any ideas, because you're going to have to find your own transportation. You won't be alone with Anne under any circumstances. And no more shopping trips."

Michael nodded. "Well, no more shopping trips, at least, sounds like a good idea."

The bodyguard turned to Tahir. "Is this trip vital to the mission? It's an enormous security risk."

"The crystal bearers must make the trip down the Nile," Tahir explained. "The keys must be activated for the final alignment."

Arnold shook his head. "Activated? I don't see how lollygagging around a bunch of old temples is accomplishing anything. And it certainly won't do you any good if you've got a dead crystal bearer."

"They will not kill her. By now, I'm sure our opponents realize the people are a vital link in this technology."

Arnold frowned.

Michael prudently kept his mouth shut.

"Talk to Anne," Tahir suggested. "Perhaps she can explain things to your satisfaction."

"I don't take my orders from Anne," Arnold said. "I'll discuss this with Dr. Abernathy. For now, I must have exact information about where we'll be going. Try to hit the temples when they are the least crowded."

Tahir agreed.

Arnold took a step closer and stuck his face into Michael's. "I'll be watching you."

* * *

ANNE SAT on the deck of the yacht Arnold had hired, looking out at the river and the temple of Kom Ombo. They were waiting for the tourist boats to leave and for Michael to arrive. He'd told her he would hire a driver and meet them there.

"It's only about forty miles from here, and the museum will pay," he'd reassured her. "But I do need some pocket money, so I'll have to go to the bank before I can check out. They got my credit cards as well."

She hadn't wanted to leave him standing in the New Cataract lobby with a bandaged forehead, and yet, after the attack last night, something had changed. Thinking back, she remembered the morning they'd gone to the Isis temple, how her shirts had been crumpled up in her drawer. She was always neat with her clothes. Maybe someone had broken into her room looking for the crystal. And before that, when she'd gone to hear him speak in New York, then out to dinner, her apartment had been ransacked. Could it all be just a coincidence?

She had to consider the possibility that Michael might be working with the Illuminati. After all, he knew a great deal about Western metaphysical orders and their secrets. Perhaps his job at the museum had been arranged to give him a plausible cover for his work with the group. Even with this, those brown eyes still lit a fire in her. And the way he always pushed his hair off his face, the spring in his step. Why did she keep falling for the wrong men? She sat back and took a deep breath, trying to put these thoughts out of her mind. The family was investigating Michael and if he had any connection to the shadow forces, they'd find it.

Time to focus on the mission. What were they doing today? Tahir had told them this was a fear initiation, but sitting in the warm sun, looking out at the peaceful waters of the Nile and the orderly village garden, a verdant strip next to the river, she found that hard to imagine. She could imagine building a villa here and basking in the sun all through the winter months, raising a couple of children with—Damn it, she had to stop thinking about him.

Anne went down to her room and rubbed ointment into her bruised shoulder. She'd come out of the attack relatively unscathed. As far as she was concerned, that had been her fear initiation. She sat on the bed and took out her sewing kit and an old T-shirt. She cut a few pieces of fabric from the shirt, took out her bras, and began sewing a pocket inside each one. If she tucked the crystal inside, any one frisking her might miss it. At least it would slow them down. Just as she was finishing, someone knocked on her door.

"Tahir is asking for you," Arnold said.

"Be right there." Anne tucked the crystal in its new pocket and got dressed.

When she arrived on the upper deck, Michael and Tahir were sitting on deck chairs, talking together as usual. She felt a stab of jealousy. Michael knew so much more than she did. He was an Egyptologist and had studied the occult sciences all his life. She was definitely playing catch-up. She sat down in the chair next to Tahir.

He addressed them both. "We'll have an opportunity to do our ritual soon. This last tourist boat is just leaving." His statement was confirmed by a series of loud horn blasts as the large white boat began to back out from the dock. Tahir waited for quiet. "Another boat may show up soon."

"Let's go then." Anne grabbed her pack with her water bottle and headed toward the gangplank.

They walked up a small hill, past the gardens, toward the temple, beautiful golden stones and columns at the top of the hill. A group of booths lined the road on the right, displaying the usual colorful *gallabiya* and silk scarves, the shelves full of statues and jewelry.

"This is a temple dedicated to two Neters," Tahir said. "Sobek and Horus. Sobek has the crocodile head and is probably the origin of the images of the dragon. Horus, of course, is the enlightened male, the resurrected Osiris."

"What does Sobek represent?" Anne asked.

"This you will feel for yourself."

Tahir bought tickets at the booth, and they walked into the temple in silence, down the hypostyle hall, past columns with beautiful reliefs of the Neters. This was becoming familiar to Anne, the silent procession to what Tahir called the Holy of Holies, the power spot always toward the back of the temple. Once they were there, rather than forming a circle, Tahir gestured for Anne to stand inside a nook. He positioned her precisely facing east, then chanted a short phrase. At the end of this, he drew a symbol over her third eye and said rather severely, "Do not be afraid."

Anne detected a hint of laughter in the green eyes above his poker face. He led her to an opening in the ground and gestured for her to enter.

"I'm supposed to crawl down there?" Anne asked.

He shushed her and pointed again.

Well, what could happen? She had already been attacked and almost abducted by two men, her room had been searched, and she was in love with the wrong man.

She crawled down through the opening and found herself in a tight tunnel. On her hands and knees, she crawled forward, trying not to stir up too much dust. As she moved, she became intensely aware of her spine, the movement of her arms and legs, the rhythm of her crawling. She imagined she had a tail, small crooked legs, and an enormous mouth. Just as she was beginning to enjoy herself, a huge fist of energy smashed into her back, almost flattening her, lighting her solar plexus on fire. The energy ran up her vertebrae with a rush of exhilaration. Anne yelled as the energy crashed out the top of her head. Then she began to crawl rapidly, exulting in the movement, in the energy braiding itself into her own. Ahead, a light indicated a hole in the tunnel. Anne crawled out and found herself only ten feet away from the original opening. She lay down in the dust and laughed.

Soon Arnold crawled out, then Michael who sat beside her with a bemused look on his face. Anne couldn't stop laughing.

"So much for fear," commented Michael, looking wryly up at Tahir.

Michael stood and offered Anne a hand up. Arnold stepped forward, but she took Michael's hand. She pulled herself to her feet, aware of the strength of his grasp. She looked into Michael's brown eyes, lit with amusement. She felt a rush of pure lust. Yielding to her impulse, before Arnold had time to react, she pulled Michael to her and kissed him hard on the mouth. Then she pulled away and said fiercely, "If you betray me, I'll kill you."

* * *

MICHAEL WALKED BESIDE Anne toward the temple of Edfu in the light of a full moon, the perfect romantic situation under ordinary circumstances. But these were far from ordinary circumstances. Arnold strode right behind them, watching Michael's every move. Michael studiously ignored him. He watched Anne, trying to understand her shifting moods.

She had told Tahir the temples were certainly beautiful, but she wondered what any of this had to do with the crystals and opening the Hall of Records. He had repeated that the sites formed an energetic combination lock, opening layers of consciousness as they moved down the Nile toward Giza. Anne had nodded, trying to be patient.

Michael knew the process they were involved in was much more than a vacation. They were undergoing a series of powerful initiations with a man trained in the oldest spiritual system in the world. Michael was certain that in the past students had prepared for months, perhaps years, before going through this work. And they'd had much more intellectual training, the benefit of a functioning metaphysical system. He and Anne, on the other hand, were hitting these temples one per day.

The pressure of this kind of spiritual work sometimes created irritation, prying out deeply buried emotions and exposing them to the light. Plus the planets were moving into the star alignment. He could feel it beginning.

They were being purified at a rate neither of them had ever experienced. She'd told him she had meditated all her life, but that was different from the concentrated work he'd done. She must be feeling the strain even more than he, and he was definitely off his game. To top it off, someone had tried to abduct her. Still, he couldn't help feeling sad at the doubt he now saw in her eyes. He thought they'd connected in New York when they'd both had that flash of the life in Egypt.

Tahir had gotten permission to visit the temple late at night so they could be alone. It seemed some of the guardians at the sites were members of his order and held him in high esteem. Michael wished he knew the subtleties of this mystery school, but being initiated by Tahir was a high enough honor. The vendors' booths near the temple were all closed and, instead of the mad dash from the docks by too many carriages drawn by variously treated horses, they'd had Michael's driver take them.

The moonlight drenched the columned walkway surrounding the courtyard. Michael could almost see through the veil of time to the past when priests had walked over these limestone floors in flowing robes, faithfully observing the ceremonies of the yearly cycle. Tahir walked past the stone statue of Horus as the falcon, down the middle of the temple, then turned to the right. They followed in the silent darkness, flashlights guiding them. Tahir went through a small hallway, then up a few stairs into a side room. He stopped and pointed to the ceiling. Michael turned his flashlight up and a spectacular painting of Nut shone down at them, her hands and feet on the Earth, her back forming the sky.

"This is a temple dedicated to Horus. Kom Ombo is dedicated to both Sobek and Horus. It harmonizes the animal and spiritual man. The temple we are in now is a calendar," Tahir explained. "Look at Nut, the sky mother, you remember?"

Anne stared up, her mouth slightly open, awed by the painting.

"You see around her head the paint is light blue, representing daylight. On the other side, the paint is dark blue and dotted by gold stars. Night. Now look at the barges beneath her. How many?"

Anne and Michael squinted up at the ceiling, counting. "Twelve," they said together.

"Yes, the Egyptian calendar had twelve months of thirty days. Then there was a five-day festival, days out of time, so to speak. There are thirteen major chambers in this temple, twelve for the months and another for the festival days." He turned and walked down the stairs, back into the temple. They passed empty rooms.

Tahir stopped near the back. "There is also a room for the Neter on his wooden barge. During the festival, the high priest of Edfu traveled downriver to the high priestess of Hathor in Dendara. Their sexual alchemy brought the rains and the flooding of the Nile on which all life depended. During the dynastic times, she came to him. Everything was reversed."

Something stirred in Michael's memory, Anne with dark hair stretched out on an altar, but Tahir was still talking.

"This ritual started in early dynastic times. In the old days, every man and woman when they came together embodied these Neters."

He turned. "In the front of the temple is another chamber for the healers. There you will find ancient remedies inscribed on the wall."

"Do people still make them?" Michael asked.

"Some do," Tahir answered.

They walked in silence back to the Holy of Holies and Tahir gestured for them to sit against the tall altar stone. Michael closed his eyes and was immediately light-headed. Tahir began to chant, and Michael felt his astral body stir. As the chant continued, he lifted out of his physical body and flew above the temple. Below him lay the town, a tapestry of tiny stars against the dark. In this dimension, the temple was lit with a brilliant white light. He looked to the south and saw through the distance more points of light. Behind him he sensed still more, a string of chakras on the flowing spine of light that was the Nile.

Tahir's voice was suddenly back in his ear and Michael opened his physical eyes to see Anne's slender form sitting cross-legged, her palms turned upward on her knees, her eyes closed earnestly, a slight wrinkle of concentration between her brows. Michael felt a rush of tenderness for her. He'd have to remind her not to try so hard, to just allow things to unfurl naturally. He could sense the strength of her psychic talent, the lifetimes of spiritual work she'd done. She was an adept, even though she was worried about how slowly her talents were unfolding now. From his perspective, she was developing at lightning speed. He thought back to what he'd just seen, the series of lights glowing next to the flowing luminosity of the Nile. He would share this vision with Anne. Perhaps it would reassure her.

She opened her eyes and saw him looking at her. She frowned.

Michael sighed. When would these Le Clairs realize he was not the enemy?

"This temple is usually seen as the cyclical calendar of the year, but there is another calendar that is connected to our mission."

Anne nodded eagerly.

Michael watched her out of the corner of his eye.

"Let's go back to Nut."

They scrambled to their feet and walked back to the small room that held the magnificent mural. Michael switched on his flashlight again and the gold gleamed rich in the beam of light.

"Every day Nut gives birth to the sun in the morning. This is why her head is always in the west, her feet in the east. In this phase, the sun is called Kheper, the scarab beetle that pushes its ball of dung. We are born with all that we need to survive. The sun travels through the sky on the body of the Great Mother . . ." He reached for Michael's flashlight and shone it on the navel. ". . . here. This is the adolescent stage of the sun called Ra, represented by the ram." He pointed his index fingers from his forehead to imitate horns. "Ra is called the stubborn, because he thinks he knows something, like my teenage sons." Tahir rolled his eyes. "Then the sun travels to her heart. Here he is called Oon, the Wise. He is starting to know something now." Tahir chuckled.

"In the last stage of the day, the sun travels to her throat. Here he is called Aten, the Wiser. In Aten, the sun is in its full flowering. The day is complete, all is accomplished. But . . ." He raised his eyebrow dramatically. ". . . then Nut swallows the sun." He shone the beam of light on her mouth and, indeed, there was the sun in the process of being eaten. "This is called Amen. The sun travels through the body of Nut to be reborn in the morning, but outside all is dark.

"This process not only describes the cycle of the day, it also describes the cycle of a man's life—or a woman's," he said, glancing at Anne. "We are born, we think we know something, then we learn. We go into the west and travel in a place hidden from this world. Perhaps we are reborn."

"So the Khemitians believed in reincarnation," Anne said.

"There is no death." Tahir handed the flashlight back to Michael and raised his index finger. "This cycle also applies to a much larger circle the Earth travels through. Human civilization goes through phases of greater and lesser knowledge. In the Awakening, the light dawns and human consciousness begins to grow from Kheper into Ra and then Oon. It flowers in full enlightenment during the time of Aten. Aten is always followed by a time of darkness, a night of human ignorance in which everything is reversed. Violence and greed rule."

"Ah," Michael said.

Tahir nodded. "We are living in the time of Amen, the time of darkness. But it is time for the dawn."

"My grandmother said something like this," Anne said. "She said it was the end of a twenty-six-thousand-year cycle, only the Vedas say it's much longer. How long does Amen last?"

"However long it is, it is long enough." Tahir waved his hands as if he would have nothing to do with counting days or years. "All the wise ones know the sun is being reborn." He reached out and grasped both their hands. "This, my friends, is our task. It is time for the Awakening. It is time to revive the great temples of Khemit. When the six come together in Giza in the old land of Osiris, the Earth will be opened to the light. It will be the dawn."

The three gripped hands, the warmth of a united purpose filling their hearts. Michael's eyes were moist. Surely, they would succeed. It was as inevitable as the sunrise.

At that moment, Arnold's phone rang. Michael had forgotten him completely. Arnold flipped the top up and answered. His voice faded as he walked toward the front of the temple.

The three followed him slowly, savoring the harmony that had been restored among them. When they went outside, they found Arnold sitting in front of the granite statue of Horus, the Falcon. "Michael," he called.

Michael stiffened. "What is it now?"

"That was Abernathy. You've been cleared. You can move your things onto the boat."

19

Long after midnight, the captain set sail for the locks at Esna. Anne and Michael sat up on deck watching the banks of the Nile slide by in the light of the full moon, finally alone.

They talked companionably for a long while, avoiding serious topics, shy now that the barrier between them had been lifted. Around half past two, Anne couldn't contain her yawns any longer. "I guess I should get to sleep. Tahir says we'll reach Luxor midmorning, if we get through the locks immediately."

"What new adventures does he have planned for us?"

"He said something about searching for instructions in the Hathor temple. Time for bed. See you in the morning."

* * *

ANNE WOKE LATE. She pushed back the cabin curtain and looked out. They were approaching a large town. When she arrived in the galley, Tahir and Michael were in their familiar position, heads together, talking. The cook handed her a heaping plate and a cup of tea. She sat at the counter next to Michael.

"Welcome to Luxor," Tahir said. "As soon as we dock, I want to head to Abydos. It's a bit of a drive."

"Another initiation?" Anne asked.

"Osiris," Tahir answered, "and then Dendara, into the crypts. It will be a long day."

They docked at the end of a queue of boats, the yacht dwarfed by the cruise ships. Once the gangplank was stretched to the next boat, they walked up and through a series of ships, each brimming with tourists. Arnold and Bob each took one of Anne's elbows and escorted her through the crowd.

"They're just as interested in Michael and Tahir," Anne whispered to Arnold.

"Dr. Abernathy won't skin my hide if *they* get hurt."

"I will," Anne said sweetly.

Tahir had rented a van to accommodate them all. Even so, the ride was long and dusty, but Tahir entertained them by answering questions. Most of it was about the finer points of Egyptology and the many mistakes of academics. Anne listened with one ear and watched the countryside unfold—the plots of crops, date palm fields, children riding donkeys. Tahir explained how the Khemitians hadn't told the Greeks the truth about many things because the Greeks were conquerors, trespassers in their land. The same was true in so many other places. Then he explained how the hieroglyphs still weren't interpreted correctly.

"Wait a minute," Anne interjected. "What about the Rosetta Stone?"

"Even that is based on the Greek. The Rosetta Stone contained three languages—hieroglyphic, demotic, and Greek. So Champollion's translation was still based on the Greek's understanding of the symbols," Tahir explained. "Schwaller was correct in his claim that the hieroglyphs had layers of meaning."

"Like ancient Hawaiian," Michael said.

"Exactly," Tahir said, getting ready to expound further, but they had arrived.

The van turned down a dusty street crowded with low buildings. The temple stood pristine at the end of this ramshackle street. No gaily colored booths here, just yellow brick houses, local shops, and more dust. Tahir bought tickets as usual, then led them toward the temple.

Two men sitting on the front step, dressed in long, white *gallabiyas,* stood up and opened their arms. "Tahir Nur," they shouted.

Tahir hugged and kissed the two men ceremoniously on both cheeks. They spoke together for a while, then one man said to Anne, "He is my uncle."

Anne had heard this claim at almost every temple. "So you're like George Washington?" she teased Tahir.

Tahir's forehead wrinkled.

"The father of your country."

He laughed. "Let's go."

Anne was preparing herself for the initiation, but Tahir began to talk as he went. The two guardians followed behind, listening intently. "This temple was built about six thousand years ago. The actual power spot is in the ruins to the north."

"I've been meaning to ask about the Holy of Holies," Michael said. "What ceremony was used to create the power spot?"

Tahir laughed. "Humans do not create the Holy of Holies, the Earth does." He sat down on a stone just inside the temple walls. "These sites are built around naturally occurring power places on Earth. Each spot has flowing water, natural crystal, and volcanic rocks. For thousands of years, people came to these spots to energize themselves. All could come; there were no restrictions. But as people began to fall out of consciousness, when Amen began, some tried to control these places out of fear. First, they erected a wall around them and declared that only some could come in. All the others had to stay outside the wall." He leaned over and drew a square in the sand with a dot in the middle. "But this wasn't good enough for the new priests, the Hanuti."

"Hanuti means priest?" Anne asked.

"Originally, the ones who handled the dead, but when the priests became businessmen, I apply this term to them all." Tahir paused, then said, "After the wall, they built the courtyards and pylons." He drew this in the sand. "The common people were not allowed in here either, only the 'great' Hanuti. After that, they built the walls and outer gate, and only the priests could come into the temple. The people were allowed into the courtyard on holidays, but only outside the temple." He drew a temple enclosure in the sand. "And so religion was born." He scowled. "In Aten we do not need religion. Everyone is equal. We are the same consciousness." He looked from Anne to Michael. "This is part of our work, peeling away the layers, returning the power spots to everyone." He stood and walked toward the first pylon of the temple, then stopped and pointed up. "The infamous helicopter."

"Helicopter?" Anne asked.

"Some of the New Agers think this is a helicopter," Michael explained.

Anne craned her neck to see the carvings Tahir was pointing to. They were at the very top of the column, difficult to make out. She moved her head from side to side. "I can see it."

Tahir shook his head. "But the other side is not the same. I think it's a fraud."

"But aren't you a New Ager, Tahir?" she teased.

I am a Now Ager. Now is the only time there is," he declared.

Michael shrugged at Anne when Tahir turned away. She smiled back. Apparently Michael had a different opinion about the glyphs. They followed Tahir into the temple, down the right-hand side, then into one of the rooms.

Anne stopped and gaped. Never had she seen such beautiful work. The walls gleamed with soft blues, greens, and golds. Perfectly preserved carvings of the Neters peopled the walls of each of the small rooms. Now she recognized some of the scenes. In one, Sekhmet held out her necklace to Osiris. In another, Thoth, holding two staffs topped with snakes, held an ankh to Osiris' nose while Isis held his hand.

"Stages of his life," Tahir explained, as they walked from room to room.

Next the conception of Horus was depicted, Isis hovering above the prone body of Osiris, a swallow. Horus stood behind the scene, witnessing his own begetting. Anne could imagine life here, gracious and unhurried among these beautiful, softly glowing walls.

Halfway down the south side of the temple, Tahir took another turn and walked down a long hall decorated with a carving of some sort of long barge. He made no comment, but walked out into the sun and down a slight hill. A set of stairs led down into another temple, this one like a basement to the first. They could only go so far. The floor was covered in water.

"What's this?" she asked.

"The Osireion," Tahir said. "What does it remind you of?"

Anne considered the huge blocks of granite poised atop equally large granite pillars. "Stonehenge."

Tahir nodded his approval. "Michael?"

"I always thought it looked like the Sphinx temple."

"Good," he said. "You both see more than the Egyptologists. They think this was built at the same time as that." He pointed behind him at the temple they'd left.

"Not possible," Michael declared. "I've always thought this was older."

Tahir patted Michael's shoulder affectionately. "Good boy. The architecture is completely different. This temple"—he pointed down—"is over fifty thousand years old. It has been around for almost a full cycle, just like Tefnut." He turned and put his finger to his lips. "Now we walk."

They scrambled over more sand after the old mountain goat, as they'd affectionately dubbed him. Anne's calves were aching before he reached a wall. The guardians opened the gate and they all walked to the back of another ruin. The group sat in the sand and joined hands. As Tahir chanted, Anne felt the familiar spiral of energy spread through the site, but she didn't see anything. Michael had suggested she not try so hard, so she relaxed and enjoyed the energy, trusting that the initiation was working. Her crystal, tucked safely away, tingled slightly as if to reassure her.

They walked back to the van through the crowded village, much to Arnold's chagrin. As always, the children rushed up to them, looking for gifts, and Michael gave out many pens. One little boy kept coming back for more and more. "Ah, a serious scholar," Michael teased. The boy just smiled, not understanding.

They piled back into the van and started the drive to Dendara. Anne sat snug against Michael. She closed her eyes and leaned her head back, resting. She kept seeing a bright white light. She opened her eyes, thinking the sun must be on her face, but the van had tinted windows. She closed her eyes and the glow reappeared. Suddenly, she realized it was Michael's astral body she was seeing. She relaxed against him, allowing the glow to resonate with her own energy. The drive took two hours—too fast for Anne.

The temple of Dendara stood in an even more remote site, the beautiful remains next to a few scattered houses. As soon as they arrived, a group of children ran up to the van with cat's eyes woven from colorful yarns for sale.

Tahir intervened. "When we are finished."

The children ran off toward the guardians who were approaching.

Arnold looked around. "I'm starving," he announced. "Isn't there anyplace to eat?"

Tahir went to the back of the van and pulled out a large box. "Lunch."

Michael and Arnold carried the box to the temple entrance and put it down. Anne dusted off a low stone just inside the *mamisi* and pulled out small white boxes, each containing chicken, cheese, and a roll.

"Well, at least there's cheese," Anne said to Michael as he inspected the fare. She counted. There were enough for the temple workers as well.

A hopeful dog trotted over to their picnic, his coat only patches on bare skin. Anne couldn't eat anything with those pleading brown eyes watching her, so she ended up giving him her entire lunch. The dog gobbled it up, then turned to Michael, who cheerfully gave up his piece of chicken.

"Don't give him the bones." Anne took the leg and pulled the meat and connective tissue off, feeding the dog by hand.

After their meager meal, Tahir took Michael and Anne back to the gate of the temple and pointed up. "Do you see?"

Anne studied the arch of the gate. "It's a scarab."

"Yes, but what is different?"

She squinted in the afternoon sun, studying the scarab. Suddenly, she realized she was looking at the stomach of the scarab, not its back. "It's upside down," she said.

"Exactly, and what does that mean?"

She looked at Michael, who shook his head, meaning "he asked you, not me." It came to her. "This is a place where secret teachings were kept."

"Exactly."

Tahir turned and walked back into the temple. They followed him. This time Arnold opted to wait with the guardians in the front, hoping to explore the shisha pipe one of the older children was bringing from the house, but their new four-legged friend followed them into the temple.

"We will do our initiation first, then go into the crypt." Tahir touched his finger to his lips, a flicker of excitement in his green eyes.

Anne walked behind Michael. The rooms on their right were dark beneath the stone roof. She wondered what treasures were hidden there, but Tahir didn't stop until he reached an empty room at the exact end of the temple. Here they formed a circle and, out of the soft receptive darkness, Tahir's chant rose, awakening the stillness into vibration. This time the spiral took Anne back in time.

She heard the sound of girls' laughter, the scuff of sandals on stone floors. A breeze from the west, moist with the promise of rain, lifted her now dark hair. Her vision expanded outward. Flowering trees draped their trailing limbs over the outer walls, promising fruit and perfume oil. On the north side of the temple, women walked down stone stairs into a lake, their colorful robes fluttering in the breeze like birds. From the top of a stone building, she looked out at an expanse of blue water. The sound of footsteps came from the stone steps below. Another woman emerged from the building and walked over to stand by her side. "Has he come yet?"

"There's been no sign."

The scene shifted. Now it was late at night. Listening into the darkness, she heard water dripping from oars, then a boat slide up on the shore. She ran quietly down a flight of stone steps, beneath the sacred wheel of stars, past teaching rooms, their carvings mute in the night, down more steps, then along a long corridor to the west end of the temple. She opened a small door and walked down to the river.

The dream, Anne thought, *this is the dream.* She looked up and found Michael's eyes fixed on her. With a shock, she realized he was seeing exactly what she was.

In the past, he waited by the boat, wrapped in a dark cloak. She ran into his arms.

After a minute, the man who was also Michael pulled back and looked into her face. "It's done," he whispered.

She shivered against him.

"It was necessary." He stroked her hair. "Meanwhile, you must guard these." He placed something in her hand.

Anne looked down and saw three crystal keys. "The night is always so long," she said.

"I will come again with the flood." He bent his head toward her and she kissed him good-bye. He returned to the boat.

The woman turned and reentered the temple. In the present moment, Anne turned and followed the vision. She found a hall that led to the west end of the temple. At the end of the hall, the temple guardians waited, the grate pulled back from the stairs. She climbed down into a narrow passageway and crawled through, emerging into a narrow hall-like chamber. The walls were covered with scenes and text. Anne walked forward and saw the priests, with the elongated light bulbs and a baboon, holding up daggers. She turned back and walked past Michael who had followed her until she came to a relief of Sekhmet.

She stood and looked at Michael with shining eyes. "Do you remember? You brought them to me and I hid them here."

"Yes, and now they've come back to us." He gathered her into his arms. "And you have come back to me." He kissed her lips tenderly at first, then deeper, past and present folding together into the eternal now.

When time began again, Anne realized Tahir was standing some distance away next to the opening of the crypt. She gently pulled away from Michael.

Tahir walked toward them.

Anne bent down and pressed a stone next to the floor. The stone shifted revealing a small chamber. "This is where I hid the crystals long ago when I was high priestess here. Michael brought them to me and I put them here for safekeeping."

Tahir bent down to examine the cavity.

"All three?" he asked

"Yes."

They all knelt in the sand, Anne behind Michael, allowing the trained archeologists room to work. She peered anxiously over his shoulder.

"It looks like there's a jar here." Michael's voice was muffled. "It's large enough to hold a scroll." He reached into his backpack and pulled out a pair of latex gloves. He turned to her. "Do you have anything like a soft brush in your pack?"

"Only a hairbrush."

"Are the bristles plastic?"

"No, I think they're natural."

"Good, would you sacrifice it for the cause?"

Anne promptly dug her brush out of her pack and handed it to Michael, who painstakingly cleared sand from the jar. When at last the jar was free of the sand, he picked it up and inch by inch removed it from the hollow. He looked around. "What is the cleanest wrapping material?"

"We are taking it?" Tahir asked.

"We need a controlled environment to open this jar. By the looks of it, it's at least two thousand years old and the scroll, if there is one, could be even older. It could disintegrate immediately if there is a breath of wind. The humidity should be carefully controlled. We really need a lab, but then we couldn't keep the contents secret."

"I'll have to get permission from the keepers here."

"I thought you were the head of your order."

Tahir shook his head. "It doesn't work that way. These people are the descendants of the people who built this temple and made these scrolls. We must have their permission to remove anything."

Michael nodded. "You're right, of course."

"I will go for them now." Tahir stood and walked back to the opening, then squeezed through.

Michael sat back on his heels, looking at the jar in his hands.

Anne pulled a sweater from her pack. "Will this do?"

"It will cushion it somewhat."

"Is there anything else in there?" Anne asked.

Michael turned back to the small chamber and started to brush the sand back grains at a time. On the third sweep, he knocked against something.

Anne pressed forward, her heart pounding.

Slowly, taking what seemed to Anne to be an exorbitant amount of care, he pulled out a granite tablet.

"Excellent," Michael breathed.

"What's on it?"

"I can't really see, but if the scroll doesn't hold up, this should help us."

Michael handed the tablet to Anne, then continued brushing back the sand. After ten minutes, he was satisfied the hollow was empty.

By this time, Anne could hear the guardians talking amongst themselves, then footsteps sounded on the stone steps. Soon three temple guardians were crowded together with them in the narrow passageway.

Michael held out the granite tablet for their inspection.

Anne pointed to her rolled sweater holding the jar as Tahir talked animatedly. "They have given permission for us to take the jar and tablet. They understand our mission. I promised to return them when we have finished."

"Of course," Michael said.

"And to make a copy of the scroll if we can."

Again Michael agreed.

"Let's get back to the boat then," Tahir said.

On the ride back, Tahir wrapped the granite slab in a piece of soft cloth and decisively put it away. "We'll wait until we can pay proper attention."

The ride seemed to last forever. Anne asked questions, but Tahir's answers were monosyllabic. When they arrived at the dock in Luxor, they made their way as quickly as possible to the boat. Anne cleared a table in the common sitting area. Michael carefully placed the jar on it and Tahir took out the granite tablet.

"Close all the windows," Michael directed Arnold, who for once obeyed him. "Now we'll see what condition this scroll is in." He took a penknife and ran it gently around the lip of the brown earthenware jar. Sand fell out. "Good, it's fairly clean." Then he began slowly prying the top off. After a few turns, he looked up at Anne. "In my suitcase I have a small jar of liquid. It's got a museum label. Could you get it?"

Anne started to get up, but Bob was ahead of her. "I'll get it," he called over his shoulder.

Michael continued to turn the lid, then stopped again. "It's stuck."

Bob returned carrying a small vial, which he handed over to Michael.

"Thank you." Michael looked around. "A cloth. I need a strip of cotton."

Anne ran to her room and came back with the remnants of her old T-shirt. "Will this do?"

"Excellent." Michael wet the cotton with the liquid, then moistened the exposed area under the lid. He waited a few minutes, and then tried the lid again. It started to move.

"How can you stand this?" Anne burst out.

Michael smiled. "Archaeology requires nerves of steel." Finally, he raised the lid. "Pray," he said.

They leaned closer.

"Don't breathe on it."

They obediently sat back.

He looked inside the jar and his shoulders dropped.

"What?" Anne cried.

Michael spread clean brown paper on the table, then tilted the jar, pouring out dust and small fragments of parchment. Michael carefully sifted through the fragments using soft-tipped tweezers. After a full five minutes, he sat back, eyes closed. "Nothing."

"Then we're lost," Anne said.

"It is a disappointment, but it is not the end. This is older still." Tahir unwrapped the granite tablet and started to pore over the hieroglyphs. After just a few seconds, he said, "Here is the *djed* pillar, the symbol for Michael's crystal."

Anne saw a forked staff topped with what looked like a jackal's head.

"But mine is topped with the Star of David," Michael objected.

"Originally, it must have been the *djed,* the backbone of Osiris," Tahir said. "Later they put the symbol for the sacred formation the six keys must form to open the site."

"Formation?" Anne asked. "You mean we stand in a star shape?"

Tahir nodded, then went back to his study. In a few minutes, a smile lit his face. "The ankh is on the opposite side at the top. And here's the lotus at the bottom." Tahir's voice crackled with excitement. "The first triangle."

"Okay," Anne said, "yours has the ankh, but mine is topped with the fleur-de-lis."

"Which was originally the lotus. Sekhmet carries the lotus staff," Tahir explained.

"What does it represent?" Anne asked.

"The opening of consciousness," he said, still squinting at the tablet.

"I thought the *djed* pillar was traditionally associated with the *was* and the ankh," Michael said.

Tahir nodded, still not taking his eyes off the granite. "Here is the *was.*" He pointed to a glyph below the *djed.*

"I've seen many Neters carrying the *was,*" Michael said.

"What is a *was?*" Anne asked.

"A scepter with the head of Set. It symbolizes mastery over duality," Tahir explained. "And here is Seshat, across from it." His forehead wrinkled.

"Seshat?" Michael leaned over to see for himself.

"You didn't expect that? What is Seshat?" Anne asked.

"Who," Michael corrected her. "Seshat is the Neter of form."

"I thought that was Khnum," Anne said.

"Khnum forms the human body," Tahir answered. "Seshat takes the sound of her consort, Djehuti, and reflects to him the form those sounds create."

Anne looked from Tahir to Michael, completely lost. "We haven't gone to those temples," she said. "Does this mean the ceremony won't work?"

Tahir didn't answer, but sat staring at the granite, lost in thought.

"I'll explain in a minute," Michael whispered to her.

Silence descended on the group. Michael watched Tahir intently.

Finally, Tahir shouted, "I've found it. *Nefer*. The glyph completing the second triangle is *Nefer,* harmony." He clapped his hands together.

Anne saw an oval with a long cross stuck in the top.

"*Nefer?*" Now it was Michael's turn to frown. "Doesn't that mean 'beautiful' or 'good'?"

Tahir shook his head. "Again the Greeks. *Nefer* means 'harmony.' You see . . ." He gestured for Anne to come closer. "In this case, the was represents Djehuti."

"Djehuti is better known as Thoth, the one who brought the symbols. He's often depicted carrying a scribe's tool," Michael said.

Again Tahir shook his head. "But this is later. Sound comes before symbol. Djehuti creates the sacred sounds."

"Oh." Anne was beginning to see. "And Seshat, the feminine, gives them shape."

"Exactly!" Tahir grabbed her arm in his excitement. "The sound creates the form, and the two together . . ." He raised his hands into the air. ". . . harmony, creation of balance."

Michael was still frowning.

"Look," Tahir said, "look at the glyph. It represents the lungs and larynx. The source of the sacred sounds in humans."

"Oh, my," Michael said.

"Sound opens the Hall," Tahir said. He turned back to the piece of granite. "Now, what are these?" Around the original six symbols stood the forms of Neters. "Sekhmet, Ptah, Isis. These are the principals supervising our triangle."

Anne rocked back and forth, trying to contain her excitement.

"Horus?" Tahir held the slab directly under the light. "It is rubbed off. "Hathor definitely, so it is likely Horus. And the last is gone completely."

"Oh, no," Anne said.

But Tahir was smiling. "We have discovered the directions for forming the key. It is a great triumph. The rest will take care of itself."

20

---

*T*homas paced back and forth in front of a warm fire in the library of the Rosicrucian Order's retreat center in Freiburg, Germany.

"The Vatican had the crystal and now it doesn't. Do you think the crystal might have changed hands during the war?"

Franz Maier, the archivist, sat back in his armchair. "That is a distinct possibility. There is someone we can check with. Gustav Kepler knows the Third Reich's metaphysical archives better than anyone. I'll call him."

Thomas let out a sigh. "You don't know how grateful I am, Franz. It's vital we bring all the crystals to Egypt by February first. If we don't find all the crystals, the world will remain in darkness for thousands of years."

"I don't know about you, but I've had enough of it. I'm ready for the promised dawn," Franz said. His urbane tone stopped Thomas in his tracks.

"I'm taking this too seriously, am I?"

"It's as serious as, how do you Americans say, a heart attack?"

"Yes," Thomas said.

"But you are well trained, my friend. You must not focus on defeat."

Thomas squared his shoulders. "Point well taken."

Franz stood. "Our library is at your disposal, as are all the considerable resources of our order."

Thomas felt as if a weight had been lifted from his shoulders. "Thank you, my friend."

"I'll go make that call." Franz left the library, closing the door softly behind him.

Thomas walked over to a desk by the window and placed his index finger on the security reader. It scanned his print. Such state-of-the-art technology seemed anachronistic in this centuries-old castle, but the place had been tastefully renovated. He was grateful for the modern plumbing.

Within seconds, the computer granted him access to the archives and he typed in his first search term. In a flicker of light, a list of all the scanned documents containing the word popped up on the screen. Thomas clicked the first and started to read. He spent the greater part of the morning in this manner. Not once did his fingers touch the fragile scrolls or handwritten books of the collection.

He found the history of the Rosicrucians' crystal, the one Michael Levy carried, along with several accounts of the two keys guarded by the Templars. The story of the torture and murder of Jacques de Molay made for gruesome reading, but his suspicions were confirmed. The order had decided to leave some artifacts for the church to confiscate, hoping they wouldn't realize the bulk of the Templar treasure had already been taken to Scotland. He found no mention of the stone after its capture.

Around eleven, Thomas sat before the computer screen, but stared out at the bare trees in the park beyond the windows.

"Gustav can see us tonight."

Thomas looked up from his reverie, surprised he hadn't heard Franz approach. "Excellent. Did he say anything?"

"I didn't want to broach the subject on the phone, but he knows our visit concerns the Nazi archives. Any luck?"

"My suspicions about why the order allowed the church to take the crystal were right," he said. "Otherwise, nothing."

"Too bad, but we both suspected this would be the case. I was going for my daily constitutional and wondered if you'd care to join me."

Within five minutes, the two men were walking along a paved path that took them through the estate's formal garden. The only green spots were the box hedges and evergreen trees in the distance. They followed the path through an arched gate into an extensive herb garden, now a series of brown beds marked with black metal signs carrying the names of various plants.

Thomas broached a new topic. "I've heard now from two sources about a legend concerning another of the keys."

"Yes?" Franz tucked his nose under his muffler for a moment to warm up.

"It concerns Akhenaten's mother, Tiye. The story goes that one of Tiye's relatives took the key to wisdom back to the mountains when he left Amarna after Akhenaten's death."

"Sounds vague."

"So many of the clues concerning the keys are vague. My own family legend only states that the crystal will be used to restore the flow. What flow, how, and where have remained a mystery for centuries. We've just now confirmed the place is Egypt, probably the Giza plateau, and the time is in approximately two weeks."

"'The key to wisdom,'" Franz repeated. "'Restore the flow.' Tantalizing phrases. Do you think the mountains refer to the Himalayas?"

"I believe so. The best evidence suggests Amenhotep, Son of Hapi, who was one of Ahkenaten's teachers, came from the north of India or perhaps Tibet."

"If it's Tibet, we may have difficulty. The Chinese have destroyed many temples along with their libraries. Scores of monks have been murdered. The sect with the information you're looking for may be almost gone."

"You're right. I just hope the cosmic forces will lead me to the right person."

"We have a few houses in that area. We'll contact them and see if they have any information."

Thomas stopped and turned to Franz. "Thank you, my brother. Without your help . . ." He turned his palms up.

"We're committed to the same fight. It is my deep honor to assist the bloodline."

"As it is my duty to serve," Thomas replied.

* * *

THAT SAME MORNING in Cairo, Karl Mueller stood outside Mr. Spender's door, bracing himself. Spender had ordered him to secure a second crystal for another test and he'd failed. So far. He'd badly underestimated the Le Clair security team. Even Anne, as it turned out, could hold her own, at least against the locals he'd hired. Another miscalculation. He thought the local team would escape Arnold's notice. That part had worked. As for the rest, they'd botched the job. Those men would never work for him again. Or anyone else, for that matter. Next time he'd take care of the bitch himself.

Mueller took a deep breath and pushed the door open. Spender glanced at him out of the corner of his eye, but didn't stop what he was doing. A bad sign. General Ahmed sat in one of the chairs in front of Spender's desk. Mueller stood and waited for his boss to deign to notice him.

After several minutes, Spender said, "Take a seat."

Mueller obeyed instantly. Attitude was for amateurs.

"I've invested a good deal of money in your training, Mr. Mueller. However, we do have extensive resources at our command. Can you tell me why I should keep you alive?"

"The mission has experienced setbacks," Mueller began.

"Setbacks are one thing. Failure is quite another." Spender's voice was flat. "I expect a precise report."

"Yes, sir." Mueller tightened his stomach and began again. "I failed to retrieve a second crystal, as instructed. After searching the rooms of all the subjects, it was determined they were carrying them on their persons."

Spender took a breath.

Anticipating his objection, Mueller continued. "They did not put them in the hotel safe or rent any boxes in a bank. Nor did they leave them in Cairo. I'm certain of that."

Spender took out a cigar and put the tip in the cutter, then looked up.

"The Le Clair security team is top-flight, so I subcontracted with a local terrorist cell to take a crystal."

Spender cut the tip of the cigar and smiled. His eyes remained cold.

"Our intel did not indicate that Anne Le Clair had any martial arts training. As it turned out, she was skilled enough to slow the team down and her security reached her in time."

Spender lit his cigar. The click of the lighter closing sounded loud in Mueller's ears. Spender took a leisurely puff, then took the cigar out of his mouth and admired it under the light. He looked up and said, "Go on."

"Given this new information, the plan is to take the Jew's stone. He returns tonight."

"What do you think, Ahmed?"

"Let's try with two crystals this time," the general said.

"I agree," Spender said. "Swap Marchant's stone with our duplicate again. Perhaps the crystal is coded to its Keeper in some way. Two that we know of have been passed down in families. It could be the DNA has some effect."

"This may be," Ahmed said, "but what about Marchant's stone? Didn't his family recently acquire it?"

"The family had ancestors who were Templars. The father said he was reclaiming a family heirloom."

Ahmed nodded.

Spender turned to Mueller. "Get a DNA sample from both."

"That's already taken care of, sir."

Spender raised an eyebrow in inquiry.

"I took samples from Marchant when we had dinner together."

"Good. And Levy?"

"I can get a sample when I steal his crystal."

"I don't have to tell you this is your last chance, do I?" Spender crushed the expensive cigar in the ashtray on his desk.

"No sir." Mueller stood, and his body automatically snapped to attention. "Will that be all, sir?"

Spender regarded him like a snake watches a frog. "For now."

* * *

"THIS MORNING we finish our initiations in the south," Tahir said. "We fly back to Cairo this evening."

Anne squinted at him over the rim of her coffee cup. They'd stayed up almost all night deciphering the granite tablet. Around three o'clock, Tahir had suggested they get a few hours' sleep. He'd roused them shortly after dawn, looking calm and rested. She was beginning to believe that Egyptians didn't need sleep.

She climbed into the cruise boat they were docked next to, by now an expert at negotiating the ramps. Michael ran up behind her and together they hurried through the lobbies of several more ships, their crowds of tourists just eating breakfast. When Anne and Michael reached the dock, they ran up the stone steps to street level. Anne heard Arnold calling her name, but she didn't look back. On the street, Michael grabbed the first carriage, an older two-seater pulled by a contented chestnut. They drove off, relishing their rebellion.

Anne snuggled under Michael's arm and half-listened to his sightseeing commentary.

They arrived at Karnak too quickly. Michael paid the driver; then they walked arm in arm down to the temple gates and waited like commoners of old. Five minutes later, Arnold and Tahir arrived in another carriage, and Arnold stalked up to Anne, frowning deeply.

"What was that stunt all about? Just because Michael has been cleared doesn't mean you can go gallivanting off alone with him. You are still in danger."

Anne was grateful when Tahir showed up brandishing their tickets. "We shall approach the Holy of Holies in silence," he said and walked off, effectively silencing Arnold.

The group followed behind him like a row of ducklings.

Anne gazed up at the obelisks rising behind the rows of columns, all deeply engraved with various Neters she couldn't make out yet. After the psychic experience she'd had in Dendara yesterday, she didn't expect much from today's initiation. Her usual pattern was a few days of quiet. She'd be lucky if she even felt the spiral of energy that usually answered Tahir's chant.

Tahir veered off toward the left, walking across a span of sand and rock. She glanced down to be careful of her footing, and when she raised her eyes again she saw a woman walking toward her from the temple, dressed in long flowing robes and carrying a basket of flowers.

"Welcome home," the woman said.

Anne looked into the woman's face and recognized—herself.

Suddenly, the temple walls blossomed with color, the trees leafed in an instant, and the sand turned green beneath her now sandaled feet. Around a corner, the scent of flowers from a verdant garden filled the air. Water splashed in a fountain and a woman sitting on a bench looked up at her and smiled. Their group of four in the present was joined by a long procession of men and women in the past, all carrying baskets overflowing with red, yellow, pink, and blue blossoms, all chanting in a complex harmony that pebbled Anne's flesh. Brilliantly colored birds flew among them and perched in the trees, adding their song. The chant was but one part of the deep harmony, the complete openness of one heart to another, the perfect accord of that community of many that was one.

Tears flowed unchecked down Anne's face as she walked in both times, reliving the age when they had all lived in full consciousness, open to the singing birds, the shining faces of the flowers, the majestic river slowly winding through the land, the Sun beaming down on his Earth, the galaxies swinging in great spirals, and all life, here and in the higher frequencies, creating a great symphony of oneness.

Now they all made their way through a corridor formed by stone columns, a soft dun in the present-day sun, leaping with color in the past. They approached a sanctuary. Anne passed the flat, dusty altar outside the shrine, went through the entry room and into the chamber on the right. There she stood beneath a pinprick in the limestone ceiling illuminating the face of the Neter Sekhmet. But Anne did not see the statue. She saw the Neter herself, gazing down through layers of space and time, a look of deep compassion on her face.

Anne's knees buckled. She fell at the great one's feet and wept. From her poured all the pain of separation she'd ever felt in this life. The perfect peace of the past filled her and covered the cuts and bruises like a golden unguent, healing in an instant all the aches, all the fears, all the yearnings for what she could never name until now.

Stand up, dear one. Sekhmet's voice was a golden bell in her mind.

Anne rose.

Let me bless the key.

She took the necklace from its hiding place and laid it on the flat top of the lotus staff that ended just under the goddess's breasts, in the fierce heart of the great lioness.

Take my hands.

Anne placed her flesh hands over the stone hands of the Neter and closed her eyes. From somewhere far above, an enormous river of light flooded the chamber. Anne felt as if she were standing in a column of honey, thick and golden, vibrating with the voices of a thousand bees.

When time began again, Sekhmet spoke her blessing: *Go and awaken the world.*

Anne took her crystal and stepped back, only now seeing the dark granite statue with the lioness face topped by the solar disk. She turned and noticed Tahir and Michael standing near the back wall of the chamber, both their faces wet with tears. Anne knew what to do next. She walked up and escorted Michael to the feet of the Neter, then withdrew. Michael placed his key in the same niche and Anne felt the portal open again. She closed her eyes and watched the great lioness bless her son. Then Tahir took his place and again the golden radiance filled the chamber.

When Tahir finally stepped away from the statue, Anne turned and walked back through the entry room into a second chamber on the left of the shrine. In the past, a gold statue stood there, cloaked in something. She looked closer and saw the figure was wrapped in his own wings. Individual, exquisitely carved feathers gleamed under the pinprick of light. In the present, the room was cold and empty, filled only with dust.

"Where is he?" Anne turned to Tahir.

"He is gone now. The Christians or the Muslims"—he shrugged as if it didn't matter which—"destroyed the statue long ago."

"Ptah?" Michael asked.

Tahir nodded. "Pater to the Romans, our father. And Sekhmet, the Power."

Anne knew she was ready.

* * *

THAT EVENING as Anne, Michael, and Tahir boarded a plane for Cairo, Thomas and Franz sat in the comfortable home of Gustav Kepler. Gustav was a much older man than Thomas had expected, well into his nineties. He wore a velvet smoking jacket. The skin on his hands was almost transparent with age, as thin as onionskin paper, but he still had a full head of wispy white hair that framed his face in a wild cloud reminiscent of Einstein. Gustav was attended by a granddaughter who tucked a blanket around his legs. He bore the fuss with dignity. She placed a bell beside the old man, said something to him in German, and left.

When the door clicked shut, Franz leaned forward slightly and spoke loudly. "Gustav, let me introduce Thomas Le Clair from the American family."

Thomas took the old man's hand. "It is an honor to meet you, sir."

"The honor is mine, Mr. Le Clair." Gustav's voice was worn with years of use, but his eyes were bright. "It is a rare pleasure to serve the bloodline."

Thomas had a fleeting wish for the anonymity he enjoyed at home. "We all serve the light, sir. Please, call me Thomas."

"Please, please, sit down." Gustav gestured toward a sofa and another armchair forming a semicircle in front of the fire his granddaughter had settled him next to.

Thomas sat across from Gustav and Franz settled on the sofa.

"How may I help you?" Gustav asked.

Franz nodded for Thomas to take the lead.

"Franz tells me that you're an expert on the metaphysical holdings of the SS."

Gustav studied Thomas for a long moment. "You want to know, but are too polite to ask, if I was a member of the SS."

Thomas felt his cheeks growing warm. "I apologize for not controlling my thoughts more carefully."

Gustav dismissed Thomas's apology with a wave of his hand. "It is a legitimate question. The SS was a group of the blackest magicians the world has ever seen." He sat back in his chair. "I was born in Munich and, just after the first war, I became involved in a group exploring metaphysics. I was a teenager. Himmler, who was older than I, recognized my talent."

"You knew Himmler personally?"

"Oh, yes," Gustav said. "I was his protégé for about a year, but as I progressed, I began to realize my mentor lacked a proper understanding of the work, so I left the group and looked elsewhere for teachers. Several years later, I became a Rosicrucian."

"How fortunate you escaped."

Gustav nodded. "Yes, I am grateful I had the courage to break from him. But . . ." He held up a finger. ". . . when the Thule Group gained political influence, a decision was taken to place an agent in their midst. I was the perfect candidate."

"That must have been difficult."

"It was only through divine protection that I was able to complete my task."

"So you approached Himmler?"

Gustav's eyes had a look of sadness. "My task was to convince Himmler I'd had a change of heart. And I was able to do so. He never let me into the heart of the group, thank God. Imagine what I would have been forced to participate in. I'm still burdened by the thought of how many I might have saved."

"Your work was invaluable in bringing down the Third Reich," Franz said in a strong voice. "We can only be grateful that you were willing to pay the price."

Gustav reached over and pressed Franz's hand, then continued. "I helped organize the Thule Group's records and I smuggled out a copy. Those have been left with me, but on my death will go to the order."

Franz nodded. "We are grateful."

Gustav turned to Thomas, "So I ask again, how may I help you?"

"I am searching for an artifact, a crystal necklace once in the possession of the Templars but sacrificed on Black Friday to the church. We've determined the necklace is no longer in the possession of the Vatican."

"And you want to know if the Reich took it?"

"Exactly." Thomas settled back in his chair.

"This necklace, can you describe it?"

"I've never seen it myself, but records say it is a small point, maybe three inches long, topped with a was design worked in gold."

Gustav's eyes widened. "A *was* design?"

"Yes, the crystal was originally from Egypt and we think the original design it bore has been continued."

"I know this necklace."

"Yes?" Thomas sat forward eagerly.

"Indeed. According to the archives, Himmler had it for some time. I always wondered why he bothered with it. I never found any information about its virtues."

"It is one of a set of six crystals. One, topped with a fleur-de-lis, has been entrusted to my own family. Our legend tells us it is to be used to 'restore the flow.'"

Gustav sat forward, his eyes bright again.

"The second is held by a Levy."

"Ah, the priesthood," Gustav breathed.

"We believe so. I'm told it's topped by a Star of David. A third never left Egypt. I don't know its emblem. I haven't been able to locate the other three, but written records say the Vatican held one. Another legend suggests that a fifth crystal, called the 'key to wisdom,' was taken to the East by one of Tiye's relatives. The sixth seems completely lost."

"An intriguing story," Gustav said. "I appreciate your trust. Have you been able to find more about what these crystals do?"

Thomas crossed his legs. "My family has always believed they form a key to something that has been locked away, hidden at the setting of the sun to be brought to light with the dawn."

"You think the time is now?"

"Astrological evidence suggests the time is February first."

Yes?" Gustav sat back, a frown on his face. "A new age is upon us, but who can say how long the transition will take. Greed and violence have not abated. Do you not fear whatever you uncover will fall into the wrong hands? The Reich only sailed across the ocean."

"You are right, sir. Dark magicians are still among us, and yet the signs have been frequent. I feel a deep urgency to find the other stones. We believe these keys are a vital part of restoring the light. We fear if we do not restore the flow, the Earth may remain in darkness for an entire cycle."

The three fell silent, the only sound the crackling of burning wood. Thomas shifted in his chair. A log on the fire popped.

Finally, Gustav spoke. "This we must prevent." He pulled a key from the pocket of his jacket and pointed to a large desk on the other side of the room. "The bottom drawer on the left."

Franz found a drawer full of files.

"The fourth one back."

Franz retrieved the file and gave it to Gustav, who put on a thick pair of reading glasses and began to go through the papers.

Thomas sat forward and took a deep breath.

Finally, the old man pulled a single sheet out and held it under the lamp beside him. "This particular crystal was taken by U.S. Intelligence."

"Damn," Thomas blurted out. "Then the Illuminati must have it."

"An officer by the name of Marchant."

"Who?" Thomas sat bolt upright.

"A Gary Marchant. Claimed his family had Templar roots and had been searching for the stone since it was lost." Gustav studied Thomas's face. "You know something of this man?"

"I know one of his descendants. He lectures on sacred geometry, has written a book on Egypt. To think the crystal was right under my nose." He stood and started to pace in front of the fire.

"This does not seem to be good news."

Thomas turned. "I don't trust him. Never have."

"Where is he now?"

A slow smile broke across Thomas's face. "In Egypt, lecturing at a conference."

"It would seem, Mr. Le Clair, you have located your fourth crystal and it is exactly where it should be."

Part Three

I Am The Light

21

On Friday night, Anne sat in the back of a large lecture hall in the Mena House listening to the first night of what the conference organizers were calling the Egypt Extravaganza. Their flyer claimed that all the important voices in the alternative field would be speaking. Anne recognized a few names from a reading list Thomas had given her. Academics didn't seem to mix with this group, although there were some Ph.D.s—one in geology, another in physics. Michael was the only speaker who bridged the gap between the two worlds, with a degree in Egyptology from one of the best schools and a position at a prestigious museum side by side with his book, dubbed New Age by most, definitely not read by his traditional colleagues.

On this first night, each speaker had two minutes to give a synopsis of his or her presentation. Only a few remained. Paul Marchant was still talking after ten minutes, when the emcee walked up to him and said, "Thank you, Mr. Marchant. I'm sure everyone is anxious to hear your information. Next we have Joe Whyte, an engineer." Marchant blinked like an owl at the man, then walked off stage.

Two women, Debbie and Rita, had plopped themselves on either side of Anne right as the program began and gave a running commentary on each speaker.

"I don't know what to think of this next guy. His stuff makes sense, but everybody knows the Great Pyramid was a temple of initiation. He claims it was a power plant," Debbie said.

"Really?" Anne said politely. Michael held Joe's theories in high regard.

"Now this guy," Debbie pointed to a name in the program, but held it too far away for Anne to see. "He traces the Illuminati all the way back to the Nibiruans."

"The who?" Anne asked.

"You know," Rita said, "the slave drivers of the planet Nibiru? The one that has the strange orbit between Mars and Jupiter? Who bioengineered the human race by splicing their DNA into early humans?"

"Excuse me?"

"You've never read Kramer, I see," Debbie said. "Don't worry. We'll fill you in on what you've missed."

"Anyway," Rita said, "he claims the Illuminati are going to do a blood sacrifice in the Great Pyramid during an alignment in the next week."

"Blood sacrifice?" Anne was beginning to feel like a parrot.

"They stay in power by sacrificial murder, don't you know? They prey on the true bloodline. Like Princess Diana. She was part of the bloodline. Her car was tampered with and her driver drugged. But the important part is the date."

Debbie said, "An important alignment. They've done these throughout history. Hitler did mass killings on certain important dates. And even in America, the murder of President Le Clair."

Anne froze.

"They're members of the bloodline, too. That was a ceremonial sacrifice," Rita said.

Anne had registered in her married name, hoping for some anonymity. Clearly these women hadn't recognized her face.

The emcee was now at the microphone thanking Joe Whyte. She'd missed everything he'd said.

"And now it is my great honor to introduce a man who has traced the roots of the Western metaphysical traditions to the ancient Egyptian mystery schools, Michael Levy."

As Michael approached the microphone, Debbie whispered in her ear, "Isn't he a hunk?"

"Quite attractive." Anne was pleased she could find a point of agreement.

"I just read his book, but he doesn't know all the connections between the Illuminati and international shadow government. He seems to think some of the organizations are still pure. The Masons are completely corrupt, have been from the start," Debbie added.

Anne picked up her purse. "Can you excuse me? I'm afraid I have to go to the ladies' room." She left the room, then walked up the hall and stood outside an open doorway so she could listen to Michael without interruption.

"We can trace the Rosicrucians back to this same source, the Essenes. In Islam, the line runs through the Sufi mystics." Michael's eyes kept returning to Anne's empty seat.

He should be more careful, she thought.

They still had two crystals to find and had agreed it was likely the Keepers of these keys would be drawn to Giza as the alignment neared. The three planned to keep their public contact with each other to a minimum while they investigated, hoping to draw the other Keepers out. Thomas had contacted her to confirm that Paul Marchant held a key. She'd been a bit surprised, but in retrospect it all made sense. They'd agreed she would try to make a connection with Marchant.

Anne stepped forward slightly so she was visible to the stage, but not the audience in the back. Michael's eyes flickered toward the movement and his shoulders relaxed. "All these traditions had their birth in the Egyptian mystery schools." He looked around for the emcee. "I think that is sufficient."

The host walked forward, a bit surprised. "Short but promising, yes?" he said to the audience, and they burst into a short round of applause. Michael nodded in recognition, then took his seat in the speaker's section in the first few rows.

"Next," the emcee continued, "I'd like to welcome our special guests from Guatemala who will be explaining connections between the Egyptian pyramids and those of their ancestors, the Maya."

Anne was curious about this group. There were three in all, two men
and a woman. They all walked to the front, but to Anne's surprise the
woman stepped forward to speak. She was short and round, dressed in
white with a brilliantly colored scarf wrapped around her head.

"Hello." She stood on tiptoes to speak into the microphone.

A technician rushed out from behind the stage to adjust the stand for
her.

"Thank you." Her voice now rang through the room and she took a
step back. "My name is Maria Lol Ha and I come from a small village in
Guatemala. I am a healer and teacher there. Jose and Enrique are warrior
priests from my village."

The two men nodded gravely and Maria continued. "We are honored to
visit this ancient land of Egypt. The Maya have existed much longer than
the anthropologists believe. In our legends, when the Maya first came to
this planet, we went to four sections of the Earth. Egypt was one of them."

There was a murmur in the crowd.

"In my talk, I will explain the connection between ancient Egypt and
Maya peoples." She paused, then leaned forward again. "Thank you."

The emcee walked up to the mike. "Thank you again," he said as the
three Mayans left the stage, the two men flanking Maria. "The schedule for
the conference is in your brochures, but generally, we'll be going to sites
in the mornings, have lunch near the site, then lectures in the afternoons
or evenings. Tomorrow we'll tour Sakkara and the Step Pyramid with our
guide, Tahir. This man is well versed in the ancient spiritual traditions.
I'm sure he'll amaze you."

Yes, he will, Anne thought. She spotted a white turban in the front,
as Tahir stood. He raised his hand to greet the audience, then sat down
again.

The emcee continued, "Now we're all in for a treat. We're adjourning
just down the hall for our opening party. You can talk personally with the
speakers you've just met. We've got an open bar, Middle Eastern treats,
plus a local group will be playing and . . ." he paused dramatically, "there
will be belly-dancing lessons for the ladies."

"No guys?" someone shouted.

The host stuck his mouth closer to the mike and shouted, "Oh, and the gentlemen, too," but his words were lost in the noise of scraping chairs and rising voices.

Anne stepped back from the side door and made her way through the crowd toward the party to seek out Marchant. When she arrived, the room was already stuffed with people, half milling around the buffet tables and lined up at the bar. The other half had surrounded the celebrities.

She spotted Michael toward the back of the room surrounded mostly by women, Debbie and Rita among them. Rita seemed to be holding forth, but Anne knew Debbie would jump in as soon as her other half took a breath. At least she'd be free of them for a while. Anne bought a bottle of sparkling water from the bar and strolled around the room, casually joining the group around Marchant.

"Do you really think your work will stop the pole shift?" This question came from a blond dressed in a belly-dancing outfit.

Marchant seemed oblivious to this display of flesh. "That's exactly right, but my work must be funded quickly. Otherwise the Schumann frequencies will rise too high to make a correction."

"What happens then?" A brunette with silver at the temples leaned forward, her dress revealing cleavage.

Marchant turned slightly toward her, then focused on some point close to the ceiling and started to talk. "This flip will happen quickly for a geological event, perhaps even in a couple of days. Such a rapid shift will create enormous winds well beyond hurricane velocity that will destroy forests and towns. The Earth's tectonic plates will be crushed together in some areas and pulled apart in others. The earthquakes will be devastating."

Anne surveyed his audience. Almost everyone in the crowd was wide-eyed with a sort of gleeful horror.

Marchant continued, "The face of the continents will change, not just from the quakes, but from the tsunamis. The tidal waves will be unprecedented. These quakes will be off the Richter scale. The Earth as we know it will be gone, most of humanity wiped out."

"I know a bit about grants. I might be able to help you put together a few prospects," a young man in the group offered.

Suddenly, Anne felt a tingling in the small of her back. Every morning she put up a shield of protection just as Grandmother Elizabeth had directed and asked for a signal if any psychic attack was directed her way. Pretending to move so she could hear Marchant better, she walked to the other side of the group and surveyed the crowd that was now in front of her. There were the Mayans, smiling at the group around them, patiently answering questions. She looked back up the right side of the room and found a man staring at her, his dark eyes slits of pure malice.

He saw that she had noticed him. "Illuminati," he mouthed silently.

Anne shuddered.

"You must be cold," Marchant said.

Anne jumped, surprised to have attracted his attention. "Yes, I left my shawl in my room. The nights in the north are so much cooler."

"So you did go to the south," he said. "I looked all over for you."

This earned her haughty stares from the blond and brunette.

"I'm afraid I must apologize for missing our appointment," she began. "But perhaps we could meet to discuss your project."

"Oh?" Marchant blinked.

"I believe we share some mutual interests."

He stared at her for a long minute.

"I'd like to join that meeting," the young man said. "About those grants—"

Marchant ignored him. "I think you're right," he said to Anne.

"We'll be in touch then." She nodded to the group, turned, and walked out of the room.

* * *

THE NEXT MORNING, the group toured Sakkara. Once they were out of the buses and the camel jockeys chased away, Tahir arranged the group in a circle outside the door of the complex. "Please, take hands. We can have two circles, there are so many."

Anne looked around for Marchant, but he was nowhere to be found. Apparently, he was skipping the morning tours.

"I'll chant in the ancient language still taught by my people." Tahir's voice carried through the crowd. "The meditation will bring us into harmony with this place. Then walk in silence through the columns and we'll gather on the other side."

Someone took Anne's hand. "This is exciting." She recognized Debbie's voice. "This is one place I don't remember."

"I do." Rita stepped into the circle next to Debbie. "It wasn't the Nefertiti life, though."

"Really?"

"No, I think I was a healer priest."

"Tahir is ready to begin," Anne whispered.

The two quieted down and Tahir began his chant. Anne felt the complex open to them and, as soon as he'd finished, she turned and walked through the series of columns. There were no visions, only a deep sense of calm. She could hear Debbie whispering to Rita behind her. They followed her everywhere, through the courtyard as Tahir explained how the cobras at the tops of the columns had formed an energy field over the site, even into the healing niches as he explained how the patients were diagnosed and healed through sound.

Anne couldn't concentrate with all the chattering, but she had to admit they were entertaining. Debbie, as it turned out, was convinced she'd been Nefertiti and Rita had been her mother-in-law, Tiye, during the reign of Akhenaten. It was interesting that Akhenaten had such a following. She could hardly scorn their beliefs. Hadn't she remembered two past lives in Egypt herself?

Michael seemed to have shaken his female fan club and had taken his usual place at Tahir's side. While the others went in to meditate in the chamber of the three niches where negative and positive energies were harmonized into wholeness, Tahir took Michael over to one of the roped-off tunnel openings and began to tell him an animated story. Anne tried not to resent her self-appointed guardians. They helped her cover. Besides, Michael would relay Tahir's story to her later.

After everyone had gone into the chamber, Tahir took the group off to a mound on the north side of the Step Pyramid and here did his meditation. Apparently, this was the real Holy of Holies. Again Anne saw nothing and her crystal lay quiet against her heart, but later on the bus ride to their lunch place, Anne overheard a couple talking quietly to each other.

"It was all water," the woman said, "little islands surrounded by water. I came to be healed and afterward took a boat to this very mound where I made my offering."

"Yes," the man added, "and I saw the whole healing complex when it was still operating. It was so beautiful, with statues of the Egyptian gods all lined up."

Back at the hotel, Rita and Debbie invited her to a special channeling session, but she begged off. The evening was taken up with a lecture by Joe Whyte, who explained in the careful detail of a skilled engineer exactly how the pyramid had functioned as a power plant. Her skepticism about Whyte's ideas gradually waned as he laid out his case, explaining how the structure was built to resonate in harmony with Earth's natural energy field, how that energy was stepped up through Helmholtz resonators. The pyramid produced hydrogen gas and microwaves, serving as both a source of energy and a communication device. His argument that advanced machining techniques had been used to create many of Egypt's artifacts seemed indisputable.

It was quite late when he finished, and Anne wandered back to her room, vaguely aware that Bob was following at a distance. The message button on her phone was lit, so Anne buzzed the front desk. The message was from Paul Marchant inviting her to join him the next night for dinner. She left a message for him that she'd meet him around seven.

Then she called Michael. "I'm invited to dinner."

"That's good progress."

"How about you?"

"I'm afraid I have to do museum business tomorrow night. One of our patrons has invited me to his home. But I can't let Mr. Marchant be the only man to wine and dine you in Cairo. May I have the pleasure of your company Monday night?"

"But we can't be seen together."

"It's a big city, my dear."

"I'd be delighted."

"Excellent. I'll see you Monday night then. Good luck on your date."

"It's a business meeting. By the way, what were you and Tahir talking about this morning?"

"Oh, what a story. Best told over dinner."

"No fair."

"I promise to make it worth the wait."

"See you then."

* * *

THE TOUR GROUP spent the next day on the Giza Plateau. Again Marchant didn't come. Michael and Tahir were inseparable, teaching together. Anne enjoyed seeing the Sphinx again, but got no message. How could she hear with Debbie and Rita chatting away? Tired and dusty in the afternoon, she decided to take lunch and an Egyptian nap in her room. She woke around five. After a shower and long meditation, Anne met Marchant in the lobby. Arnold had agreed to tail them.

"I was hoping for some privacy and made reservations in town. I hope that's all right with you," Marchant said.

"An excellent idea." Anne smiled graciously.

"Shall we go?" He offered Anne his arm.

Once they were in their taxi and under way, he turned to her and asked, "So you've changed your name?"

"Oh, Greene. It's a married name."

"You're married?" Marchant asked, his tone of voice remaining the same.

"Divorced, actually," Anne tried to sound warm and inviting. "The family name attracts too much attention. I'm glad I didn't use it. I've discovered Mr. Kramer thinks my family is in hip deep with the Illuminati and planning a blood sacrifice in the Great Pyramid soon."

Marchant laughed. "That man has pieces of the picture, but he doesn't see the whole."

"I'd like to hear your idea of the whole," Anne said.

"Yes," he said, "I was hoping we could share some information."

They arrived at the Raoucha and Kandahar, twin restaurants serving Lebanese and Indian cuisine, and were ushered into a back room, where they took a table. Marchant ordered for them both and Anne decided it would not be helpful to voice any objection. Arnold stationed himself at a table just outside their room, where he had a view of her and the main area of the restaurant.

Marchant took up their conversation again. "Did Mr. Kramer give a date for this blood sacrifice you're to participate in?"

Anne hid her surprise by coughing a little after she swallowed a sip of chai. "I didn't hear this from him, but two of his fans. They did mention these events are timed with important planetary alignments."

He nodded. "Anything specific?"

"They aren't that sophisticated, I'm afraid. How about you? Do you know of any important alignments coming up?"

"My work is important to the future of the planet." Marchant suddenly took a new tack. "I know this sounds rather megalomaniacal, but I've studied all my life. Did you ever feel you were put here to fulfill an important mission?" He looked full into her face.

"My mother gave me a thoroughly rational education. It's only recently that I've discovered such a feeling."

"Really? I thought you'd trained all your life, given your background."

As they ate their dinner, Anne treated Marchant to an abridged story of her childhood and adolescence. "It's hard to escape public service as a Le Clair. But combining that with spirituality is something I'm only recently learning about."

Marchant studied her for a moment. "Are you frightened you haven't mastered enough to pull it off?"

Anne hesitated before this invitation to divulge what she knew.

"How about a trial run?"

Anne stared at him, her fork halted in midair.

"I know where it is, but I can't get in by myself. Time is of the essence. There are certain . . ." he searched for a word, "interests who want to take control."

"Yes?" Anne set her fork down and gave Marchant her full attention.

"I can't open the room without another key."

Anne was stunned by this revelation. She'd imagined a game of cat and mouse, not this straightforward admission. Unless it was a trap. She reached out to him with her mind, feeling his energy like a cop patting down a suspect. He was hiding something, but about this, he was telling the truth.

His eyes took on a speculative gaze. "How long did you say you'd been training?"

Anne laughed despite herself. "Politicians learn that almost by instinct. I've just honed it a bit."

"Well?"

Anne smoothed the napkin in her lap. "Tell me about this room." "Not here," Marchant said. "But I can take you."

"Why me?"

"Simple deduction. Michael's too competitive."

"Michael? Michael who?"

"Please, if we're going to work together, we have to be frank."

"All right."

"His ties to the museum could be a cover for the shadow forces."

"I hadn't thought of that. But why do you think my family isn't involved in that group?"

Marchant sat forward, his lean frame taut with purpose. "Because if you were, they wouldn't have assassinated your uncle."

"I see." Anne couldn't think of anything more astute to say.

"We must work together to stop these people from gaining control of this ancient technology."

What technology? And he knows of a room? Clearly, they'd underestimated Paul Marchant.

"When?" Anne asked.

Marchant sat back with a sigh of relief. "I'll let you know. Keep yourself free of commitments. We may have to act on short notice."

* * *

AS SOON AS Anne got back to the hotel, she called Michael's room and left him a message to meet her at Tahir's house, then took a cab there herself. Arnold had agreed the limo compromised her cover, but he insisted on accompanying her. It was quite late, but Tahir was sitting on the floor in his living room with Shani and two teenaged boys.

"I'm sorry to barge in like this," she began.

I'm sorry to barge in like this," she began.

"Come in." Tahir put a cushion on the floor next to him. "It's good to see you. Our home is your home."

"Thank you." She took a breath. "I've got news."

The boys excused themselves, but Shani stayed. Tahir nodded for Anne to continue.

As she talked, her intensity eased and her words flowed more slowly. Tahir packed tobacco into the bowl of his *shisha* pipe while he listened. Before she got very far, Anne heard the front door open and Michael walked in.

He greeted Tahir and Shani, then turned to Anne. "Did you strike gold on your date?"

"It wasn't a date," Anne said, watching him settle onto his cushion. "I have news." Anne started again, this time telling the story more slowly.

When she finished speaking, Tahir said, "A room. I've heard stories about the excavation at the south end of the plateau." He dropped small coals onto his tobacco, then took a deep draw from the pipe. He sat back and exhaled huge plumes of smoke through both nostrils, looking exactly like a dragon. He passed the pipe to Michael, who took a small puff out of politeness, and offered it to Anne. She shook her head.

"We hear information on these secret digs from time to time from the villagers. Who else would they hire to help them? I heard that a large underground temple was discovered some years ago. I stumbled onto a smaller one as a teenager."

Anne's eyebrows peaked.

Michael said, "The story he told me at Sakkara. Perhaps you want to tell her yourself."

Tahir took another puff from his pipe before continuing. "When I was about sixteen, I entered a tunnel near the Step Pyramid at Sakkara. I spent the whole day walking, crawling, sometimes swimming through a huge underground system of tunnels. After hours and hours underground, only occasionally seeing sunlight through the holes above, I crawled back up a large opening and came out on the Giza Plateau."

"But—all the way from Sakkara?" Anne's eyes were wide.

"Yes, eight miles."

"My God. A whole series of underground caves from Sakkara to Giza?"

"Not caves, tunnels. The plateau is filled with them. And they extend north as well as south. Many years ago, the Nile was in the west. The tunnels were drilled out of the limestone bedrock so water could be brought to the sites." He paused and looked at Anne. "Do you remember the Osireion?"

"Behind the temple at Abydos?"

"Yes. Remember how it is a whole layer lower than the front temple?" Anne nodded.

"After my first discovery, I snuck back to the Giza tunnel and explored beneath the plateau. These tunnels are not the only structures buried beneath the sand. I think they've uncovered a temple that in the ancient days stood at the south end of the plateau. I've heard stories about this room Paul Marchant told you about. In the back of that temple sits the Hall of Records."

"Oh, my God!" Anne sat bolt upright. "But that means the Illuminati already have access."

"No." Tahir knocked the ashes from his pipe onto a plate next to him. "The gate to the Hall is guarded by ancient technology they do not yet understand."

"What kind of technology?" Michael asked.

"It is an energy field," Tahir said, "that cannot be penetrated by force. It must be opened with the keys."

"Does it take all the crystals to bring down the shield?" Michael asked.

"Based on what we discovered at Dendara, the Hall itself cannot be opened without all six crystals."

"That's a relief." Anne sat back. "Then if I go with Paul, we won't be able to get in."

"You won't be able to activate the site," Tahir clarified.

"Should I go with him then?"

"Not without me," Arnold interjected.

"Arnold's right," Michael said. "It's clear Paul is working with the shadow government. Otherwise how would he have gained access? You can't trust him."

"We need to know exactly where the entrance is," Tahir said. "I can't crawl around under the Giza Plateau like I used to. I'd prefer not to send my children, given that the Illuminati are actively working the site. It would save time."

Michael looked at Tahir again. "What do you think is in the Hall of Records? Marchant seems to think our mission is to uncover some kind of Atlantean technology."

Tahir packed his pipe again. "I don't believe in Atlantis."

"What?" Michael stared at Tahir. "You can't be serious."

"I am perfectly serious."

"But all the metaphysical traditions document the existence of Atlantis. It's supposed to be the source of the Khemitian civilization."

Tahir shook his head. "Tell me the story and listen to it yourself as you do."

Michael sat back and began to recite the familiar story. "Supposedly, right before the fall of Atlantis, people left the island and sailed to the East. When they arrived in Egypt, they taught the people their technology and built the Sphinx and pyramids, leaving the technology and records they'd brought with them in a chamber beneath the Sphinx. A sort of time capsule, so to speak."

"What did these Atlanteans look like?" Tahir asked.

"Well, supposedly they were Nordic types. Tall and blond."

"And these Khemitians?"

"They were supposed to be Africans."

"Right, so enlightened white people came and taught the ignorant savages of Africa everything they knew and were the fathers of Khemitian civilization?"

"Oh." Michael smiled. "I see the problem."

Tahir placed more hot coals on top of his tobacco and took another deep draw from his pipe. After his famous exhale, he said, "That's not the only problem, that the story is racist. When did Atlantis fall?"

"About twelve thousand years ago."

"And how old is the Sphinx?"

"Much older."

"Exactly so." Tahir offered the pipe to Michael, who took another small puff. "Now, what did I tell you about the cycles of civilization?"

Michael eyes turned inward in thought.

Anne watched this exchange, enjoying the parade of emotions over Michael's open face.

"You said that humanity goes through cycles of enlightenment and ignorance. That we are entering the awakening, when humanity is becoming aware again."

Tahir nodded. "Is all of humanity awake during Aten?"

Michael's eyes widened. "Yes, of course."

"Then what about Atlantis?"

"Okay, I see what you're saying. This is the story of the fall into ignorance, not the beginning of civilization."

"Precisely. During Aten, the entire globe lives as one family sharing all knowledge. Each land uses technology that is appropriate to the specific area. Stonehenge in England, Tiahuanaco in Bolivia, and the pyramids in the land of Osiris."

"The land of Osiris?" Michael frowned.

"The sites in northern Khemit, stretching from Dahshur in the south to Abu Roash in the north. The series of pyramids. *Bu Wizzer*, in the ancient language. The land of Osiris."

"Oh, yes. These sites all worked together."

Tahir sat back, a look of satisfaction in his eyes.

"So then what are we looking for in the Hall of Records?"

"This is enough for tonight. In just a few hours, I must lead the group through the Cairo Museum. Contrary to popular belief . . ." He glanced at Anne, his eyes laughing. ". . . I do sleep."

Anne stood and gathered her things to go.

"Go with Paul Marchant," Tahir said. "We'll have to work with him and should try to befriend him. You seem the best candidate for the job."

"I'll let you know when he contacts me. Good night."

"Good night." Tahir stood and ushered them to the door.

They took a cab back to the hotel. The birds were beginning to stir when she and Michael stopped outside her door.

"We'll have dinner tonight then?" Michael asked.

"A date?" Anne teased.

"Yes," he murmured and bent to kiss her. Suddenly, the *mu'adhdhin* began his call to prayer, startling them both. Michael drew back without his kiss. "Tonight then," he repeated.

"Tonight," Anne whispered.

* * *

ANNE WENT to bed just as the sun was rising and slept until noon. She missed the museum tour, but Michael could take her another time. After a late lunch, she wandered toward the conference lecture hall. Glancing at her program, she saw Jake Kramer was scheduled to speak, the man who believed Egyptian civilization had been built by aliens. If Tahir rejected the idea that white Atlanteans had built Khemit, she could only imagine what he'd say about this theory.

She leafed through her program to read the bio of Mr. Kramer. Her eyes fell on his picture and she stopped dead in her tracks. Here was the man who had glared at her and mouthed the word "Illuminati" during the party on the first night. She didn't want to subject herself to his accusations once again.

A Monday afternoon next to the pool suddenly sounded lovely, except she didn't think it would be warm enough to swim. Or perhaps a visit to the salon. She stretched out her hands and examined her fingers. They looked like she'd been doing exactly what she'd been doing, digging through the sands of Egypt for a solid week. Then again, Michael was an archaeologist. Maybe he preferred this look. Laughing at herself, Anne walked back to her room and made an appointment to get her hair and nails done. She wondered if Dr. Abernathy would approve of such an indulgence—taking time away from saving the world just to look good.

Around half past seven, Anne walked through the lobby of the Mena House. Many eyes turned to watch her. Bob followed at a discreet distance.

"Hello, Cleopatra," one of the bus boys said as she walked by.

"*Sukran,*" she said. Her evening dress was the color of a light sky. Sapphire earrings sparkled from beneath her wheat-blond hair that now hung in carefully arranged curls. A royal blue and gold silk shawl from Aswan completed her outfit.

Michael had given her an address where she was to meet him at eight. She gave it to the taxi driver, who maneuvered through the familiar streets of the village onto the road to Cairo. Instead of crossing the bridge, the cab made its way through a street lined with large houses and immaculate gardens, then drew up to a large boat landing. A striped awning covered the dock. Next to the wide gangplank stood two young Egyptian men dressed in toga-like pants, formed by a pleated cloth wound around the waist and cinched with a large belt and golden buckle. They were bare-chested except for replicas of traditional necklaces strung with red, lapis, and light-blue beads setting off golden ankhs.

Michael stood just inside the boat entrance, scanning the crowd for her. She paused on the walkway to look at him. He wore a three-piece blue suit that made him look every inch the sophisticate, but Anne knew better. She knew the strength and agility hidden beneath that suit, and the sensitive heart hidden beneath that. In a characteristic gesture, Michael pushed his hair out of his eyes and at that moment their eyes met. A smile broke out on his face. It was as if the sun had come up. A rush of warmth filled Anne. She stepped onto the boat and Michael took her hand.

Michael nodded to Bob, who discreetly melted into the crowd. "It's marvelous how he does that," Michael said. He held Anne at arm's length, taking her in. "You look stunning."

If anyone else had looked her up and down, she'd have been insulted. But her body responded to Michael like a flower to the sun.

"Shall we go in?" He offered his arm. They walked into a long room filled with tables arranged around a central stage. The staff carried in dish after dish of steaming food, filling two long buffet tables. Enticing aromas floated in the air.

Michael escorted her to a small table next to the window near the bow. He pulled back her chair. A bottle of champagne and two glasses sat in the middle of the table.

She glanced up. The ceiling was painted like Nut's sky, a deep blue sprinkled with gold stars. A row of golden lotuses graced the sides of each panel on the ceiling. "Just like the old days," she said.

"I'm glad you like it. It's a bit touristy, but that ensures no one we know is likely to stumble across us."

"I didn't see Paul Marchant all day," Anne began.

"Shhh," Michael touched her lips with the tip of his finger. "No business. Tonight is just for us."

Anne was taken aback. Their quest had so consumed their time together that for a second she couldn't imagine what to say to him. "This business, as you call it, has changed my life. I'm not the same woman you met in your uncle's jewelry shop."

"It was fate."

"Pardon me?"

"I almost didn't come into my uncle's store that day. I had a great deal of work in the museum. I asked him to try to find someone else. But then something kept nagging me to go, so I changed my mind and told him I'd do it. It was just a feeling I had, that it was important to be there." He reached for the champagne bottle.

"So the two crystals were reunited."

He filled both their glasses. "The two Keepers were reunited." He lifted his glass. "To the most exciting woman I've ever met."

Anne paused, surprised. Finally, she said, "Why, thank you, sir." She clinked her glass on Michael's and they each took a sip. "I wouldn't have thought you'd find a rational lawyer who does political work for her family firm so intriguing."

"As you said, you're not that woman anymore. Even though she was very intriguing, too. It's been a pleasure watching you learn."

Anne shook her head. "All these compliments. My goodness."

"I had to hold so much back from you in the beginning. Then I was under suspicion." Suddenly, he laughed. "I couldn't believe what you said to me at Kom Ombo. 'If you betray me, I'll kill you'? Just after you gave me a passionate kiss."

Anne shifted in her chair. "After the attack in Aswan, I realized there were several coincidences I was overlooking just because—"

"Yes?"

"Because I was attracted to you." She looked up at him.

Michael reached out with his forefinger and started to stroke Anne's hand.

His touch made Anne aware of every inch of her skin. "I knew in my heart you were innocent," she said. "After Aswan, I thought back and realized I'd been with you the night my apartment was broken into. Then again the day my hotel room was searched. My head told me to be careful."

"After a broken heart, our intellects often want to take charge to keep us from pain. But the head is not such a good judge of relationships," Michael said. "I've wanted you ever since the first day I met you."

She looked into his deep brown eyes. Here was a man who'd endured humiliation and suspicion but remained steadfast, who'd waited while she learned what he'd studied all his life, with never a hint of condescension or impatience. Here was a man who had become her best friend.

Then she realized the boat was moving and raised her eyes to a beautiful view of the Nile. The dark water danced under the lights from the bank. Across the expanse of river, several more boats steamed along, some full of reveling tourists like this one, others carrying just a few passengers, others plying their trade. The gulls had gone to sleep. Inside, people were beginning to line up at the buffet tables.

Michael squeezed her hand. "I've ordered the vegetarian special for myself. Would you like to try it also or would you prefer the buffet?"

Anne stretched back in her chair, feeling much too relaxed to jostle elbows with the crowd. "I'll have what you're having," she said. "At least you asked."

"Excuse me?"

"Marchant. He just ordered for me."

Michael laughed. "He doesn't strike me as a man with much panache. But . . ." He pulled a mock stern face. ". . . no business."

Anne held up her hands, palms forward. "No business."

Michael instructed the waiter to bring two of the vegetarian plates and soon the two were sampling an amazing array of international vegetarian delicacies—keefta balls from Persia, stuffed grape leaves from Greece, a delicate pasta funghi from Italy, a light curry from India, and of course falafels, pita bread, hummus, and olives from Egypt. She hadn't thought she was hungry, but this was the best meal she'd had in Egypt so far.

When they finished, Michael asked, "Dessert?"

She looked over at the buffet table. Several groups were crowded around it still.

"I'll do the honors," he said.

"I don't usually."

"Tonight we're celebrating." Michael pushed back his chair and went to the table, returning with a small plate of various chocolate treats. The mousse was the lightest she'd ever had, and they each finished off with a bite of a dark chocolate torte.

Waiters began circulating, clearing plates, offering coffee and aperitifs. The band appeared and began playing a slow dance tune.

"May I have the honor?" Michael held out his hand.

"It would be my pleasure." Anne allowed him to lead her onto the dance floor. Her shoulder tucked perfectly under his arm as if they'd been made to fit together. They moved toward the side of the dance floor, away from the growing number of couples. A late moon slowly rose over the Nile.

After a few slow numbers, the band brought out a belly dancer. Michael and Anne drifted away from the fast tempo to an upstairs deck. They stopped at the bow, Anne nestled under Michael's arm. She shivered in the cool wind off the river and Michael pulled her under his coat.

"Better?" he whispered in her ear.

"Yes." She laid her head on his chest, listening to his heartbeat. She felt the hard edge of his crystal beneath his shirt. Anne wished that they didn't have to go back to the pretense of not knowing each other, to the task laid out before them.

The boat reached a line of tall hotels and started to turn around. "No," she whispered. "Not yet."

Michael reached down and put his hand beneath her chin. He tilted her head up and bent down to kiss her. The kiss began softly, his lips touching her like a honeybee testing a flower, then swiftly deepened. A warm rush of desire filled her. She leaned into him and felt his body respond.

His mouth moved to her ear and whispered, "I've waited all my life for you." His voice was thick with desire.

"I feel like I've known you for centuries, like I'm coming home."

They walked around the top deck as the boat voyaged back down the Nile. About halfway back, they returned to their table and watched the river slip by. Neither felt the need to speak. Once the boat had docked, Anne walked out onto the gangplank with Michael, as if in a dream. On the street, he hailed a cab. Bob quietly slipped into the front. She'd forgotten all about him. With her head on Michael's shoulder, the trip passed quickly.

As they were pulling up to the Mena House, Michael said, "Perhaps we shouldn't be seen together. Do you want to go in first?"

"I suppose," Anne answered languidly.

Michael reached across her and opened her door.

"Good night then," she said.

"Good night."

Anne slipped through the lobby, avoiding the groups of conference participants standing around in clusters. She saw Marchant in the distance, but he turned his back to her, indicating this was not the time. She went to her suite.

"Good night, Bob," she said at the door.

"Good night." He opened the door to the adjacent suite. "Sleep well."

She didn't think she could sleep, not with the currents of desire coursing through her body. She stretched out on the bed, pulling her silk shawl over her. After a minute, she heard a knock. She sat up, her heart pulsing. Through the peephole she saw the familiar brown curls gleaming in the hallway light. She opened the door.

Michael looked at her, his eyes filled with desire.

"Come in," she said. She heard Arnold's door open, then close again.

Michael took her into his arms and kissed her almost violently, lifting her off the floor and carrying her to the bed. But once there, he slowed down, savoring a long, deep kiss. He turned her over and unzipped her dress, kissing her long back, then gently lifted her hips and drew the dress off. Anne sat up and loosened his tie, pulled it off, and threw it next to her dress. Then she unbuttoned his shirt and opened it, burying her nose in the nest of brown hair on his chest, breathing him in.

His hands cupped her breasts and he looked into her eyes. "My Hathor priestess."

She smiled. "If only I remembered now what I knew then."

"Let's see if we can remember," he said, and he kissed her again, his hands stroking her body.

Anne gasped and pushed herself against him, eager now. Michael quickly pulled off the rest of his clothes and stretched out beside her, kissing her lips, her neck, her breasts, her belly, then back up again. Anne pushed herself beneath him and they joined their bodies together.

As they moved, the present melded with the past. The intense sweetness of their bodies opened all her senses and she remembered him coming to her, the Tantric rituals of the temple, connecting to the earth, the river, bringing the flood out of the dampness of their lovemaking. In England, she lay on a stone altar, his body over her, his head crowned with the horns of the sacred deer. Even further in the past, he sat on a bed hung with silk curtains and she wrapped around him, a vine to his tree.

He traveled there with her in his mind, aware of it all—their bodies joined and aching in the present, their souls free of time, dipping into their past like swallows. The intensity built until there was no more thought, only waves of energy climbing the two spines of one consciousness. They climaxed together, releasing the energy up and out into the vast dome of the sky.

22

The next day, Thomas Le Clair sat outside the Tibetan Buddhist temple in Dharamsala, India, waiting for an interview with Lama Tenzin. Thomas accepted the chipped white cup filled with tea that his guide offered him.

Thomas's trip from Germany had been long, but not as long as the trip the refugees in Dharamsala had endured when they'd left their homes in Tibet. His guide had showed him around the village, school, hospital, and crafts center. The Tibetan refugees had accomplished a miracle and Thomas would leave a large contribution at the end of his visit.

He leaned back against one of the trunks of the banyan tree that shaded him. The sounds of chanting wafted out to where he sat and he closed his eyes, letting the sound carry him inward. His breath quieted and the muscles in his back and neck relaxed.

Some time later, Thomas realized all was quiet. He opened his eyes to find his guide approaching with a man dressed in the deep red robes of this sect. Thomas unfolded his legs, putting the tingling of one foot out of his mind, and stood to greet the monks.

"Mr. Le Clair," his guide said with a slight bow, "Lama Tenzin."

Thomas folded his hands together and bowed lower. "Namaste."

"The lama asks if you would accompany him to his office.

If it is agreeable with you, I will serve as your interpreter."

"I would be honored," Thomas said.

The guide nodded to Lama Tenzin, who led the way down a flagstone path flanked with calla lilies. He walked through a low door. Thomas followed and found himself in a small room looking out on a garden. Lama Tenzin gestured to one of the pillows surrounding a low table, and Thomas took a seat, tucking his legs beneath him once again.

Lama Tenzin spoke to the guide, who then asked, "How may we help you, Mr. Le Clair?"

Thomas took a long breath, then began his story. "I belong to a family that accepted a spiritual responsibility long in the past, and the time to fulfill an important part of that obligation is drawing near. We are in possession of an important artifact, a crystal. The legend surrounding this stone tells us that one who can unlock the crystal's secret will use it 'to restore the flow.' These are all the instructions that remain about the stone. The rest has been lost over the centuries."

As the monk translated, Lama Tenzin's gaze retained the same friendly openness from before, as if he were not surprised by Thomas's recitation.

"My family has researched the history of the stones over the years, and our information indicates there are six crystals that must be used in conjunction to accomplish their task. My sister has become the new Keeper of our crystal and, based on her experiences, we think she is the one we have been waiting for.

"Our astrologers alerted us to an important alignment occurring on February first. We call it a Star of David alignment, two intersecting triangles. This, along with other indications, suggests the time has come."

Lama Tenzin listened to the translation, then said something to the guide. The guide laid out a piece of paper and pen. "Can you draw this alignment?"

Thomas drew the alignment, indicating the signs. "I'm not familiar with Tibetan astrology, so I've indicated the Western names."

The lama studied Thomas's drawing for a moment, then nodded for him to continue.

"We believe we've discovered four of the crystals. One is held by a man who is a descendant of the Hebrew Levite priesthood. Another by a man whose father took it from the Nazis at the end of World War II. We haven't traced his genealogy, so don't know more about his family's origins."

Lama Tenzin spoke with his guide for a moment. They seemed to be clarifying what Thomas had just said. "Please continue," the guide said.

"The fourth is in Egypt, kept by a family with ties to the original wisdom schools there. Recently, I did some research in the library of a well-known metaphysical family who kept documents away from the Inquisition."

The lama and guide spoke together, then the guide said, "Something like our own experience now."

Thomas agreed. He paused for a moment out of respect, then continued his tale. "In this library, I discovered a scroll that suggested a Tibetan master served in the court of the ancient Egyptian king Akhenaten with the title Amenhotep, Son of Hapi. As you may know, this king was murdered and his followers fled Egypt. Amenhotep returned to his homeland and the scroll suggested he carried with him an important artifact."

Lama Tenzin sat forward, his eyes intent on Thomas's face.

Thomas had the sensation that the man could see to the bottom of his soul. He didn't flinch under this scrutiny. "This artifact was referred to as 'the key to wisdom.' Three of the other crystals have been traced back to this same moment in history. I believe the Tibetans may be holding a fifth crystal."

Lama Tenzin and his guide spoke for a long time.

Thomas schooled himself to patience, something he had thought he was gifted with until he sat with the Tibetan Buddhists. Then he realized he was still in elementary school.

Finally, the lama and guide looked up at him. The guide said, "Lama Tenzin believes your request is important and your heart is pure."

Thomas bowed his head behind his joined palms.

"He says you should travel to the Samye Monastery between Tsetang and Lhasa. This is our oldest monastery and, if this information is available, the monks there will have it."

Again Thomas thanked the men.

"Of course, we cannot accompany you since we would be immediately arrested, but there are travel agencies that specialize in treks to Tibet. This would be the best cover for you. Tomorrow I can put you in touch with the right people. Tonight you will be our guest?"

"It would be my pleasure," Thomas replied.

The guide stood and bowed to Lama Tenzin. Thomas followed suit.

"Please accept my thanks for your help," Thomas said. "This work is vital to the world's well-being."

The guide translated this, then the lama replied in Tibetan. The guide said, "Lama Tenzin agrees. He says he is pleased to serve the light, but he wishes to do a ceremony for you before you leave. Tomorrow morning. Then we will see the travel agent."

"Your blessing may well make the difference between success and failure." Thomas bowed low.

The ceremony took most of the next morning. Thomas quelled the thought that kept repeating in his mind, that the Star of David alignment was only eight days away, and focused on the long chants. After two hours, Thomas nodded off. Those hard mats hadn't been conducive to sleep last night. A blast from the ra-long horns woke him with a rush of adrenaline. From the corner of his eye he saw Lama Tenzin laugh. Thomas smiled at himself and sat up, regaining his focus. After another half-hour, Lama stood and anointed him with sweet-smelling oil and gave him a prayer scarf. Although the ceremony had taken a good chunk of time, it had been powerful and Thomas felt a shift in his energy. He was lucky to gain the blessings of such a high lama for their mission.

The rest of the afternoon was spent getting visas. He was able to cut down on red tape by spreading a lot of money around. In India, he understood this was business as usual. Next he consulted with Ralph, the family's pilot, about filing a flight plan. Luckily, he still had the family jet. That would save time. When his guide pulled their car into the airport, Thomas noticed a blue BMW he'd seen earlier outside the government office. Most of the vehicles in India were buses or mopeds. The few cars were left over from the British, so this one had CIA written all over it.

Or even worse. But why would they deliberately stand out? Were they trying to intimidate him?

"I think that car is following us. Can you slow down so I can get a look at the driver?"

"Of course. People who visit Lama Tenzin are often watched."

"I'd like to get a look at him if I can."

The guide pulled the car over, pretending to read the signs, and the Beemer drove past them. The driver looked European or American. Thomas couldn't make out the color of his eyes or hair underneath his Fedora, but he had a large hooked nose that should make him easy to identify.

Once the arrangements were made for the next day's early morning flight, Thomas returned to the monastery, where he stayed the night. Tossing and turning on the mats, Thomas finally got up around two o'clock and walked out toward the road. The blue car was parked across from the main entrance to the temple.

Not even trying to hide.

* * *

ON TUESDAY MORNING, Anne woke in Michael's arms and without a word they moved together again. This time there was no cosmic event, no blending of lives, just Anne and Michael together in the present moment. Their lovemaking was gentle, like the mourning doves calling to each other outside their window. When they lay still again, Anne whispered, "Our timing is terrible. Now I have to go make eyes at Paul Marchant."

Michael traced the line of her collarbone, then ran his fingers gently down her sternum and around each nipple. Anne turned over on her side and pushed against Michael, relishing the warmth against her back. He shifted position and entered her again. Afterward, they drifted back to sleep.

Some time later, the phone rang. Michael grunted as she moved to answer it.

"Wake-up call," she said, and closed her eyes again.

"Do you want to go to Dahshur today?"

"Hum?" Anne turned back to him sleepily.

"To Dahshur. That's where the conference is going."

She frowned in imitation of a petulant child. "Do we have to get up?"

Michael kissed her forehead and said, "We have business to attend to."

"Business. I much prefer no business."

"Tahir wants us to take the crystals into the Red Pyramid."

"Haven't we done enough initiations yet?" Anne turned over and looked up at Michael.

His eyes took on a mischievous gleam. "I'm surprised you're not eager to see Paul. I thought you had a date."

Anne pinched him.

"Ouch."

"It's not a date. Besides, Mr. Marchant doesn't grace the tours with his presence."

"I need to go, though."

"Oh, all right."

They showered together and Anne thought they'd have a third round, but it was not to be.

"You need to refuel," she teased.

Michael kissed her deeply, the warm water running down their bodies. After a minute, he pulled back. "Tonight."

"That's a date." She stood for another minute in the warm water, taking it all in. Finally, they were together. And it all felt so normal. Not the usual jostling of preferences, the compromises. Michael fit like tailor-made clothes.

Michael dried off, then picked his wrinkled pants off the floor and pulled them on.

"Let's hope no one's watching," he said, as he opened the door to Anne's suite and peeked out.

Arnold stood in the hallway pretending to read the paper. He turned to him and said, "The coast is clear."

Anne changed and headed for breakfast. Arnold sauntered behind her, his head turning from side to side as he surveyed the grounds.

"Michael was not observed," he said.

"Good." She took in his slight smile. "What?"

"Nothing."

After Anne filled her plate at the buffet, Debbie and Rita waved her over to their table. "Where were you?" Rita asked.

"You missed it," Debbie said. "His presentation was incredible."

"Who did I miss?"

"Kramer!" Rita looked at her compatriot. "Honestly, she's impossible."

"You look awfully relaxed this morning. What did you do?" Debbie asked.

"I took the day off. I knew I could rely on you to tell me what I missed."

The two embarked on a detailed explanation of Kramer's conspiracy theories, relieving Anne of any explanations. She saw Michael come in and a rush of warmth filled her. She turned her eyes back to the two women, trying to pass off her reaction to Michael as shock at Kramer's revelation of how the Masons were running the United States military.

They talked all the way to the Red Pyramid. Halfway up the steep climb to the pyramid's entrance, their breath gave out. Anne saw Paul Marchant get off the second bus. When he came to the first steps of the climb, he gallantly offered a hand to Maria Lol Ha, ignoring the two warrior priests who walked in front of and behind them.

What's he up to, she wondered.

The door to the inside of the pyramid was a third of the way up the side. Once there, they had to climb back down two hundred fifty feet into the bowels of the structure. This took all her attention. The passage was just under four feet high and, after last night's workout, Anne's thighs started to burn. She was in the middle of the group, so she couldn't stop to rest. She stretched her legs as soon as she arrived in the first chamber. Many in the group climbed the steps at the other end of the first chamber to view the smaller cavities, but Anne sat on the stone floor waiting for Tahir to begin. He placed them in a triple-layered circle for his ritual. She leaned gratefully against the limestone wall and Tahir began his chant.

This was not his usual brief chant. He went on, his volume intensifying until the echoes and harmonics from his voice seemed to vibrate the massive structure. The vibration spread under the pyramid and stretched to the north and south, seeming to make the land itself shiver. The crystal tucked next to her heart pulsed in harmony with the energy. She felt other small points of vibration in the room, one where Michael sat. One coming from Tahir. Another vibration joined in, then a fourth. More small points of pulsation started. Now there were more than six. Apparently, the pyramid was resonating with every crystal in the room, new or old. And this group had plenty of crystals.

Anne relaxed again, enjoying the celestial choir she heard in her mind, the frequency much too high for her physical ears. Finally, Tahir's voice grew quieter, then stopped altogether. Anne reluctantly opened her eyes to find Maria looking at her. The woman nodded, then looked away.

The chanting had attracted other tourists and a whole group clogged the passageway. They started to move into the chamber once Tahir stopped, and suddenly the place was entirely too crowded for Anne. She started the long duck-walk out of the pyramid. Rita was right behind her, talking again.

"Wow, did you feel that? I thought the whole place was going to shake down around us."

Anne just nodded, out of breath. Her euphoria gave way to her lack of sleep. Once they emerged from the pyramid, Anne found a rock to sit on, admiring the view on this clear day. The Step Pyramid rose in the distance and even farther north the pyramids at Abusir. The Giza pyramids stood faint on the horizon. So that's what she'd felt.

The group finally piled back on the buses and went on to the Bent Pyramid, where Tahir explained his theory of this structure. "Egyptologists say the builders of this pyramid got to a certain point and realized they'd made a mistake. The structure would not stand at the angle they'd started with, so they simply changed the angle.

"This is foolishness. The ancient Khemitians, living with all their senses open, did not make these kinds of mistakes. This pyramid was built this way for a reason. Seneferu is supposed to have been the king who commissioned this pyramid along with the Red Pyramid and the collapsed pyramid at Meidum, but Seneferu has a different meaning. *Neferu* is the plural form of *Nefer*, which means 'harmony,' like the harmony of vibration we just experienced in our ceremony. When you put the Sen in front, you get *Seneferu,* which means 'double harmony.' This pyramid resonates to two frequencies. It has a double voice."

A group of about ten had latched on strongly to Tahir's teachings, forming a circle around him. They fired questions. The wind had picked up, making it difficult for those farther away from him to hear. Michael, of course, was stuck to him like glue. Anne would hear it all tonight. She smiled in anticipation.

The group stopped for lunch at a picturesque open-air restaurant, complete with mud-brick ovens and an aviary full of pigeons. Marchant continued to court Maria and the two priests walked beside her like herders, one on each side. Michael sat with Tahir one table over. His eyes brushed over Anne momentarily and she stirred in her seat.

She turned to the duo who had joined her at a long table. "So who's scheduled to talk this afternoon?"

"That gorgeous man over there talking to our guide."

"Michael?" Anne's voice must have betrayed something, because both Rita and Debbie stopped eating and looked at her.

"She's got a crush," Rita said.

"Definitely."

Anne felt the heat rising to her face. "I'm not the only one who finds him attractive."

Rita looked over at Michael. "I'll bet half the group has made an offer."

"I heard him speak in New York. And that other guy," Anne said.

"Which one?" Rita asked.

"The one talking to the Maya. I forget his name."

"Oh, Paul Marchant. Definitely not a dreamboat, but he's smart. What do you think of his theories?" Debbie asked.

"I'm not much of a math wiz," Anne said, relieved the conversation had veered away from Michael.

"Sacred geometry is the key to all the sites," Rita put in.

"But what is the practical use of this fancy math?" Anne asked.

"The entire universe is structured on the principles of sacred geometry. The same harmonics are repeated on all levels, from the galactic right down to the molecule. If your city or home is built using the same structure, it will resonate harmonically with the entire universe. There's a guy who proved that the emotion of love actually makes the heart chakra resonate in a harmonic of the golden ratio."

"So it would be easier to enter higher states of consciousness," Anne concluded.

Rita and Debbie looked blank for a second.

"I suppose so," Debbie said.

Luckily, it was time to board the bus. The heavy meal affected the duo and they soon dropped off to sleep. Anne was grateful for the quiet. Michael was on the other bus with most of the speakers and Tahir.

She decided to attend Michael's talk that evening. No sense calling attention to herself. Once she was back in her room, she called Michael, but he wasn't in. There were no messages from Dr. Abernathy. She wondered how Thomas was doing in the East. She thought of going to Tahir's but, after two large yawns, decided a nap would be the best way to spend the rest of the afternoon.

When she woke, the sky was darkening. After a shower, she hung the crystal around her neck rather than tuck it away. No one was going to attack her tonight. Then she walked into the lecture hall just as Michael was being introduced, and slipped into an empty chair in the back, unnoticed by Rita or Debbie who had secured seats close to the front. Rita kept craning her neck over the crowd, looking for Anne. There was an empty seat next to them, but she couldn't imagine listening to their commentary during Michael's talk.

She was not disappointed. Michael gave his usual stellar performance, carefully tracing the major metaphysical traditions back to ancient Egypt. The audience listened, quiet, absorbed looks on most faces.

Toward the end of his talk, Michael said, "All my life I've found evidence of a living wisdom tradition in Egypt, but with all my trips I've been unable to meet with anyone who had knowledge of this group, much less actually meet anyone from it. Until now."

Expectancy filled the room, like someone had tightened a hidden string in the audience.

"On this trip, I have been privileged to meet a man trained in the ancient tradition of Khemit, a man who has shared some of these teachings with me and with you. This man, ladies and gentlemen, is none other than our guide, Tahir Nur Ahram." He pointed to Tahir, who stood and nodded, shyly accepting the burst of applause. "Do you have anything you'd like to say?"

Tahir shook his head and started to sit down, but the applause doubled. Some shouted for him to speak. Tahir rose from his chair again, an imposing figure in his dark *gallabiya*. His white-turbaned head rose above the crowd, who were now on their feet cheering.

Once on stage, Tahir leaned into the mike and said. "I thank you, but I give you these teachings when we are at the sites. I do not have anything to add to Michael's wonderful talk. He took the words I would have spoken."

People had lined up at the mikes and proceeded to ask questions. A man about forty asked, "How can you claim that an intact tradition exists here? It's been centuries."

Tahir nodded. "Egypt has been under the influence of foreign ideas for a very long time, but our teachings have been passed down orally for thousands of years in secret. I do not say we remember everything, but the sites hold the knowledge. They have spoken to many of you."

"You claim the ancient Khemitians built the pyramids, but how could they have had the ability? Who taught them?"

Tahir repeated the teaching of the five stages of the sun. Then he said, "During Aten, all humans have full consciousness. All the senses are open and the encyclopedia of all knowledge is open to everyone."

More questions followed for Michael: "Kramer explained the Masonic stranglehold on the American government, yet you claim they come from this wisdom tradition. How can you reconcile this?"

"Mr. Kramer is a meticulous researcher and a man of great integrity, but we disagree on this point. Certainly, some Masonic lodges fell into dark practices and their presence in the military has been confirmed. It seems logical that some may be working with a more hidden group of international interests. But these are a minority. Most of the lodges still follow the old ways."

Anne sighed. How much longer? He still had to sign books, but he was obviously enjoying himself. He was a born teacher. His eyes shone as he listened to each question. His answers were thoughtful, pitched for the understanding of that particular individual. She'd have to share him with the world, but why so soon? She sat in the back, waiting for their time alone.

After another ten minutes, the emcee intervened, "It's getting late and tomorrow our indigenous wisdom keeper"—the man smiled self-consciously—"will be taking us to Abusir. Michael will be signing books in the lobby and you may ask him questions during the rest of the conference."

The audience clapped long and hard, then reluctantly gathered their things and started to leave. Anne sat across the lobby, watching. After another hour, Michael was finally alone. He gathered his briefcase and stood looking around. She sent him a psychic nudge, just to see how sensitive he was. After a second, he turned and looked straight at her. *Your room?* The question from him formed in her mind.

Yes, she sent, delighted at their communication.

Anne walked toward her room slowly, allowing Michael time to stash his briefcase and extra books in his room. She rounded the corner near her room and heard footsteps behind her. Her body warmed at the sound and she turned, prepared to step into his arms.

Maria Lol Ha and her two priests stood there instead.

Anne came up short.

Michael turned the corner at just that moment.

Maria looked from Anne to Michael and said, "Good. I want to talk to you both."

Desire for her second night with Michael wrestled with curiosity over this mysterious pronouncement, but Anne was too well schooled to allow any of her tumult to show on her face. She offered her hand to Maria.

"I'm Anne—Greene. It's a pleasure to meet you."

The woman shook Anne's hand, "Thank you."

Michael offered his hand and started to introduce himself, but Maria said, "I know who you are. I know who both of you are."

Anne shot a quick glance at Michael, who shrugged.

"Can we talk somewhere in private?" Maria asked.

"Certainly." Anne glanced at Arnold, who'd appeared from the shadows.

"Your room is the best," Arnold said.

Maria took a step forward.

Anne quickly said, "I must apologize. This man is head of security for my family. There have been attempts on my life while in Egypt. He must clear everyone."

This euphemism was lost on Maria, so Anne said, "He needs to search you and your friends."

The two men stepped in front of Maria.

"Of course, your guards may search us as well," she added.

Maria spoke to her two guards in their own language. After a few exchanges, she nodded.

Arnold frisked the two men, then walked toward Maria, but they put up their hands. "No."

"I'm sure she is fine," Anne said.

Arnold went into his room and returned with a small metal detector. "Is this acceptable?"

One of the men nodded.

Arnold passed the metal rod over Maria. "She's clean," he whispered to Anne.

"You must search Michael," Anne whispered back.

"Oh, right." He did the same to Michael, whose eyebrows arched.

Anne bit her lips to keep from laughing. "Please, come in."

She ushered the group into the sitting room in her suite. The two warrior priests stayed outside and motioned for Arnold to do the same. He agreed.

When the three were seated, Anne said, "May I offer you anything?" This situation was perplexing, not to mention inconvenient.

Maria shook her head. "We have a task to accomplish."

Anne looked at her blankly.

Before Maria could explain herself further, there was a knock at the door.

Anne walked to the door and put her eye to the peephole. She opened the door to reveal Tahir.

"Tefnut told me to come," he said rather breathlessly. He hurried into the room, then stopped in his tracks when he saw Maria.

Anne closed the door behind him. "It's all right. She wanted to talk with us."

Good," Maria said when she saw Tahir. Then she reached beneath her white blouse and pulled a necklace over her head. Dangling from it was a three-inch clear crystal point.

"Oh, my God!" Anne groped for the chair behind her.

Michael reached beneath his shirt collar and pulled out his crystal.

Anne's fingers closed on the chain of her necklace and she pulled it over her head.

"*Hum De la la!*" Tahir exclaimed—"praise be to God"—and he took his own crystal from around his neck and held it out. "Four are found," he said.

"Five," Anne said, "counting Paul Marchant's."

Michael turned to the Mayan woman. "May we examine your stone?"

Maria stretched out her hand in answer.

Michael bent over the artifact, carefully examining the setting but leaving the stone untouched in Maria's palm. "It's the image of Seshat, the seven-petaled flower."

"*Aiwa!*—yes!" Tahir said.

"Seshat?" Maria asked.

"She is the consort of Djehuti, the sacred scribe, the bringer of sound. Seshat gives form to the sound," Tahir said.

Yes." Maria sat forward. "The Maya call this Hunab K'u, the giver of movement and measure. I wish to share with you the story of my people and these stones. To the Maya, this is a seven-pointed star. It represents the star system our ancestors came from, the Pleiades."

"Star system?" Anne asked.

Maria nodded. "When our ancestors came to this planet, they went to four areas of the Earth. One of them was Egypt, and this group was called the Naga Maya."

Tahir nodded. "I know of a small temple south of Sakkara called 'Maya.' I will take you there."

Maria nodded her thanks. She settled back in her chair and her voice took on a formal, storytelling rhythm. "Long ago, before the worlds were separated, all the descendants of the star people lived in harmony with the Earth and with each other. We were one member of a large family of star nations. Elders from those nations came here to teach us and left behind a gift of themselves, children who mixed the traits of the star elders with those of Earth's people. We lived in a golden age, connected to the other star systems and dimensions.

"The technology"—she stumbled over this word—"that kept this flow alive was built in stone. Temples were raised at certain power spots to . . . make bigger?"

"Amplify," Anne said.

"Yes, amplify the energy with flowing water and crystals. These temples kept the Earth connected to the galactic river of energy. Certain crystals were brought from the home worlds and given to the star children to link the temples with each tribe's place of origin. A crystal from the Seven Sisters." She held hers up.

"But all knew this golden age would not last because of the path our sun takes in his journey around the center of the galaxy. We go through sections of space that cannot support full consciousness and we pass through times of strife. The star elders left before the sun reached this place. Then when the signs of decline began, the tribes separated the keys. They turned off the sites to spare those star nations who remain always in the light. Each star clan took its crystal and hid it away, keeping the story for their proper use secret."

Maria's eyes shone. "We have come almost to the end of this time of darkness. The sun travels to a place of light, and the light will grow and grow until we once again take our place in the galactic family. Our job is to restore the flow to one of the greatest power spots on Earth."

As Maria spoke these words, a deep shiver ran the length of Anne's spine, and this shiver had nothing to do with Michael's proximity. It was recognition that awoke with these words. Her eyes filled. Maria reached out and took Anne's hand. Warmth flowed into her and the tears spilled down Anne's cheeks unchecked.

Tahir broke the silence. "Your tradition teaches that these crystals come from other planets?"

"Yes," Maria said. "My people come from the Pleiades. Michael's crystal is from the people of Sirius. Your crystal, Tahir, is from Vega in the Lyran system, the origin of most humanoids."

Tahir sat staring at Maria, his mouth open. Anne had never seen him amazed by anything before.

"Vega," Michael repeated.

Maria spoke with such assuredness, it was difficult to doubt her. "Anne's crystal is from a planet the Western scientists have not charted. It is the source of the cat and bird races, a planet of great winged cats. Paul Marchant's crystal is from the great intellects of Orion."

"Well, that makes sense," Anne said. "He's all brain and no heart."

"Yes," Maria said. "That is why the Orion races came to this water world, to grapple with emotion."

"And the sixth crystal?" Tahir asked.

"We do not know who holds it, but the stone comes from Antares."

Anne roused herself from contemplating Maria's story. "Thomas is on the trail of that crystal. He found a scroll that indicates it might have been taken to the East. He's in India now."

"We pray for his success," Maria said, "because there is a danger."

"What?" Michael asked.

"The turning of the Earth cycles is natural, part of our sun's path around the center of the galaxy. But it is necessary for humans to reconnect the temple sites to amplify the link. This is how we are vulnerable. It is possible for these links to be used to send destructive energy back through the loop, to affect the star nations that have already ascended. There is a plan to use the Orion crystal to override our mission."

Anne shook her head. "I'm not sure I understand."

Michael sat forward, his knuckles white on the arm of the sofa. "Some group could stop the Awakening?"

"But Tahir said that isn't possible." Anne looked at him now for confirmation.

"This is my understanding," Tahir agreed.

Maria continued. "Just as we are members of a huge force that has incarnated at this time to help the Earth return to the light, there is a group of souls who have come here to stop it. They wish to use this communication link to bring down the temples of light on other worlds as well. If they succeed in taking over our mission, the body that rules over these ascended planets is prepared to destroy Earth to stop this from happening."

"Destroy Earth?" Michael jumped to his feet. "How could this be possible?"

"It is quite possible," Maria's voice was steady. "Once the link is reestablished, they can send a pulsed energy wave back through the link that will rip the planet apart. The entire galaxy cannot be risked. We must not allow these dark forces to win. Our very existence depends on it."

23

---

*A*nne stretched out along the length of Michael's body, luxuriating in the feel of skin on skin. She nestled her head in the crook of his arm, content after their early-morning lovemaking. Their two crystals sat together on the nightstand, refracting rainbows onto the walls from the east-facing window. But her peace was short-lived.

"What do you think about it?" she asked.

"I think this is the most wonderful morning of my life." Michael burrowed beneath her hair and kissed her neck.

Anne smiled. "I mean Maria's story."

"Oh, that." Michael flipped over onto his back. "I don't know what to make of such ideas."

Anne turned over and propped her head on her elbow, looking down into his face. "Scientists pretty much agree that given the distances involved in interstellar travel, the amount of fuel needed would be double the size of the craft itself. The energy requirements are simply prohibitive."

"According to our current level of scientific understanding, Ms. Scully," Michael added. "Haven't Joe Whyte and even our Mr. Marchant convinced you the Khemitians were more scientifically advanced than we are? We still don't have cranes to lift the heaviest blocks in the Great Pyramid. Most people don't realize we still couldn't duplicate it."

"So how did these aliens get here?"

Michael reached up and traced the bridge of her nose. "Maybe they used some laws of nature we don't understand yet. Quantum physicists theorize that space travel could be achieved by bending space in front of the craft, creating a stable space-time bubble for the ship to travel in."

"Maybe, but what about her claim that the shadow forces plan to use the Giza power spot to affect other planets?"

Michael shrugged. "So many people have predicted global catastrophes, but none of them have materialized."

"The shadow government seems interested in power, plain and simple. Controlling the Earth's energy sources and the global economy."

"Is that all?"

Anne smiled at his tone. "And any government that gets in their way. But planets in other dimensions? It seems like a fairy tale to me."

"A month ago you would have considered some of your visions fairy tales."

"That's true."

"We'll just do our job. That way we'll never have to find out if she's right or not."

Anne turned to face him. "Maybe we should skip the conference today."

"I think it's best if we go. Keep our cover."

"Do we still have a cover? Maria knows. Marchant suspects something. Somebody attacked us in Aswan."

"Good point," Michael conceded.

"It seems strange, going shopping. That's not how these adventures work in the movies."

"What should we do instead? We're waiting for our initiation, waiting for Marchant to contact you, waiting for Thomas to find the last key. All our efforts to find it here have turned up nothing."

"Has Tahir scheduled our time in the pyramid?" Anne laid her head on his shoulder.

"Saturday night, around midnight."

"We'd better get some sleep tonight. I haven't had a full night in a while."

"I don't regret a minute of it." Michael pulled her to him again.

* * *

THOMAS PEEKED out the window of the monastery before going outside. Through the early morning fog, he could make out the same blue car that had followed him yesterday. Apparently, they'd spent the night outside. The same car followed him all the way to the airport. He decided ignoring it was the best policy. He was glad Steve, his security man, was along. It looked like he might need him.

During the flight to Lhasa, Thomas forgot about his tail. The mountain peaks piled higher and higher on top of each other, reaching beyond the sky straight for heaven. The rising sun turned them a deep rose.

Once they landed, Steve rented a Land Rover. They were blessed with clear skies and good roads. This time they were followed by a jeep. On the ferry, Thomas tried to get a good look at who was following them.

Steve advised against it. "Pretend you don't see them. Let me handle it."

They arrived at the Samye Monastery in the early afternoon. Lama Tenzin had furnished Thomas with a letter of introduction. Upon presenting this to the main office, he was ushered in to see the Rinpoche, who listened carefully to Thomas's story, interrupting him several times to clarify points. Thomas was impressed with the man's grasp of history. He seemed well versed in the European metaphysical traditions and their struggles. His understanding of Egyptology was strong as well.

Finally, after Thomas finished his story and the Rinpoche seemed satisfied, the monk said, "I need some time to go through our library. Can we meet tomorrow?"

Thomas swallowed his objection. Only seven days remained before the alignment. Thomas took his leave, and he and Steve drove back to their hotel in Lhasa. This time the jeep followed more closely. The man with the Fedora and hooked nose sat in the passenger seat. A Chinese military officer drove.

It was dark by the time Thomas got back to the room. He put in his daily progress report to Dr. Abernathy; then he, Ralph, and Steve went in search of a restaurant. The ubiquitous jeep appeared when they'd walked only half a block.

Steve nodded his head toward them. "They're just trying to intimidate us. Apparently, they do that sometimes to people who seem to be involved with the monks."

"I'm not worried about them. I've seen worse." Thomas had a bad headache from the altitude, even though he'd drunk a great deal of water. They went into the first place they found and, once they were seated, the waiter brought them each a cup of yak butter tea. With all his travels, Thomas had never mastered this particular taste, but it was impossible to refuse. With his headache, he just hoped he wouldn't get sick. He forced down a few sips of the liquid and nodded his appreciation to the waiter. He was grateful when a rice, vegetable, and bean dish smelling strongly of curry was placed before him. The food helped his head and he felt a bit more substantial by the end of the meal.

After receiving some helpful tourist hints from the waiter, none of which they had time to pursue, the three men gathered their coats. Thomas pushed open the door and saw the jeep parked directly in front of the restaurant. Steve stepped forward, putting Thomas and Ralph behind him. They took two more steps and more jeeps rushed from down the street, jumping the curb on either side of them and coming to a screaming halt. Men dressed in Chinese military uniforms jumped out of the vehicles and pointed automatic rifles at them.

"Don't resist," Steve whispered and raised his hands in the air.

Thomas took a step back, but ran smack into the closed restaurant door. One of the soldiers stepped toward Thomas, brandishing his rifle. Thomas raised his hands. "What's going on?" he asked, looking around for someone in charge.

The man in the fedora climbed out of his jeep and sauntered up. He stuck his face into Thomas's and said, "You're under arrest."

"How can you arrest me? You're not with the Chinese government," Thomas said.

The man nodded for the soldiers to handcuff the three men.

"What's the charge?" Thomas shouted, trying to pull his hands away from the soldiers who'd grabbed him.

The man spat on the sidewalk just in front of Thomas's boots. "Take him away."

* * *

EARLIER THAT AFTERNOON in Egypt, the conference group arrived in two buses at the Khan el-Khalili market in downtown Cairo. Tahir went to the middle of the plaza and waited for the group to follow. A large circle formed around him and a flock of hopeful pigeons pecked around their feet.

Tahir pitched his voice so everyone could hear. "Several hundred years ago, this was a slave market. The people were held in the rooms above the ground floor." The group's eyes followed the closely packed buildings up several stories. "Now it is a much happier place, the best shopping in Cairo—jewelry, clothes, statues, papyrus. Enjoy yourselves and don't be shy about bargaining. It's expected. I'll be in this teahouse if you have questions." He pointed to the first alleyway. "We'll meet back in the plaza in two hours. The alleys twist and turn, so don't get lost." Tahir walked across the plaza, where he was greeted by the restaurant owner and given a prime seat.

The group milled around, the adventuresome already making off toward the narrow alleyways. Anne set off for the far lane to look for the papyrus shop where Michael planned to meet her. She found it quickly and stopped in front of the store.

"We have fine silks," a man behind her said. "Very good price."

"Replicas from the museum store. Much better price," another called out.

Anne spotted a restaurant a few stores down and took refuge there. The waiter approached her table.

"Mint tea," she said.

He nodded and went back to the kitchen. She sat back in her chair, relaxing. From her vantage point, she could see down the narrow alley crammed with shops, workers, and tourists. The air carried snippets of Japanese, French, German, English, and Arabic. The windows of the shops gleamed with color.

A man in his early twenties stepped into the teahouse and approached her table. "Such a beautiful—"

"Go away," Anne said in a firm voice.

"But it is such a waste for a beautiful woman to sit alone."

"*Imshee!*" Anne shouted. "Scram!"

Several men at another table looked up. Arnold materialized beside her wooer, who turned and made his escape. Arnold sat down at a nearby table. The waiter brought her order and Anne sat sipping tea, enjoying the display of humanity that poured past her table, careful to avoid eye contact with any men. A knot of Japanese tourists went by, the latest in camera equipment hanging from their necks. A European couple walked by, the woman dressed in short shorts. Several eyes followed her. A boy around ten offered blue-glazed, mass-produced scarabs. She shook her head.

"There you are." Michael's voice surprised her. "I thought we were going to meet in the papyrus store."

"The shopkeepers started in on me."

Michael shook his head. "Things used to be different, but with the economy, people are getting aggressive."

"Let's go contribute to Egyptian prosperity. We can't do anything to save the world right this minute." Anne put an Egyptian five-pound note on the table and took Michael's arm.

"We hardly know each other, remember?"

She put her hands in her pockets. "Who are you buying presents for?"

"No one."

"What? Here you come to Egypt and don't bring anything home for your family?"

"I come to Egypt a lot. They're tired of my trinkets."

"My family will expect something. Assuming we make it back and the world is still intact."

"I'm planning on it."

"So show me around."

They entered the papyrus shop and the owner greeted Michael like a long-lost brother. Michael turned to Anne. "This is my very special friend. She's looking for quality and I brought her to you."

"What are you looking for, madam? Anything in particular?"

"Show her your Nut." Michael turned to Anne. "His colors are excellent."

The man pointed to the samples hanging on the walls.

"Oh, that one. I've never seen a double one like that." After forty-five minutes, Anne left the shop with three double Nuts, one Isis with her wings spread wide, a Ma'at, and several generic court scenes. She jostled several passersby with her cardboard tubes. "Maybe I should have asked him to ship them."

"It's not too late. Let's go back—"

Two men ran smack into Michael.

Michael let out a yell. He dropped the package he was carrying and grabbed his arm.

"What's the matter?" Anne stepped closer to him. Michael's face was pale, his eyes registering pain. "What happened?" She took his hand away and saw blood.

"They took my crystal," Michael said.

"Oh, my God!" She looked around, but the two men were gone.

Arnold was at her side.

"They've got the crystal," she repeated.

Arnold took off.

"Let me see." Anne guided Michael into a side alley and took off his jacket. "Roll up your sleeve."

There was a round hole in the middle of Michael's forearm. The flesh was white immediately around the puncture wound, then an angry red. The bleeding had already slowed.

Arnold reappeared. "It's no use. They're gone."

"They stabbed him." Anne pointed to Michael's arm.

Arnold checked Michael's pulse and pupils. "How do you feel?"

Michael blinked. "It hurts."

"Are you dizzy?"

"No."

"Can you breathe?"

Michael nodded as he gingerly lifted his shirtsleeve away from the wound.

"Any stomach cramps?"

"No."

Arnold's shoulders relaxed. "Then it probably wasn't poison."

"Poison?" Michael looked up at Arnold in alarm.

"But we need to keep you under observation. Let's get a taxi. I've got a first-aid kit in my pack." He started walking Michael out of the market toward the square.

Anne followed. The man from the papyrus shop ran after her. "Is he hurt?"

"Just a scrape. Somebody wasn't being careful." She handed him the tubes and her business card. "Can you mail my packages?"

"Anything for my friend."

She opened her purse. "Here's two hundred pounds."

"But this is too much."

"Keep the change for your trouble."

The man hesitated.

"Please." Anne turned and ran after Arnold and Michael.

"*Sukran,*" he called after her.

They quickly found a cab. By the time they were halfway across town, Michael's arm had stopped bleeding and the pain had lessened.

"Did you see anything?" Arnold asked them both.

"Nothing," Michael said. "My back was turned."

"And you?" Arnold looked at Anne.

"Two men. One was just under six feet tall, the other shorter. Both wore dark-blue *gallabiyas* and white turbans. I think one had a beard."

"Any distinguishing markings?"

Anne's forehead wrinkled, then she shook her head. "I can't remember anything."

"Nothing to go on," Arnold said.

"They got the key. What the hell was this all about?" Michael pointed to his arm.

"We still haven't ruled out an assassination attempt," Arnold answered.

"Assassination? Why would anyone want to kill me?"

"Let's see," Arnold said. "You're involved in a plot to change world power. You've become romantically involved with a Le Clair."

"All right." Michael looked from Arnold to Anne. "But if they wanted to kill me, they'd have used a different weapon or stabbed me in a vital organ."

"Not necessarily," Arnold said. "They didn't want to create a scene in such a crowded place and risk getting caught. If I were doing it, I'd use a slow-acting poison or something to induce a heart attack later."

Michael stared at Arnold, speechless.

"Don't worry," Arnold added. "I can test your blood for most slow-acting agents once we get to the hotel."

"I see." Michael found his voice. "What if I am poisoned?"

"I have the antidotes for most agents commonly used in espionage circles."

"Do you have a tank hidden away somewhere?"

"Not necessary." Arnold kept a steady eye on Michael.

Michael looked at Anne, who just shrugged.

They rode in silence for a while and Michael closed his eyes. Arnold leaned forward, but Anne put her hand on his shoulder. "Let him meditate."

After seeing that Michael's breath was even, Arnold leaned back.

"Why him? Why not me?" Anne whispered.

Arnold shook his head. "Who can say? He's involved with several high-profile spiritual groups."

"High profile?" Anne said. "You'd barely heard of them."

"But Dr. Abernathy knew them. You can bet the Illuminati know them and have some kind of conflict with them. It's all speculation at this point. We don't have any evidence."

The taxi pulled up in front of the Mena House and they rushed to Michael's room. They opened the door to find all the drawers emptied into the middle of the floor and his books strewn on the bed.

"For pity's sake." Michael sank onto the floor.

"Check to see if anything else is missing."

Michael searched his briefcase and looked through the papers scattered over the bed and floor.

Anne turned. "Arnold, go get the blood kit."

He left without comment.

"I'm sorry, Anne." Michael sat on the floor amidst the contents of his overturned drawers, his face pale beneath his tousled dark hair.

"What are you sorry about?" Anne sat next to him and took his hand.

"My crystal, what else? Who do you think did it?"

"The shadow government's black ops men. Who else?"

"I'd like to find the bastards." Michael tightened his grip on her hand.

Anne gently pulled away from him. She opened the torn sleeve and looked at his arm. The red had faded, but it was swollen now. "It's better."

Michael sat with slumped shoulders, his eyes filled with sorrow. "What are we going to do?" he whispered.

"We'll figure something out." She'd never seen him like this. She tried to inject her voice with optimism. "It'll work out. It has to."

"I can't do anything without my crystal."

"Are you certain we need all six?"

He nodded. "Looks like we're going to find out whether Maria's right or not."

Arnold returned with a medical kit. "Come, sit in this chair. Hold out your arm."

Michael complied, his movements wooden.

Arnold swabbed Michael's arm and drew blood into a syringe. He opened a case, revealing a series of vials, each with a different colored liquid in the bottom, and began injecting small amounts of Michael's blood into each one. "The results will take about fifteen minutes." He turned to Anne. "I suggest you consider allowing Michael to move in with you. Otherwise, I'll have to secure this room as well."

Anne turned to Michael, who was looking more cheerful. "But what about our cover?"

"We've been spending nights in your room anyway. We'll just have to be careful coming and going."

Anne nodded.

"Good," Arnold said. "Bob and I will search everything before we move your things."

"You don't have to wait on me," Michael objected.

"We need to sweep the room and your personal possessions anyway. There may be several bugs."

Michael nodded. "Let me know when you're ready to pack."

"I want you to rest," responded Arnold. "You've been attacked, remember?"

Michael sat back in his chair and dropped his hands in a gesture of surrender.

Arnold looked at his watch, then walked over to the various colored vials.

Anne crowded in to see.

"You're in my light," Arnold said.

Anne sat back, holding her breath.

Arnold held each vial up to the light, his eyes squinting. Finally, he stood up. "There are no agents present in your blood that I can identify."

"What does that mean?"

"It means there may be something present we don't know about," Anne explained. "Or that somebody just punched some flesh out of your arm—" She stopped, eyes wide.

"It could be," Arnold said.

"What?" Michael asked.

"Maybe they just wanted a sample of you to use with your crystal," Anne said.

Michael sat back heavily in his chair. "These people are really twisted."

* * *

DR. ABERNATHY was in the firm's library when his secretary rushed in. "There's an urgent message, sir."

"Can't you put it through?"

"I think you'll want to take it in your office."

He got up and walked down the hall with his secretary. "Who's calling?" he asked.

"Assistant director of the CIA."

Dr. Abernathy hurried to the phone, closing the door behind him. "This is Abernathy. What's happened?"

The voice at the other end identified himself, then said, "It is my duty to inform you that the Chinese government has arrested a Mr. Thomas Le Clair in Tibet."

Abernathy's breath caught in his chest. "What's the charge?"

"Espionage. It's always espionage in Tibet."

"Is anything being done to seek his release?"

"The State Department will receive the report at the end of business today."

Abernathy looked at his watch. Two o'clock. Three hours.

"Can I have the details?" Abernathy wrote down the particulars of where Thomas was being held and by whom. "Thank you." He punched line two and dialed Spear. When his secretary had put him through, he told him the news. "What's our best option?"

"Call Katherine."

"Katherine? She's the last person we need on this."

"She's friends with that senator who toured China last year. That's our best bet for fast action."

"I'll call her."

He buzzed his secretary. "Get me Katherine Le Clair, please." She had a married name, but nobody used it. The phone on his desk rang. His secretary said, "She's on the line, sir." A beep announced he was connected. "Katherine, I've got bad news."

"What's happened to Anne?"

"It's not Anne. It's Thomas."

"What's happened?" Katherine's voice was sharp.

"He's been arrested in China. Tibet, actually."

There was a pause. "Tibet?" Katherine's voice had dropped an octave. "Arrested?"

"Spear thought your senator friend could help. The one who toured China last year."

"Oh, Rodman. Excellent idea. Give me the particulars and I'll call right away."

Dr. Abernathy repeated the information he had.

"What do you think they want with him?"

"He's been to the monasteries asking questions about one of the keys. Went to Dharamsala in India, then flew to Lhasa."

"Did they arrest any of the monks he spoke to?"

"I don't have that information."

"You should lodge a formal protest at the State Department. It will help speed things up."

"I'll do that, but you'll probably have him out before the paperwork goes through."

Katherine chuckled. "I'll let you know."

Dr. Abernathy hung up the phone and sat back in his office chair. Katherine could be all business when she needed to be, and Dr. Abernathy was grateful that this emergency had catapulted her into that mode. Politics still operated on friendships, favors, and grudges.

Rousing himself, he turned to his computer to check his e-mails. After decrypting Arnold's report, he read that Anne and Michael were continuing their relationship. Why couldn't she have waited? He just hoped their intelligence on Michael was complete. He didn't want any nasty surprises in that arena.

Arnold next said that a woman from Guatemala had revealed she held another crystal. Dr. Abernathy nodded his head. The Maya. That made sense. Excellent news. Just one more to find. This shed some light on the possible motives for Thomas's arrest. Anne's group now had four crystals under their control. Perhaps the Illuminati were trying to shift the balance of power back in their favor. That meant they probably knew where the last crystal was hidden and had plans to secure it.

He buzzed his secretary. "Joan, get me an appointment with our contact at the State Department, for as soon as I can get down there. Tell him it's an emergency."

"Right away, sir."

The computer emitted a series of beeps that signaled a top-priority transmission. Dr. Abernathy clicked on the relevant message and tapped his foot as it cycled through the decryption process. It was from Arnold. "Michael attacked in market. Key stolen. Strange wound on arm like punch biopsy. No poison. Please advise."

He stared at the computer screen, adding it all up. Thomas arrested. Michael's crystal stolen. The Illuminati were making their move seven days before the alignment. The anxiety he'd felt dissolved into a clear focus. He didn't want to fly down to D.C. for a meeting, but Thomas's life might depend on him doing just that. Was his old enemy trying to divide his attention, divert him from their real target? He'd double security on Anne.

He had to admit Michael was as good a target as she was, perhaps better, considering he'd trained all his life for this task. Compared to Michael, Anne was a beginner. Dr. Abernathy's last suspicions about Michael Levy evaporated. He rubbed his temples. He had to figure out the Illuminati's next move before they made it.

24

*D*r. Abernathy's cell phone rang early Friday morning, waking him from a deep sleep. He groped for it on the nightstand, almost knocking over the lamp. He pushed a button, but it just kept ringing.

"The one on the top left," Grace mumbled from her pillow.

He found the right button. "Abernathy here."

"I've been released." Thomas's voice flooded his ear.

"Thank God." He turned to Grace. "Thomas is out of prison." "What a relief." She sat up and grabbed his arm.

"Where are you?" Dr. Abernathy asked.

"In Lhasa still. We're still waiting for our flight plan to be approved. We'll be in New York tomorrow, I guess, or maybe Sunday. I'll call you when I know exactly."

"Are you all right?"

"Not a scratch, but they were about to start in on me when somebody interrupted them with a telegram. How did you get me out so fast?"

"Your mother," Dr. Abernathy said, his voice warm. "God bless Katherine. She called her senator friend, the one who toured China last year."

"Mother comes through once in a while."

"You should call her immediately. I'll bet she hasn't slept."

"I will. There's one more thing. I'm concerned about the Rinpoche I visited in the Samye Monastery. He may be in danger just because I went to see him." Thomas emphasized these last few words.

There's something he's not telling me. "We'll look into it."

"Good," Thomas sounded reassured.

"Can you send me an e-mail with the particulars?"

"If I get my computer back."

"I see. Is this line secure?"

"Steve scrambled the signal."

"Tell me his name." Dr. Abernathy looked around for something to write on. Grace handed him a pad of paper and a pen. He took down the information. "I was scheduled to fly down to D.C. this morning. Perhaps I need to take the trip after all."

"Definitely," Thomas said, his voice firm.

"I'll get right on it." Dr. Abernathy took a deep breath. "I'm very glad you're all right."

"Thanks. I'll see you soon."

"Good-bye." Dr. Abernathy looked at the clock. Five o'clock glowed in green letters. "If I lie back down, I'll never get up again."

Grace kissed his shoulder. "I'll make coffee while you're in the shower."

"I don't deserve you."

"I know."

* * *

ON SATURDAY EVENING close to midnight, Anne and Michael stood in the dark entrance to the Great Pyramid, ready to complete their last initiation. Tahir had invited Maria to join them. They numbered four key holders, but only three crystals.

"I feel like I'm missing a limb." Michael leaned against the massive stones.

Anne put her hand on his shoulder. "I think Tahir's right. They'll bring your crystal the night of the alignment."

"Then why steal it to begin with?"

"So they can perform weird experiments?"

Michael's eyes widened.

"Who knows?" Anne regretted her attempt at a joke. "They won't harm it permanently. They want to open the room as much as we do."

Michael prodded the ground with his foot.

"At least Thomas was released."

"True." Michael made an effort to sound cheerful.

"How's your arm?"

"It's nothing."

"I'll bet it still hurts."

"Just a dull ache. I'm fine, really."

Tahir climbed the steps to the entrance with his daughter Shani and a guard. This man pulled out a large key and opened the gate to the pyramid. Tahir handed him a wad of American dollars and whispered some instructions in Arabic, then turned and gestured for the group to enter.

"After you, ladies." Michael bowed slightly.

Anne followed Shani through the doorway. Crouching down, she started the climb. "Are we going to the King's Chamber?"

"Yes, although it's really the Central Chamber. No one was ever buried in here."

"So you don't believe the tomb was raided?" Anne's voice echoed in Mamoun's tunnel just inside the door.

"No original burial has ever been found in any pyramid."

"Ever?"

"No, but the archaeologists keep insisting they were all tombs."

Anne ducked down to enter the three-foot, eleven-inch-high ascending passageway. They climbed in silence. Shani stopped at the Grand Gallery and waited for Anne, who stretched her back, then climbed the wooden steps.

At the top, Shani said, "You first."

Anne bent low and entered the King's Chamber, a large granite rectangle with a long stone box at one end. Shani followed behind her, their footsteps loud as they walked to the center. When Michael and Maria joined them, Tahir began to speak.

"Welcome to the Central Chamber of the Great Per-Neter." His voice reverberated off the walls of the chamber. *"Per-Neter* means 'house of nature.' *Pyramid* comes from the Greek word *pyramidos,* meaning 'fire in the middle.'"

Anne shifted her weight, curious that Tahir was lecturing before the ritual.

"Per-Neters vibrate in harmony with the Earth's basic frequency. When they were fully functioning, they amplified that vibration to create a resonant harmonic field that assisted in the opening of human consciousness. The temples, the Per-Bas, were located around the pyramids. The people gathered there to open their awareness fully."

He paused. When the reverberations of his voice died down, he looked at Maria and said, "The pyramid also created energy for the civilization, as well as radio and microwaves that kept our planet connected to other worlds."

Does he think there was interstellar contact or is he just being polite? Anne wondered.

"When the Earth was falling into the age of darkness once again, an accident or natural cataclysmic event occurred that shut the pyramids down. You can see the cracks in the ceiling here and here." He pointed.

Anne looked up and saw repairs reinforcing the area around the cracks.

"During this age of darkness, the pyramids have been used as initiation chambers by those who struggled to remain in higher states of consciousness." Tahir looked at Michael. "Your metaphysical traditions are correct, but they do not realize that the pyramids were used differently during the age of light, the age of Aten."

Michael nodded.

"We are standing in the most highly vibratory environment on the planet. This entire structure was built to enhance vibration. This room floats on a bed of crushed crystal. The ceiling and chambers above receive the energy and further amplify it. Tonight we will use this great vibration to complete your initiation." He gestured for them all to join hands. Tahir closed his eyes, visibly gathering himself, then started to chant in his ancient language.

The sound awakened the pyramid. That was the only way to describe it. Anne felt the structure take her measure, like a doctor diagnosing a patient. Her crystal grew warm against her skin. She knew Michael must feel the loss of his. The chant went on, reaching beneath the pyramid, resonating the whole plateau. Anne started to feel light-headed. After what seemed like a long time, Tahir stopped his chant and waited for the echoes of his voice to quiet. But Anne felt a hum continuing just beneath hearing range.

"Everyone sit," Tahir said.

The sound of scraping feet filled the chamber. Anne wedged a small pillow she'd brought from her room beneath her and crossed her legs lotus style, leaving her spine straight and relaxed.

"We're going to turn the lights out now so the sound of the generator won't interfere with our work. The darkness will open your eyes to the higher dimensions. Everyone will have a turn in the box. When I touch you on the shoulder, follow me. Don't worry. I know my way around. Meanwhile, relax and allow yourself to tune into the energy of this site."

Tahir began his chant again, and this time Shani joined him, creating a harmonic. They sang louder and the sound reached inside Anne's skull and vibrated her very bones. The sensation was so deep she almost panicked, but she forced herself to keep breathing. A river of energy flowed up her spine, bringing an inner light.

The Sphinx turned around and smiled at her. But it wasn't the Sphinx of today. The statue had the face of a lioness crowned with the solar disk and she was surrounded by water. Rounded green hillsides sloped in the distance. Nine pyramids gleamed white in the sun. Above the flat top of the Great Pyramid, a glowing white crystal hovered, but it was not physical. Somehow Anne knew this stone completed the pyramid in a higher frequency.

Two men stood on a hill nearby, staffs in their hands. She recognized Michael and Joe Whyte in a previous life, two of the priests who ran the site. Her vision telescoped and she saw that the ends of the sticks they carried were similar to the staffs held by some of the Neters. *Vril sticks.* The name was instantly supplied. Through these wands, the priests amplified and directed energy that ran up their legs from the earth and entered their crowns from the etheric dimensions. As soon as Anne's attention went into the crown chakras of the two men, her own activated. She looked up through layers and layers of worlds, all pulsing in harmonic frequencies. Just at that moment, Tahir tapped her on the shoulder.

Anne stood and, to her surprise, she remained in this altered state. She felt as if she were fourteen feet tall. The room was full of light now, a soft, glowing light that revealed other faces, other bodies, all crowded together in the Central Chamber. The granite box gleamed white. Anne lay down in it. Cynthia stood at her feet, smiling down at her. At her head stood a radiant being, her eyes shaded with powdered lapis, her lips red as coral, holding an ankh to Anne's nose.

Isis.

Yes, daughter. It is time.

Tahir leaned over the box and directed sound into her heart chakra. At the same instant, Isis raised her wings. Anne's chest blossomed like a red rose. The whole pyramid became one pulse of overwhelming energy.

The Sphinx reached back through the ground and up through the pyramid. *Where do you want to go?*

Before Anne could think, the great cat grabbed her and launched her into space. Anne streamed through the galaxy, her energy like the stars around her.

A memory surfaced. She sat inside a two-story crystal looking out at her pod, the other workers in the Crystal Matrix Chamber of Atlantis. It was the end, and they were leaving in exactly the same way she'd just been hurled into space. She watched herself attune to one frequency of the rainbow of colors that was the crystal and travel along it back to a planet deep in space. Once there, she looked down at her body and found fur, four legs. She stretched her arm and it unfurled, a wing. Other beings exactly like her surrounded her on all sides, purging her system of any dissonance.

Anne hovered in space, at the spot where the past and future connect, feeling the flow of the galaxy. It was pure bliss. The enormous, overpowering intelligence watched her. Then she saw herself hovering over her mother while Katherine writhed in labor. Two tall beings of light stood next to her, whispering. *You will find the stone. You will restore the flow. The return of the Age of Light depends on this work.*

She understood her mission. She knew there were hundreds more coming in with her, thousands of souls thronging into bodies ready to contribute their light to the Great Return. Ready to embody and heal the deepest wounds, ready to bring love to the darkest hates, ready to lose and then rediscover themselves. All to bring back the light.

Remember, remember, the light beings sang as she was pushed through the birth canal into a room with harsh lights and grating noises.

Still hovering in space, Anne watched as a stream of energy flowed from the center of the galaxy down through chakras far above her crown, chakras she'd never known existed, into a point arm's length above her head where it sat like a dove on a chalice, waiting. She knew what she was to do.

As Anne reentered her body, Isis looked into her spirit eyes and smiled. The Sphinx purred, the sound a rumble under the ground. Cynthia stood at her feet. Thomas stood beside her, radiant in his astral body.

It was worth the sacrifice, Annie. It was all worth it, he said.

Where did you come from? she asked, but he only smiled.

Anne opened her physical eyes to see Tahir bending over her, still lit by the glow of spirit. He nodded his approval and offered her a hand out of the box.

Michael was next.

* * *

PAUL MARCHANT BOWED his head to allow Karl Mueller to take off his blindfold and opened his eyes to the sight of the front of the underground temple. Mueller pushed him toward the passageway into the Blue Room, as Marchant had started to call it. Once through the passageway, Marchant stopped, but Mueller kept walking. Anubis glared after him, but Marchant could see that Mueller was oblivious. Marchant silently asked permission to enter the temple and received a nod from the great being. He apologized for the ignorance of those accompanying him.

Soon they will not be welcome, the jackal sent.

The "they" Anubis was referring to included a small cluster of men who stood in front of the blue curtain of energy talking among themselves. One of them turned when Marchant and Mueller approached. He was dressed in a blue designer suit and expensive leather shoes. The others wore military uniforms, some Egyptian, some American. The man in the blue suit addressed him. "Mr. Marchant, we meet at last. My name is Spender. I'm in charge of this mission."

Marchant shook his hand. "Pleased to meet you." He pushed some firmness into his voice.

"We've devised a little experiment tonight. Your first effort to open the room produced some result, but it seemed to me, based on the tapes, that you simply couldn't produce enough energy with just one crystal."

Tapes? Marchant schooled his face to remain calm. *What if they taped me when I came alone? What if they're going to open the Hall now and dispose of me? No, he thought, if they'd recorded my visit, they'd have done something by now.*

"So . . ." Mr. Spender pulled something out of his pocket with a flourish. ". . . we've secured a second crystal."

Marchant stared at the stone dangling from Spender's fingers. He'd only read about the other keys, never seen one. Not even Anne's. His whole being burned to examine it.

"In due course," Spender said, as if aware of his thoughts. He put the crystal back in his pocket. "Our research tells us the stones are tuned to the DNA of certain families, so we've secured some genetic material from the bearer. We want you to do what you did before, but this time I will join you using the second key."

"We can try that," Marchant said. He hoped his voice sounded normal.

As Spender talked, Marchant tried to get a glimpse of the crystal's setting. This might give him a hint whose it was. He doubted it was Anne's. He couldn't imagine these men getting past that hulk who guarded her to get a sample of her DNA, much less steal her crystal. He'd read in an ancient manuscript that the settings of all the stones were different, indicating their lineage. His own was topped with the was symbol, signifying authority.

But before he could get a close look, Spender draped a piece of dead muscle over the top of the crystal and tied it in place.

Marchant recoiled, then caught himself, trying to suppress his revulsion.

"Ready?" Spender smiled slightly at his pale face.

"Certainly." Marchant took his own crystal out and tried to collect himself.

"Well?" Spender asked.

"We need to meditate for a moment," Marchant said. "We can't just launch into it like we're opening a can of Spam."

"Then proceed." Spender laid stress on this last word.

Marchant closed his eyes, fighting the panic rising in him. He had to control this situation. A second crystal could very well bring down the curtain, but he didn't want this to happen. They'd barge in and disturb things. No one else should enter the room before the alignment. As the Orion crystal holder, it was his place to be first.

Calling on his years of study, Marchant steadied himself. He placed his awareness on his breath, allowing the natural rhythm to steady him, then started to breath deeper and faster, focusing his attention on his solar plexus. After about thirty seconds, his stomach glowed. Marchant opened his mouth and started to chant. Spender joined in, slightly off key. Out of an offended aesthetic, Marchant turned his head and chanted into Spender's ear, correcting his pitch.

In response to the correct sound, specks of gold began circling inside the blue energy field. Marchant held his crystal out toward the curtain and the dark blue started to lighten. Spender mimicked his gesture, holding the flesh-swathed crystal to the field. The curtain immediately darkened.

Spender frowned and started to chant louder. The gold specks slowed. He turned to Marchant. "What's wrong?"

Suppressing his irritation, Marchant pulled Spender's hand back about a quarter of an inch. He held his own crystal up, showing Spender how the stone needed to be grounded at the root in the energy center in the palm, the point an extension of the index finger. He started the chant again. Spender adjusted his grip on the crystal and added his voice.

Again the gold specks circled, but Marchant could tell already it wouldn't work. The decaying muscle draped over the crystal was dampening its energy, not activating it. He also knew Spender wouldn't accept his word for it, so he continued chanting. The DNA had been a good idea and if he were handling both crystals, he could energize the piece of flesh enough to make it work. But he wasn't going to tell this man what to do.

After a few more minutes of chanting, the curtain lightened again. Spender, getting excited, pushed his crystal forward, and the energy field darkened. They tried again. And again. Marchant's head throbbed with the unreleased energy he was holding.

* * *

WHILE ANNE LAY in the stone box in the Great Pyramid, Michael tried to feel what was happening to her, but he couldn't make the connection. Ever since the theft, he'd felt flat and clumsy, his consciousness wooden, his psychic abilities wrapped in layers of thick wool. He never imagined he depended on the stone so much. Without it, he was second-rate, maybe third.

Anne thought maybe they'd drugged him, used some new compound Arnold didn't know about. But Michael knew deep in the core of his being he couldn't open the Hall of Records without his key. The mission would fail. Instead of ascending into the light, the Earth would fall into a deeper darkness. Even though Michael knew the dangers of succumbing to despair, he couldn't fight it off.

I'm sorry, Mother, he sent to the Sphinx.

No comforting voice answered back.

Michael jumped when Tahir touched his shoulder. Michael unfolded himself and walked over to the stone sarcophagus. For him, it might as well be a tomb. But as soon as he lay back in the stone box and Tahir leaned over him, directing his chant into Michael's heart, his consciousness spread out in a flash along the entire grid line.

A deep vibration rumbled through the plateau and the Bent Pyramid in Dahshur started singing in a double frequency that mimicked the

328 • Theresa Crater

harmony Tahir and Shani still chanted. Next the Red Pyramid added its voice. Then the complex of harmonics wove an intricate pattern into the land as pyramid after pyramid chimed in, some of them still standing, some existing now only on the etheric plane. A violent surge of energy shook Michael's spine, knocking out any remaining blockages. He became a channel of pure, white light.

And then he found it. His crystal. It was somewhere beneath him, just to the southwest. He heard chanting. He reached for his key and found something dead and wet wrapped around it, dampening its clear, sweet vibration. He recoiled from the touch.

What the hell?

He probed deeper. Beneath the barrier, the stone was intact, still singing its song in a faint pulse. Then the answer came to him. The crystal was wrapped in a dead scrap of his own flesh, the piece of his arm they'd punched out. They were trying to activate the key using his DNA pattern. Someone was breaking into the Hall of Records. He had to stop them.

From a lifetime of habit, Michael sent a stream of awareness to the crystal and made contact. The crystal answered with a surge of energy.

* * *

SUDDENLY, Paul Marchant felt the crystal in Spender's hand spring to life.

The curtain in front of him turned from robin's egg blue to sky blue and then a bluish white. What had happened? He shifted his awareness from his own key to the one in Spender's hand and found Michael.

You've got to get out of here, he sent.

What the hell is going on? Michael asked.

Get out of here before you bring down the curtain.

Isn't that what you want?

No, not now. They'll destroy everything. We can't let them succeed.

Marchant felt Michael's awareness withdraw like a wave back into the ocean. The curtain darkened again.

Spender turned to him. "What are you doing wrong?"

"Me?" Marchant's nerves were frayed. "I'm not doing anything wrong. It's that slab of dead meat. No energy can flow through that."

Spender regarded him through narrowed eyes. "Your life is in my hands, Mr. Marchant."

Marchant stood perfectly still. This man was a killer, not personally, but his Doberman was right behind him in the form of Mueller. "Yes, sir," he said automatically.

"That's better. Now what are you doing wrong?"

Marchant took a breath to say something, anything to assuage this man, then stopped. He had to be careful. He didn't want to antagonize Spender further, but he desperately wanted this experiment to fail. He took a breath. "The DNA sample was a good idea. The crystals do seem to be keyed to certain genetic strands." He paused. He thought this was true, but he still wasn't certain. "But the sample itself is dead. There's no energy in it. The DNA is not functioning. It can't respond to the sound."

Spender studied him through narrowed eyes. "Try again," he commanded.

Trying not to betray any emotion, Marchant centered himself and started to chant again, deeper this time. Spender joined in slightly off-key, and this time Marchant didn't bother to correct him. The curtain remained a dark blue, as unperturbed as a remote mountain lake.

With a growl of frustration, Spender stabbed his crystal into the energy field. Without breaking, the curtain curved around the stone, coalesced, and snapped back into place, sending Spender flying. He landed heavily a few feet back. Mueller jumped to his side and offered him a hand up, but Spender ignored him. He stood and dusted himself off, taking his time.

Marchant stared at the ground, avoiding his eyes.

Spender walked back to his side. "Now what?" he asked, his voice harsh with controlled fury.

Marchant looked up from the dusty floor to see the curtain had turned an ominous dark blue, the color of a brooding thundercloud.

"I asked you a question, Mr. Marchant. You are our resident expert." Spender's voice suggested he thought otherwise.

"The energy field cannot be opened by force. It will absorb any violence directed at it and send it back tripled." His voice trembled. "Surely your engineers tried that already or I wouldn't be here."

"We hadn't tried with the keys."

"The keys work through establishing a harmonic resonance with the curtain. Clearly, two crystals aren't enough."

"How about two crystals with two Keepers?"

Marchant blanched. Perhaps Spender had felt Michael. Marchant studied his face, but saw only a well-bred mask. Almost in a whisper he said, "Why not wait for the alignment? Even if we get the force field to come down, this room may not open into the actual Hall unless the planetary alignment is exact."

"May, Mr. Marchant? I deal in certainties."

"I am certain that . . ." He groped for a word that wouldn't antagonize Spender any further. ". . . your sample won't work." He pointed to the decaying muscle.

Spender studied him for a full minute, his eyes glacial. Finally, he said, "Then we'll try with a live specimen."

Marchant stared, trying to imagine what the man meant.

Spender turned to Mueller. "Escort our guest back to his room."

* * *

MICHAEL OPENED his eyes to see Tahir leaning over him, a quizzical look on his face. Michael started to speak, but Tahir gestured him to silence. The ritual was not finished. Maria still had to go into the box. Michael took his place in the circle and tried to settle back into meditation.

At last, Michael heard Maria climb out of the box and take her place in the circle. After a few minutes, Tahir and Shani stopped chanting and the group sat in silence a bit longer, allowing everyone to return to this time and place.

Michael heard the hum of the generator and squinted against the harsh white light that invaded the nurturing womb they'd been sitting in. When he could open his eyes again, he found Tahir staring at him. "I'd like to hear from Michael first."

Michael recounted his experience.

"Now we know why they took your stone," Tahir said, his voice serene.

Michael was glad the rest of the group was still in such an expanded state. The experience had shaken him.

"We know something about Marchant's intentions," Anne said. "It seems his loyalties are divided."

"Between the Illuminati and himself," Shani said. "I don't think he wants us to succeed either."

"What does Marchant think we're doing?" Anne asked.

Michael sat up straighter, easing his back. "I'm not sure. He said he was afraid of them opening the Hall of Records and destroying things. He thinks the alignment is crucial to opening the Hall correctly."

"He wants control of what is in the Hall," Tahir said. "He's still thinking materialistically."

"What is in it?" Anne ventured.

Tahir gave his standard answer. "Some things must be experienced."

"You won't tell us, even now? When the Earth's future hangs in the balance?"

Tahir regarded her for a long minute. She felt like the Sphinx was looking deep into her soul. "There can be no telling. It is an experience. Trust yourself and the universe."

Anne sighed, exasperated. "What should we do?"

"Talk to Marchant," Maria said. "Try to wake him up. Get him to realize what is at stake."

"I doubt he'll come over to our side," Anne said.

"You have to talk to him." Michael pointed his index finger at her. "He's made overtures to you. Get him to show you the room."

"Why me? He's contacted you now."

"He might assume I was asleep and connected with him on the astral plane. He may think I won't remember."

"Paul can tell us who has your crystal. Perhaps he's open to a deal," Tahir said. "Anne is our best chance."

"I'll try."

Maria spoke up. "My vision took me back to my ancestors of long ago. I saw the ancient cities before the deluge. I might be able to figure out where we need to go, but I'll need time to do the calculations."

"Would a computer help?" Shani asked.

"I'm not familiar with computers."

"I can help you," Shani said.

"Good," Tahir nodded and looked around at them. "Remember your visions. Our hope lies in them. We'll meet at my house tomorrow night."

* * *

AROUND NOON, Paul Marchant slumped in a chair in front of Spender's massive mahogany desk. His eyes kept straying to the gold-leafed statue of Horus elegantly displayed beneath a single spotlight. It was an original, at least thirty-three hundred years old, most likely just one of many artifacts the man had gleaned for his own personal collection. His head ached from last night's effort. He tried not to rub his temples.

Spender watched him with his usual crocodile smile. Mueller was nowhere to be seen.

"Sleep well?" Spender asked.

"Not really," Marchant admitted. "I never sleep well after doing psychic work."

"I slept like a top." Spender stroked a cigar, but made no move to light it.

That's because you didn't do a goddamn thing, he thought. If Spender was the best the Illuminati had to offer, then he'd badly overestimated the enemy.

"Last night didn't go well, Mr. Marchant. I hope you won't make us regret bringing you on board."

Marchant shifted in his chair. "I can only assure you I did my best. We simply didn't raise enough energy to bring down the curtain. We'll control the situation during the alignment."

"I want to get in before that, Mr. Marchant."

"I understand." He shifted again, irritated by how Spender kept drawling out his last name.

"I've brought you here today because I want you to have an even better understanding that any plans you may have made behind our backs will come to nothing."

"What plans?" Marchant asked. "Do you think I'm stupid enough to try to double-cross the Illuminati?"

Spender pushed a button on a panel near his right hand and pointed to a bank of monitors. The wall filled with images of Michael unzipping Anne's dress. Marchant's stomach clenched as he watched Michael deposit kisses down her naked back, then pull the dress down over her hips. The two moved together. Spender cocked his head for a better view.

Finally, the images stopped. After a minute of heavy silence, Spender looked at him. "Just in case you were harboring any illusions, Mr. Marchant."

He tightened his jaw, saying nothing. Had he only imagined Anne's interest in him, or was she playing him for a fool, dropping crumbs to entice him to reveal his secrets while giving herself shamelessly to that overrated Jewish mystic? It wasn't that he was interested in Anne sexually. He was just sick of playing second fiddle to the Rosicrucian Order.

Spender interrupted his reverie. "Let's make sure we don't have any more failures, shall we?"

Marchant fought the urge to wipe the smug look off Spender's face.

"That will be all for now."

* * *

THAT EVENING, Anne made her way across the grounds of the Mena House in search of Paul Marchant. Her head ached from the extremes of awareness she'd passed through in last night's ritual, the euphoria of her vision, the chill of fear about the Illuminati opening the Hall. She remembered her training with nostalgia. Dr. Abernathy had insisted she get plenty of rest between such heightened states to keep her balance. Now she felt like an athlete in the middle of playoffs. There was no time to integrate her experiences, weave her visions into her ordinary consciousness. She had to roll out of bed and perform again.

Anne opened the door of the restaurant and flinched at the noise. All the conference participants seemed to be shouting at the top of their lungs. She took a breath to steady herself and walked in, looking for Marchant. She found him alone by the windows, tucked behind a potted plant, drinking coffee. His face had a pinched look and his shoulders were hunched. He wasn't feeling any better than she was.

She stepped up to the table. "Do you mind if I join you?"

Marchant brightened visibly when he saw her. "Just the person I wanted to talk to."

"I'm flattered." Anne tried to sound energetic. She pulled out the chair opposite him and sat down.

This is too easy, she thought. *What's he up to?*

He leaned across the table and said in an undertone, "I've made arrangements for tomorrow night."

"Isn't Monday cutting it a bit close?"

"Couldn't be helped." Marchant's eyes darted around the restaurant, then back to her. "They're watching me pretty closely."

"Who, exactly?"

"I think you know the answer to that." He looked around again. "Let's get some privacy." He stood without waiting for an answer and walked toward the door.

She could only guess last night had shaken him and he was willing to take chances.

He held the door. "This way." He headed for the pool. Once they'd gotten some distance from the building, he sat on a chair beneath a tree. Anne sat next to him.

Marchant looked around again, then said, "We'll meet at midnight near the Sphinx. It's closer that way, but be prepared for walking. Bring your crystal, but leave your bodyguard behind."

"Bodyguard? What are you talking about?"

Marchant pointed to Bob, who was sitting on the grass nearby, looking for all the world like an enthralled tourist.

"I don't know that guy," Anne said.

"Then why is he always around you, him or that big wrestler guy?"

"He's attending the conference. What wrestler guy are you talking about?"

"The other one who's always around you, who followed us to the restaurant that night."

Anne sat for a minute, not knowing what to say.

"Sneak away. Surely you can do that."

"I'll come alone." She couldn't imagine how she could accomplish this. How was she going to work Michael's crystal into this conversation?

"Good," Marchant said. "Let's not be seen together any more. We'll meet—"

"There they are." Rita's voice rang out. She stopped in front of them, breathless. "We've been looking all over for you. Did you hear the news?"

Debbie arrived just after her cohort. She nudged Rita. "Told you they'd get together."

"We were just discussing my theories," Marchant began, clearly flustered.

"Right." Rita rolled her eyes. "Did you hear the news?"

"What news?" Anne asked, giving up on a cover story.

"The Illuminati did a blood sacrifice in the Great Pyramid last night."

Anne just stared, so Rita continued. "It was to prepare for the alignment, to ensure the Earth stays enslaved to the Anunnaki lords."

"A blood sacrifice," Anne repeated. "I thought they were going to do that during the planetary alignment."

Rita shrugged off this objection.

How these two could guess anyone had done a ritual in the Great Pyramid last night was beyond her, but where did they get these ridiculous ideas? This sounded more like the gruesome ceremony performed in front of the Hall with the dead slice of Michael's flesh.

"It was a double sacrifice," Debbie said.

"Double?" Anne frowned.

"Yes, Thomas Le Clair was killed in a plane crash just last night."

Anne felt as if the all the air had been sucked out of her.

"—blown up, I'll bet. CNN says it was an accident. Pilot error or something. But I think the Illuminati killed him, just like Princess Diana."

Anne couldn't breathe.

"Anne? What's the matter?" Rita asked.

Anne turned and ran. She heard Marchant say, "Thomas Le Clair is her brother, you idiot."

"Her brother?" Rita's voice was fading.

Bob was beside her in a flash. "What happened?"

She grabbed Bob's hand. "Where's Michael? I have to find Michael."

Bob turned Anne toward him and put both hands on her shoulders, forcing her to look him in the face. "What happened?" he repeated firmly.

Anne stared into Bob's brown eyes, her mouth opening and closing like a fish out of water.

"Anne." He shook her. "What happened?"

"Thomas. He's dead."

"What?"

"A plane crash."

"That can't be. We would have heard."

They both looked up to see Arnold approaching them. The look on his face said it all.

"No!" Anne pushed against Bob. "No. Not Thomas."

Anne allowed herself to be led back to the room. Within minutes, Michael was at her side. "I just heard. I'm so sorry."

Arnold and Bob left them alone.

"It can't be. How can it be?" Anne searched Michael's face for an answer.

Michael shook his head.

"But I just saw him."

"What?" Michael's eyes sharpened.

"Last night. I saw him. He was standing at the bottom of the box, with Aunt Cynthia." Anne dropped into a chair as she realized what she was saying. "Oh, my God!"

Michael knelt on the floor beside her.

She looked at him, her face bewildered. "He said it was worth the sacrifice."

"What?"

"He said it was all worth it."

"What did he mean?"

"That we'll succeed." Anne stared at Michael, white with shock. "My brother is dead. They killed Thomas." Her face crumpled.

Michael picked her up and carried her to the bed where he cradled her as she wept. She cried fiercely for a long while, then lay limp and silent.

A knock on the door roused her. "You'd better answer it," she whispered. "It might be Arnold with news."

Michael walked to the door. "Yes?" he called.

"Miss Anne, por favor?" A thick Spanish accent revealed the identity of the visitors.

Michael opened the door to the two Mayan priests.

"Por favor, have you seen Maria?" Enrique's eyes scanned the room.

"No." Michael opened his mouth to ask for privacy, but the anxious eyes of the two men stopped him. He tried to step outside to speak with them, but Anne sat up and pushed her hair out of her face. "Please, come in."

Jose and Enrique stepped inside the door.

"What's happened?" Michael asked.

"Our room, it has been broken into. Everything is on the floor. The furniture turned over."

"Is anything missing?"

"Si, señor. Maria is missing. And her crystal."

25

---

*P*aul Marchant walked back to his room after hearing the news about Thomas Le Clair. It was too bad, really. The man had been a great reservoir of knowledge, respected by all in the metaphysical community, even his family's enemies. The plane had gone down in the Indian Ocean. Now what had Thomas been doing in the Far East? He fumbled for his keys, opened the door, and reached for the light switch.

"About time."

Marchant jumped back, smashing into the edge of the door. Karl Mueller sat in the dark, cool and calm.

"Jesus, you scared me to death."

Mueller smirked. "Get your things. We've got a job to do."

"For God's sake, wasn't last night enough?"

Mueller stood up and barked, "Get your things."

Marchant fought to control his anger. "This is unwise. Intensive psychic work takes a good deal of energy. You have to rebuild that before trying again."

"I have my orders."

He took a breath to explain, but Mueller interrupted him. "Take it up with the boss. Follow me outside in five minutes. I'll be two blocks down the street."

"Sieg Heil," Marchant muttered.

"Excuse me?" Mueller stuck his face into Marchant's.

"I'll be there," Marchant said in a monotone.

"Yes, you will." Mueller turned on his boot heel and slammed the door behind him.

Soon Marchant was bouncing around in the back of a black jeep, his arms folded across his stomach. He rode in silence, trying to imagine what Spender had planned. His last words had been ominous, but if nothing had changed, this was a waste of precious time and energy. After twenty minutes, the jeep pulled behind the security office on the Sphinx side of the plateau. Mueller brandished the blindfold.

"Is that necessary at this point?" he asked.

Without an answer, Mueller wrapped the blindfold around Marchant's eyes and the jeep sped off, knocking Marchant back against the seat. He rode in darkness, seething at the way this moron dared to treat the holder of the Orion crystal. When he did open the Hall, he'd pay them back. He could play their game for just one more night.

The jeep stopped with a screech of brakes. Mueller grabbed Marchant's arm and pulled him out of the jeep. Once out, Mueller gave him a shove, and Marchant stumbled, falling to his knees.

"Get up." Mueller pulled him to his feet, grumbling, but guiding him more carefully down the stairs. Just inside the underground temple, he jerked off the blindfold. Marchant looked over the lake at the massive pillars in the back.

Yes, he thought, *I'll tie you between those and have you flogged.* He walked to the tunnel to the inner temple and bent low. On the other side, he paused, asking permission of Anubis.

Mueller pushed him. "Let's go."

This man needs to die, he sent to the noble jackal.

Anubis made no comment.

Marchant took two steps toward the blue curtain and stopped dead in his tracks. Standing in front of the curtain, hands tied behind her back, was Maria Lol Ha, her mouth taped closed. A chill of fear crept through him. With her, Spender just might succeed.

"Mr. Marchant." Mr. Spender stood up, wiping the sand from his immaculate blue suit.

Marchant felt a surge of rage at this urbane, self-satisfied amateur mystic. He'd devise something truly torturous for this one.

"As I said, a live sample." He pointed to Maria as if she were an exotic breed of cat, then he brandished Michael's crystal. "I hope you've taken our little chat to heart. Shall we proceed?"

"This is not wise. We should have waited a day before making another attempt. This type of work requires a great deal of energy—"

"Enough," Spender's voice penetrated to the core.

Marchant bit back his retort and turned his attention to Maria. He'd scanned her before. She was powerful. This time they were going to get in, he was certain. What was he going to do? With numb fingers, he took his crystal from around his neck and positioned it in his hand.

Maria's eyes widened.

Spender nodded and Mueller ripped the tape off Maria's mouth, taking a piece of lip with it.

"No, you mustn't do this." A trickle of blood fell on her chin. "The timing is not right. Without the alignment, the stargate might misfire. We may destroy it."

"What is she talking about?" Spender looked at Marchant. "Stargate?"

"Why don't you ask her yourself?" he said.

Spender looked surprised by this idea. He turned. "Well—what is your name?

"My name is not important, but the success of this mission is."

"What exactly is your mission?"

Maria studied him, her body trembling, but her eyes remote and calm.

Spender took a step toward her. "Answer me."

She squared her shoulders. "To bring the Earth into the Fifth Age."

"The Fifth Age . . ." Spender looked at her with contempt. "What kind of New Age nonsense is this?"

"New Age?" Marchant asked. "She's Quiche Maya."

Spender waved away this objection. "We're within three days of the alignment. The influence of any astrological configuration can be felt a full three days before and three days after the exact alignment. It's time to open the Hall of Records." He looked at Mueller. "Untie her hands."

Mueller cut the cord with his knife. Maria flinched, but didn't make a sound.

Spender turned and held Michael's crystal out to the blue curtain.

Maria caught Marchant's attention, then glanced up quickly at the ceiling. Looking up, he saw them for the first time. Tiny dots on the ceiling. Outlines of constellations. His mouth fell open. How could he have missed them before? Then he saw he was standing beneath Orion and smiled. At least his instincts were functioning. Maria deliberately moved away from the Pleiadian cluster and took her place beneath Antares. Marchant moved to the Vega triangle.

Spender looked over his shoulder. "No more procrastinating. Let's get this curtain down."

Marchant started to chant and Maria joined in, a sweet fifth above him. He frowned slightly, and she came down to his tone. Spender added his quavering voice.

The curtain responded with its now familiar sequence. Specks of gold appeared in the dark blue velvet, then started to swirl. The curtain started to change color, turning from the dark vibrant blue of an ocean to the color of cornflowers, then to a summer sky, and finally to a white tinged with blue. Without a hitch, as if it indeed were the time, all color faded from the curtain, and then with a swoosh, the energy field disappeared altogether.

Marchant's mind focused like a diamond. He had finally gained access to the Hall of Records. He was performing his appointed task, the task he'd been born to do. But Spender was right in front of him, ready to steal it all.

"Ah," Spender said, as if a jar he'd been trying to open had finally given way. He stepped forward into the circular room.

The room was smaller than Marchant had thought, probably thirteen feet from the center in all directions. He'd expected stale air and dust, but the room was fresher than the temple outside. He looked up at the ceiling, searching for vents, but found none. Instead a gold astrology wheel, more elaborate than the one from Dendara, captured his eyes. He traced Orion's belt, the Seven Sisters in their lopsided cluster. On the floor beneath him lay a beautiful tiled mosaic depicting a star tetrahedron, the main Star of David outlined in lapis blue, a second one offset in light turquoise. He paused beneath the Orion constellation, suddenly light-headed.

His vision blurred, then doubled. He saw himself in the past, a tall Egyptian priest holding up his crystal. Five others stood in formation around him, each holding up a crystal, each chanting a sound that was an elaboration of a basic weave of the quantum fields making up this area. His heart was heavy with the duty they performed. Marchant stepped forward to stop it and the vision disappeared.

He blinked and saw Spender walking the perimeter of the room, his filthy fingers probing the pristine yellow sandstone. A wave of nausea washed through Marchant. He felt as if Spender were handling his privates. It took every ounce of self-discipline he possessed to stop himself from ripping the man away from the walls and throwing him to the ground.

Mueller stepped forward and Marchant whirled. "No." He pointed his finger as if this alone would stop further invasion.

Spender looked up and chuckled. "Wait outside. Keep your men prepared."

Mueller stood at the threshold of the sanctuary, his black boots poised to trample the opened flower of the most sacred temple on Earth.

"Now, Mr. Marchant." Spender looked the two Crystal Keepers up and down. "How do we get past this vestibule?"

"Please, come back to the center." Marchant felt an inexplicable urgency to get the man away from the walls.

Spender did as he asked. "Well?"

Marchant looked at Maria. "Where's the door?"

Something in her eyes closed against him.

"Do you know?" he urged.

She shook her head.

"I must attune to the room." Marchant closed his eyes and again the room opened to him. He was inside the bell of a delicate flower, walking in the heart of a nautilus spiral. The room was as fragile as an embryo, but with the same power of new life. He should have taken off his shoes.

He sent out a psychic probe and the room responded with a swirl of energy, like iridescence, suggesting he move to a different spot beneath the wheel. But he resisted. This might indeed open the wall. The chamber withdrew its suggestion and simply stood, pristine and radiant. Marchant fought back tears. There was nothing he could do to prevent the rape that was about to occur.

A wave of energy spiraled out from Maria. As it passed through him, he saw a jaguar in his mind. She was weaving a protection spell. He only hoped she was successful.

Marchant asked silently, *Where is the door?* And received back an impression of the ceiling. He'd keep Spender away from there.

"Mr. Marchant, you're trying my patience." Spender's voice broke the threads of awareness he'd spun around the room.

Marchant opened his eyes.

The jaguar crouched, just out of vision.

Every cell in Marchant's body revolted against what he knew he had to do next. Setting his teeth against the growing nausea, he said, "Let me examine the walls."

Please forgive me, he sent, and stepped out of his place in the star formation on the floor. He was immediately dizzy, as if he'd moved from a high altitude to sea level in one step. The air was thicker, resistant. He walked clockwise around the outer perimeter of the star, then coming full circle, stepped to the outer wall, extending his senses into the limestone. Such beauty floated to the surface of his mind, the living walls of a well, a portal into other frequencies, other dimensions, themselves alive with harmonics of the one song that would open this space.

His own crystal was singing now, picking up one note and amplifying it, reaching down his arm into his heart, filling it, then brimming over and spilling down to the earth, sending a jet spurting through his head into the sky. Marchant shook himself like a wet dog to break his enthrallment to the stone. He stuck his left hand into his pocket and pulled out a scrap of red silk. He wrapped his crystal in the silk, cradled it inside a black velvet bag, and shoved it back into his pocket. The song receded to the background.

Marchant shook his head again, then began his probe. He expected only his initial impression to be confirmed, that the door to the Hall of Records was in the ceiling. Tomorrow he would find the lock and open it. He circled the room inch by inch, Maria and her jaguar watching his every move, Spender a step behind him. He went around completely, then motioned to Spender. "The door is directly across from this one, at the apex of the bottom pyramid."

"Pyramid?" Spender growled.

Marchant pointed to the floor, then walked around the perimeter of the star to the tip. He winced when Spender walked directly across the star tetrahedron to the far wall.

"But it isn't a physical door as we understand it. It manifests only at certain times."

Spender laughed. "Come now, Mr. Marchant, I know you're just trying to keep the treasures safe so you can come back and plunder them yourself. We recruited you because of your expertise. We need you to help us bring this Atlantean arsenal online, not just open the door to it. We must trust each other."

"Then you'd better tell your messenger boy to treat me with more respect," Marchant burst out.

Spender laughed again and patted his arm. "Has Karl been misbehaving? He'd better hope he hasn't done anything to jeopardize our work here." He shot a deadly look over his shoulder. "Now, how do we open this second door?"

Marchant mustered up an image of himself as a child confessing to his mother, and spoke from that place. "No one wants to open this door more than I do, Mr. Spender. There's nothing more important to me than getting in there without the Rosicrucians and the damned Le Clair family telling everyone what to do. But we simply have to wait."

"But I'm not willing to wait, Mr. Marchant." Spender looked up at Mueller. "Bring the explosives."

"No!" Maria lunged at Spender. The jaguar swept through him at the same instant.

Spender blinked and looked down at this chest.

"Explosives?" Marchant was on the edge of panic. "That is impossible."

"I assure you it is quite possible." Spender said.

"I have to agree with Mr. Marchant."

All heads turned to this new voice. A man stood in the entrance to the small chamber, tall and straight, obviously used to command. He was dressed all in black, and the only color to him was a shock of silver hair that he'd pulled back in a ponytail. The accent was British, upper class.

"Mr. Cagliostro." Spender walked across the room diagonally, causing Marchant to wince again, and offered to shake hands.

Alexander Cagliostro? Marchant looked at the man carefully. *No, it couldn't be.*

Cagliostro just looked at Spender's extended hand. "What exactly do you think you're doing?"

"Opening the Hall of Records, as instructed." Spender stood straighter, like a soldier reporting in.

"With explosives? Looks like I got here just in time." He held out his hand, palm up. "The crystals."

Spender opened his mouth to say something, but thought better of it. He handed Michael's crystal to Cagliostro, then turned and snapped at Marchant, "You heard him. Give the man your crystal."

"This stone is keyed to me. No one else can—"

"Now." Spender gestured toward Mueller.

To prevent more people invading the sanctuary, Marchant handed his crystal to Spender without another word. He would have preferred to give him his heart. Maria did the same. Spender gave the stones to Cagliostro and stepped back.

"These two may go." Cagliostro pointed to Marchant and Maria.

"Karl—" Spender began his order.

"Karl needs to stay."

Spender bit his lip. "You two. Take the woman back to the compound. You," he pointed to the jeep driver, "take Marchant back to the hotel."

"Remember to blindfold them both," Mueller said, as he tied Maria's hands behind her back.

Marchant and Maria were led away.

Mueller squared his shoulders and schooled his face not to show the satisfaction he felt. Cagliostro would finally get this operation back on track.

"I've checked the room. There's no obvious door, but Marchant thought it would be here."

"Be silent." Cagliostro removed his shoes, then took the three crystals in his right hand and walked around the small room clockwise. When he realized Spender was still there, he frowned and pointed at the door.

Spender got out of his way.

He walked around a second time, then spiraled his way into the center, where he sat in perfect lotus position and closed his eyes. He sat for a long time.

Mueller shifted his weight as silently as possible. Spender stared at Cagliostro. Finally, the man opened his eyes. "We'll have to wait for the alignment. Did you actually think you could open the Hall of Records with force, Mr. Spender?" He didn't wait for an answer, but got up in one fluid movement.

Martial arts, Mueller thought. *He's studied at least one form.* Not only was this man deadly with his mind, he could probably fight physically as well. He felt more respect for Cagliostro.

As soon as Cagliostro left the small room, the blue energy field snapped back into place with a swoosh. Without so much as a glance at the sound behind him, Cagliostro collected his shoes, walked down the six steps of the inner temple, and stood in front of the Horus statue. Spender and Mueller followed.

"Now, Mr. Mueller. Is everything arranged?"

"Yes, sir." Mueller snapped to attention. "We have operatives in place to take out the heads of the Families after we secure this site."

"The story to discredit the Le Clairs?" He glanced at Spender.

"Ready to be released," he said.

"And you're certain this is the way into the Hall of Records?" Cagliostro raised an eyebrow at Spender.

"There's no other place. We've combed the plateau for four decades. Mapped every nook and cranny. This is the place, all right."

"You'd better be right." He walked out of the temple without another word.

Mueller was still wondering how he'd found it.

* * *

THE NEXT MORNING, Anne woke like a deep-sea diver, swimming slowly to the surface. On the way up, she met the memory of Thomas's death and almost turned back, but she knew she had to keep going. When she broke the surface, the rest flooded in around her—Maria's disappearance, the theft and misuse of Michael's crystal, the need to deceive Marchant, their mission to reopen the Hall of Records.'

They still didn't know exactly what this entailed. Maria had insisted they were saving the world from eternal darkness, that if the return to the light was stopped, the planet would be destroyed by highly advanced alien civilizations. As outlandish as this sounded, Anne couldn't shake the story. Something about it rang true, especially after her memory of the cat planet during the initiation in the Great Pyramid. She tried to focus on Thomas's last words to her there, but the odds seemed insurmountable.

Michael crawled back into bed beside her, his breath smelling of mint toothpaste.

"I feel so lost without him," she whispered.

Michael kissed her forehead. "We just have to keep putting one foot in front of the other, for Thomas."

"I wish you'd known him."

"I did know him, sweetie."

Anne turned over and looked up into Michael's brown eyes. "Really?"

"My group met with him several times. He knew more about ancient metaphysical societies than anyone I've ever met."

"I used to tease him unmercifully. I said at least the people who were nuts over Dungeons and Dragons knew they were playing a game. What did I call it, his obsolete research? Now my life depends on it."

"He had the strongest sense of honor I've ever seen, like it was an integral part of him."

Anne kissed Michael's rough cheek. "That was my brother. Is," she said firmly. "He seemed certain we were going to succeed, but I just don't know how, with two crystals gone and the one he was searching for permanently out of reach."

"We don't know that."

"What?"

"The last crystal may turn up yet."

You're like him, you know. The eternal optimist, no matter the stakes."

"That's one of the greatest compliments you could ever pay me."

"It's true." Anne lay back on the pillow. "So, Mr. Levy, what should we do now?"

"Take a shower."

Once they were up and dressed, Arnold called. "May I come over? There re some new developments in Maria's kidnapping."

"Please do," Anne said.

As soon as she hung up the phone, Arnold gave a warning knock on the door between the two adjoining suites, then came in and took a seat on the sofa in the living room. "We searched Maria's room thoroughly."

"Any clues?" Anne asked.

"One fingerprint."

"You can take fingerprints?" Michael asked.

Arnold nodded. "I found a match in the army's database." He laid a file on the coffee table.

"The army? How did you get access?" Michael asked.

"We have connections with the Secret Service. The print belongs to an Adam Ardsen, born in Detroit, Michigan. This is the really interesting part. He died four years ago."

Anne leaned forward. "He what?"

"Died."

"But—" Anne frowned. "So what does this mean?"

"It means," Arnold patted the file in front of him, "this man works for the shadow government."

Anne's cell phone rang. "Now what?" The screen read "No data sent." She answered it.

"Annie. Thank God you're all right."

"Mother," Anne's eyes filled with tears again, but she blinked them back. "How are you?"

"My baby. They've killed my baby, Annie. First my brother, then my sister, and now my baby."

"I know."

Katherine sobbed into the phone and Anne allowed her own tears to fall, finding strength in expressing her own grief.

When her mother's storm of emotion subsided, Anne asked, "What's happening there? Do you know anything more?"

"I only know one thing. It's open season on Le Clairs and I want you home."

Anne closed her eyes. The last thing she needed was a fight. "Are they going to be able to recover—" She couldn't bring herself to finish the sentence.

"We'll know in twenty-four hours. Did you hear me?"

"I heard you."

"Well? Do I have to come get you?"

Anne laughed. Michael and Arnold both jerked their heads up to stare at her. She shrugged. "What can I say? You know I have a job to do here."

"Anne Morgan Le Clair Greene, if you don't get back here to your grandmother's estate where we can protect you—" Katherine's voice choked. "Please, Annie."

"I can't argue with you. I just can't." She hesitated, then said, "I saw him, Mother."

"Who?"

"Thomas."

Katherine was silent for a moment, then in a low voice she asked, "What do you mean?"

"I saw him in the Great Pyramid during our initiation. He was with Aunt Cynthia. He was a brilliant white light. He told me it was worth the sacrifice."

Katherine cried quietly.

"Mother, I have to do this. Otherwise what are all these deaths for?"

"They're for nothing, that's what. For old stories. For—"

Anne interrupted her. "You're just trying to convince yourself. You don't really believe it."

Katherine was silent again.

"I'm sorry, Mother, but you know in your heart what I'm saying is true."

"Let's not fight. I just don't want to lose all my children."

"You won't. I promise."

"You'd better be right."

Anne laughed through her tears. "I promise. I swear on Thomas's memory."

"I'll see you soon then." Katherine hung up.

Bob walked into the suite from the adjoining one. "There's an e-mail for you, Anne." He handed her a printout.

Anne,

I'm coming immediately. Do not leave the hotel under any circumstances until I arrive.

Roger Abernathy

"Everybody's telling me what to do." She let the page slip onto the floor. Michael picked it up and read it.

"I can't say I disagree with him."

"Then who is going to go with Marchant? You? What are you going to say to him? 'The Le Clairs won't let my girlfriend out of her room, so I'm going in her place.' I'm supposed to be interested in him, remember?"

"I remember," Michael said quietly.

"I'm sorry."

"It's all right."

"Well, we took a shower. Now what do we do?"

Michael smiled down at her. "Let's see what Tahir has uncovered."

"He'll have to come here." Arnold looked up from his file. "I'm under orders."

Anne threw her hands up into the air. "Fine, just fine and dandy."

"I'll go see if he's with the conference. I may have to stay. This morning is the speakers' panel. Everyone is expected to participate."

Anne looked at Arnold. "Can I go?"

He just shook his head.

"I'll go find Tahir," Michael said. "Or Shani. They may have news."

Arnold nodded. "Bob is going back over Maria's room just in case we missed anything." He turned to Anne. "I'll be next door if you need me."

While they were gone, Anne paced up and down the length of the suite, pausing occasionally to look out the windows at the sun climbing the pyramids. Her stomach ached and she finally realized it was hunger. She ordered room service and sat to meditate before it was delivered, but she found no peace, only pictures of Thomas playing in her mind like a family movie.

She got up from meditation and switched on CNN. On the television screen, different images of Thomas played. His life as New York's most eligible bachelor. His affair with Nina Young, the famous actress. Katherine had approved of her. His public life as a scholar. Then it all started, the cover story about his reckless driving and piloting, how he often flew the family jet himself, about the bad weather that day. A supposed family friend confessed her worries over Thomas's recklessness in the air. Anne knew this particular woman would say anything to be associated with Thomas, even the government's lies. She switched off the set. There would be time for nostalgia later. Or not. Then it wouldn't matter. She'd be with him.

Breakfast arrived, but after a few bites, she lost her appetite and sat sipping tea, simply waiting. What was she going to do if Arnold refused to allow her to go with Marchant tonight? She'd never been successful at giving him the slip. If Tahir had been able to find a way into the room, then it would be all right. If not, there was no choice. Perhaps Dr. Abernathy would arrive by then and realize she had to go. Or she could slip Arnold one of his own sedatives. No, she couldn't do that to Arnold. He'd see reason.

Michael came back around lunchtime with Tahir and Shani, whose faces were sad. Tahir leaned across the coffee table and took her hand. "We are sorry to hear about your brother. He was a wonderful man."

Shani nodded.

"That's right. You met him, too."

"Yes, I enjoyed our time together. Michael shared your vision of him," Tahir said.

"I hope that was okay," Michael said.

"Of course," Anne said. "What do you think it means?"

"That we will succeed. What choice do we have?"

Anne looked into Tahir's strong face and drew courage. "None."

He nodded and sat back on the sofa, his gaze taking in the other three. "I have a general idea where the temple is located, but these shadow government soldiers have the villagers scared for their lives."

"What do you mean?" Arnold asked.

"It seems they killed one worker already. He talked about what was happening on the site and his story ended up on a New Age website. He was dead within twenty-four hours. Found in the garbage dump."

"And the people are certain he was killed because of the story?" Arnold asked.

"No doubt. A few days later when a few other workers had been discussing this man's death and what he'd said, a gang of thugs rousted them out of their homes in the middle of the night, took then out into the desert, and beat them. They left them there to crawl back home. After that, nobody was willing to talk."

"Even to him," Shani said.

Arnold frowned, not understanding.

"He is the village elder," she said as if this should explain everything. In response to the blank looks around her, she continued. "The head of the village. He is consulted in most matters. To refuse to give him important information—this has never happened before."

"Instead they advised me to live to fight another day."

"And what if there isn't another day?" Anne asked rhetorically.

"This is a problem," Michael said. "Did you learn enough to find the entrance?"

"I have a good idea where it is, but the main entrance seems to be heavily guarded. From my early days of crawling around in tunnels, I have an idea how to sneak in. I want Michael to come with me."

"Tonight?" Michael asked.

"Yes." Tahir turned to Arnold and Bob. "Will one of you come along for protection?"

Arnold looked at Anne. "Bob can stay here with Anne. I'll go."

"But what about Paul Marchant? We've worked hard to get him to trust me and now he's planning to lead me into the temple."

"Haven't you been listening? The place is crawling with shadow forces," Arnold said.

"Paul says he can get us in alone."

"You trust him?"

Anne hesitated. "No, but—"

"But?" Arnold raised his eyebrows.

"What if they can't find it? We have to know. The success of the mission depends on it."

"The success of the mission depends on you staying alive." Arnold narrowed his eyes.

Anne opened her mouth to protest, but Tahir cut in. "What if you go with her? You and Bob?"

"Then who protects Michael?" Anne asked. "And you?" she added as an afterthought.

Tahir smiled. "I will keep him alive."

Anne felt the red creeping into her face. "I'm sorry. It's just that—"

"No need to apologize." Tahir dismissed her embarrassment with a wave of his hand.

"I can't guarantee her safety down there." Arnold shook his head. "I don't know the terrain, how many guards they have posted, their training—"

"If we fail, I might as well be dead," Anne said.

"How do you know that? You don't really know what this Hall of Records consists of. You don't know exactly what you're supposed to do. How can I sanction you taking such a risk for so many unknowns? My job is to protect the family."

Anne stood up. "My family exists to perform this mission. This mission is more important than my life, than the lives of my whole family, the lives of everyone in this room."

Arnold opened his mouth to object, but Anne overrode him. "Why does my family exist at all? I'll tell you why. To pass down this crystal." She held the stone up in the air. "My family has endured exile, persecution, torture, and death to keep this crystal safe. For five thousand years. We've succeeded, and the time has come to use it. And you're trying to tell me that, after all that, when the last piece of the puzzle is within reach, I'm supposed to sit in my room just because I might get hurt or killed?"

Arnold squared his shoulders. "If you're dead, how are you supposed to do your job?"

Anne softened her voice. "They won't kill me, Arnold. They need me to open the Hall of Records."

Arnold looked around at the others. "What am I supposed to do? These Le Clairs could talk a bunch of cats into swimming the English Channel."

Michael chuckled. "You have my sympathy."

Arnold grinned wickedly. "You may need mine later."

Michael looked up at Anne. "I sincerely hope so."

26

That evening, Tahir slipped one of the guards a handful of Egyptian pounds and this man opened the gate in front of the Sphinx compound. Tahir thanked him, and he and Michael walked past the great cat, skirted the outer wall, and made their way up the causeway toward the pyramids.

Go quickly, the Sphinx whispered.

Tahir lengthened his stride and Michael hurried to keep up. He smiled, remembering how Anne had nicknamed Tahir "the old mountain goat" because they both had trouble keeping up with him in the south. Compared to recent events, those days seemed innocent and carefree. They would go south again, as soon as this business was finished. He wanted to see the sorrow in Anne's eyes melt to the happiness he'd grown so attached to.

Tahir stopped next to a large culvert covered by a metal grate. He reached into his capacious pockets and produced an old-fashioned skeleton key.

"Down there?" Michael asked.

"If I can do it, so can you." Tahir lowered himself over the edge and started to climb down, finding small niches in the limestone for his feet and hands.

Michael followed, making sure of each step before he took it. Once down, Tahir unlocked the grate. Each man grabbed an end and pulled. It was heavier than it looked, but after the second attempt, they propped it up against the wall they'd just come down. They sat on the edge to catch their breath.

After a minute, Tahir looked up. "Ready?" Without waiting for an answer, he eased himself over the edge.

Michael looked down into the dark pit. "Down there?" he asked again.

Tahir's laughter echoed in the tunnel.

Edges of rocks jutted out here and there, making for good footholds. The two inched their way down the tunnel. Finally, the climb straight down turned into a slope and then flattened out. The passageway was similar in size to the ascending chamber in the Great Pyramid. Michael duck-walked his way forward, Tahir close behind. After two hundred yards or so, the tunnel turned again. Michael lay down to rest his cramped thighs.

Tahir sighed as he lowered himself to the ground. "I wish I were a teenager again."

When Michael's legs stopped burning, he crouched again. This time Tahir took the lead. The tunnel veered to the left, then dropped straight down again. Climbing down was almost a relief. At the bottom, they found themselves in a passageway about nine feet high and broad enough for the two of them to walk side by side.

"I remember that this passage branches off a few times."

"I'll have to trust you. I've lost all sense of direction," Michael said.

They walked for a while in silence. At the first turnoff, Tahir paused, shining his flashlight on the limestone, then the floor. "Somebody's been down here."

The sand was marked by many footprints, some sandals, some the tread of boots or sneakers.

"Lots of somebodies," Michael said.

They added the imprints of their own shoes. The tunnel turned twice and emptied them out into a large cavern. They walked forward and came to another tunnel that emptied into this space. Then a third.

"Can you find your way back?" Michael asked. His voice echoed eerily.

"Not to worry." Tahir swept his light over the entire area. It widened farther down and they walked toward this space. Soon they came across a large granite box, the same shape but larger than the one in the King's Chamber. No one was in sight and they relaxed their guard.

"What is it?" Michael asked.

"According to the Director of Antiquities, this was the tomb of Osiris."

"The live special on television?"

"That's the one."

"So that's where we are then. What do you think it was?"

"The ancients pumped water through these channels from the old Nile in the west, well over ten thousand years ago." Tahir shone his light farther into the cavern. "Let's go back."

They retraced their steps and found their original tunnel.

"How do you keep from getting lost down here?" Michael asked.

"I got lost many times, but Tefnut always told me how to get out," Tahir said. "But tonight, we're under a deadline."

Michael followed behind him for another five minutes, the light creating a yellow halo around Tahir. Soon they came across a right turn.

"Shall we?"

"I'm just following you," Michael said.

They struck off into this new tunnel. It took two more turns to the right. Michael had a sense of height and stopped. "What's up there?"

Tahir shined his flashlight and they saw a small opening high above their heads.

The tunnel took another turn and suddenly narrowed. Tahir got down on his hands and knees and crawled forward. About twenty feet in, he called back over his shoulder. "Rubble."

Michael crawled back and waited.

Tahir emerged and stood up. He brushed the sand from his *gallabiya*. "Let's hope it's not behind that pile of rocks. We can't move them with our bare hands."

Tahir grunted. "Let's go back."

They reached the main tunnel again, then walked in silence for a few more minutes. Michael heard the sound of running water. "Listen."

Tahir paused. "They spent ten months pumping out that first chamber."

"Are we going to have to swim?"

"I did when I came up from Sakkara, but probably not here." Tahir chuckled. "Our director says these tunnels were swimming pools for the royal family."

"Swimming pools? Around the tombs? What will they think of next?" Michael almost ran into Tahir, who was standing still in front of a tunnel that ran off to the left.

"Let's try this one. Be alert. We don't know who else may be crawling around down here tonight."

"Okay," Michael said and followed Tahir down a slightly narrower tunnel, otherwise identical to all the others they'd come through. The sound of flowing water grew louder and Michael smelled moisture in the air. The tunnel made another turn and there it was, an underground stream flowing in its own bed of evenly cut stones. The tunnel widened and they walked side by side, trying to hear any sound above the stream.

In another fifty yards, hieroglyphs appeared in the limestone. Michael stopped to read them out loud:

Out of nothingness I return.
From darkness arises the light.
The green grain stretches to the sun
And is cut down again.
All hail Osiris.

Farther in they found incised reliefs, first Osiris, which made sense based on the previous text, then Isis, of course. Next came Ptah and Sekhmet, and, finally, Horus and Hathor. Around the next corner, the tunnel gave way into an enormous cavern lit by electric lights. They stopped dead in their tracks.

A thrill ran through Michael. "This must be it," he whispered.

Tahir nodded.

The sound of rushing water quieted to a trickle again. Looking off to his right, Michael saw the stream emptied into an underground lake. Just in front of the lake lay an enormous statue of Osiris.

* * *

AROUND MIDNIGHT, Anne waited in the shadows next to the Sphinx enclosure. She'd avoided attracting any attention from the villagers who were still up and about, but the cats pillaging the Dumpsters had spotted her. One brazen calico fawned at her feet. Checking the ground beneath her first, Anne settled into the dust and scratched the cat behind her ears. Arnold had insisted she carry a small handgun, an unaccustomed weight tucked in a holster in the small of her back. She knew both he and Bob were some- where close by, but even the cats couldn't find them.

Footsteps approached, and Anne sank deeper into the shadows. The lid of the far Dumpster squeaked as it was lifted and Anne heard the wet thud of a bag, kitchen garbage perhaps. The man didn't bother to close the lid. Soon after he left came the softer thuds of cats jumping down to investigate this new offering. The calico, ignoring the possibility of more food, turned on her back, exposing her stomach. Anne took comfort in the cat's rumbling purrs.

The next set of footsteps walked past the line of Dumpsters to the end and stopped. The cat ran. The streetlight illuminated Paul Marchant's tall, thin form and Anne stood to show herself.

"You came," he said simply.

"Of course. This is important."

"I thought that with Thomas—" Marchant stopped, not knowing what to say.

"He would have wanted me to complete this mission."

Marchant nodded, awkward for some reason. "I've bribed the guards, so we should have no trouble."

"Can I contribute?"

"Excuse me?"

She reached for her wallet.

"Oh, that's okay, but thanks."

Anne sensed something was wrong. Marchant was usually more self-absorbed, never this polite. She stepped out of the shadows and looked around. No one was in sight, but she knew this was an illusion. Arnold and Bob were close by. She only hoped Marchant hadn't been trailed by the dead man who still left fingerprints. Or even worse, sold out to the people who'd hired him for the best safecracking job in fifty-two thousand years.

"This way." Marchant walked back to the Sphinx enclosure to a small gate off to the left. A padlock hung on the latch, but he gave it quick tug and it came loose. He opened the gate and stood back for Anne to pass.

With a nod of thanks, Anne walked through and Marchant replaced the padlock with a click. They passed a group of buildings, now dark, then rounded a corner. A series of low hills to the right of the road obscured the view. Marchant skirted around them, staying close to the deeper shadows. He pointed toward the open desert on the left. "The sand is too loose," he whispered.

For fifteen minutes, the only sound was the swish of sand beneath their feet. Finally, Marchant crouched down behind a small hill, gesturing for her to join him. Anne saw a dark patch in the sand ahead, but was uncertain if it was a shadow or a hidden structure. They watched in silence. Soon a man dressed in a dark *gallabiya* appeared from the shadow and walked toward them. So it was a tomb or set of stairs.

"The guards have taken a break," the man whispered to Marchant.

Marchant slipped the man some baksheesh and the guide gestured for them to follow him. They ran across the clear space and the man climbed down.

Anne followed him down a worn stone stairway, Marchant right behind her. There was a turn to the right, then another set of stairs. Anne felt a growing sense of energy the deeper they went. One more set of stairs took them into what looked like an underground cave. A faint light glowed in the distance.

The guide stopped here. "The guards expect me to be here. I told them I was supposed to do some work tonight."

"Thank you." Marchant turned to Anne. "This way."

She wondered briefly how Arnold and Bob would get in, but dismissed the thought. The guide was no match for them. She followed Marchant along a dusty path. A hint of dampness reached her nose. After about fifty yards, the natural cave walls gave way to limestone blocks. Anne's fingers, lightly touching the wall, found incised reliefs. The light was brighter here, but not enough for her to see clearly. She shined her flashlight onto one of them and found Sekhmet looking back at her. She felt a surge of confidence.

"Turn it off," Marchant whispered.

Anne did as he said, then followed behind him. They approached a turn and the light grew brighter. They rounded the corner and Anne stopped dead in her tracks. "Oh, my God!" Before her stood an ancient temple that had been at ground level ages ago. Two small replicas of the Sphinx flanked broad limestone steps, eternally guarding an expansive plaza.

Marchant walked down the steps, hugging the side, and stopped by one of the Sphinxes. Anne followed. He crouched down behind the statue and looked around. "It's clear," he whispered.

They walked onto the plaza. Anne heard the trickle of water and, looking to her left, saw a lake. At the other end of the plaza, a series of columns held up a roof now covered from above by the sand of the Giza Plateau. An enormous statue lay on its side toward the back.

"This is beautiful," Anne breathed.

"Yes," Marchant said, but he didn't give her any time to take it in. "This way." He headed toward the right side of the plaza, following a path of footprints in the sand.

Anne heard a sound behind her and stopped. She turned to look out over the plaza. Nothing moved. Maybe Bob had made a misstep.

"What?" Marchant asked.

"Oh, it's amazing, this place."

"The entrance to the Hall is this way." Marchant started to walk toward the far right side again.

Anne turned to follow him, but the sound of running feet on stone made her whirl around. Three men dressed all in black rushed toward her.

"No!" Marchant shouted. One of the men ran past Anne and kicked Marchant in the solar plexus, doubling him over. The man followed this with two fists like a sledgehammer to the back of his head. He fell and didn't move again.

Anne didn't wait for the two remaining men to attack her. She ran toward them, then crouched, coming up with a punch under the first man's jaw. He staggered back, but regained his balance and kicked at her knee. She danced out of the way and reached back to pull her weapon, but the second man moved in with a punch to the head. She thought she heard someone scream her name, but she didn't have time to look. She ducked under his arm, then swung back with a blow to the kidneys.

Now the third man joined them. Anne whirled and tried to push one man into the next, then kicked back as another came at her from behind. He avoided her kick and grabbed her, pinning her arms. She could hear someone running across the plaza. The other two came at her in front. She leaned against the one holding her and kicked the ones approaching. They fell back for an instant, long enough for her to break the third man's hold and roll free. Anne pulled her gun as she came up, holding all three at bay.

"Arnold," she screamed. "Bob. Where are you?"

She stood facing the plaza, the three men circling her. Something smashed into the back of her head and a galaxy exploded inside her eyelids as she fell.

* * *

"ANNE!" Michael sprang across the statue of Osiris, his body a blur across the plaza. Tahir was close behind him. She was putting up a good fight. He stretched out to reach her. A man ran from out from a hidden passageway and hit Anne on the back of the head. He picked her up and slung her across his shoulder.

Arnold materialized from nowhere, Bob right behind him, guns drawn. "Drop her," Arnold shouted.

The man whirled and fired. He was quick, even carrying dead weight.

God, she better not be dead, Michael thought.

Arnold rolled and took careful aim, getting off one shot. The man fired again. Arnold grabbed his arm. His gun fell to the floor. Michael leapt for the man holding Anne, but he was grabbed from behind. He jerked around and landed a solid blow on one of the men. He heard more gunfire behind him and a horrible scream that ended abruptly. He turned to see Arnold and Tahir racing up the stairs after the four men, one still carrying Anne's limp body. Bob lay on the plaza floor, a pool of blood growing under his head. Michael tore up the stone steps and around the corner, where he ran into Arnold and Tahir standing with their hands in the air.

A man pointed an assault rifle at him. "Hands up." Six more men carrying assault weapons blocked the exit. "Don't move," the first man said. "I'm authorized to use terminal force."

Arnold growled.

They were dressed in black uniforms with no insignia. The leader's accent was American.

"That woman is an American citizen," Michael said. "She's being kidnapped."

The man's eyes had the same cold glint as the metal of his gun. Michael took a step forward.

The man stuck the rifle in his stomach. "I said don't move."

Michael stepped back. They all stood with their hands up listening to the receding footsteps. Michael thought he heard an engine start. Still they waited. After what seemed an eternity, the leader said, "Sit down with your backs to each other."

Arnold sat against Michael. Tahir crouched near. "I said sit." The man threatened to kick Tahir, who immediately sat all the way down. Two of the other men tied their hands behind their backs with plastic cord. "Feet together," one commanded. They bound their ankles with the same cord.

The leader checked each of them. Apparently satisfied, he stood and said, "Move out." The men turned and ran up the stairs.

"Quick," Arnold said in a low voice to Michael, "in my pocket is a knife."

Michael maneuvered himself around and tried several times to put one hand into Arnold's pocket, but his bonds were too tight.

"Keep trying. Anne's life depends on it."

Michael pulled his hands apart, biting his lip as the cord cut into his flesh, but it stretched enough for him to reach into Arnold's pocket. He felt something cold and flat and pulled it out. He placed it carefully into Arnold's hand.

Arnold quickly cut himself free, then Michael and Tahir. "Go see about Bob," he ordered. "I'll track Anne."

"But—" Michael began.

"No buts. Do as I say." He disappeared up the stairs.

Michael and Tahir ran back down the stairs to Bob, who lay motionless. The pool of blood had grown alarmingly. Tahir leaned down and checked for a pulse, then shook his head. He closed Bob's eyes. Paul Marchant was nowhere to be found.

"What should we do?"

"We have to carry him out. We can't allow the authorities to find this place yet."

Bob's body was still warm and flexible. Michael took the dead man by the shoulders while Tahir carried his feet. Bringing him up the broad steps and through the passageway was relatively easy compared to carrying him up the narrow sets of stairs. By the time they had him lying on the desert sand, they were both panting and wet with sweat.

Michael pulled out his cell phone. "Do you know the number for the police?"

"We need to carry him away from the entrance."

"But won't the police know we've tampered with the evidence?"

Tahir patted him on the shoulder. "Leave that part to me."

They hefted Bob once more and carried him across the sand and around two hills. Finally, Tahir was satisfied. Michael handed Tahir his phone. He looked at it and handed it back. "You dial." He gave Michael the number for the antiquities police. When it was ringing, Michael handed the phone to Tahir. He had a brusque conversation in Arabic that was too fast for Michael to follow.

Michael sat with his head in his hands, only now feeling the bruises from the blows his assailants had landed. He reached out with his mind for

Anne, but received no impressions. She couldn't be dead. The Illuminati needed them all alive. He kept telling himself that. He studied the face of Bob, this man who'd watched him with hooded eyes for the first part of the trip, then exchanged jocularities with him on the second half. The desert sky was ablaze with stars. He felt a surge of rage at the neutrality of the universe.

"They're coming." Tahir handed Michael the phone.

"When?"

Tahir shrugged. "When they get here." He squatted on the sand.

"What's our story?"

"I told them Anne was kidnapped and her bodyguards tried to stop it."

"Well, that's true, but what about the crime scene?"

"This is Egypt. The antiquities police already know what happened. Don't worry." Then Tahir moved closer to Bob and, closing his eyes, began a soft chant.

Michael closed his eyes and listened. The song unfolded beneath the desert stars like a soft flower and eased Michael's heart somewhat. He wondered whom Bob had loved in his life, if he'd left behind a wife and children. His thoughts turned to Thomas, of the last-minute terror of the plane plummeting into the ocean. He remembered the last time he'd seen him, with Guy, in fact, discussing some minutiae about how the Rosicrucians had been connected to the Masons in the past.

Tahir stopped chanting.

Michael recited the Mourner's Kaddish, the Jewish prayer for the dead, one for Bob and another for Thomas. Then on impulse, he added a third for Cynthia. When he finished, he opened his eyes to see Tahir watching him. "Too many deaths," he said.

"There is no death. We all go into the west."

"But these weren't natural deaths. They were murdered, all three of them."

"Yes, still they have left their dream of separation and rejoined the great All in All."

The sound of car engines reached them and they both stood. Two sets of headlights came toward them across the desert. As Tahir had predicted, the police asked perfunctory questions, put Bob's body in the back of one of their white jeeps, and gave Tahir and Michael a ride back to the Mena House. The *mu'adhdhin* had just started the call to prayer when they walked into the lobby.

Now to find Anne. He would not sing the Mourner's Kaddish for her. They went straight to her suites and knocked on Arnold's door. A distinguished gentleman with steel-gray hair and wearing an ascot opened the door.

"Michael. And Tahir. Come in."

Michael stepped into the room with Tahir close behind him. "And you are?"

"Roger Abernathy." He shook hands with them.

Arnold came into the room, an ice pack tied to his arm. "Bob?"

"I'm afraid, bad news," Michael said.

"The police have his body," Tahir said.

Dr. Abernathy looked over at Arnold. "I'll notify the office to make the necessary arrangements. We should take a moment to remember our fallen colleague, but we need to be sure the list of dead doesn't grow. To the business at hand. I suppose there's no use pointing out that you all disobeyed my direct order."

"She insisted," Michael said. "We had to find the entrance to the Hall of Records."

Dr. Abernathy turned on Tahir, "And you didn't know where it was?"

"Not exactly, no."

"Why not?"

Tahir looked at his large hands for a moment, then up at his inquisitor. "My order went to great pains to hide the entrance. Egypt has suffered under many occupations and we've had to be in hiding since before the Greeks. Most Egyptians don't even know we exist. We meet in caves. The exact location of the Hall of Records was lost."

"You've had your whole life to find it."

Tahir studied him. "Did you know when you were born that the prophecy would be fulfilled in your lifetime?"

Dr. Abernathy looked down. "No, you're right. I apologize. It's just— we've lost Thomas and Bob. Now Anne—"

"She isn't lost," Michael said forcefully. "They won't kill a Keeper of one of the keys. They want to open the Hall as much as we do."

"How can you be sure they haven't opened it already?" Dr. Abernathy asked.

"My own experience, for one thing." Michael described what had happened during his initiation in the Great Pyramid.

"So you're saying Paul Marchant held back, that he could have opened this curtain if he'd wanted," Dr. Abernathy said.

"Yes," Michael continued. "Plus Anne told me Marchant was desperate to take her there. He said they had to get in before the Illuminati did. He was afraid they'd do irreparable damage and make our mission impossible. That's another reason we thought she should go."

"Bob and I were right behind her," Arnold said, "but there were a dozen men waiting in ambush. We were delayed getting to her."

"A dozen?" Michael did a double take.

"Do you think Marchant was in on it?" Dr. Abernathy asked.

"I don't think so," Michael said. "He sounded enraged when the men came running out. They attacked him, too."

"But he was gone when we went down for Bob," Tahir said.

"You witnessed the attack?" Dr. Abernathy's tone was cold.

"We'd been crawling around tunnels for hours searching for the temple I saw in my vision. We'd just emerged on the other side of the underground lake when we heard Marchant scream. I ran as fast as I could." Michael smiled at Arnold. "She had three of them under control until that fourth guy snuck up behind her." His shoulders fell. "I didn't reach her in time."

"So it wasn't really necessary for her to go at all," Dr. Abernathy said.

Arnold squared his shoulders. "What's done is done. You can fire me later. What we need to do right now is work out a plan to get Anne back."

"And Maria," Tahir said. He explained this to Dr. Abernathy.

Dr. Abernathy looked around at everyone. "So this is the situation as it stands now. The Illuminati stole Michael's crystal and kidnapped Maria and Anne. Marchant's been working for them all along. That means they control three of the five crystals we know about. The sixth is still missing."

"What was Thomas doing in Tibet, anyway?" Michael asked.

"Tracking down the last crystal. He found an obscure reference to one of Tiye's relatives taking a key to wisdom back to the East. He met with a Rinpoche at the Samye Monastery outside Lhasa looking for information. This Rinpoche was going to do some research and get back to him the following day, but Thomas was arrested right after this meeting. We secured his release the next day through diplomatic channels, but they shot his plane down." Dr. Abernathy's voice caught. He paused, then continued. "The Rinpoche he spoke with is now missing."

"So they may have him as well," Michael said.

Dr. Abernathy steepled his fingers. "It's within the realm of possibilities."

"It's a mistake to think the Illuminati control the crystals just because they have physical possession of them," Tahir pointed out. "Your own experience makes this clear, Michael."

Dr. Abernathy raised his eyes. "Make no mistake. The Illuminati are going to bring in their big guns now."

"What are you talking about?" Michael asked.

"The man running the operation here is talented in espionage, not psychic work. That is why he couldn't make your stone work. They'll bring in their best for the alignment."

"Who?" Michael asked.

Dr. Abernathy looked him square in the face. "Alexander Cagliostro."

Michael blanched. "Does he really exist? I thought he was a myth used to scare apprentices."

"Indeed he does exist, Michael."

"Who is this man?" Tahir asked.

"The most powerful black magician the world has seen for some time. Now the head magician of the Illuminati. His family fled Italy a few centuries ago and masqueraded as English aristocrats under the name Ravenscroft. Cagliostro has since returned to his original family name."

"How do you know him?" Michael asked.

Dr. Abernathy studied him for a moment. "He was my teacher."

Michael sat in stunned silence. Then he asked, "My God, how did you escape his influence?"

"It's a long story, better told another time."

Michael nodded. "Tomorrow night the alignment begins. They'll bring all the Keepers and the crystals to the room. We'll meet them there."

"You mean you'll just walk into their hands?" Arnold looked from face to face.

"What else can we do?" Michael answered. "We need each Keeper working with his or her own crystal to open the Hall. Once we begin the ritual, the balance of power will shift. They can't control what will happen then."

"Cagliostro may change that," Dr. Abernathy pointed out.

"He may, but is there any other choice?" Michael looked around the room.

"I agree with Michael," Tahir said.

"I already met with the ambassador about this. Tomorrow morning I have an appointment with the president. I don't think it will do much good."

"The police aren't going to make any progress against the international shadow government," Arnold said.

"I know some men who work for them," Tahir said.

"Good, go to them," Dr. Abernathy said.

27

*A*nne watched as a woman dressed traditionally in a full-length, black kameez and hijab left two unopened bottles of water and took the untouched breakfast tray. Anne picked up the first bottle and searched for puncture marks. Finding none, she opened it and drank. Her mouth was dry and cottony from some drug they'd given her. She made herself stop before draining it. The room had no mirror, but her left eye was almost swollen shut and her right cheek twice its normal size. No broken bones, but a deep purple spread over her thigh and hip.

She tore a corner from the one blanket they'd given her against the cold of the desert night and wet it. Gingerly, she dabbed her face, cleaning out the sand that had stuck in her wounds. Once the blood stopped flowing again, she washed out her makeshift facecloth and hung it to dry from the black bar on the window.

Outside she saw the sandaled feet of people and the gray legs and black hooves of donkeys. Occasionally, a soft-footed camel glided by. The metal barring the window was solid, the screws shiny new and completely out of reach. There was no chair or table, just a straw mattress and one blanket. She supposed she could tie the blanket to the bars and pull herself up, but then what? She had no tools. They'd emptied her pockets. Oddly enough, they'd allowed her to keep the crystal.

She sat down to meditate, hoping to clear the remaining cobwebs from her head. Then she could think of a way to escape. Or perhaps make psychic contact with someone in her group, tell them she was all right, give them a beacon to trace.

After about twenty minutes of dull, sleepy meditation, her mind cleared somewhat. Anne could tell she'd need more water to wash the drug completely out of her system. She had to be ready for tonight. She assumed they would take her to the temple for the ritual. Who knew what would happen once the crystals were activated? She sent out a tentative psychic probe, but was met with a dead space all around her. They'd erected some kind of dampening field around the room. She had to break through it. She composed herself to try again.

Two sets of footsteps approached and a key scraped in the lock. A compact, muscular man pushed the door open. She recognized him as the person who had watched her during the luncheon speech at the UN. Most likely the dead man who left fingerprints. He grabbed her hands and tied them, then reached beneath her hair and unfastened the clasp of the crystal necklace. He handed her crystal to a second man, who was dressed in an expensive blue suit and Armani loafers.

He spoke first. "I'm here to explain to you what is going to happen now, Ms. Le Clair."

He looked like the man Michael had described who'd held his crystal during the attempt to open the Hall of Records.

"We've been fighting this war for a millennium," he began with relish, pacing back and forth in front of her. "We keep killing your messiahs—Akhenaten, then your illustrious ancestor. We took his message and twisted it to serve our empire, but that eventually fell and your sickening vision was trotted out again. So we deposed the Merovingian Dynasty and replaced them with the second Holy Roman Empire."

He turned on his heel and looked at her. "Your kind doesn't die, it seems. You just scurry into hiding like rats. The world believes our last attempt was defeated." The ghost of a smile crossed his lips. "But as your dear departed brother tried to explain to you—"

Anne inwardly flinched at the mention of Thomas.

"—we just took the Third Reich over the ocean and reestablished it in the land of the free, the country founded on the principles you hold so dear. Freedom. Democracy. The pursuit of enlightenment is what they wanted to say, those Freemasons, but they decided to call it happiness." He stuck his face down into hers. "Haven't you figured out yet that people are too stupid to govern themselves? To say nothing of understanding the high spiritual mysteries. They need a firm hierarchy. They need authoritarian leaders, a priesthood who tells them what to believe and keeps them in line through fear for their eternal souls."

"But it's a lie," Anne said.

He straightened up and started pacing again. "Who cares? It's not important for them to know. It's important for them to be controlled. They can't handle the truth."

Anne listened, repulsed yet fascinated, like a mouse staring into the eyes of the snake that's about to devour it.

"You must know by now that recent world events have been carefully staged to allow us to solidify our hold on global resources. All those ignorant people have laid down their lives, begging us to take the responsibility of thinking away from them."

A tear escaped Anne's battered eye. He must think she'd be dead by tomorrow or he wouldn't speak so freely. Right now, she couldn't see how to prevent that.

"We've taken your uncle's legacy, all his lofty ideals"—he waved his hands in the air—"and used them for ourselves. Tonight we're going to end this battle of ours, Ms. Le Clair." He held up a crystal on a gold chain.

She saw the glint of a star. It was Michael's.

"Tonight we shall triumph. We'll open the Hall of Records and take control of the Atlantean technology that will ensure our world domination. Then we can stop all this pretense of democracy. The laws are already in place. We control most of the world's governments, and those we don't will quickly become insignificant. Enjoy your last day on Earth, Ms. Le Clair."

He stepped aside and a third man walked into Anne's cell. This one was new to her—tall and elegant, his hair pulled back in a silver ponytail. Beneath two eyebrows black as ravens' wings were dark, piercing eyes.

He wore black beneath a cape held together with an elaborate brooch of Celtic design and carried a black walking stick topped with a clear quartz ball. He looked completely out of place in Egypt. The air around him crackled with power.

"We meet at last, Anne Morgan Le Clair," he said.

He spoke the Queen's English in the most genteel accent Anne had heard since her year at Oxford. She made no response.

Spender handed him the crystals and left.

"You attempted to clear your head and have already tried to send a message, but I've warded the room, you see." He looked down his nose at her. "Our little Annie, just now beginning to learn what she should have studied oh so long ago. I see the seed of jealousy we planted in Katherine's heart sprouted and grew fruit. Otherwise, you might have out shined them all." He closed his eyes.

Anne jerked back, repulsed by the sudden presence of the man's mind in her own.

"You do have talent."

She shut her eyes and tried to push him out.

"Now, now. Don't be rude."

She took a breath, pulled herself into her very core and pushed out with a wave of white light.

He laughed and continued his probe.

Anne's eyes flew open. She hunched over, trying to protect herself.

His eyes were still closed, his face tilted slightly up. "Ah, yes. Many lives in Egypt. You were there at the closing of the Hall. You kept the keys safe in Dendara and again in Avalon. A priestess at the Isis temple—what did the Christians call them? Prostitutes. Women who gave themselves to any passing stranger. All in the name of your goddess." He opened his eyes and studied her, a vivisectionist observing the effect of his experiment.

"You and your lover are remembering those practices now, but we of the Illuminati have never forgotten them." He leaned his face close, a suggestive smile on his lips. "Perhaps I will finish your education in these matters."

Anne shuddered.

"Or did my former student probe you? These techniques are most effective in forcing open the psychic abilities of young girls."

Anne's face was a blank.

"Roger." He imitated a submissive, feminine voice. "Your Dr. Abernathy."

Former student? Anne thought. *And he claims to know Mother, to have influenced her feelings toward Cynthia.*

"Or is he still treading the same old tiresome path of virtue?"

Who is this man?

"I thought you'd never ask, my dear. Where are your manners? My name is Alexander Cagliostro."

Anne's mouth dropped open.

"I see my reputation precedes me." He seemed pleased with her reaction.

Anne fought for self-control.

"Now, shall we get down to business?" He looked around for a place to sit.

Mueller stepped outside and brought back a café chair, which he placed across from Anne. Cagliostro eyed the seat, then, deciding it was sufficiently clean, settled into it.

Anne steeled herself.

"Tell me everything you've learned about the crystals and the Hall of Records."

Anne straightened out her legs and leaned against the wall. "I know much less than you imagine."

Cagliostro nodded.

Mueller stepped up and backhanded her, splitting her lip.

She explored the cut gingerly with her tongue.

"Don't worry. I won't damage you enough to spoil our evening's festivities. I find a little pain sharpens the senses." He motioned for Mueller to step back. "Tell me what you know."

I only found the temple last night. What could I possibly know?"

Cagliostro nodded, and again Mueller slapped her across the face, knocking her head hard against the wall. Anne's ears rang.

"Careful of her head. Tell me what you know," Cagliostro repeated, and this time Mueller punched her in the stomach.

She gasped for breath.

Mueller stepped back, his hands behind him, almost at attention. She sensed a wave of pleasure from him, then another mental probe from Cagliostro. He nodded to Mueller, who hit her again.

"Tell me what you know." Cagliostro enunciated each word carefully.

"I told you. I just discovered the temple last night. It was my first trip."

Another nod elicited more blows. A trickle of blood ran down her neck. Her side caught with every breath.

"Tell me what you know," Cagliostro said again.

She went over it in her mind, trying to see if any of it would betray them, would put that final power into the hands of the Illuminati. Her hesitation earned her a punch to the kidneys.

"Tell me what you know."

Anne doubled up on the floor, trying in vain to protect herself. Mueller kicked her already bruised hip. She screamed.

"Tell me what you know."

Cagliostro continued to ask and Mueller continued to pound her. Anne lost track of time. Finally, she lay on the floor of her cell, aching all over, her breath ragged. With the next blow, she passed out.

Annie. Thomas hovered over her, radiant with light. *Even this man has a place in the plan. Tell him what he wants to know.*

Thomas. She reached out for him, but found only thin air. Something jerked her awake. Another kick to her hip.

She struggled to sit. "Okay." Blood sprayed from her mouth when she spoke. "I'll tell you." She wiped her lip on her shoulder as best she could.

Cagliostro leaned back in his chair and crossed his legs, draping his cloak over them fastidiously. "I'm waiting."

"I only discovered the entrance last night with Paul Marchant."

"Two nights ago," Cagliostro interrupted. "You've lost a day."

Anne grimaced, remembering the drug. Her words came in short gasps as she continued. "The local people lost the knowledge. He wanted to open the curtain. He says there's some kind of blue energy field closing off the entrance that only the crystals can open. But we never got that far. We were attacked."

"And?"

"Paul seems to think it's an entrance to a larger room that holds Atlantean records and artifacts. Machines, maybe weapons."

"Yes?"

"Maria thinks it's a stargate that will reconnect the Earth to a galactic grid system." She stopped here.

"There's more." Cagliostro's eyes were closed.

"Our Egyptian informant refuses to tell us anything. He says the Hall of Records can't be explained in words."

Mueller stepped forward.

Anne curled up, anticipating another blow.

Cagliostro opened his eyes. "Wait."

Tears welled in her eyes and she angrily blinked them away. She would not feel gratitude toward this man. "We've tried everything to get him to talk to us, but he says it's something that must be experienced." She looked Cagliostro square in the face. "And don't go rounding him up, because he didn't even know where the temple was. Why else do you think I risked my life to find it?"

Cagliostro probed her mind and Anne bore the violation as best she could. "She's telling the truth. Let the woman clean her up."

Mueller turned to fetch her.

Cagliostro shook his head. "You're pitiful, you and your little investigative team. You know nothing. And you expected to open the Hall of Records? It's a good thing I've arrived."

Mueller returned with the Egyptian woman.

Cagliostro looked down at Anne and said, "Try to make her look decent. There's nothing more common than a woman who's been beaten black and blue." With this, he pocketed the two crystals and left. At least the stones were together again.

Michael sat in Anne's suite. As the day progressed, the pressure of the alignment grew stronger. He felt the temple pulling him. He hadn't slept. Last night they'd driven around the village and into Cairo, searching for psychic impressions of either Anne or Maria, but come up with nothing. The city was too densely populated.

Michael had returned to Anne's room and gone into trance, holding one of her silk shawls. He kept running into a blank wall, some kind of dead space. He tried to trace the source of the ward, but had no luck. He asked for a guide to show him, but no one came. Around midmorning, he'd suddenly gotten a deep chill, as if someone had walked into the core of his being. It took him a long time to regain his balance, and the threat of an imminent presence never left him.

Dr. Abernathy returned around noon from his visit to the president, who had been formally sympathetic and completely useless. It was more than the two Mayan priests received. Jose and Enrique had talked to the police again and got only vague reassurances. They had no embassy to go to. Dr. Abernathy had included Maria Lol Ha's kidnapping in his discussion with the president, but he held out no hope for help from the government.

In the early afternoon, Tahir arrived, dog-tired, with no leads. The villagers who worked for the project told him Anne was probably being held in a secret American military facility near the Cairo airport. Arnold had scoured all the government databases he could gain access to, looking for blueprints, schematics, anything to help him in a rescue mission, but found nothing. The base didn't exist officially and the files were well hidden.

"Going in there with no information would be suicide," Arnold said. "We should wait for them to contact us."

But they heard nothing. No telephone call. No e-mail. No demands. No ransom. Nothing. Just as Dr. Abernathy had anticipated. "They'll be expecting us tonight. The alignment is most exact just after eight o'clock. When does the sun go down?"

"Around half past six," Tahir said.

"We'll start for the site just after that."

"There has to be something we're overlooking," Michael said, "something we could do."

"Well, if you think of it, please let me know," Arnold said.

"We're doing everything we can," Tahir said.

"If they hurt her—" Michael began.

"You don't think I'm worried about that?" Arnold snapped.

"Enough," Dr. Abernathy said. "We're all on edge. None of us have slept, but we have a job to do. I want everyone to get some rest. I'll call you when we're ready to go."

Back in Anne's room, Michael reached a hand over the expanse of the king-size bed. His whole being ached for her. He couldn't lose her now, not after he'd patiently waited to earn her trust, not after he'd watched her grow from a skeptic to a practicing mystic, not after he'd fallen in love. He turned on his back and tried to slow his breath, but he knew sleep was impossible. He sat up and folded his legs beneath him, determined to meditate, but his mind scattered like a novice's. Finally, he turned to prayer. He pleaded for help from any being willing to assist the Earth's return to the light. At last he felt presences gather around him, sending streams of light, reassurance, strength. But the sinister specter that had been with him since his crystal was stolen hovered just out of reach, draining away his confidence.

Sensing that the time was near, Michael got up and laced up his boots. He had nothing to bring except a water bottle that he put in his backpack. He had to depend on the Illuminati to bring his crystal. He shouldered his pack just as Arnold knocked on the door.

"It's time."

The six men—Michael, Tahir, Arnold, Dr. Abernathy, Jose, and Enrique—crowded into Arnold's rental and rode in silence to the Sphinx side of the plateau. Arnold pulled up near the guardhouse. An antiquities police-man waved him over. Arnold rolled down the window, one hand on the revolver on his hip.

"Le Clair party?" the policeman asked.

Arnold was speechless.

Dr. Abernathy rolled down the back window. "Yes."

"You may proceed. Keep it on the road. You'll have to walk a short way in."

"Uh, thank you," Arnold said and pulled past the gate.

"Just as I thought," Dr. Abernathy said.

"Don't let down your guard," Arnold said. "Just because they've invited us in doesn't mean they won't kill us once we get there."

"Agreed," Dr. Abernathy said.

They drove around the low hills, then passed the spot where the police had loaded Bob's body just two nights before, an eternity ago. Around the next curve, they found four jeeps parked. Arnold pulled over and they climbed out. Arnold gathered them around. "I'll go in first. Who knows how to use a gun?"

"This is a high spiritual ritual," Michael objected. "We can't go in there armed."

"If we don't go in there prepared to fight, we'll all die. Who knows how to use a gun?"

"I'll take one." Dr. Abernathy reached for the revolver. "I'm a sharp-shooter. But I have to agree that the crystal holders should not go in armed."

Michael tucked a small flashlight into his pocket, hoping it wouldn't be noticed, as Arnold handed pistols to Jose and Enrique.

"No one is to use these until after the ritual," Dr. Abernathy instructed.

"They'll just frisk us and take them away," Arnold said.

"Maybe," Dr. Abernathy conceded, "but there is power in surrender."

Arnold stared at him.

"There must be no violence. Absolutely none." Abernathy looked at Arnold's uncomprehending face. "We'll all learn something tonight."

The group walked toward the shadow in the sand that marked the entrance to the temple. As they came closer, a low wall and the steps materialized out of the darkness. They tiptoed down, Arnold leading. At each turn, he peeked around the corner using a small mirror with a bend in the handle, then waved them forward. At the bottom of the steps, Arnold paused and listened intently. The cave was silent except for the distant trickle of water. He nodded and inched his way forward, crouched low. The cave walls gave way to limestone blocks. Arnold stopped and listened again.

The pull of the temple grew stronger. A faint singing reached Michael. Tahir and Dr. Abernathy looked around for the source of the sound, but it was obvious Arnold heard nothing.

Arnold glanced back. "What?" he mouthed.

Just at that moment, soldiers rushed the group from all sides, as if they'd just stepped out of the walls. Three soldiers seized Michael, pulled him back against the wall, and shoved two assault rifles into his stomach. Two soldiers stopped Dr. Abernathy, weapons bristling. Four men lay unconscious on the ground around Arnold, who was now held down by at least eight others. Michael looked back toward the steps. Jose lay on the ground, his eyes wide open in surprise at the men pointing guns at him. Michael couldn't see Enrique. Three soldiers held Tahir. At a nod from their leader, the men marched the group into the open plaza of the temple.

They walked down a set of stairs flanked by two replicas of the Sphinx. A man dressed in an impeccable blue suit stepped from behind one and said, "Welcome, gentlemen." He pointed to Tahir. "Take his crystal."

One of the men holding Tahir patted him down.

"It's around his neck," the man snapped.

The soldier pulled the crystal from around Tahir's neck, breaking the gold chain. He handed it to the suit.

"This way, gentlemen."

He turned and walked down the right wall of the chamber to a tunnel. They all squatted down and made their way through.

At first Michael found it difficult to move with three men holding onto him, but with each step into the tunnel, the song swelled in his mind like a siren's call. They emerged from the passageway and Michael stopped before a living, breathing Anubis. The men continued to drag him forward, but he looked back over his shoulder until the great jackal nodded his approval.

Michael turned forward and found himself staring into the face of the Great Mother Isis, who held her ankh to his nose. Osiris stood across from her, his blue-tinged skin glistening. He held the crook and flail over Michael as he passed. Horus stood behind his father. He passed one of his golden wings over Michael as the soldiers dragged him forward, blind to the higher vibrational beings surrounding them. Across from Horus stood the Lady Hathor holding a sistrum. When Michael looked into her eyes, a thousand voices swelled in song, adding their complex harmony to the chant rising from the end of the chamber.

The great lioness Sekhmet looked down at him through several dimensional layers. *Be strong, my son, she said. Your time has come.* She touched him with her lotus staff. Father Ptah stood across from her, his golden wings wrapped around him, his blue face smiling down. When Michael passed, Ptah unfurled his wings and touched Michael's crown with his staff. Michael wanted to fall to his knees, but someone was holding him up, pushing him forward. He heard the sound of voices, but had trouble focusing on the words.

A man dressed in a black cape stood in front of a blue curtain studded with stars. Michael's mind melded with the curtain, but Ptah, who stood beside him now, whispered, *Not yet.* Michael focused on the magician in front of the curtain.

The man spoke. "Roger Abernathy, we meet again."

"Alexander Cagliostro." Dr. Abernathy acknowledged his former teacher with a nod, then stood in the midst of his captives, silent and calm as a deep spring.

"Where are your manners? Aren't you going to introduce me?"

"This is my assistant, Arnold—"

"I'm not talking about your hired gun, idiot. Take these three away." Cagliostro waved his hand at Arnold, Jose, and Enrique.

Arnold struggled, managing to throw down two more men before he was subdued again. Eight men held Arnold while two tied him up and dragged him out of the room. Six more men pushed Jose and Enrique behind them.

"I've been waiting for this opportunity to finish our little quarrel," Cagliostro continued.

Dr. Abernathy said, "I'm sorry our parting was not more amicable. I was young and brash. Please accept my apology for condemning your choice of paths."

"It's too late for apologies. While you've been wasting your time protecting the spawn of the pretender, I've mastered my craft. Tonight we'll put an end to you and your kind."

"The sun is rising, Alexander. Even you, powerful as you are, cannot stop it."

"Enough. Now, which one of you does this belong to?" A crystal dangled from his right hand.

Michael's awareness snapped into the physical dimension, completely focused on the stone. So this was the specter who'd been threatening him from the edges of his mind. Michael took a step forward.

At the same time, Paul Marchant stepped out of the shadows. "You can't keep it. You have to give it to him."

"Be silent." Cagliostro glared at Marchant. "Michael Levy. Levite priest turned museum curator."

Michael's whole being yearned for the stone, to hold it and join in the song around him.

Cagliostro took a second crystal from his other pocket and looked at Tahir. "Tahir Nur Ahram. Last guardian of the knowledge of the Eye Tribe." He regarded Tahir's worn *gallabiya*. "How the once-illustrious house has fallen."

"There is no last, just as there is no first," Tahir replied, as if instructing a child.

"Watch and learn." Cagliostro turned slightly and snapped his fingers.

Two pairs of soldiers stepped forward from the shadows on the left side of the inner temple. One pair held Maria, pale but unscathed, between them. Anne stood between the other two, her left eye black and puffy, her right cheek swollen.

Anne looked at Michael, and her mouth formed a crooked smile around her swollen lower lip. "Michael, it's good to see you."

"What have you done to her?" Michael turned on Cagliostro like an enraged bear.

Cagliostro glanced at him. "She can do her job. We are all accounted for except for the elusive key that Thomas died so valiantly trying to find. I think my presence will more than compensate. Shall we begin?" He held up Michael's crystal.

Michael fought to control himself. If he wanted to help Anne, he had to stay alive. And the curtain was singing to him more strongly than ever. They had a job to do that was more important than his life. But Anne's? He had to find a way to save her. He moved up the six stairs and took his crystal from Cagliostro. As soon as he touched it, the song surged in his mind, almost knocking him down. He grounded himself with an effort and walked back to the star tetrahedron outlined in blue tile on the temple floor. A soldier walked with him, gun aimed at his head.

"Tahir." Cagliostro held up another crystal.

Tahir did as Michael had done, and a soldier followed him, gun cocked and ready.

Marchant moved down the stairs and a soldier moved with him. "Please call your man off. I've cooperated."

Cagliostro shook his head. "You conspired behind our backs. Now shut up and do your job. Bring the women."

He handed each her crystal and the soldiers took Anne and Maria to the star formation. Soon the crystal holders stood on the tiled floor of the temple with their crystals and attendant soldiers.

Michael moved deep into trance, the song of the curtain moving into his body, vibrating him down to the bones. He took off his shoes, barely registering the reaction of the man guarding him, and placed them at the edge of the temple. The others followed suit.

Michael's vision blurred. Energy forms swam in the air all around him. But something wasn't right. He felt compelled to move. Maria caught his eye and looked up. An enormous golden astrology wheel filled the ceiling. Sirius, yes. He moved beneath the Dog Star. The others moved also, Maria to the Pleiades, Anne beneath the cat planet in the far reaches of space, Tahir beneath the triangle of Vega, and Marchant beneath the belt of Orion.

As each Keeper moved into place, the energy of the temple built like layers of music, one track intensifying the next. Cagliostro stepped into the Antares position and the energy twisted. Michael winced against it, but knew they must go forward. The planetary alignment built to a crescendo. The Hall of Records must be opened now.

Five Illuminati adepts moved from the shadows of the large statues, three men and two women. One was Miriam. She smiled at Michael, then stepped beside Anne. The rest took their places next to the other

Keepers. With a glance at Cagliostro, they closed their eyes and entrained their minds with the Keeper they stood next to. Michael's whole being recoiled from the creeping malice trying to take control. He pushed back against the tendrils snaking around his mind, gathered up all his rage, and hurled it at the man beside him.

The man smiled and his grip strengthened.

No, Michael. Ptah's mild voice reached him. *Bring him to the light.*

Michael turned to the wise one. Their eyes met and his mind melded with the Neter, lifting him out of his temporary identity as Michael Levy. He was the consciousness that watched, eternal and unchanging, one facet in the great jeweled awareness that was everything.

The other Keepers felt Michael's transformation through the link and they followed. As he slipped into a higher consciousness, so did they. Now as facets of one mind, each took a crystal in their right hand, aligned it with the index finger, and pointed to the middle.

Cagliostro pulled a crystal out of his pocket and did the same. A stream of pollution poured into the circle. Ignoring him, Marchant spoke a phrase in a language Michael recognized as Atlantean. It had no effect. This chamber was much older. Atlantis was one ring in the ancient tree of history. Tahir chanted in the ancient language of his people, and the phrase reverberated in the chamber, awakening memories, faint half-life figures of the past.

Marchant sounded a note, Maria another, a fifth higher. Each instinctively knew their tone and a beautiful harmony filled the chamber. The blue curtain sang with them, melting in one instant from a dark navy to sky blue. In another instant, it became transparent and, with a small whooshing sound, folded in on itself and disappeared.

The five moved as one up the six stairs into the small, precious chalice of a room, taking their places on the smaller star tetrahedron laid out in tile on the floor. Each stood tall, arms up, waiting for the flow of cosmic energy from the galactic core handed down through the star tetrahedron of planets in the alignment.

Beside each Keeper, several octaves higher in dimensional frequency, stood a Neter in the lighter blue star tetrahedron, adding its voice, holding up the sacred flame. Ptah stood with Michael, Sekhmet with Anne, Horus with Tahir, Osiris with Marchant, and Isis with Maria. Now they were ten. Cagliostro took the empty place in the formation, but Hathor waited by the entrance.

Something coiled at the bottom of the Nile, down deep near Elephantine, woke, and stretched its head. Power stirring from far south flowed downriver, gathering force as it came. From Khnum's island and the island of Biga it flowed, from the root of physical form to the womb of the world, then to Kom Ombo, where the great crocodile dove in and swam northward. The river of power rolled on through the great temples at Karnak, Dendara, Abydos, and Edfu, the essence of each temple they'd visited joining the flow, braiding in its particular frequency, its special light. The vast flood reached Giza, the crown jewel in the spine of the Nile, and the Keepers were inundated. Just as a river surrenders to the sea, all their limitations simply washed away.

A door opened in their unified mind, an ancient door containing certain knowledge. Everyone knew at once.

The Hall of Records had no physical existence. There were no artifacts, no weapons, no scrolls filled with lost knowledge. They themselves were the Hall of Records. They would awaken and the Earth would awaken with them.

Anne smiled at Michael and held her crystal aloft as she'd held the lit candle in the Christmas Eve service as a child. It had all been practice for this moment.

Marchant laughed out loud, astonished as all his plans crumbled into dust, but his heart soared as he embraced his real destiny.

Tahir smiled. Now they knew. The quest was over. Every single human being was a living, breathing library of cosmic knowledge. All humanity would return to this high state of consciousness, this exquisite unity that could never be written down, that had to be experienced, just as Tahir had said. Just as the first lines of the Tao said, and the Rig Veda. Hadn't all sages said this down through the ages?

Their vibration reached such a height that the five Crystal Keepers blinked out of sight. The soldiers looked around frantically.

Cagliostro looked at the Illuminati standing in the circle. "Find them." They all closed their eyes.

The Sphinx, the Great Mother Tefnut, now gathered up the river of energy that flooded the Giza Plateau and pulled it into herself, where she modulated it and pulsed it out to those mother planets, those grand, realized civilizations that had bent down eons ago and lit the wick of Earth's own planetary family. They smiled down. "They are awakening. The children are awakening," and their love streamed through the galaxy into the very heart of Earth.

Now.

Now was the time to take that flow of perfect love handed down through the alignment and anchor it deep into the enormous crystal waiting in the cavern beneath this temple. They saw it in their one mind, a mirror image of the granite pyramid above, a crystal pyramid 454 feet high, its base just beneath them, its point reaching deep into the Earth's crystal grid system.

How such a crystal could exist was beyond Michael, but he knew it was there, just as he knew he loved Anne, had loved her for centuries, and would love her again.

She returned a surge of energy to him.

The Keepers raised their crystals and sang the song of the Awakening, the new song of the ascended Earth.

But a voice was missing, a stone was absent, and in its place a malevolent, gaping maw spewed forth hatred and violence. Beneath that was fear, the quivering, all-consuming terror of a newborn infant thrown onto the garbage heap, never knowing a mother's arms, never realizing its place in the universe. Once grown, rising up and grasping the nearest weapon, forcing its will on the world. "I'll show you. I'll get you for what you've done to me."

The Illuminati blinked into view and merged again with the Keepers they were matched with. The knowledge flooded them. Now Cagliostro knew as well, the Illuminati adepts all knew there was nothing to uncover, no warehouse of Atlantean technology to ensure the impotent dream of world domination shared by those who refused to face what they had done in their ignorance.

"No!" His voice ripped through them.

The six Illuminati reached through the minds of the Keepers and found—light. Two recoiled, Cagliostro and another. The remaining four merged into the cosmic intelligence, diving in with abandon, shedding their fear and hope. There was nothing amiss in the universe.

"No!" Cagliostro screamed again. "You don't have to surrender."

"There is nothing to fear," one of them said.

Cagliostro reached into this man's body with his mind and stopped his heart.

The soldiers heard Cagliostro's voice, but couldn't find him. To the Crystal Keepers, the soldiers moved in slow motion, as if through molasses.

The five Keepers dug deep into their love and redoubled their song. The Neters sang several frequencies above them. The universe, a many-tiered birdbath of dimensions, sang with them. They had to reach a peak to receive the energy in the crystal hovering in space above the Great Pyramid. It would beam the energy to their own crystals and they would transmit it physically to Earth. But the alignment was already moving apart. Time was running out. Without the sixth crystal, its Keeper, and the voice of the Hathors, they would fail. The perfection of their union started to crumble. A wave of grief swept through them all.

Suddenly, beyond all hope or reason, a circle of light appeared just outside the small chamber. Through it stepped three Tibetans, two monks and one nun. The sound of overtone chanting rose from them. The nun took a crystal from beneath her robes, positioned it in her hand, and kicking off her sandals, entered the temple. She took her position beside Cagliostro, who reached out with his mind to kill her. She brushed him off like a fly and added her voice to the chant. Hathor stepped beside her and thousands of upper-dimensional voices joined in.

Everything happened at once.

The chant, now complete, built to a crescendo and peaked. The crystal atop the Great Pyramid, an ethereal point that gleamed only in the higher dimension, unseen by the physical eye, now loosed the cosmic energy from galactic center. This light flowed into the crown of each Crystal Keeper, down each spine to each heart where it entered each crystal. As one, the Keepers pointed their keys to the center of the star beneath their feet and a million gigawatts of galactic energy flooded the Earth, reawakening the eight-hundred-mile-wide crystal at the Earth's core. This crystalline heart pulsed once and that stream of energy spread through every crystal, every ley line in the planet. The Keepers spasmed and fell back, completely sated.

"No!" Cagliostro screamed again. "Stop them."

The Keepers popped into view and the soldiers reached for the stones.

Paul Marchant turned toward the man trying to tear his crystal from his hand and hit him with a bolt of searing white light.

"Stop him," Cagliostro ordered.

Three soldiers pointed their weapons at Marchant and pulled the triggers.

He saw the bullets flying toward him in slow motion. He smiled as he watched them come, the consequences of his attempt to own this sanctuary for himself. The bullets tore through his chest, jerking him back fully into the physical dimension. But they were too late. Already he could feel it, feel the spread of the light, feel the Earth's grid system coming back online. He fell, offering his life in restitution. Tefnut took him into her heart and returned him to Nut.

Spender screamed as Marchant fell, and one soldier opened fire before he realized who he was shooting. The bullets crashed into Spender at the same spot that Maria's jaguar had jumped through him just a few days earlier. He blinked in surprise and looked down at his chest. He fell, dead before he hit the floor.

"Michael," Anne shouted. "Michael, we've got to get out of here."

"Stop them," Cagliostro screamed.

More soldiers poured through the tunnel and thronged up the steps. Five men surrounded Maria and she stood with her hands up, an enormous smile on her face.

"Anne." Michael grabbed her hand and pulled her through the crowd, willing the soldiers not to see them. Two men grabbed Anne. She twisted away, kicking their legs out from under them. Anne and Michael ran down the stairs and scrambled on their hands and knees through the tunnel.

Once through, they raced across the plaza without looking back. Bullets flew around them. They dived behind the fallen statue of Osiris.

"This way." Michael headed into the labyrinth of tunnels, following the stream that fed the lake. When they could no longer see the lights in the chamber, Michael risked turning on his flashlight. Thank God he hadn't been searched.

They ran until their lungs burned, following turns in the tunnel as they came, now right, now left, praying they would find a way out. As they ran, they lost their higher connections. They came back to being just Anne and Michael, running for their lives and fully aware of their bare feet. Finally, they could run no farther and stopped, leaning against the tunnel wall, gasping for breath. When their breathing quieted, they listened. They heard silence, then a voice from far away. "Where are they?"

They ran again, up tunnels, around turns, finally reaching an ancient set of stairs. Anne stopped. "Where are we?" she whispered.

"I have no idea." Michael panted behind her.

"Which way should we go?"

"We need to go up eventually. Let's try these steps."

They started to climb, carefully picking their way around fallen boulders and debris. They climbed for a long time, slowly picking their way upward. No voices came behind them. The euphoria of their ritual had worn off completely, leaving Anne aching all over. She climbed, holding her ribs. "How much farther?"

"Want to rest?"

"No, we need to get out of here."

They climbed another twenty-odd steps and ran into a wall of stones and smaller debris.

"Now what?" Anne asked.

"Looks like a dead end."

Anne sank down on the top step, cradling her head in her hands. "I don't know how much longer I can go on."

Michael moved closer to the stones. "Wait."

"What?"

"Come here. Put your nose here."

Anne stuck her face into the crack between the stones and took as deep a breath as her ribs would allow. She laughed, then grabbed her side. "Ouch."

"What?"

"I never thought I'd be happy to smell camels."

"If we can move some of these stones, maybe we can get out."

"Or we could start an avalanche and be crushed to death."

"True, but we've had good luck tonight."

Carefully, Michael dug out the smaller debris from around two stones. Anne moved up beside him.

"No, you rest."

"But—"

"Please."

"All right." Gratefully, Anne leaned back against the wall at a good distance from Michael.

After ten more minutes of digging, a stream of fresh air blew down to Anne. She moved up beside him.

"I think I can see the sky," he said, and continued to move debris out of the way, careful not to dislodge any large stones. Finally, a narrow but clear passage lay before them.

"I'll go first just in case we're crawling to our deaths," Michael said.

"You'd better stay alive," Anne said.

"Here goes." Michael started to move through the tunnel he'd cleared. Anne watched his body disappear as he pulled himself up. Seconds later his head reappeared. "Come on." He reached a hand down and helped Anne up.

She stretched out on the ground, grateful to see stars again. Michael leaned against a new brick wall of some kind. After she caught her breath, Anne sat up and looked around. "Where are we?"

"I'm not sure." Michael looked up. "Oh, my God!"

"What?" Anne asked.

Michael pointed up.

An enormous head loomed in the night sky above them. They were sitting against the foreleg of the Sphinx.

"Oh, my God!" Anne repeated.

Goddess, corrected Tefnut.

Anne and Michael burst out laughing.

"Shhh, someone will hear us," Michael sputtered.

Anne doubled over laughing, then grabbed her ribs.

Michael snorted.

"Stop," Anne protested.

"I can't help it. I guess Edgar Cayce was right."

"Why? There was no Hall of Records, not like he said."

"Yes, but we've just opened the stargate and here we are beneath the right paw of the Sphinx."

"Tefnut is her proper name."

Michael pulled Anne to him and kissed her tenderly, careful of her swollen lip. Then he held her arm's length away and looked deep into her eyes, the one almost swollen shut. "You are the most beautiful woman in the world."

"I look like a punching bag."

"Anne Morgan Le Clair Greene," he said, "will you marry me?"

Anne's voice caught in her throat. Then a twinkle appeared in her one visible eye, "Hathor priestesses don't get married, remember?"

"How will you explain that to the press?"

Anne smiled, "Okay, but what will your uncle say?"

"My uncle?" Michael's voice rose.

Anne shushed him. "Quiet. You'll attract the police."

"What has my uncle got to do with this?" he whispered.

"Well, he kept telling me that you respect family."

"So?"

"So I'm not a nice Jewish girl."

"I beg to differ."

"What?"

"You're descended from one of the world's most famous rabbis from the tribe of Judah, and on your mother's side from the tribe of Benjamin. How Jewish can you get?"

"Then I accept." Anne kissed him.

392 • Theresa Crater

Michael took her in his arms and held her against his heart. "I hope I never come so close to losing you again."

"Me, too." She leaned into him, content. "I think we did it."

"I think you're right."

"Paul Marchant didn't make it."

Michael nodded. "But it was an honorable death."

Anne pulled away and struggled to her feet. "Come on. Dr. Abernathy and Arnold will be beside themselves." A shadow crossed her face. "If they made it out."

"I didn't feel anyone else die. I was in such an expanded state, I think I would have known."

"But I lost it about halfway through our escape."

"True." He looked at Anne, who was leaning against the Sphinx. Her face was black and blue, her eye and lip swollen. She was holding her side. "Let's get you to a doctor."

They walked out from the paws of the Great Mother, down the wooden path and to the gate. Michael lifted her over and they walked hand in hand across the front road, past the Pizza Hut franchise and down the street. A knot of people stood on the sidewalk.

Suddenly, Dr. Abernathy whirled around. "Here they are."

The group ran toward them. Anne recognized three of the Illuminati adepts standing with Tahir. Shani was the first to reach them. "Are you all right?"

"We're fine. No broken bones," Anne said. "Did everyone make it out?"

"Everyone except Paul Marchant."

"Some of the soldiers ran after you. The rest rounded us up. Looked like they were going to execute us on the spot." Dr. Abernathy shook his head.

"What?"

One of the Illuminati spoke up. "Cagliostro suddenly collapsed. Even he has limits." She smiled. "I assumed command and told the captain of the squad it was all over. We just walked out."

"Where are the Tibetans?" Anne asked.

The nun stepped forward. Putting her hands together, she bowed to Anne and Michael.

Anne returned the posture in greeting. "Namaste, but how did you know?"

"Your brother. He came. We knew it was time."

"But how did you get here?"

The nun only smiled and stepped back. The three Tibetans looked at each other, then closed their eyes. A circle of light appeared and the three stepped into it and simply disappeared.

Everyone gaped. After a long silence, Anne looked around and asked, "How did they do that?"

Dr. Abernathy shrugged. "There are stories about teleportation, but I never really believed them." He looked at her. "We need to get you to a doctor."

"There's a doctor's office down the street."

"But it is the middle of the night," Tahir said. "The hotel has someone on call."

The group hailed taxis, which could still be found even at this hour. They piled in and Arnold called ahead, asking for the doctor. They arrived at the Mena House in about fifteen minutes. The group went to Anne's suite. They sat on whatever was available—the couch, chairs, the floor.

Anne turned to Tahir. "Did we do it?"

"The Hall of Records has been opened. The Awakening has begun."

"So what happens now?" Anne asked.

Tahir sat on the floor and out of habit looked around for his *shisha* pipe. Finding nothing, he said, "This is the time of the dawn. Earlier was the time of transition, like when the *mu'adhdhins* call everyone to prayer. The quickening of the light woke you all." He included everyone in a sweep of his hand. "Now more will awaken, then even more as the sun rises above the horizon. Some like to sleep in." He winked at Anne.

She smiled.

Tahir continued. "Those will wait until the sun has climbed halfway up the sky. It is a natural process, like all things. Human beings will begin to live in harmony with each other, with the environment."

Maria nodded. "The Earth is safe. The star elders will begin to return to help us teach. We have done a good thing."

"We should toast the success of our mission," Anne said.

"And our engagement," Michael announced.

"Congratulations!" came from several people.

Michael called room service. "Champagne, please."

The doctor arrived and ushered Anne into the back room. Shani went with her.

"Let's see what's happening in the world." Someone turned on the television.

"It may take some time," Tahir cautioned. "The sun hasn't even come up."

Thomas Le Clair's face filled the screen. Then the coverage switched to a shot of a helicopter pulling a piece of twisted metal out of the ocean. "Wreckage of the Le Clair family jet was found this morning off the coast of India," the reporter's voice began.

The group watched as the helicopter flew to a larger boat with the piece of the plane. Then the scene shifted. "In China, officials announced plans to open negotiations with the Dalai Lama."

"I can't believe it," one of the Illuminati said.

"The light is spreading quickly," Maria said. "Soon the world will be at peace and we can turn our attention to solving problems rather than killing each other."

Michael switched off the set. "A moment of silence for our fallen—Thomas, Bob, and Paul."

Michael closed his eyes, as did several of the others. As the room quieted, Michael's senses deepened. He felt the vibration of the pyramids just outside, familiar but now somehow different. His awareness reached out to merge with the energy. It was higher and lighter, sweeter somehow. He opened his eyes to see Maria's face.

She smiled at him. "Do you feel it?"

He grasped her hands. "We've done it."

"Yes, but it will still take some time. Do not be discouraged if it doesn't all happen overnight."

Anne walked back out of her room, a patch over one eye, her arm in a sling. "Nothing broken." She looked at the expressions in the room. "What?"

"China has announced peace talks with the Tibetans," Michael said.

"You're kidding."

"It's true. We just closed our eyes for a moment," Michael continued. "The energy of the plateau has shifted significantly."

"So our mission was a success," Anne said.

Tahir nodded. "We have opened the Earth again. The sun will rise."

"Good." Anne looked from face to face and her forehead wrinkled. "But there's something else."

"They found Thomas's plane." Michael's eyes slid from her face.

Anne nodded. "He's still with me, though."

Michael looked up at her again.

"It's okay, Michael. I'll miss him, but this is what we do, the Le Clairs. This is who we are."

A knock sounded on the door. "Room service."

Dr. Abernathy opened the door and a waiter rolled in a cart. Arnold signed for the delivery and Michael grabbed the bottle and opened it with a loud pop. The champagne ran over the top of the bottle and everyone grabbed a glass. Shani poured.

Once everyone's glasses were full, Anne held hers in the air. "To the Awakening."

Voices answered her from around the room. "To the Awakening."

Acknowledgments

I want to thank the many people who have helped to make this book possible. My deepest gratitude and love go to my life partner, Stephen Mehler, who took me home to Egypt, who introduced me to the indigenous wisdom tradition of that ancient land, who read my unpublished work and encouraged me to keep writing, and who loved and supported me through the process of writing, editing, and finding a publisher. My deep thanks go to Abd'El Hakim Awyan for his knowledge, wisdom, and patience, and to JoAnn Parks and Max for introducing me to Stephen and helping me find myself again. I also must thank Sekhmet for her love, support, and guidance.

Special thanks also go to Christopher Dunn and his wife, Jeanne, for his ideas about Egypt and for accompanying us on the path; also to John DeSalvo for his support and friendship, and all the independent Egyptologists and theorists whose ideas I've brushed against in this book. I am deeply grateful to Stephen Simon and the Spiritual Cinema Circle community for helping me believe my dreams can come true, and to Neale Donald Walsch for suggesting Hampton Roads. I also thank Andrea and Mark Pinkham of Body, Mind, Spirit Journeys for all they do to take people to the sacred sites of the world, and all those at the Clan Sinclair Study Centre in Noss Head,

Scotland, for their tolerance of the stories being written about their family.

Special thanks go to my critique team, Traci Morganfield, Carol Valera Jacobson, and Susan Johnson, as well as the members of the Science Fiction Studio at Metropolitan State College of Denver. Thanks also to Broad Universe, Rocky Mountain Fiction Writers, the Northern Colorado Writers' Workshop, Women's Voices, and all my writing teachers, including Joanna Russ, Valerie Miner, Irena Klepfisz, and Chuck Schuster.

I also want to thank family and friends who have encouraged me, including Aldrin, Shaniqua, Ashley, Aldrin Jr., and Aubria Gresham; Sunny and Bob Mehler and family; Phyllis and Ron Hoffman and family; Marylee and Joe Swanson; Ruth Adele; my parents, Ralph and Lois Crater, who wondered why their child kept saying she wanted to be a writer; Eddie Crater; and the felines who sniffed, poked, and purred the book into being—Thea, Persephone, Ting Li, Wizzer, Parsifal, and Arwen.

Finally, an enormous thank you goes to all the great people at Hampton Roads for their excellent work, especially Frank DeMarco for his insightful editing.

About the Author

Award-winning author Theresa Crater brings ancient temples, lost civilizations, and secret societies back to life in her visionary fiction. Her novels include The Power Places series, *Under the Stone Paw* and *Beneath the Hallowed Hill, The Star Family* and *God in a Box* Her short stories explore ancient myth brought into the present day. She blogs with the Visionary Fiction Alliance and Women Write the Rockies, and is a member of Sisters in Crime and the Independent Authors Network. Currently, she teaches writing and British literature in Denver.

For more information:

Website: theresacrater.wordpress.com

Twitter: twitter.com/theresacrater

Facebook: www.facebook.com/tlcwrites

Good Reads: www.goodreads.com/author/show/498934.Theresa_Crater

Pinterest: www.pinterest.tlcwrites

Linked In: www.linkedin.com/in/theresa-crater aa540410

Books by Theresa Crater

CPSIA information can be obtained
at www.ICGtesting.com
Printed in the USA
BVHW040147190819
556200BV00016B/367/P

9 780997 141313